I0725279

FICTION
OR
PROPHECY

ANGELO THOMAS CRAPANZANO

ISBN: 978-1-961017-12-2 (sc)
ISBN: 978-1-961017-13-9 (e)

Rev. date: 04/27/2023

CONTENTS

DEDICATION

This book is dedicated to Richard and Patricia Stiff, my best friends and neighbors. Their friendship and support is a highlight of my life.

ACKNOWLEDGMENT

I wish to thank Richard Stiff for the many intellectual discussions we have had together. The discussion we had on terrorist interrogation led me to write this novel.

CHAPTER ONE

Nowhere to Go

IT WAS LATE IN THE afternoon on a chilly spring day in April. A light spring wind stirring through the garden brought the heavy scent of roses through the open door and into the family room. Two friends were sitting in the family room drinking a pre-dinner drink and discussing politics. Bill was an inch, perhaps two, over six feet and powerfully built but had a very pleasant disposition. He was handsome, clever, with a comfortable home next door to Mike and Annie They had been neighbors for six years. The men got along well, but what really made the friendship strong was that their women had hit it off immediately.

"What do you find wrong with negotiations and finding a middle ground?" said Bill, goading Mike.

"Because that really is appeasement," said Mike. "Appeasement has never worked."

"Why do say that?" questioned Bill.

"Check your history," responded Mike. "Appeasement has never worked. It only gave the enemy time to build their army. Look at World War II. By appeasing Germany, we gave it time to build the greatest army of the time. A mistake on Germany's part lost the war for them, but if run intelligently, they would have won. I give credit to God though. When a nation turns away from God, it is destroyed."

"What has God to do with it?"

"Look at Israel. Every time it turned its back to God, God sent an enemy to defeat it. Our officials think this is a kid's game," continued Mike. "Look at the fuss they made over our interrogation methods. This is not a game. The terrorist's only aim in life is to kill as many Americans as they can. You can't appease a group that believes so deeply that they are willing to die for their cause."

"Are you saying that you believe in torture to get the information we want?" asked Bill.

"There are many ways to get information," answered Mike. "Why not use truth drugs? I know that they say it's against their rights. Why should a non-American terrorist murderer have rights under the constitution that they don't believe in and are trying to destroy?"

"What good have our interrogation methods, whatever they are, done for us?" asked Bill.

"I know that the liberal news media doesn't tell you everything," responded Mike, "but the information I received from a conservative publication listed two American structures that were saved from the information obtained through interrogation. One, I believe, was the Golden Gate Bridge. However, Bill, the information that concerns me is the information they received just before all the fuss about interrogation. The terrorist bragged that they had developed a backpack nuclear bomb. He said that they were going to simultaneously nuke the ten biggest cities in the USA. When asked why, he said that after bringing the US to its knees, they could destroy Israel once and for all. Our officials think that he was just trying to scare us. Well, I can tell you that it scares me."

"You don't think that they could actually get away with something so unbelievable. How would they get into this country undetected?"

"Now Bill, I know you are kidding. You know better than that. If two million Mexicans can come into this country every year, you don't think *ten* would have trouble?"

"Don't you think you are exaggerating the possibility?" argued Bill. "Aren't you being very pessimistic? The chance of that happening is like the chance of you getting hit by a lightning bolt."

"Go ahead and close your eyes," said Mike. "Think of me when it happens."

"How about both of you opening your eyes and coming up here? That is if you have solved the problems of the world," said Sally, Bill's wife. She was leaning over the railing dividing the kitchen from the family room. There were six steps from the family room to the kitchen. Bill took them all at one leap.

"I will not have to be called twice for Annie's pasta," said Bill. "The best path is from her Sicilian hands to my German stomach."

"Sit down and behave," said Sally.

"I know how you like my pasta sauce," said Annie "That's why I made it especially for you."

The next morning, Mike packed a small overnight bag and his attaché case and was ready to go to his book signing.

"Are you going to see Tara while you are in Chicago?" asked Annie.

"Why would you ask that?"

"Well, she was your first love, and she lives in Chicago," said Annie. "I remember that she was your first love, I remember that you were engaged to her, and I also remember that she dumped you for someone else."

"Well then, you should also remember that I chose you," said Mike. "Besides, she is probably married now. How would I know her new last name?"

"So you have thought of this, have you?" said Annie showing her jealousy.

"Honey, you're jealous of someone I knew ten years ago," answered Mike with a smile on his face.

"You told me when you proposed that you loved her with all of your heart, and you asked me if I could live with that."

"Perhaps that was true when we first got married, but we have had ten wonderful years together. It all changed when you gave me a fantastic kid," said Mike, getting serious. "Have I ever given you reason to doubt my love for you? Have you ever thought that I didn't do everything I could to make you happy?"

"No, you have been a model husband," said Annie.

"And you have been a sweet, loving wife," said Mike pulling her to him. He wrapped his arms around her and kissed her lovingly. "I wouldn't give up one minute of our years together. Besides it's been over ten years since I've seen Tara. She is probably fat with seven spoiled kids. However, honey, if you are worried, I will call and cancel my trip. You are more important than a book signing."

"Don't be silly," said Annie. "I trust you. So go and please drive carefully." Mike kissed her again with a passionate lingering kiss.

About fifteen minutes later, he entered Interstate 80/90, which took him directly into Chicago. It was a six-hour drive to Chicago, and it was after ten when he left. It was a boring trip that gave him a lot of time to think. After he got up to speed, his mind went back to his conversation with Annie. He wondered what Tara looked like and what she was doing. He had loved her with all his heart. He had planned his whole life around her and was devastated when she stopped writing and wouldn't take his calls. He waited for two months to hear from her. He remembered that he had packed to go to Chicago to win her back but his mother and sister talked him out of it. They told him that if she had another boyfriend, he would only make a fool of himself. They said that he should get some facts first. That's when he decided to call her best friend, Laura. Laura told him that Tara had gotten back together with her old high school boyfriend whom she loved desperately. She also told him that they were planning their wedding for June.

Suddenly, Mike began to feel his love for Tara returning, and he felt a strong desire to see her again. He remembered that he had never loved anyone as much as he loved her either before or after her. There was a magic he felt with Tara that he had never felt before.

Suddenly, he felt guilty. What was he doing? He loved Annie. His duty was with her. He tried to shake thoughts of Tara from his mind, but her image kept popping up. He tried to think of Annie and how they met instead. After Tara, he had to get away. He decided to take his mother to Jeannette, Pennsylvania, where his aunt Millie lived with her Italian husband, Alfred Morelli. While there, he met Alfred's brother who had a daughter named Anna Morelli, who was about four years younger than Mike. It was pretty obvious that Annie had fallen in love with him. Mike had little ego left and needed to be loved, and in the two weeks they were there, Annie showered Mike with love that he had never experienced before. In his state it filled a need he had. He thanked God that she turned out to be as wonderful as she was. Mike felt his love for her swell in his heart. He felt better now.

He had driven almost five hours when he saw a car pulled off the road. A young woman was behind it waving a white hanky. Mike had not noticed while deep in thought, but there were a lot fewer cars on the road than he had expected. He pulled up behind her and stepped out of his car.

"Are you having car problems?" he asked her. It was a dumb question, he thought. He was stunned by her beauty; she was well built and had gorgeous light-brown hair.

"It started to miss and finally stalled. I have no idea what the problem is," she said shyly.

"Well, open the hood and let me take a look," said Mike. She complied, and Mike looked the engine over. "There doesn't seem to be any leaks and the oil is okay." He reached over and disconnected one of the spark plug wires. "Turn over the engine," he requested. After she tried to start the car Mike pulled out from under the hood and waved at her to stop. "I see your problem," he said, replacing the spark plug wire. "You don't have any ignition."

"Is that serious?" she asked.

"Well, without a spark, your fuel will not ignite."

"What should I do?" she asked, becoming nervous. "I tried to call for help, but my cell phone is dead."

"Don't worry, I won't leave you stranded here," said Mike. "Let me take you into the nearest town and see if we can get someone to tow your car to the nearest mechanic."

"Would you do that? It would be so kind of you," she said, sounding a little relieved. Mike pulled out his map and looked for the nearest town.

"Look here," he said pointing to the road on the map. "There is the little town of La Porte, here just off the interstate on Route 39. It looks large enough to have a tow truck and a mechanic. Get in and we will go and see."

"My name is Sarah Anders. I'm on my way to Chicago for a meeting. I have to be there by seven tonight."

"My name is Michael Mills. I'm an author. I have a book signing in Chicago tomorrow afternoon. I wanted to get there early so that I could sort of case the area."

"Good," said Sarah. "I'm glad that I'm not holding you up from your appointment."

"That's no problem," responded Mike.

About twenty minutes later, they entered the main street of La Porte. About two miles into town, they saw an AAA sign in front of a garage and gas station. Mike pulled in.

"What can I do for you?" asked a middle-aged man dressed in a mechanic's uniform.

"My car stalled on me on Interstate 80. Do you think you can get a tow truck to pick it up for me, and do you do auto repair service here?" asked Sarah.

"Yes to both questions," said the service man. "My name is Bob. As to whether or not I can fix your car depends on what is wrong with it. Let's bring it in and we will see."

"Mike, what are your plans?" asked Sarah. "Are you going to continue your journey?"

"I don't know," said Mike, hesitating to think about it. "I hadn't thought about it. I hate to leave you stranded if, for some reason, he can't fix your car."

"Would you mind waiting until he looks at my car then? If it can't be fixed right away, perhaps I could hitch a ride with you to Chicago so I don't miss my meeting. It is an extremely important meeting."

"Sounds like a good plan," said Mike. "I don't mind waiting. In fact, why don't I go with you? Remember, all of your possessions are in my car."

It was almost five when the mechanic finished evaluating the auto problem.

"I'm sorry to tell you that you have ignition problems, and I don't have the part to fix it today. If you want, I can order the part and have the car ready within the next couple of days."

"What do you think, Mike?" asked Sarah. "Will you give me a lift?"
"Of course," said Mike. "Let's get going if you want to make your

seven o'clock meeting."

Once they were on the road, Sarah turned to Mike. "I'm sorry to put you through all this," she said apologetically.

"Nonsense," said Mike. "It brought some excitement to an otherwise boring trip."

"How many books have you written?" asked Sarah.

"This is my fourth book," he answered, "but this is not my prime source of income. I am an electronic engineer, but I quit my full time job and am working as a consultant. That gives me more time to write, which is my first love. How about you, what is your line of work?"

"I was a physics major in college. I now work for NASA in Cleveland."

"Are you married?" asked Mike. He was sorry he had asked almost before he had said it. He didn't want her to think he was hitting on her. He didn't wait for her to answer. To recover, he said, "I'm married to a very wonderful woman. We have been married for almost ten years, and believe it or not, we feel like we are still on our honeymoon. We also have a nine-year-old son."

"That sounds wonderful," said Sarah. "No, I'm not married. I had a young man who I cared for very much. He joined the air force, and I haven't heard from him since."

"How long ago was that?" asked Mike

"It was over ten years ago," she said

"You'll meet the right guy. You will know him when your stomach gets butterflies and you get a lump in your throat. I still feel the magic flow through my wife and I when we hold hands," lied Mike. Tara was the only one that made him feel that way.

"That's the way I felt with Tom," confessed Sarah. Then, distracted, she asked, "Why did those two cars flash their lights at us?"

"I don't know," said Mike. "Sometimes it's a warning that a police trap is ahead. It's no problem, since I am not exceeding the speed limit."

"The other thing that is puzzling," Sarah noticed, "is that there isn't much traffic on the road, especially this close to Chicago."

"I wonder what that is ahead," exclaimed Mike, ignoring her comment. "It looks like a blockade." Mike slowly approached the police cars blocking the interstate. It was the state police. The officer nearest them walked up to the car.

"I'm sorry," he said, "but the roads to Chicago are all closed. No one is allowed into the city."

"What's the problem?" asked Mike.

"All I know is that we got a call from our captain to close all the roads into Chicago. There is some kind of danger for anyone entering the area. That's all I know."

"Well, how long will the road be closed?" asked Sarah. "I have an important meeting in Chicago."

"Lady, there isn't going to be any meeting in Chicago tonight. I don't think there are any people in the city. Not being able to get any other information, they turned around and headed back to La Porte.

On the way, Mike told Sarah about the story he had heard about the terrorist's threat of nuking ten cities. They discussed it for a while, but they both dismissed it as unlikely. In La Porte, they went to the gas station to see what progress Bob had made on Sarah's car.

"It's the funniest thing," said Bob. "I haven't been able to contact anyone for the part. The phones must be down in this area. I can call my home here, but I can't get my normal contacts here in Ohio. I finally got a call in to a place in Utah. However, that would take a week for the part to get here by mail. I thought that I'd wait until things cleared up so I can get the part from my regular source in Chicago."

"That's okay," said Sarah. "My meeting has been canceled anyway, I think."

"I think my book signing has also gone south," said Mike.

Sarah walked to the other end of the station to a public phone to make a phone call. Mike took the opportunity to call Annie on his cell phone. There was no answer, though he got through to Annie's cell phone. Sarah came back shaking her head.

"That's funny. I couldn't call my office either. It didn't even ring. I will have to charge my cell phone and make my call."

"What makes you think that your cell phone will work? I couldn't get through to my wife, cell phone to cell phone."

"My phone will work," said Sarah with a smile on her face. "I work for the government. My service is through the satellite."

"Well I believe you will have plenty of time to charge it tonight. I'm not driving home in the dark. We better see if we can get motel rooms for the night. Then, lovely lady, I am inviting you to dinner."

"Those are the best words I've heard today"

"I know. It's been a pretty lousy day up to now."

"The biggest regret I have is that, because of me, you haven't been able to get into Chicago," she said sadly.

"Don't start adding up the points yet," said Mike. "We don't know what happened in Chicago. There could have been some kind of massive explosion. You may have saved my life."

"You're right," she answered, deep in thought. "We don't really know what happened. It had to be something devastating to stop all traffic into the city."

They found a small motel and got individual rooms. They agreed to meet in the motel lobby at eight. It was a little after eight when Mike showed up.

"I thought you had stood me up," said Sarah, kidding.

"I fell asleep," said Mike still in a daze. "I tried to watch TV but the one in my room doesn't work."

"Yes, mine didn't work either; I wanted to catch the news for some information as to what happened in Chicago."

"Well, I suggest we forget about Chicago, and go get something to eat," said Mike. "I'm starved."

"Yes I'm starved too. It must be due to all the activity we have gone through today."

After a satisfying dinner, Mike and Sarah sat at the table over a cup of coffee and talked about their lives. Sarah described her childhood and how she had always loved science.

"Have you always wanted to be a writer?" Sarah asked Mike.

"No, as I mentioned before, I graduated as an electronic engineer. Writing is a hobby. I make my livelihood as a consultant. Although,

I must admit that I like writing more than engineering and also that the book income is coming up to par with my engineering income. You see, in writing I can have a fantastic adventure anywhere in the world and even into outer space. I can meet important people and travel to exotic places. Although I have only written one science-fiction book, I am told by some of my readers that I should write a sequel to it."

"I can see that you have a real passion for writing," said Sarah. "You make me want to read all of your books. I like science fiction if it doesn't get too fantastic."

"My only science fiction is within reality. You will say to yourself, 'It could happen that way.' Do you do much reading?"

"Unfortunately, I do not have the time. I don't know if I told you that I work at NASA in Cleveland. I normally work crazy hours."

"I guess that is why you are still single," said Mike, trying to find out about her love life. He didn't have to try hard. She was willing to discuss it freely.

"I was very much in love with a fellow in college. I told you about Tom earlier. We talked about marriage. He was the only man who gave me butterflies in my stomach and a lump in my throat like you had with your wife. He was the only guy and I don't think it will ever happen again."

"I don't believe that," said Mike. "Someone will come along and sweep you off your feet. You are a very intelligent woman and beautiful on top of that."

"How about you?" asked Sarah. "Have you ever felt that way with anyone besides your wife?"

"That is a very interesting question," said Mike. "As a matter of fact, it will prove my point."

"How's that?" she asked.

"Annie was not my first love. I was madly in love with a girl named Tara in college. She was my whole life. I thought I could not live without her. There was a magic between us that I had never felt before her or after her."

"Not even with your wife?" asked Sarah, showing great surprise in her voice.

"I married Annie on the rebound. She was a settled for. I told Annie all about it before we got married. She said that she could live with it as long as I promised to be true. It was a blessing from God, and some luck I guess, that Annie turned out to be such a loving up-beat person. She showered me with so much love that I couldn't help but love her back. We are now extremely happy. I love her very much. I would never do anything to hurt her. So you see, there is happiness after your first love."

"You are surly blessed by God. It probably was his plan all along," said Sarah.

"Do you believe in God?" asked Mike.

"Of course," said Sarah. "I am a born-again Christian. I am a Baptist."

"That's great," said Mike. "I'm a Baptist too. If we are here Sunday, we can go to church together."

"If we don't get to bed, we will be here drinking coffee Sunday," said Sarah jokingly.

"Dear Lord," said Mike looking at his watch. "I can't believe what time it is. Let's meet at the motel's small cafeteria for breakfast, say about nine."

"Sounds like a plan," said Sarah as she got up to leave.

The next morning, after a light breakfast they went to the auto repair shop to talk to Bob.

"Bob, got any good news for us?" asked Mike.

"No, not yet," he answered. "I can't get hold of anyone anywhere. I think the long-distance phone system must be down."

"Do they shut down the TV stations at night?" asked Sarah. "I tried to get the news to see if there was anything about Chicago and all I got was noise."

"Have you tried your cell phone?" Mike asked Bob, ignoring Sarah's comment.

"Yes," said Bob. "That seems to be down too. Perhaps the cell phone tower is down. I don't understand what is going on. My TV was off also, and that is not normal."

"So there is no chance of you getting the part for Sarah's car today, is there?"

"I will keep trying, but I don't see how I can get it today."

"If you can't find a new part, do you think you can get a used one from a junk yard in town here?" asked Mike.

"We don't have a junk yard to speak of. However, you have a great idea. If you are willing to pay for the trip, I can send someone to South Bend to see if they have either a new one or a used one at their junkyard. They have a pretty good size yard."

"Do you know what I think?" asked Sarah. "Why don't you do what you have to do to get the part? Go to South Bend if you have to. Mike and I will try to go to Chicago."

"Are you sure, Sarah?" asked Mike.

"Yes," she answered. "It is already almost eleven. I would think they have cleared up the problem by now. We can make it to your book signing, and I can perhaps go to my meeting, which I assume has been postponed."

They checked out of the motel and soon were on the road to Chicago. It was about fifteen minutes after they left when Mike noticed that Sarah, who had been quiet, had a strange terrified look on her face.

"Sarah, are you all right?" he asked.

"No," she answered with a quiver to her voice.

"What is the matter? Should I pull over to the side of the road?" he asked, becoming very worried about her.

"No," she answered. "I'm sorry. I just have this terrible feeling of monumental and eminent disaster."

"What has caused you to feel this way?"

"Everything is starting to add up," she answered. "I tried to call my office. I tried all the numbers I have and couldn't get an answer from any of them."

"I know what you mean," said Mike. "I have been trying to call my wife all morning, and I can't get an answer either."

"On top of all that," continued Sarah, "the TV stations are all out, the radios don't work, and this thing about Chicago has all the ear marks of a terrible national emergency rather than a local problem. I don't know if I should tell you this, but there is a secret base somewhere in the country that we are supposed to call in case of an emergency. I have the phone number, but it is in my vault in my office." Before Mike could answer, they saw that police cars were still blocking the road to Chicago.

"How much longer will the road to Chicago be blocked?" asked Mike of the police woman at the blockade.

"I don't know," she answered. "It depends on the time it takes for the radioactivity to subside."

"Radiation?" asked Sarah. "Was there any destruction in Chicago?"

"Ask Martha, she just arrived here to replace me. She flew over Chicago earlier this morning. Hey, Martha, these people want to know what Chicago looks like from the air." The other policewoman walked over to them.

"Chicago," she said, "doesn't exist anymore. All there is there is a great gigantic hole, which is slowly filling up with water."

"Do they know what happened?" asked Mike, as shocked as Sarah.

"All we know is that we are to prevent people from going any farther because of the radiation."

Mike grabbed Sarah by the hand and took her to the car. They were half way back to La Porte before anyone spoke.

"I wonder if this is the fulfillment of the story you told me about the terrorist claiming that they had a backpack nuclear bomb," Sarah said. "Has this happened to the ten cities that he claimed would be nuked?"

"I don't know," answered Mike. "I'm not thinking straight right now. Let's wait until this all sinks in." When they got to the auto garage, Bob came out to talk to them.

"I haven't been able to contact anyone," he said. "I sent one of my men to South Bend. He left about twenty minutes ago. He should be back in a couple of hours unless he can't find a new part. Then he will have to search through all the junk yards."

"That will be fine," said Sarah. "Mike what do you want to do? If you want to go home I will understand. I'll wait for my car."

"With what we know about Chicago, we aren't sure he will get the part. Regardless, I will not leave you stranded. We have a lot to think about. Seeing that we're both people of science, maybe between us we can figure out what is going on. I think we are better together than apart. I want to be in the position to help if I can."

"You are something special do you know that?" she said. "Well, doesn't that sound like the right thing to do?"

"I'm biased," she answered. "I have never felt so alone in all my life. I need you to be with me."

"Then it's settled," said Mike. "We better go see if we can get our rooms back. We will have dinner here tonight. We have a lot to discuss. Tomorrow we will go to church together and pray that God will help us through this. We will ask God to direct us to do his work. Then after church, if your car is not fixed, we will both head for Cleveland. What do you think?"

"Sounds like a plan," she said.

They met for dinner that evening at a small cafe across from the motel. They were quickly seated and ordered their dinner.

"I've been thinking about what you said about the terrorist's threat," started Sarah. "It just doesn't make sense. Why nuke ten cities? How could that help anyone?" When Mike didn't answer her she continued. "That would just send us into a full-blown war with everything we've got. It would make better sense to nuke our army and air force bases. That way we couldn't retaliate. What do you think, Mike?"

"We really don't know what they have done," responded Mike. "Was it one city or a hundred cities? If it was only one or two cities that they nuked, then perhaps it was meant to aggravate us like they did with the twin towers. If it was really more cities, then I wonder what our officials' are planning. What is our military doing? My conclusion is that I don't have enough information yet. We just have to wait until we do."

"I guess you're right," agreed Sarah, "but I have this very strange feeling, like I'm expecting a terrible disaster to occur. It's like the feeling I had earlier as we drove toward Chicago."

"I know what you mean," said Mike. "I have the same type of feeling, like I haven't heard the worst part yet." They both sat in silence for a while.

"Let's change the subject," said Sarah. "Not knowing will drive us crazy. Tell me about your life." They spent the rest of the evening talking about their childhood days.

CHAPTER TWO

A Long Way Home

SUNDAY MORNING CAME AROUND SOONER than Mike would have liked. Waking brought back all the questions he had, with no

chance of a quick answer to any of them. Mike got up and met Sarah for breakfast.

"Have you any new thoughts on the current situation?" asked Sarah. "I don't even know what to call it."

"No, I don't." Mike responded as if he was deep in thought. "At this time, I am just thinking of my family. How are my wife and son? Was Cleveland one of the ten cities? All I have is more questions."

"I know," said Sarah. "I don't want to think of all the possibilities. Finish your coffee, then let's find a church and ask God for the answers or at least the wisdom to do the right thing. It's a little past ten. The motel pamphlet, I believe, stated that the service starts at ten thirty."

They found the Baptist church and attended the service. They both said a number of silent and private prayers. The sermon was especially appropriate, asking the members to trust God, reminding them that he is always in control and that all things will always come together for good. When the service was over, they went to the auto repair to see what Bob had to say.

"I'm sorry," said Bob. "My man came back without the part. The parts houses said they didn't have it, and the junkyard people said they didn't have the time to search their junked cars for the part. They said if they found one, they would call us. I think that the part cost is too low for them to spend time looking for it. I'm sure that if they find a slow time during the week, they will look for it."

"We have to get back to Cleveland," said Sarah. "We can't wait for it at this time. Could you just store the car for now until you can get the part? We will come for the car at a later date."

"That will be no problem," said Bob.

"What do we owe you for the effort that you have put in so far?" asked Mike.

"Don't worry about it," he answered. "We can settle when you come back for the car. After all, if you don't come back I have the car for collateral." They shook hands, and Mike and Sarah went back to the motel. They gathered their things, paid the bill, and left for Mike's car.

"Are you sure you want to leave your car here?"

"What other choice do I have?" she answered. "I can't stay here not knowing what is happening. He may never get the part. Besides, I have to get back to my office and see if I can help. In case we are in a full-fledged war, I have information that our military is going to need. Anyway, it's only a cheap foreign car." Without another comment, they were soon going east on Interstate 90. It was after one when they left. Mike tried several times to call Annie with no results.

"I don't understand why she doesn't answer her cell phone," said Mike. "We spend a lot of money so we can each have a separate, personal phone, and when I need her to answer it the most, she doesn't answer it."

"Maybe she was somewhere where she didn't want it to disturb her so she turned it off and forgot to turn it back on again. I'm sure she wasn't worried about you," said Sarah, knowing that what he said was unreasonable and was said under extreme frustration. "Have patience that all will become clear in a few hours."

Mike realized what he had said had no basis in truth. He knew something must have happened to her or her cell phone. "I hope it's just that her cell phone went bad." He also knew that this was improbable.

"Do you want to stop at South Bend for an early lunch and some gas?" asked Sarah trying to change the subject.

"No, it's too big a city. I don't want to get all tangled up in their traffic. We have enough fuel to get us to the next town. Elkhart is only about fifteen miles past South Bend. We just passed the exit for South Bend anyway, so it isn't too much farther."

"You know this area pretty well," said Sarah. She was pleased that she was able to change the subject.

"Yes, I've traveled this road a few times to visit my sister."

It was after two-thirty. Mike was getting anxious to get home before dark. They had been driving about two hours when they came through a hilly part of the highway toward a flat part of the country. There were still some large rocks along the sides of the road and in the center strip that they were driving through. Sarah had fallen asleep and awoke as he turned coming down one of the hills. It was Sarah who noticed it first.

"What is that coming at us?" she asked. "It looks like our air force is on the job."

"I don't know," said Mike as he bent forward to get a better look through the windshield. "They don't look like our fighters."

"Why are they flying so low?" asked Sarah. She grabbed on to her seat belt as Mike swerved drastically. Mike had seen the dust in front of him, and, thanks to his military experience, was able to recognize that the planes were shooting at them. As he swerved onto the soft shoulder, just missing one of the rocks, he heard the bullets rip through the rear roof and across the rear seat.

"What's happening?" asked Sarah in deep panic. "Are they shooting at us?" Without answering, Mike stepped on the brakes, steering the car near a large group of bushes on the side of the road. He hit a button on the dash to open the trunk.

"Sarah!" he yelled. "Quick, get out, grab whatever you can carry out of the trunk, and run and hide by those rocks." Mike reached into the glove compartment, grabbed his Swiss knife and his binoculars, and ran to the trunk. He took one of the books out of the box he had in the trunk and threw the box with the rest of the books in the bushes. He grabbed his attaché case and suitcase and threw them in the bushes also. He then placed the book he had kept against the gas pedal. The engine roared at top speed. Then Mike opened the driver's side window and placed the gear in drive. The car took off, almost tearing Mike's arm off. Mike then noticed that the aircraft had turned around and was approaching him. He didn't have enough time to get to the rocks, so he jumped into the bushes. He had just made it as the aircraft began firing at the car.

The auto was hit directly, but continued down the road, slowly going onto the soft shoulder, then into the field toward a small wooded area about two hundred feet down the road. Mike heard the familiar sound of a rocket igniting. He hadn't noticed, but a second aircraft had followed the first and shot a missile at the auto. The missile hit the trunk and blew the auto into a thousand pieces. Mike stayed hidden until the aircrafts had turned around and headed west again. He picked up the books, his suitcase, and his attaché case and headed for the rocks. When he got there, he could not find Sarah.

"Sarah!" he yelled in panic.

"I'm here!" yelled Sarah. "I'm between the rocks, under the far one." Mike walked between the two large rocks. It was very narrow. He didn't see Sarah.

"Sarah, where are you?"

"I'm here," she answered. Mike saw her hand appear from under the rock on his right.

"How did you get under there?" asked Mike.

"Bend down," she said. "There is a lot more room under here then the end where you are." Mike set down the items he was carrying and slid them under the rock.

"Can you hide these under there?" Mike set down the items he was carrying.

"No problem, I have my suitcases under here," she said as the items disappeared. Mike turned sideways and dropped down to the opening where Sarah was. He was able to slide into the opening. As soon as he was settled, he felt Sarah's arms and body enfold him.

"What is happening, Mike?" she asked, sounding like she was fighting tears.

"I think those were Russian MiGs, and I recognized at least two

Chinese fighters."

"What does all this mean?"

"I don't really know," he responded. "It looks like we are being invaded."

"Is that possible?" she asked.

"What I am afraid of is that our country has been so lax and over-confident that we have neglected to see the obvious."

"What exactly are you saying?" she asked, wanting a more definitive answer.

"Well," said Mike. "I think that it wasn't only the cities that they nuked, it was all the army, navy, and airbases that were nuked, and perhaps many cities. They didn't say that they only had ten backpack nuclear devices.

"Oh Mike," said Sarah now in tears. "What are we going to do?" "We wait and pray," he said. "I still hear the aircrafts flying above

us. At present, at least we are safe." At last, after what seemed like hours, the sky was silent.

"I don't hear them anymore," said Mike. "Let's get out of here and start walking. I think we were near the Ohio border."

"What has happened to your car?" asked Sarah. "Can it still be used?"

"Didn't I tell you? The car got blown to a thousand pieces. We are on foot from here to the next city." They had barely walked away from the rocks when Mike held Sarah back with his hand.

"What's the problem?" asked Sarah. Mike was looking through his binoculars.

"I think that the whole enemy army is out there coming our way," he answered. "The smoke I saw out in front of us is what triggered my suspicions." He handed the binoculars to Sarah. "Look for yourself. What do you see?"

"It looks like a column of tanks, trucks and thousands of foot soldiers, as far as I can see, north and south of us." Mike took back the binoculars and analyzed the situation.

"You're right," he said. "There is no way we can get around that army. We are safer under the rock." They were in no hurry to get under the rock until they heard the sound of the aircraft retuning. They quickly hid under the rock, and Mike peeked out so that he could see what was going on.

"How long do you think it will take them to pass us?" asked Sarah. "Well it looks like they are moving at about twenty or thirty miles an

hour," he said as he started to slip out into the open. "Where are you going?" she asked.

"When we were out there, I saw this big rock. I think I would like to place it at the end so that no one can look under this rock."

"Won't you be seen by the aircraft?"

"I don't hear them anymore. I can move the rock before they come back."

Mike was gone longer than Sarah wanted. She was about to call out to him when she noticed that it was getting a little darker due to the rock being placed at the end of the hiding area. A few minutes later he slid in beside her.

"You will not believe how heavy that rock was," said Mike as he settled in. "On top of my having problems moving the rock, the army is almost here. I think we are safe here until they pass."

"With all those men, vehicles and tanks it will probably take hours." They waited for what seemed more than an hour.

"I better go see what is going on," said Mike as he started to slip out from under the rock.

"Won't they see you if you go out there?"

"No, I'm going to the other side of the rocks to look over them. I'll keep hidden behind them."

He slid out and moved slowly west away from the army. He leaned over the rocks as inconspicuously as he could. Using his binoculars, he observed every movement they made and analyzed every bit of information he gathered. He was putting two and two together, arriving at intelligent conclusions as to what their general mode of operation was. Having seen all that he needed to see, he slowly slid back under the rock, next to Sarah. Sarah didn't ask any questions. She just waited. She knew that Mike would tell her every detail of what he saw.

"First let me tell you that they are not moving anymore," he started. "They are settling in for the evening. All that noise we heard came from four bulldozers that cleared a landing field for the aircrafts. There are eight airships. They are all parked on the northern end of the landing field. The field is located east of the army. I guess that is for self-protection. They probably feel that the area they have already destroyed will be safer. The amazing thing is that all the ends of the rows are coming in toward the middle. I would think that they will need at least three hours for them to gather in one large area. What I think is that they do that so that they can replenish their weapons and eat together. There are over twenty trucks parked near the road. It looks like they are waiting for their supply lines to show up. I could see smoke rising from several spots in the area. There is one large tent in the center about a mile south of us. Then, there are hundreds of smaller tents coming up all over the place. The large tent has the Chinese flag on top of it. The Russian flag is beside the tent. All the tanks are on the west side of the army area. A couple of tanks are almost next to our rock."

"I wonder when they will be marching again tomorrow?" asked Sarah, sounding like she was out of breath.

"I believe that they will not start moving until the end divisions are back in line again. It took three hours for them to get here, so I suspect it will take the same amount of time for them to get back in place. I imagine that they will start very early in the morning, and the line will not move forward until all are in place. My guess is that they will eat a big breakfast and skip lunch." "I can't believe that they could do this every day," added Sarah. "They have moved pretty fast to get this far. They couldn't move this fast if they did this ever day."

"You make a very good point," said Mike. "They may gather only when the supply line comes in. They may get enough supply each time for a few days."

"I guess we have to wait until morning," she said, snuggling up to him. "I hope you don't mind if I use your shoulder for a pillow."

"Let me get my jacket from my suitcase so I can use it as my pillow." That done, they settled in for the night.

It was still dark out when Mike was awakened by the activity outside their hiding place. He lay there awhile, listening, when he heard the all too familiar sound of the trumpet. In fact, he could hear many trumpets at different levels of loudness. He assumed that each division had his own wake up call. Mike wondered what time it was. It was too dark for him to look at his watch.

Just as he was about to give up, he noticed a light at the narrow entrance to their location. It wasn't very bright but bright enough so Mike was able to read his watch by sticking his hand by the entrance. It was four-thirty. Mike guessed that one of the vehicles or tanks had turned on its lights. It was about a half hour later that he heard the heavier noise indicating that the larger vehicles were starting to move. The noise woke Sarah.

"What is happening?" she asked.

"I think that they just ate breakfast and are starting to spread out again. It took about three hours for them to congregate. Remember they stopped at about six and ate about nine. Then they all went to sleep between nine and nine-thirty. They had about seven hours' sleep and woke about four-thirty. It is my guess that they will start moving forward about eight."

"As many as there are of them and their equipment," said Sarah, "they will be moving over us for about two hours. We will be here until ten."

"You will be surprised at how fast they will move," said Mike. "However, it will be about an hour or more before we can come out. They will have to be out of sight, and don't forget, they will have a rear guard following at a good distance behind them."

"Do you think we will be able to get home today?" asked Sarah.

"It all depends on if we can obtain a vehicle. Even then it will be difficult."

Mike's prediction turned out to be very close. After the main body passed by without detecting them, the rear guard followed about twenty miles behind, going around thirty miles an hour. It was a little after eleven when they came out from under the rock.

Sarah took a big deep breath of air. "It feels so good to be out in the open," she stated.

"The only thing I feel is hunger," said Mike, "Remember, we didn't have dinner last night."

"Well I can solve that problem," said Sarah with a smile. She slid back under the rock and returned holding a bag in her hand.

"What do you have there?" asked Mike in astonishment.

"It's the leftovers from yesterday's lunch," she said. "I wasn't going to leave it behind."

"You are amazing. Do you know that?" he said.

"You can have half of the soft drink that I kept." said Sarah. Mike took a sip of the soft drink.

"It's still cold," he said while taking another sip.

"It was pretty cold in the cave last night," she said. "I would have frozen if it wasn't for you. You are very warm blooded do you know that."

"That's because I was hot over you," said Mike, kidding her. Sarah thought that was pretty funny. "Why are you laughing? How many guys do you know that spent a night in a cave with his arms wrapped around a beautiful woman?"

"Oh, stop it already," said Sarah, embarrassed. "Shut up and eat your burger." After they finished their burgers and the soft drink they started across the field. Sarah took only her handbag, and Mike took his attaché case.

"We will leave the suitcases here," said Mike. "They will be safe. We probably have a lot of walking to do. Best we don't load ourselves down."

They stayed close to the edge of the road where there were plenty of shrubs to hide under in case the aircrafts returned. However, they saw no one. They did see a few cars, but they had been shot up and were not drivable.

They crossed the field that had been plowed for the landing strip. Mike checked around with his binoculars.

"There are some tanker trucks still on the runway," said Mike. "I think that the aircrafts land here every evening until the next time they come together and plow a new runway."

"Do you know what really scares me?" asked Sarah. "We haven't seen a car come or go on this otherwise busy super highway."

"I know," responded Mike. "Have they exterminated everyone from here to the ocean?"

"Dear Lord, I hope not," said Sarah. "Although, I'm sure they have done a lot of damage." After a moment of silence she added. "How fast are we going walking?'

"Well we are walking somewhere between two and a half and three miles an hour. I remember that the distance between Interstate 69 and the last tollbooth on the Indiana Toll Road is about twenty five miles. We had passed Interstate 69 and traveled about ten miles when we got hit, so I will guess that we are about ten to fifteen miles from the tollbooth. Let's assume that if we have twelve miles to go at an average of three miles an hour, it should take us about four hours to get to the toll booth. That is about two to three miles from the Ohio Turn Pike."

"Four hours and we are still only near the Ohio state line," said Sarah, feeling depressed. "What would it take to get home, a month?"

"Well, it is about two hundred miles to Cleveland from there so at three miles an hour—"

"Stop," she said interrupting Mike. "I've heard enough. I can do the math myself."

"The answer to the problem is that we must get transportation," continued Mike. "About two miles from the toll booth is the little town of Metz. I've been there before for fuel. If we cut across the farm land as soon as we see the toll both sign, we can save a little time."

It was a little after four when they saw the sign that said, "East Point Tollbooth Two Miles Ahead."

They turned south and cut through the field that had recently been plowed. There was no one in sight. It was about six when they reached Metz. The town had been terrorized. Six men and five women were moving bodies from stores and the road, and loading them on a flat truck that, apparently, was the only running vehicle in town. Some stores were completely destroyed. Mike assumed that they had been shot up by the tanks. Without a word, Mike and Sarah helped them.

When the truck was overloaded, the driver commented, "Let's take these and come back and check for more."

"Thank you," said one of the women. "Where did you guys come from?" she asked as she nodded toward Mike and Sarah.

"We were attacked on the road and managed to survive," said Mike. "We came here looking for food and a vehicle."

"The truck is the only thing that is drivable," said the woman. "They destroyed everything else. Do you guys have any ideas as to what is happening?"

"No," said Mike. "We are just as mystified as you are." Mike decided not to tell them what he suspected. Why kill any hope they may have. They were at least, for the present, rising to the challenge.

"As for food and lodging, help yourselves. Most of the store owners were killed as well as the poor souls that were shopping."

"Were the residential areas also hit this hard?" asked Sarah coming out of her shock.

"They blew up some of the homes and searched through the rest. I don't know what they were looking for."

"How did you people survive?" asked Mike.

"Most of us hid in our basements or fruit cellars. They were in a hurry and didn't search thoroughly.

"Will it be okay if we find some food and stay here, someplace for the night?" asked Mike.

"Of course," said the woman. "We have pretty well cleaned the downtown area. We are going to go from house to house to see if we can help. We are going to have a survivor meeting tomorrow after we take care of all our neighbors that were killed. You are welcome to attend."

"No," said Mike. "We have our own families that we are worried about. We will leave first thing in the morning."

"God go with you," said the woman as she left.

"I see a store that looks like a grocery store just down the street," said Sarah. "I think that there is a haberdashery just next door where we can get a blanket for the night."

"Good thinking. It's so good to have a woman around to take care of the necessities."

"Stop the silliness and let's get something to eat."

They walked down to the store. The meat counter glass top had been shattered and the food was covered with glass. Some of the cans on the shelves were shot full of holes. but a few were still intact. They found some soup and some paper cups and had enough to fill their needs. They found the cooler. It was still cool and the meat was still good, but the electricity was out so they had no way of cooking.

They also looked around for food for the morning. They found some milk in the cooler and some cereal on the lower shelves. With that taken care of they went to sleep.

Mike woke up at the first sign of light; he hadn't slept that well. Sarah woke up as soon as she sensed that Mike had moved.

"Let's have some breakfast and get moving," said Mike. "This place gives me the creeps."

"Yes," responded Sarah. "It is very depressing. I'm ready."

They ate breakfast and were soon on the road back to the highway. They walked in almost complete silence. However, their minds were not at rest. Mike's thoughts were on his home, on Annie and Ben. Was Fairlawn in the same state as Metz was? If so, were Annie and Ben able to hide in their basement? Was Ben still in school?

Sarah's thoughts were on her office. Was it bombed out of existence? What happened to the other employees? Would she be able to retrieve the secret base phone number? If she couldn't then she has failed her country. She knew the importance of the meeting in Chicago. She had information that was critical to her country's defense. They had been walking for about two hours when Mike stopped.

"There, can you see it?" Mike asked, pointing slightly to his right. "It's the Westgate Tollbooth. It's at the beginning of the Ohio

Turnpike and the Ohio border." As they hurried to get there, Sarah was first to notice that it was deserted.

"There isn't anyone around," she said, realizing that the help they thought they would get there would not materialize. "What do we do now?"

"We keep walking," said Mike sadly. "What is our next stop?"

"I don't remember any small cities on the way to Toledo. However, if I recall correctly, Toledo is about 60 miles from here. At three miles an hour, we should get to Toledo about this time tomorrow," said Mike sarcastically.

"How far is Toledo from Akron?"

"About 130 miles," said Mike, expecting a load of explicative. "Why do you ask?"

"I just want to know if we would get there this month."

"Still have your sense of humor," said Mike. "That is a good sign. We will find transportation I guarantee."

It was about two in the afternoon when Sarah saw a car in the field not far from the road. It looked partially hidden in the high grass.

"Look," she said. "It's a car off the road." She ran to it. "It doesn't look damaged at all." Mike walked slowly behind her to the car and tried the doors.

"The doors are locked," he said. Sarah was walking away from the car, into the field. "Where are you going?"

"I see that the grass here has been trampled," she said. "I want to see where it leads. It may be the owner's trail." She walked about 100 feet and yelled to Mike. "Mike, come here. I think I found the owner." Mike ran up to her. There at her feet was a woman face down in the dirt.

"Look through her purse," he said. "It's there by her side. Do you see it? See if you can find the keys." Sarah slowly and carefully pulled the purse from under her. The strap was around her shoulder. Sarah pulled it out as if she was afraid to awaken the woman. She looked through its contents.

"There's nothing here," she said sadly. Then, thinking the situation over, she asked, "Why would she stop to lock her car when someone is shooting at her?"

"I think you are smarter than you know," he said hopefully. "She was running from a plane, so what would you have done with the keys?" He then walked up to the woman's left hand that was extended above her head. He slowly lifted her hand. There in her fist were the keys. He struggled to pull the keys from her grasp. Her hand was as stiff as the hand of a stone statue. He was finally able to free them.

"I guess she didn't have time to put them away," said Sarah. "She must have locked the car as she was running away from the aircraft that was shooting at her."

"That's the way I figure it. Look at where she was running to," he said, pointing about a hundred feet ahead of them. "She was headed for those woods. I bet that if you shift the dirt around here you will find many bullet slugs."

"Too bad she couldn't make it," said Sarah. "I wonder if she has a family. Does she have any children? I'm going to put her purse back under her. That way, when someone finds her, they will know who she is and perhaps be able to notify her family."

"For now, let's walk back to the car," said Mike. "Let's find out if it runs and how much gas it has." They walked back to the car. Mike opened the door and tried the keys. The engine started right away. He checked the gas gauge. It had about a quarter of a tank.

"It's a compact so it probably will get good mileage," suggested Sarah.

"It will at least get us to the nearest gas station," responded Mike. "Our biggest problem is getting the car out of this field." He then put the car into gear and tried to move it forward. They could feel the tires slip on the grass. Mike tried to rock it back and forth. It moved very slowly forward and then stopped. It wouldn't move any farther forward no matter what he tried.

"What are we going to do now?" asked Sarah starting to worry.

"We are going to see how strong I am and how good a driver you are," said Mike. He got out of the car and motioned for Sarah to get into the driver's seat. "Now, you are an intelligent woman, so listen carefully. I want you to give it gas very slowly. When you feel it slipping, release the gas and then slowly reapply it again. I'll be pushing the car from behind. Don't rock it as I did. You will run me over. Do you understand?"

"Gotcha. I know what to do."

"Good girl." Mike got behind the car, and as he applied pressure he yelled to Sarah, "Go!" Sarah did exactly as Mike had instructed her. The car started to move. Sarah was smart enough to know that she couldn't make large steering moves. Slowly, the car moved onto the shoulder where the wheels grabbed the gravel and moved onto the road. Sarah moved over to the passenger seat as Mike caught up to the car. He noticed that she had moved, and so he climbed into the driver's seat.

"We make a great team, don't we?" he asked.

"I take it that is a form of a complement?" she asked.

"You bet," he answered with a smile. "You were terrific. You did exactly what was needed, even things that I forgot to mention."

"Thank you," she said. "It's nice to be appreciated."

"Just remember one thing," he reminded her. "I couldn't have done it without you."

"What do you think I would have done without you?" she added. They drove for about half an hour when Mike saw the sign for Route 80.

"I remember this area," said Mike. "There is a small town just off of the turnpike. You can see it from the highway. I'm going to stop there." He took the exit ramp and headed for the town.

They were shocked at what they saw. The town was completely destroyed.

"It's no wonder," said Sarah. "This town is so close to the highway. Have you noticed that the highway has not been damaged at all, yet everything else has been badly damaged?"

"What are you suggesting?" asked Mike.

"What I'm thinking is that they have a reason for keeping this road in good shape. Perhaps they will need it for their supply line."

"I never thought of that," said Mike. "I'm glad you brought it up. Here we have been traveling and feeling safe, what do you think would happen if we ran into their supply line? I'm sure they will be traveling with sufficient protection. It makes sense that they would make sure that they wipe out everything around the highway."

They pulled into the center of town and into a gas station.

"There is no one here," said Mike. "I think that there might be some survivors because all the bodies have been removed. There are probably a few farmers left who have cleaned up as much as they can and then went home."

"Look," said Sarah, filled with fear. She was pointing to the field east of their position. "Are they coming back?" Mike grabbed his binoculars and looked out at the dust that Sarah was seeing.

"It's a farmer that is plowing his field. He is probably getting ready for his spring planting."

"How can he go back to work like nothing has happened?

"What else does he have to do?" said Mike. "He has to live. Besides he probably has no idea of what is going on outside of his little world."

"You see if you can get some gas," she said, having settled down. "I'll go see if I can find some food." Mike couldn't pump gas because the electricity was out, so he went into the gas station to look for a generator. These little towns generally had independent generators that gave them energy. He found one behind the station. Unfortunately, it had been destroyed by the invading troops. Mike then went down the street until he came to a small hardware store. It had been badly destroyed. However, Mike found the piece of plastic tubing he was looking for. He also found a five-gallon can.

There were several cars parked along the road in town. They were all heavily damaged and not drivable. However, most had undamaged gas tanks. Mike used the plastic hose and siphoned sufficient gas to fill their car. Just as Mike was replacing the gas cap, Sarah walked up.

"I have four sandwiches with salami. I also brought along the whole salami that I cut in half to take home. Also, I found some fruit and soda to drink. "

"Good girl. I also have a full tank of gas," said Mike. "I had to siphon the gas from the damaged cars."

"Let's eat here," suggested Sarah. "It's too hard to eat while we're moving."

"I like that idea," he said. "We have to keep our eyes on the road to make sure we don't run into the supply line." They ate silently in the car, and, when full, they headed back to the turnpike. Just as they approached the entrance, Sarah spotted some movement on the highway. The road went up a small hill, and anything on the top of the hill was visible. Mike, figuring it was the supply line, quickly turned the car around and drove it into the gas station building out of sight.

"Wow, that was close," said Sarah. "I think God is still with us. What would we have done if we had been on the turnpike? Where would we have hidden?"

"Your idea of eating here saved us," said Mike. "We have to be more careful. I think your assessment that they kept the roads in good condition for their supply line was correct. I think that after this one passes, it will be pretty clear the rest of the way."

It was about a quarter to five when the road was clear enough for them to continue home. The next half hour passed with little conversation. They were approaching Toledo. When they got to the Toledo bypass, they could see most of the city. They were amazed at the destruction they saw. Most of the larger buildings were gone. Only the foundations were visible. Mike and Sarah could see some activity. The local inhabitants were probably still removing bodies from the streets and cars. Mike stepped on the gas and sped through the area as fast as that little car could go. He wanted to get away from there as fast as he could.

"I wonder if Cleveland is the same way." said Sarah. She saw tears appear in Mike's eyes.

"I wonder if Akron and Fairlawn are the same way," he said. "We may be going home to mayhem. By the way, since you don't have a car, I think we should go to my home first so that you can take this car to your place," Sarah agreed. It was a little over 100 miles from Toledo to Interstate 77 in Ohio. It normally took two hours. Mike stepped on the gas and drove as fast as the car would go.

"Aren't you going a little too fast?" complained Sarah.

"What's the problem? There are no cops and no traffic." No more was said. Mike made it to Interstate 77 in a little under an hour and a half. From there it was about 15 miles to his home. Merging onto Interstate 77, he noticed that there were many more cars on the road, but none were running. Some had been blown to pieces, and others were just full of machine gun holes. There were no bodies to be seen. Every damaged car or damaged building that he saw affected him like a stab wound in the heart. He tried to imagine Annie and Ben running up to him with joy upon seeing him. But the image would not form in his mind. He felt a rising pain in his heart as he left Interstate 77 and headed for his house.

CHAPTER THREE

Unhappy Homecoming

MIKE TURNED DOWN HIS STREET. Some houses were badly damaged, but most were only slightly damaged and some not at all. As he approached his house, he noticed that it looked like it wasn't damaged. As he pulled into his driveway, he did notice that the front door was wide open. He pulled all the way in the back where he realized that the garage door, which was in the back of the house, was open.

"My wife's car is gone," said Mike, talking to himself. Sarah had been very quiet up to this point. "She is probably at the school to pick up Ben." Sarah knew it was too late for Ben to be in school.

"Don't you think it is strange that we don't see anyone around?" said Sarah. "This late in the day, shouldn't the children be out playing?"

Mike didn't answer. He didn't want to think about it.

"Let me go inside to see if Annie is there or if perhaps she left me a note. If she is there, I would like you to meet her." He went inside and after a few minutes came back out to the car.

"There is nothing," he said disappointedly. "I think I will go to the school to see what I can find out."

"Do you want me to drive you to the school?" asked Sarah.

"No, that won't be necessary. I'll just walk down there. You take the car and go on to your home I know that you have problems of your own. Go find out what is left of Cleveland and your home."

"Are you sure?" she asked, not wanting to leave him alone.

"Yes, I'll be all right. I'm sure that I will find a friend or two. It can't be any more different here than it was in those small towns we passed."

"Well, if you are sure," she said as she handed him his briefcase. "This is all you have here, I believe."

"That's it. Keep in touch."

"Okay," she said. She pulled out into the street and disappeared. Mike grabbed the spare keys to his wife's car and walked briskly down his street to the second intersection and turned right. Five minutes later, he was walking into the school parking lot. The sight was the same as he had seen everywhere. Some cars were badly damaged and some were untouched. He spotted Annie's car. It was in good shape. All the school's doors were open, and he heard some activity inside. He prayed that the sound he heard was from Annie. She was always volunteering to help where it was needed. Hope built up in his heart. He walked through the door to the gym. The first person he saw was Martha, a math teacher that had Ben last year. She had become good friends with Annie. Since she wasn't married, Annie had invited her several times to dinner.

"Hi, Martha," said Mike. "It's good to see that you are okay." He started to ask her if she had seen Annie but stopped. Martha had completely broken down at seeing Mike. It took several minutes before she could talk.

"I tried to stop her," she managed to say between tears. Mike began to suspect the worse.

"What happened?" he managed to ask through the lump in his throat.

"I tried to stop her," she could only say.

"Tried to stop her from what?" asked Mike afraid of what the answer would be. It took a few minutes to get her calmed down enough so she could tell Mike what had happed.

"We heard the sound of machine guns and saw teachers being shot," she said, hesitating to gasp between each word. "I ran to Annie's room. She was subbing for Miss Calardy's kindergarten class." She hesitated to catch her breath. "I grabbed Annie and pulled her to the closet in the back of the room. We lay down on the floor. Bullets went through the wall above us."

"What happened to Annie?" asked Mike, getting impatient.

"Well, when the men had left the building, we came out and looked out the windows. That's when Annie saw the men throwing the older students in the rear end of a large truck. When Annie saw one of them grab Ben to put him in the truck, Annie yelled out his name and started to run outside to help her son. I tried to stop her, but I couldn't. I tried to tell her that as long as he was safe, she should wait. It wouldn't help Ben if she got killed. She knocked me down and ran outside. I should have knocked her down. I tried to stop her!" she yelled and broke down crying.

"What happened to Annie?" he asked, starting to cry, knowing the answer.

"The guy in the truck shot her. First he shot her in the neck, and then he came down and shot her in the heart." Mike was now crying loudly. It took Martha what seemed like an hour to get Mike calmed down.

"Where is Annie now?" asked Mike as soon as he could talk. "She is in the locker room," said Martha.

"Take me to her."

"I didn't know what to do with her. I tried to call you, but no one answered. I told the undertaker who is burying most people in a large grave to leave her until last. We tried to find relatives or addresses for each person." They reached the locker room, and Martha took him to where Annie's body lay on a bench, covered with a sheet Martha had found somewhere. As soon as Mike saw her, he collapsed on top of her and cried, repeating her name over and over again. Martha left him alone with her. She stayed back by the door. She didn't know what to do for him.

It was about an hour later when the undertaker arrived to pick up more bodies. When he saw Mike, he recognized him

"Aren't you Mr. Mills?" he asked. Mike looked up and nodded. "You and the missus have two crypts in our Rose Hill Mausoleum."

"Yes," said Mike.

"I'm Jeff Morgan. Why don't you come with me now and pick out a coffin?"

"No, I don't want to leave her. I want to sit with her all night."

"We can't leave her any longer," said Jeff. "She has already started to decompose. She will start smelling bad very soon. It's even too late to embalm her now. We will put her in the coffin, and give you a few minutes before we place her in the crypt."

"No, I want more time with her. I can't let her go. Put me in the other crypt. I have no reason for staying out in the world."

"I'll tell you what I'll do: I will take her now and put her in a cold locker. You come pick a coffin, and tomorrow morning you can spend more time with her as long as she stays cool." Martha led Mike to Annie's car.

"Have you heard anything about my son?" asked Mike

"All I know is that they took him away in the truck with the other older students," said Martha. Mike got into Annie's car and soon was in his yard. He drove it into the garage and pushed the button to close the garage. Nothing happened. Then Mike realized that the electricity must be off. He got out and closed the door manually. He went into the house and sat in the family room. He knew he couldn't go to sleep. He didn't know how long he had sat there when he heard a knock on the door. He looked at his watch. It was almost nine thirty.

"Who could it be at this time of night?" he said out loud. He walked to the rear door and looked through the door window to see who it was. As soon as he recognized her, he opened the door.

"Sally," he cried and hugged her. After sobbing on her shoulder for a while, he let her in. "How are you? I didn't think there was anyone left in the neighborhood."

"There were a few of us left, but most of them left to go south where they think they will be away from the invaders. Never mind them, though, what do you know about Annie? I'm so concerned about her. She went to sub for one of the teachers. I was hoping that she got through the madmen attack at school."

Mike started to cry. "She didn't make it," he finally got out. He told her the story as Martha had told him. Sally was crying along with Mike. They hugged for a while until they ran out of tears.

"What have you heard about Bill?" asked Mike.

"I have not heard from him," she said. "He went to one of Doug Miller's plants to solve a problem there. I don't even know which one, or I would have gone there to look for him. That's why I didn't go with the others. I won't leave until I find out what has happened to him."

"How did you know I was home? There are no lights."

"I went out to the barn, and I noticed that your garage door was closed. I thought that Annie had finally found her way home."

"Speaking of Annie, will you do me a favor?" asked Mike.

"Of course, anything I can do," she said. "What do you need?" "Tomorrow morning, I am going to have a little service for Annie at nine at the cemetery. I got a coffin for her earlier today, and she will be displayed for a short time near our crypt. Could you come with me?"

"Sure, I want to," she said. "Do you have a car? Bill has one of our cars, and the invaders destroyed our second car."

"Yes, I have Annie's car. It was parked at the school and for some reason was spared. How bad was your car damaged?"

"They cut all the wires under the hood."

"Perhaps I could fix it for you, if I can get the parts." He said.

"I'll drive tomorrow if you like," offered Sally. "I will be in better shape than you. I'd be glad to do that."

"I wonder if the church is open. I'd like to get the pastor to say a few words," said Mike.

"We can stop at the church to see if it is still there. I also know where the pastor lives, so we can stop there. We will get up early and do this and be at the cemetery at nine."

"Get up early?" said Mike. "Who is going to bed?" "Mike, can I make a suggestion?"

"Sure Sally, what do you have in mind?"

"You are grieving over Annie, and I am worried sick about Bill. We are best friends. For Annie and Bill's sakes, we should stick together and support one another's needs."

"Oh, Sally, I'm so glad to hear you say that. I don't want to be alone, and we need each other."

"Then you won't mind if I stay here tonight. I don't think either one of us is going to sleep, but I don't want to spend another night by myself. We are like brother and sister, aren't we?"

"You sure can, sis," said Mike, trying to bring a little humor in their lives. It did bring a slight smile to Sally's lips, but it was more the fact that she got her wish not to be alone. She lay down on the couch while Mike pulled on the lounge handle and pushed the lounge back as far as it would go so that he was able to rest better.

"How did you get away from the attackers?" she asked. Mike told her about his trip, how he met Sarah and how, because of her, he was still alive. Sally started crying when he told her that Chicago no longer existed. He explained about the possibility that ten cities had been destroyed. He started to tell her that Sarah and he thought that all the military bases had also been destroyed, but he noticed that she had fallen asleep. He lay there thinking of his son. Where could he be? Was he still alive? He had decided that he couldn't just stay in the house. He had to do something to find his son. Exhausted from the day's effort, and so much crying, he finally fell asleep.

The next morning, Mike awoke in a daze, wondering where he was. It took awhile for him to realize that he was home. He had no idea what time it was. It was still dark outside. He lay there for a while then suddenly realized that Sally had stayed with him. He pulled open the drapes. The moon was full, and by the moonlight he read his wristwatch. It was around five. As he stood there, he caught the smell of what he thought was coffee. From the moonlight coming through the kitchen window, he saw a figure moving around the kitchen.

"Sally!" he called out.

"Mike, come up here," she said. "What are you doing?" he asked. "I'm making some breakfast."

"I'm not too hungry."

"You have to eat something if you want to do all the things we need to do today," she insisted.

"How did you find your way around and what have you cooked?" "I've been here many times, remember. Besides, after a while you can get used to seeing by moonlight. As for the food, I made some eggs. Since your refrigerator has been closed since the power went out, it is still a little cold. The eggs are still good. Sit there, in your usual place, and I'll serve you." Mike followed her instructions without comment.

"Why are you up so early? The last thing I remember, you were fast asleep on the couch."

"I know," she answered. "I woke up and saw that you had fallen asleep, so I got up and looked out the window until just a few minutes ago when I decided to make breakfast." Sally had made two eggs, toast and coffee for each. In spite of the fact Mike had said that he wasn't hungry, he ate everything on the plate.

"Where did you get the water?" asked Mike when they had finished.

"Strange as it may seem, there is water. Since it is up on the hill, they didn't go there, and we have gas too. That's how I cooked the eggs. I did everything on your built-in grill."

"You're a wonder, do you know that?" he answered. "It's good to know. That means that we also have hot water. I suggest that we take a shower, get clean clothes, and go to the church to see what condition it is in."

The church seemed to be in good shape. As they were about to leave, Sally noticed the light from a flashlight in the pastor's office.

"Somebody's in there," she said quietly. "I wonder if it's the pastor." "There's one way to find out," said Mike. They both walked to the front door. When they got there they noticed that the door had been damaged and crudely repaired. They knocked on the door. The pastor came to the door and waved them to the side door.

"Hello, Mike, Sally. What are you guys doing here this early?" he asked.

"What are we doing here? What are you doing here? We came by to see how the church was," said Mike.

"I'm here trying to straighten things out. I tried to call the other members of the council. I could use some help. I don't know if any are still alive."

"How did you escape the attack?" asked Sally.

"I was at home. We hid in the basement," said Pastor Antony. "How did your family survive?"

"Annie didn't survive, Pastor. I need your help," said Mike with tears in his eyes.

"Dear Lord," said the Pastor. "I'm so sorry to hear that. She was such a sweet person. Oh, how we are going to miss her. What happened?"

Mike told him everything he knew, and told him that he hadn't heard from Bill.

"Pastor Antony," continued Mike, "we are having a wake for Annie at the cemetery from nine to about eleven. We would like you there to say a final prayer for her."

"Of course I will be there, not only for you but for me."

"We will leave you to your work, Pastor. We will see you later," said Mike.

They left the church and drove to the bank. They were surprised to see that it wasn't damaged too much, and that they had lights inside and a couple of young women working. They knocked on the door. It was only a little past eight. One of the girls came to the door. She recognized Mike. Mike had been going to this branch since he and Annie were married.

"Hello, Mr. Mills. How are you?"

"Not so good," said Mike with tears forming in his eyes. "I lost my wife, Annie."

"I know," she said. "A lot of people have suffered losses. What can I do for you?"

"First, tell me how you were saved and how many with you were saved."

"There were five of us working when we heard the noise. Once we figured what it was, we locked ourselves in the vault. We had to stay there till morning, but we didn't care. We were safe."

"Are you going to be open for business?" asked Mike. "That is, are my checks going to be good?"

"Our window here inside won't be open for a couple of days, but your money is safe, and your checks will be honored."

"Can I ask you one more question? How do you have lights when the rest of the area is dark?"

"Well, Bob, our director, is very smart. The first thing he did was go to the discount club, I don't remember the name, and got a generator. We need one for our computers. He hooked it up yesterday, and it works great."

"Thank you and keep the faith," said Mike and they left. "They had a great idea," he said to Sally as they left. "We still have time, and I know where the club is. Let's see if we can get one."

He drove to the area. The club had been devastated. They didn't see a soul anywhere. Mike knew about where the generators would be, and worked his way through the debris to find them. Most were damaged, but he found two that were in good condition. One was gasoline powered; the other was natural gas powered. Mike figured that he was going to have trouble getting gasoline, and since they had natural gas at home, he decided to get the natural-gas powered one. Sally helped him load it in the trunk of the car. About half of it stuck out of the trunk, but who cared? There were no police around.

"Now the question is, where do we attach it, at your house or mine?" said Mike when they got home.

"Why would you even consider mine?" asked Sally puzzled. "Because, I don't intend to stay around here very long," answered Mike.

"Where are you going? You're not thinking of going south with the rest of the people?"

"No, I have to go look for my son," he answered. "I can't rest without trying. The real question is, where can the generator be attached better?"

"Mike, listen to me," she said being very serious. "First, I don't have a freezer and you do, and it is full of food that is still good and will be for only a few days. Secondly, if you are leaving, why couldn't I stay here until the electricity comes back on at my place? I only have a few items that I could bring over and place in your freezer."

"You can stay here till the cows come home.

I think the north side of my house where the air conditioner comes in is a good place for the generator. On that side of the house is the fuse box. The gas line is there also."

"Okay then, it's all set," said Sally. "Now we'd better go to the cemetery. We don't want to be late." A few minutes later they arrived at the cemetery. They found Pastor Antony already there with his wife and daughter. Annie had just been placed near the crypt. There were three sets of flowers, one on each side of the casket and a large one above it.

"I know it would have been difficult for you to get flowers," said Jeff the director and undertaker, "so I took the liberty of getting some for you. Your pastor really gave me the idea when he arrived this morning. This is the best I could do. There wasn't too much choice as you can imagine." Mike noticed that pastor's wife, Ann, was crying. Mike thanked them and went up to the coffin. He started to cry.

"Why are you leaving me? You know how much I need you." He grabbed Annie to hug her, but he was restrained by Pastor Antony and the funeral director.

"She has been in the open air too long," said the director. The pastor started praying at the request of the director. He had notified the pastor earlier that they couldn't keep the casket open much longer. Mike heard the pastor praying, but he was in a daze and didn't comprehend anything that was said. It was near noon when the director told them that the casket had to be closed and placed in the crypt.

"No!" yelled Mike. "Please let me look at her a little longer."

"I'm sorry," said the director. "We have held back now for more than an hour to please you." While the director was talking, his helpers were starting to close the casket.

"Wait," said Mike. "Let us say good-bye." The director led them all past the casket and walked them outside.

"Good-bye, my sweet Annie," said Mike as he walked by. "Wait for me. I'll not be long."

They said good-bye to the pastor and his wife, Ann. She hugged Mike and said how sorry she was. Mike and Sally started for home. Sally insisted that she drive.

"Listen," said Mike. "While we are out, let's stop at the Copley Circle. There is an auto parts store there. Let's try to get you some spark plug wires."

Sally changed direction, and a few minutes later they arrived at the circle. The auto store was completely destroyed. It had no roof. They noticed that someone was working to place a canvas cover over the building. The store was rather small so it was possible to cover it. The canvas was set on poles or the high parts of the wall that was still up. Sally parked the car, and Mike walked up to the worker.

"Hi," said Mike. "How are you doing? Trying to protect the store from thieves?"

"No," said the man. "There aren't enough people around to steal. I'm trying to protect it from the weather."

"Are you the owner or an employee?"

"My father is the real owner, but he is retired. I'm his son, so, at present, I'm the owner or at least the responsible person. My name is Ralph Richards."

"Did your father and your family survive the attack?"

"My mom and dad are in Hawaii. Since the phones are not working, I can't contact them. My wife, my daughter, and I were saved by hiding in the cave we were visiting on our vacation."

"Do you and your parents take vacations at the same time? Who watches over the store?"

"I was supposed to be home," he said, tongue in cheek. "Don't let my father know. We were on our way home when the attack occurred. We stayed a week longer than we were supposed to. What can I do for you? You aren't a builder by any chance, are you? I can't find anyone to help me put this building back up."

"No, I'm sorry. I don't suppose that the parts are okay?"
"Fortunately, it looks like the shell went through the front window and exploded only on the roof. If I can get the building in some kind of order, I know I can be back in business. From what we have seen on the road, there will be a lot of business."

"Would you possibly have spark plug wires? The attackers cut all the spark plug wires on my neighbor's car."

"I may have some, but I don't have any power, so the deal has to be cash."

"That will not be a problem." Mike gave him the year and make of Sally's car. A few minutes under the tarp, and Ralph came up with the proper wires.

"Is that your wife in the car?" asked Ralph. "She is very pretty."

"No, that is my neighbor. My wife was killed in the attack. Her husband is still missing. We are trying to help each other."

"I'm so sorry," he said. "I guess there are many people in the same situation."

"I'm sure there are," said Mike fighting the tears that wanted to come out. He paid for the wires, and they headed for home. Mike related to Sally all that had been said between Ralph and himself. When they got home, Mike excused himself and headed upstairs.

"Where're you going?" asked Sally. "Don't you want some lunch?"
"No, I'm not hungry right now. I think I want to lay down for a
while." He went up to the main bedroom. Sally felt very bad because she could hear him crying. That caused her to cry silently not only for him but in anticipation of her own possible dilemma. She was no longer hungry either.

It was about three in the afternoon when Mike came downstairs. Sally was dozing on the living room couch. She awoke when she heard Mike come down the stairs.

"Are you all right?" she asked.

"I don't know if I'll ever be all right," he said. "If you are referring to my health, I'll survive."

"Do you want anything to eat?"

"It's too late for lunch and too early for diner. I think that I'll go hook up the generator. First I have to go to store and see if I can get some supplies that I need."

"I will have dinner ready in about an hour and a half.

After dinner, Sally went down to the family room. "Mike, come down here, will you?" she requested. As Mike started down the stairs the room filled up with light.

"What..." he said in amazement. What, how?

"I found a lantern while you were looking for the generator. It was in an aisle next to the place you found the generator. I though you saw me put it in the back seat of the car."

"I never saw a lantern that bright," said Mike still in amazement. "That's because it is an LED type. It has one hundred LEDs."

"That reminds me," said Mike. "I have an LED flash light. I've never used it, but I think it will be pretty bright too." He went into his office and brought out the flashlight.

"Come on. While we have nothing else to do, let's go see if we can fix your car." Mike got the wires he had bought, and they went next door. With Sally holding the flashlight, it only took five minutes for Mike to install the wires. Sally got the keys and started the car. It kicked over without any trouble.

After a short time of small talk, they went to bed.

The next morning, Mike rose early. He wanted to get the generator working as soon as he could. He went downstairs and looked for Sally. She wasn't anywhere to be found. He figured that she was still asleep and went outside to see if the concrete, that he had prepared the day before was good enough to hold the generator. It looked sturdy enough, so he performed the job of installing the generator.

With everything turned on, he went to the generator to make sure that he was not overloading it. It was almost to its maximum. He figured that once the freezer and the refrigerator were cold, the power requirement would be reduced. Then he went upstairs to look for Sally.

She was nowhere around. It was nearly eleven. She still couldn't be in bed, he thought. He decided to go up and see what she was doing. Before he went up, he looked out of the window to the back yard. Since Sally's driveway and Mike's driveway were only five feet apart, he couldn't help looking at her back yard. That's when he noticed that her car was gone. *Where did she go?* wondered Mike.

He began to worry about her. He had no idea what was going on out in the streets. He worried that the survivors, few as they may be, could all be in need of something and not concerned as to how they will get it. Apparently, there were no police around. It could be a free for all out there.

Mike sat around, waiting for Sally to return. He wondered if he should go out to look for her. Where would he look? He got more worried with every minute that went by. It was a little after twelve when Sally pulled into the back yard.

"Where have you been?" Mike yelled at her. "Do you know how worried I've been?"

Sally looked at him with a cold stare. Mike suddenly became aware that he was out of line. "I'm sorry," said Mike apologetically. "I have no right to question your actions. You're not responsible to me. I just don't trust the streets out there. I'm sorry."

"Don't be sorry," she said warmly. "It is kind of nice to know that someone cares about my safety."

"Well, I was worried about you. Where did you go and what did you find out? I'm sure you had a mission."

"I'm sorry that I worried you. From now on, I'll tell you when I decide to go anywhere," she promised. "I just didn't want to wake you this morning. You must understand that I have to look for my husband as much as you have to look for your son."

"I understand," he said "You have every right to do what you can in that effort. What did you find out?"

"I went to my husband's boss's office first. I thought that I could find out where all of his plants are and possibly where my husband went. The building was completely destroyed. I couldn't even find a sheet of paper. Then I thought, as long as I was out I would drive down to the electric plant. There were some men working there, so I stopped to talk to them. They told me that the plant wasn't hit too bad. They would have it repaired and working in a couple of days. However, they said that providing electricity to the public was another question. They could only find about a dozen workers out of the two thousand that were employed before the attack. They also said that the neighborhood street wires are down all over the city. It will take months to get power to the public. They have to go one area at a time and with only a handful of workers. They hope that the workers will stay on. The office was destroyed. They said that they are trying to get enough power to power up the computers."

"Well, at least someone is working on the problem," said Mike. "Let's get something to eat and plan our next move. I should have prepared something, but I wasn't thinking too straight."

After they finished eating they sat down and planned their days. Mike was eager to go looking for his son, but he also felt a duty to his city. If he survived the search, he would want to come back here to live. They decided that the first place to help was in the church. Since the next day was Sunday, they decided to ask the pastor if he needed help. They didn't know how else they could help the city. Apparently, all the dead had been taken care of by the funeral parlor. They also decided that they would go to the city hall area and see if they could find a city official to ask him where they might be of help.

The next morning, they went to church. There were only about a half dozen people there. After the service, they talked to the pastor. They asked what had yet to be done to bring the church up to par.

"We have all the woodwork completed and the walls fixed," said the pastor. "All we need now are painters."

"Sal and George, who helped me with the walls and woodwork, have repairs on their own properties to take care of. There aren't too many of us left.

They said good-bye to the pastor and went to the city hall and found a young woman there. Mike recognized her as one of the office workers. When she saw them, she froze and looked like she had seen a ghost.

"Hi," said Mike as they walked into the city hall lobby. "I'm glad to see that you have survived the attack. Are there any others that are still with us?"

"Who are you?" she asked seeming frightened.

"I'm sorry," said Mike. "I am Mike and this is Sally. We live on the next street. We came to see if we can be of any service to help the city wherever there is need."

"I'm sorry," she said. "You scared me. I didn't know that anyone else had survived. The only ones I know of are Councilman Briggs and Councilman Barton, and of course me and Sandra. I'm Phyllis Wendell. Sandra is with the Councilmen. They are trying to help the necessary stores so that we can have food and staples."

"I know them," said Mike. "Bob Barton is the chairman of the council. The other is Steve."

"Do you have any idea where they are now?" asked Sally.

"I think they are at the grocery store on the strip by the discount club."

"I know where that is," said Mike. "That's the strip where I got the generator." A few minutes later they arrived at the store where the councilmen were working. Upon entering the store, Mike greeted them.

"Hi Bob, Steve, how are you guys?"

"Mike," said Bob. "How are you? Glad to see you survived. What are you doing here? Come to help I hope."

"I will help later. Presently, I'm helping paint the church. Do you know Sally Walters? She is my neighbor. She would like to help"

"We can surely use help," said Bob. He called out for Sandra who was in the back room. Bob introduced everyone, and Sally and Sandra went off to the back room where Sandra showed Sally what they had to do.

CHAPTER FOUR

Destination Unknown

IT WAS TWO WEEKS LATER that Mike finished all the work required to bring the church to its former state. He then went to work for the acting Mayor Barton. They set up a corner of a small building for a temporary drug store and another section for a temporary grocery store. They also found some employees that were capable of running the stores until they could find the owners or beneficiaries. They also found a doctor, and, after setting up a small area for his office, Mike left and went home. Sally was still working in another building and didn't get home until late. When she got home, she found Mike had packed a suitcase and placed it at the door to the garage. He was waiting to tell her of his plans.

"What's up?" she asked.

"I think I've helped the community enough," he said. "The job here will never be finished. There is too much to do. At least I helped set up the necessary activities."

"I know they are now talking about going from house to house to fix whatever needs fixing. But why are you packing your suitcase? Where are you going?"

It's time I start looking for my son," said Mike with tears in his eyes. "He is all I got left of my family."

"Oh, Mike. Do you really think you will find him?" Sally asked sadly. "Can't you stay around a little longer? Why not wait until whatever is left of our military gets things under control? I'm sure our government will soon retaliate."

"Sally, when has our government ever had things under control?" Mike didn't want to tell her that he believed there wasn't any military or government left. "I just can't sit and wait. I have to do something."

"You are only going to get yourself killed," answered Sally tearfully. "I need you. I'll be alone if you leave. You have been my strength these past days."

"Don't worry. Bill will come back soon. He is probably very busy rebuilding somewhere."

"I hope so," said Sally. "I know even if he is hurt, he will come back to me, even if he has to crawl to get here.

"Sally, why don't you come with me?" "No, I'll wait here until Bill comes back." "What will you do here?"

"I guess I'll help Mayor Barton and the rest fix the town." Just then, there was a knock on the door.

"Who could that be at this hour?" asked Mike. He went to the door and opened it. His jaw dropped in surprise.

"Sarah, I'm surprised to see you. Come on in. What brings you here?

"I've come to see what your situation is here. I need to know what you're up to before I can plan my next action."

"Sarah, I want you to meet Sally. She is my next-door neighbor. This is Sarah. Remember I told you about her."

"Yes of course, how are you? Mike has told me so much about you," Sally said.

"I'm fine. Thank you," said Sarah. "It's nice to meet you too." Then turning to Mike she asked, "Mike, did you find your wife and son?" Mike told her about the death of Annie and the abduction of his son.

"We had a funeral for Annie about a month ago," he said tearfully.

"I see you have your suitcase ready to go somewhere," said Sarah. "What are your plans?" "I need to go find my son."

"Well, I have a suggestion that may fit right into your plans. How about you, Sally, what is your situation? Are you alone or do you have family?"

"I don't have any children if that is what you are asking. My husband has been missing for over a month. I don't know if he is alive or not."

"If I'm not interrupting anything, why don't you sit and listen to my proposition. Maybe you will want to join us. Though, I only have two backpacks."

"I don't have anything to do," said Sally. They all sat around the coffee table and Sarah began.

"What is this about a backpack?" asked Mike.

"Let me start from the beginning," said Sarah. "As you know Mike, I am a government employee stationed at NASA in Cleveland. I have been working on a highly secret nuclear project. I am the only one that can operate it. I also told you that there is a highly secret base somewhere in the states that has a few of these devices. I can't tell you more about this, but I need to get to them if we are to save the country. My cell phone works through a communication satellite, so it cannot be blocked or intercepted. However, I have not been able to contact anyone at the base. The phone rings, so I know they are there, but no one answers. I will have to keep trying. Until then, I can make my way toward them."

"But I thought you said that you didn't know where they were located," said Mike.

"That's true, but I have determined where they would have most likely put it. It has aircraft capabilities, bombers, and fighter planes. Where else can it be hidden but somewhere around the mountain region of the west?"

"So what is this about backpacks?" asked Mike.

"We will leave here by car of course, but what if we can't get gas or if this car gets bombed like your other car? What would we do then? The backpacks are our alternate solution."

"What is your plan, and how will this help me find my son?" asked Mike.

"I think that we will follow them. We will see when they come together again. I have a map of US roads. When we get a chance, we will go around them. We will get ahead and, hopefully, I will be able to contact the secret base, and they could pick us up."

"What about my son?" insisted Mike.

"They will not want to take the children with them. They will be walking through cities and small towns, destroying everything in sight. Children would get in their way. I think the people who picked up the children were another group that followed behind them. I believe they want the children for a special purpose. I believe we will catch up to the group with the children if they follow behind the army. My guess is that they are headed to a planned location. I think that they want the children for farming. After all, their supply line can only go so far and for so long. They are going to need to obtain some supplies locally.

"That makes sense," agreed Mike. "What will we do if we catch up with the group with the children? Do we have any weapons, and if we do, what can the two of us do?"

"I looked for weapons," said Sarah. "All I could find was an experimental rifle and pistol. They were designed for the Cleveland Zoo to control large animals. They shoot very small darts that are about the size of the bee stinger, but they have enough drugs to knock out a lion."

"That reminds me," said Mike. "What is the condition of the Cleveland area?"

"There is no Cleveland," she said. "By this time next year, the Lake Erie beach will be from near the Airport to south of Parma to Wickliffe. That's only the hole. About 25 miles of the area around the hole has massive damage. NASA and my office have been badly burned. I had to go through the rubble to get what I was able to recover."

"How far south did the damage go?" asked Sally, worrying about the chances for her husband.

"I really don't know," answered Sarah. "The center of the bomb, I'm guessing mind you, was about twenty miles east and south of the center of Cleveland. My guess is that it was somewhere around Garfield Heights." Sarah went out to the car and got the road map of the states. They laid the map across the table where they all could look at it.

"When we ran across them, the main tent was about here," said Mike pointing on a spot on Interstate 90. "If that was the center of the army, weren't they pretty far north. Since, as I expect, they came together from the North and South toward the center, as they did in Pennsylvania. Wouldn't that cause them to miss a lot of the country?"

"It would seem that way, but look at what comes next," said Sarah. "It makes sense if they are to cover Michigan and Wisconsin. See how far north they will have to go if they're trying to cover the northern half of the country. That brings up a very important question: do they have another army to cover the southern half of the country?"

"Let's not bite off more than we can chew," said Mike. "So we can figure that when they do converge again, this is where the main tent will be?"

"That is correct," said Sarah. "Once we know where the center is, we can plan and come up behind the rear guard. Then, we can follow it to their camp and get around them somehow toward the mountains. That is where I think the location of our secret base is. If we can get ahead of them, we can get fuel and warn the people."

"What good will that do us?"

"I will continually try to contact the base, and as soon as I can talk with them, they should send a helicopter to pick us up."

"With what is going on, do you really think they will pick us up?" "Trust me," said Sarah. They need me badly." She then turned to

Sally. "What are your thoughts on all of this? You haven't said a word."

"I've been thinking about what I want to do," she answered. "It's a tough decision."

"Well, are you with me guys?" asked Sarah.

"I will go with you," said Mike. "I don't really have any other choice. How about you, Sally, have you made up your mind?"

"I think so," she answered. "I think I'll stay here and wait for Bill." "First of all, Sally," said Mike. "Do you really think he is still coming

home? If he does, you can leave him a note." "I still think I'll stay home," she said.

"Why?" asked Mike. "What have you got to lose?"

"Okay," she said. "I'll tell you. Mike, I love you like a big brother, and I'm going to miss you terribly, but the truth is, you are going on an extremely dangerous mission. I don't think you are coming back, but I have a very strong feeling that Bill is coming home. I would know if he was dead. I'm so sorry, Mike. I'll miss you dearly." She then started to cry.

"Why don't we spend the night here, and we will start early tomorrow morning?" suggested Sarah. "We can just relax today and have a big dinner because we do not know where our next meal will come from."

"Mike," said Sally, "have you truly considered the advantages of staying home?"

"I'm sorry, Sally. I can't. I have to try to find my son. I'll miss you too, and I want you to stay here at least until the electricity comes on. If you cook us a fabulous dinner this evening you can then have all the food that is left in the freezer and refrigerator when I leave. That should hold you for a long time."

"Thanks, Mike. I still wish you would stay."

"You're welcome. I wish you would come with us." That brought a sad smile on her face.

The next morning, Sally got up first. By time the others had gotten up, she had a great breakfast ready for them. After they had eaten, Sarah addressed Mike.

"You better repack," she said. "Go into the back seat of my car and get the backpack. I recommend that you pack one change of clothes, a light blanket, and whatever you need for grooming. This ensures that if we do have to use them, they will not be too heavy."

After getting the backpack he went upstairs and repacked. When he came down, he was carrying two sets of binoculars beside his backpack.

"I have a standard set of binoculars and an extra powerful set. We may need these. I also am bringing my LED flashlights. I have a very strong one and a normal one. You never know when we may need it."

"Good idea," said Sarah. "Are we ready to go?" As soon as she said this, Sally started to cry. Mike went over to her and hugged her.

"You'll see. We will be back before you know it."

"Please take care of yourself," she said between tears. "Don't take unnecessary chances."

"I won't," promised Mike. Sally then hugged Sarah.

"Please take care of Mike. Don't let him do anything foolish."

"Don't worry," said Sarah. "I'm not ready to leave this world." They all hugged again. Sally waved a last good-bye as they drove down the street. Mike looked back at her until she was out of sight.

"I think we should take Interstate 71 to Route 40," said Sarah. "If I have figured right, that would be the center of their line. That's where the main officer's tent would be when they stop and converge. That's the only time we can get around and ahead of them."

"Sounds like a good plan," said Mike. "By the way, how much fuel do we have?"

"On the way to your house I found a place that was still actively selling gas. I filled up the tank. This little four cylinder car will take us a long way before we will need refueling."

As Sarah drove down the planned route, Mike looked ahead with his powerful binoculars. He didn't want any surprises.

"Do you want me to drive?" asked Mike

"No," she replied. "I love driving this little toy. You keep looking ahead for any action. We wouldn't want to run into their rear."

They drove for a little over two hours but saw no one on the road. However, they did see massive destruction everywhere. Suddenly, Mike yelled out to Sarah, "Pull over quickly! There is a vehicle up ahead of us!"

"I don't see anything."

"And I hope they don't see anything either," said Mike. "It looks like a Jeep."

"It can't be," said Sarah. "They should be farther than this into the country."

"Why, what do you think it is?" asked Mike.

"It has to be the rear guard," she answered. "They generally follow about 10 to 30 miles behind and are constantly in contact with the main group. They provide protection from a rear attack."

"I see what you mean," Mike said. "They have only moved about two to three hundred miles in the month or so since we were attacked on Interstate 90. That could mean one of three things. First, they may have had to spread themselves too thin to cover the country from the center to our northern states. They may have to take a different approach from here on in. You know, move north and south for each step west. Secondly, they may be short of supplies and have had to wait for food and ammunitions."

"What is the third thing?" asked Sarah. "You said that there was a third possibility."

"Yes," he answered. "The other possibility, though I believe it is remote, is that they encountered resistance from our military."

"You have great field analysis capability," said Sarah with admiration.

"I think that we should proceed as if the first analysis is the correct one. It is the safest way. Also, I think that we should follow the Jeep.

It will keep us in line with them. The Jeep's actions will tell us when they will all converge again."

They followed the Jeep for several hours, always keeping far enough away so that the Jeep can only be seen through Mike's powerful binoculars. It was around noon that Mike asked Sarah to pull over. The Jeep had stopped at a small town grocery store. Sarah and Mike stopped and waited for the men in the Jeep to proceed again down Route 40. They then stopped at the same place the Jeep had stopped. The area around it looked like it had been hit by a tornado. The grocery store was left as if on purpose. There was, however, no one around. Mike and Sarah stored up enough food for that evening and the next morning and proceeded quickly, not wanting to lose the Jeep. After about another hour of driving, Mike noticed that the Jeep had stopped off the road near the town of Richmond Indiana. He directed Sarah to pull over near a damaged building.

"What's going on?" asked Sarah.

"I have no idea," answered Mike. "It's not even two o'clock yet. It looks like they are settling in the building on the outskirts of the town."

"Why would they be stopping this early?" she asked "It can't be that the army is converging can it?"

"I don't think so. I would be able to see the army. I would guess that the army is at least 25 to 50 miles away. We will just have to wait and see." They sat and waited in the car. It was about two hours later that they realized what was happening when they felt the earth tremble and saw a large mushroom cloud coming from the vicinity of Indianapolis.

"Now I understand," said Sarah. "I have to think about this. This may be the answer we were looking for. This is a sign that may dictate what we should do. I have a lot of thinking to do."

"What are you talking about?" asked Mike. "What does this tell us other than they feel that they missed Indianapolis in their original plan?"

"Precisely," she said. "What it means is that they are carrying nuclear devices to destroy cities that were missed on their first nuclear attack."

"I'm not sure I want to know what you are thinking about," said Mike.

"Don't you see?" she said. "We can turn that against them." "How can we do that?"

"Let me think about that for a while. There has to be a way. But, Mike, you don't have to go along with whatever I come up with. We can find some transportation for you and you can go your way."

"Don't you know by now that I am just as crazy as you are?" asked Mike. "I wouldn't let you go alone. Go ahead and do your thinking about it. We will both think about it. Don't you know that we need each other?"

"I was afraid you'd say that. It may be easier for one person to get away with it."

"I already have a plan that is festering in my mind," said Mike, ignoring her statement. "Let's see if we can settle in this building. I don't think they are going to move today anymore. We can eat and get some sleep. I think better with a good night's sleep."

Before they retired, Sarah took a radiation reading. It was high but below the danger level. She, however, decided that they couldn't stay in the area too long. They settled in the floor of the old building for the night. The next morning they ate what little they had that was still edible and waited for the Jeep to make its move.

"Well, have you thought of our next move?" asked Sarah.

"I guess we should talk about it," said Mike. "I know you well enough to know that you will not leave this alone. Therefore this is my suggestion. We can work from there. I think that we should wait until they congregate again. Then, we can sneak up after they have all gone to bed, and at about one o'clock, we can see if we can put the guards to sleep and crawl up to the main tent where I am sure they would keep the lethal weapons."

"There is nothing to discuss," said Sarah. "I think that you have a plan that is similar to mine. We differ only in the details."

"We can work out the details as we go along," added Mike. They talked about it until about ten when the Jeep started moving.

"I think that the army must have converged yesterday, otherwise they wouldn't have stayed here this long."

"I agree," said Mike. "We will see as we go on. It could be that they wanted to stay away from the radiation, but I don't think so. They could just have taken a distant route." It turned out that Mike was correct. The Jeep went a short way and then turned onto Route 13(.) from Route 40. They drove about 10 miles and turned onto Route 238 at Fortville. Ten minutes later they turned onto Route 32 at Noblesville.

"I think they are taking these country roads to go around the radiation as you predicted," said Sarah.

"Not only that," said Mike, "but I think that they are heading north. That's where the center of the army should be to be able to cover half of the country."

From 32 they went to 52 at Lebanon. They followed route 52 through Lafayette to a little town of Otterbein. There, the Jeep stopped at a little grocery store to get supplies. It was about noon. They stayed about half an hour and left. Sarah and Mike followed the Jeep to the store and stopped for supplies of their own. They found fresh food and ate as if there would be no dinner that night. About a half hour later Sarah got fidgety.

"Shouldn't we be going? With the side roads they are taking we could lose them very easily."

"Don't worry," said Mike. "I won't lose them, and if I did we really don't need them. I assume that the army got supplies last night. I am sure that they get their supplies by way of Interstate 80. That road takes you about a fourth of the way down from the border. I'm sure that that's where we will find the main officer's tent."

"You got it all figured out don't you?"

"Let's pray that I'm right. I figure it will be about three days before they will converge for supplies again. We will be there when they do."

They followed the Jeep up 52 to Route 24 at Kentland. They went west on 24 into Illinois, then north on Route 51 at El Passo. By four thirty they were on Interstate 80.

"That's what I thought," said Mike. "I knew that sooner or later they would lead us to Interstate 80."

"I hope that now we stay on Interstate 80," said Sarah. "I'm tired of seeing all of that destruction on the country roads. If they intend to keep 80 open for their supply line, it should be better from here on in."

"I suppose so, unless they have to go around a high radiation area. I noticed something else that shows that you are right in that they are trying to keep Interstate 80 open. Have you noticed that all the cars that are damaged lie in unnatural positions?"

"Yes, I see that some are even upside down. What does that mean?"

"It means that the road has been kept open by having a large bulldozer plow the cars out of the way."

"I would think that if it is safe enough for the supply line, it is safe enough for us," said Sarah

"I agree," said Mike. "We will see."

It was around five thirty in the evening when the Jeep stopped off the road and set up a small tent.

"Better pull over," said Mike. "I think they are stopping for the night. I see now that there are three men in the Jeep. I suspect they will sleep for six hours. Each will probably pull two hours of guard duty. That means that we'll have to get up early to keep an eye on them."

"Sounds logical to me," said Sarah. They ate what they had saved for dinner and then discussed their plans until it got dark.

"We had better get some sleep," said Mike.

"But where are we going to sleep? There are no buildings around, not even an old building like we had yesterday."

Mike pointed to the back seat.

"You can have the back seat. I'll sleep in the front." "It looks like comfort is not in our future."

"You never know what tomorrow will bring. Now go to sleep. We have to get up early tomorrow."

"I can't sleep this early. It's not even nine yet," complained Sarah. "Then just lay there and dream about how nice it will be when this all over."

Mike woke up first the next morning. It was 6:00 a.m. He rustled up some of the food they had obtained the day before and checked for any activity from the Jeep occupants. The tent was still up, and there was no movement around it. About an hour later, Sarah woke up.

"Why didn't you wake me?" she asked.

"There was no reason to wake you. The Jeep is still parked and the tent is still up." It was about eight when the rear guard crew folded up the tent and got back on the road. Sarah had eaten so they followed well behind.

"Do you think that the army congregated last night?" asked Sarah. "No, I think that they stopped for the night, but I don't think they converged. First, they are on the move too quickly, and secondly, when they converge, the Jeep will catch up to get supplies also."

They travelled down 80 into Illinois for the next two days. Each day was the same as the day before. Every morning they ate breakfast and left about eight. They ate lunch at a grocery store and then stopped moving at about six every evening. They traveled at a speed slower than thirty miles an hour at times. It was late on the third day that things changed.

"It looks like the Jeep is not stopping at six as it usually does," said Mike. "I wonder if it's time for the convergence."

"I hope so," said Sarah. "I'm getting tired of the same thing day in and day out."

Mike put down his binoculars to talk with Sarah. "Are you ready for what we have to do next?" he asked.

"I've been thinking about that," she said. "I think that it will be best if I go in alone. It will be easier for one to sneak around in the dark."

"Are you sure? I thought I would follow you in to give you cover." "What kind of cover can you give me?" she asked. "If I am detected, what are you going to do, fight the whole army?" "You have a good point."

"You would be better watching for me to come out of the area. Then if a guard catches me, you can cover me when the whole army isn't there. The worst that could happen is that you will have to fight the pilots. The army should be the width of the landing field away."

"Whatever you say," responded Mike as he leaned forward to check on the Jeep's position.

"What's the matter?" asked Sarah, noticing that Mike looked shocked.

"It's gone," he said. "It has just disappeared. Pull over and let me climb on the hood to see if I can spot them." Mike quickly jumped on the hood of the car and looked out as far as his binoculars would let him.

"Did you find them?" yelled out Sarah.

"Pull off the road and find a place by a damaged car," he said, ignoring her question and jumping back into the car.

"Why off the road? Are you afraid of blocking traffic?" she said in jest.

"Just do as I said," he responded harshly. Sarah, taken aback, found a spot between two cars that had been badly damaged.

"What's going on?" she asked.

"Get into the back seat and make yourself as invisible as you can." Sarah did as she was told and ducked down in the back seat.

"What's going on?" she repeated.

"I saw the earth-moving equipment leveling out a runway for the fighter planes. I think they are preparing to converge."

"But why are we hiding?" asked Sarah, puzzled by Mikes actions. "I'm just guessing," said Mike, "but if I were in charge and all the

planes were coming in for a landing, I would have them fly by the area behind us to make sure nothing is building up back there. At least that is what I would do."

"It's already dusk," said Sarah. "A few minutes and they will not be able to see the ground." No sooner had she stopped speaking when they heard the planes fly above them, circling around over their car and the surrounding area. A few minutes later, they could hear the planes landing.

"We can come out now," said Mike. "Let's get something to eat. After we eat we had better get some sleep. It's going to be a long night."

"Who is going to be able to sleep?" "We can lie down and get some rest."

After they ate, they did lie down to rest. Mike dozed off for a while, and when he awoke he found that Sarah had fallen asleep. She was pretty tired. Mike found it hard to go back to sleep. He fell asleep thinking about what they should do next. When he awoke it was a little past midnight.

"Wake up, Sarah," he said, shaking her to wake her. "I think it's time to go."

"I'm awake," Sarah assured Mike. "What do you want me to do?" "Let's move the car toward the air field," instructed Mike. "Let's go very slowly." Sarah did as instructed while Mike checked ahead with his binoculars.

The sky was partly cloudy. Every so often the moon would supply enough light so that Mike could see ahead. He guided Sarah until she could see the trucks that were parked along the runway. "I can see the trucks now," she said.

"We had better park the car somewhere on the side here," said Mike. "Let's grab our backpacks."

"Why do we need to bring our backpacks?" asked Sarah. "Why can't we just leave them here until we get back?"

"I think we should have everything we need with us at all times. We just don't know what will happen next. We may just have to escape with one of their trucks. Let's be safe and bring everything with us."

"Whatever you say," she answered. "I think we should take some donuts, and I'm going to fill my canteen with milk. It will give us some substance as well as quench our thirst."

"That's an excellent idea," said Mike.

When they had done what Sarah had suggested they set out on foot toward the airstrip, always going south to where they thought the main tent would be. They moved briskly when the moon was out but very slowly when the clouds covered the moon. It was so dark without the moonlight that they could not see even a foot in front of them. Soon the main tent was spotted, and they walked toward it.

"Apparently, the truck drivers have congregated," said Mike. "It looks like they get together in one tent and take turns as guards."

"It looks like they have a tent every several hundred feet. Let's go to the next one. It seems to be the farthest from the others," suggest Sarah. They slowly crawled until they were directly across from the suggested tent. "Look here," she said, pointing to a large shrub across from the tent. "This is a good place for you to hide and cover me on my return." Mike took off his backpack and set it behind the shrub. Sarah took out a small LED flashlight and handed her backpack to Mike who set it behind the shrub too.

"We will not need these for now," said Mike. "I'll hide here, but, before I do, I can help in subduing the guards."

They both slowly crawled toward the tent. They waited until the moon came out and detected a guard that was walking on the north side of the tent. Mike took aim with the rifle. As soon as the guard turned to walk the other way Mike fired. He hit the guard in the back of his neck. He fell immediately. Before he hit the ground, Sarah was in the tent. Less than a minute later she came out.

"There were three drivers in there," she said. "They are all asleep. I'm going to the main tent. You wait here. Look, if I don't come back in an hour, get into the car and take off as fast as you can."

"We will see," said Mike, not giving her statement any importance. "Don't you want me to go with you to help with the guards at the other end of the field?"

"No. What are you going to do if I get caught? Are you going to fight the whole army?" She started to leave when Mike called her back.

"Wait," he said. "Come back a minute." She came to him. "What do you want?"

"Come here." When she got close to him, he put his arms around her. "Listen, we don't know what will happen, but if things go wrong, I wanted you to know that I have strong feelings for you. You are a very special person. I love you." After saying that, Mike decided that he had gone too far. To cover for his error, he continued, "I love you like my little sister, and I have the urge to protect you, but I now have to let you go on your own. I also know that you are wise and will not take unnecessary chances."

"I love you too, big brother. You are the special one, but then I'm biased. After all, you are my brother. Don't worry. I'll be back before you know it and we will laugh about all of this." She kissed him on the cheek. He did the same. They squeezed one another tightly in a big hug, and she left him standing there.

The moon was behind a thin cloud, but she could see fairly well. In a crouched position she made her way across the airstrip. When she was almost to the other end of the field, the moon came out brightly, trapping her in the open. She fell to the ground and made herself as flat as she could. Fortunately, the guard was walking the other way. She waited until the moonlight was dimmed by the clouds. Then she crawled to the end of the field.

Just as she reached the other side, the moon came back out. The guard was almost in front of her. He saw her but was stunned in surprise. He hesitated too long. Sarah shot him in the neck. He fell over backwards. She quickly entered the guard tent and put the other guards to sleep. She then repositioned the first guard so that he was leaning against the tent. She put him as a sign to herself as to where to start back across the field.

She then moved tent by tent, hiding behind each one as she got there. She made sure that the area was clear before she moved to the next tent. Finally, she arrived at the last tent before the larger main tent. From there, she could see a guard walking back and forth in front of the main tent. She waited until the moon was nearly covered and walked up behind the guard. He never knew what hit him.

Sarah went into the main tent. It took her a few seconds before she could see anything. There were five officers inside all lying on small canvas bunks. She shot them with her stun gun to put them all to sleep for the next two hours should they survive the nuclear bomb. Using the flashlight, she started looking under each bunk. She could see under each of the four bunks near her. There was nothing under the first four of them. She was about to give up when she noticed that the farthest bunk, which was crosswise compared to the others, had a blanket over the front of it. She threw the blanket up over the officer on the bed and looked under it. There were several packages there. She could see that the two that were in front were the same. She pulled one out and lifted its cover. It was a nuclear device. She studied it for a while and quickly figured out the controls. She set it for two hours and activated it. She could hear the timer clicking. She set the other one. If one failed, the other would detonate. She pushed them under the bed again.

She was about to leave for the airfield when a thought entered her mind: *What will happen when the next guard comes to take his turn at being guard? They would find the on duty guard gone and set off an alarm.* She had to find the other guards. She looked around; there were many tents. *It has to be one that is closest,* she thought. Looking around she noticed that there was one tent that was just across from the entrance to the main tent. That made sense to her.

She silently entered the tent. Now she was sure she got the right tent because she found an empty bunk. There were three soldiers there. She put them all to sleep with her stun gun and left. As she made her way back toward the airfield, a large, dark cloud covered the moon. It became pitch black. She moved in the direction she felt was correct. She looked for the tent where she had leaned the guard against the tent, but she couldn't find it. She finally got to what she thought was the airfield, and she set out to cross it blindly, hoping the moon would come out before she ran into a guard.

Back on the other side of the airfield, Mike lay flat on his belly waiting for Sarah to come out. He was very disturbed by the darkening of the sky. He would not be able to see Sarah when she came out. He waited for what seemed like an hour. Then, as if a light came on, the moon appeared. He looked around but didn't see Sarah.

He started to worry. Would he ever see her again? Should he leave as Sarah suggested? As he lay there in thought, he heard a sound that was very familiar to him. It sounded like the noise his mother made when she was beating a rug with a paddle that looked like a tennis racket. She would hang a rug on a clothesline and beat the dust out of it. He slowly moved toward the noise.

The moon slid behind a thin cloud, but Mike could still see. As he got closer to the noise, he saw three soldiers busy doing something behind one of the trucks at the back of the truck. As he moved closer, he noticed a Jeep parked not too far from the activity. He moved behind the Jeep. He noticed that the keys were in the ignition. Suddenly, the moon came out, brightly illuminating the area. Mike was shocked at what he saw. It was Sarah. They had her hanging from the frame of the canvas-covered truck. She was completely bare. They had stripped her of all her clothes and were beating her. The shortest of the three was hitting her with the barrel of his rifle. One of the others was punching her in the face. Even in the dark, Mike could see that her face was covered with blood. He aimed his rife at the one hitting her with the rifle. He was the one doing the most harm. *Thank God he wasn't hitting her with the other end of the rifle,* Mike thought. However, he couldn't shoot. He felt he couldn't get all three. One would surely duck and call for help. He didn't know what to do.

He watched them, waiting for a break. It came sooner than he expected. Two of the men conferred together, and one of the men left for the tent. That was Mike's break. The one with the rifle bent over to pick something up from the ground. Mike shot him in his face, and he fell face down on the ground. The other man grabbed his companion to see what his problem was, and Mike nailed him in the back of his neck. Mike quickly dragged them out of sight behind the truck. When the other came out, he called out for his comrades. Mike stepped out from behind the truck, and, before the man could recover, Mike shot him in the face. Then, Mike quickly took out his Swiss knife and cut Sarah down.

"Please don't die on me," he urged. She couldn't answer because she was unconscious. He grabbed her pistol and put it under his belt. He put her flashlight in his pocket. Then he picked her up and put her over his shoulder. He placed her gently in the rear of the Jeep. He grabbed the backpacks and threw then on the floor of the Jeep. Her clothes had been all cut up, so he left them there. He covered her with his blanket and started the Jeep. It had about a quarter of a tank of gas. *That has to be enough*, he thought. Soon, he had the Jeep racing east down a country road away from the army site. He didn't know if Sarah had been successful, but he wasn't taking any chances. He had driven for about a half hour when the road ended at another country road. He turned to go south on the road when he heard Sarah moaning. He pulled onto the soft shoulder and stopped.

"Sarah," he said. "Are you all right? What can I do for you? How can I make you more comfortable?"

"Ten," she said, barely audible. "Ten," she repeated. "What about ten?" asked Mike.

"After...three," she finally finished and passed out.

"Ten after three?" asked Mike to himself. Then her meaning dawned on him. She was saying that the bomb would go off at ten after three. Mike got the Jeep back on the road and went as fast as the Jeep would go. He looked at his watch, it was a little after two thirty. He had less than a half hour to get to a safe place.

It was about five after three when he got to a little town. A sign pointing east of the town read Route 59, but he didn't have time to get there. He drove into the center of the town. He saw two buildings that were close together and figured that the best place to be would be between them. After pulling between the two buildings, he noticed that the building on his left had basement windows.

He quickly put on his backpack and pulled Sarah over his left shoulder. He grabbed Sarah's flashlight and her backpack in his right hand and headed for the front of the store. It was a drug store, and the front door was broken and left open. Mike headed for the rear of the store. As he had suspected, a stairway was there on the right side of the hall. He quickly made his way down the stairs, almost dropping Sarah. He set her down next to the north wall and covered her again with his blanket. Then he started up the stairs to get the medical items he would need to bandage Sarah.

He had only gotten to the first step when the ground and building shook as if there was an earthquake. He fell to the ground and dropped the flashlight. He found himself in complete darkness. It was also getting very hot. He crawled in the direction he knew his backpack would be. He found it and grabbed his flashlight. It was more powerful than Sarah's, and it lit up the whole room. The smaller flashlight had somehow turned itself off. Mike found that it worked fine. Mike got the Geiger counter out of Sarah's backpack and checked the radiation level. It was at an acceptable level.

He went upstairs, checking the radiation level as he went up. It got pretty close to an unacceptable level, but that didn't matter to Mike. He had to help Sarah. He checked around and found a bowl and a six-pack of water. Next, he found some Band-Aids and some large sterile gauze packages. The last thing he needed was some antibiotic ointment. After finding it, he proceeded back to the basement. Sarah was partly awake. She was obviously in pain.

"Water," she pleaded. Mike got one of the water bottles and offered it to her. She couldn't drink while lying down, so Mike tried to sit her up. She yelled out in pain.

"I'm sorry," said Mike, "shall I continue to raise you?"

"Please" she said, "don't mind me. I need water badly." Mike continued to gently bring her to a near sitting position. Mike put the water bottle to her lips. She almost drank the whole bottle.

"What part of your body hurt when I lifted you?"

"All of it," she said, "but my side hurts the most. I think my ribs are broken."

"I'm going to slowly set you down again. I have to clean your wounds."

"Okay," she agreed. Mike, as gently as he could, set her down on her blanket and covered her body with the other end of the blanket. Opening another water bottle, he emptied it into the bowl. He soaked some of the gauze in the water and wiped the blood from her nose and her forehead. Her nose had stopped bleeding. Mike spread some of the ointment on the cut on her forehead he then placed a Band Aid on it.

"Sarah," he said in a very soft voice. "I need to check the rest of your body for cuts and bruises." He was hesitant to do anything; however, it had to be done.

"Do what you have to," she responded. Mike uncovered her. He was glad that he had. There was a cut on her side and across her stomach.

"You have a cut across your side and stomach," Mike informed her. "They are not very long. They look like knife wounds. It must have happened when they cut away your clothes. I will try to cover them with gauze and tape."

After spreading some ointment over them, he cut some gauze, and taped it over the wounds. Then he checked her right side. It was very swollen and had started turning black and blue.

"What can I do for your side?" asked Mike.

"You can wrap it tightly with the gauze. It won't help but it will feel better."

"I will have to lift you up to get the gauze around you," warned Mike. She didn't answer. She seemed to be in deep thought. Mike managed to get the gauze wrapped tightly around her without too much trouble. She moaned once or twice but that was all.

"Mike," said Sarah when he had finished. "There is something I didn't tell you. I didn't think it was important before but now it may be. I went to medical school before I transferred to the study of nuclear physics. I've got a little of the medical knowledge that your general practitioner has."

"That's great, but what has that to do with me?" asked Mike, puzzled over what she was telling him.

"I need you to do something for me."

"Sure, anything you ask," said Mike. "What do you want me to do?" "I want you to play doctor."

"What?" asked Mike. "How can I do that?"

"You do exactly as I tell you to do. I will instruct you on every step." "Why?" he asked. "What is the problem?"

"I don't know if my arm is fractured, or just badly bruised. I need to know that before I can move it. The same applies to my leg."

"How can I tell that?" asked Mike concerned about the likely possibility that he couldn't do it.

"Just do what I tell you, and don't hesitate if I yell due to pain. I know that it is going to be painful. I'm ready for it, and I want you to be ready for it too."

"All right," said Mike. "Where do I start?"

"Put both of your hands on my arm just below the shoulder. Put one hand on the inside of my arm and the other on the outside. Now, slowly press up against the bone. Can you feel the bone?" she asked, showing great pain as he pressed down on her arm.

"Yes, I can feel what I think is the bone. Now what do I do?"

"Slowly work down the arm over the bruised area and down to the elbow, feeling for an inconsistency in the bone structure."

"I understand," said Mike. He started to slowly work down the bone. He could tell that she was in great pain when he got to the swollen and black and blue area. All of her muscles tightened up. He felt no inconsistencies in the bone.

"I couldn't feel any breaks or cracks," said Mike

"Good," she answered. "You would be able to feel a break very easily. However, I don't think you could feel a crack. Just to be safe, I want you to wrap my arm with the gauze just to keep it straight and stiff." Mike did as asked. When he was done she said, "Now, do the same thing to my leg." Mike covered her upper body with the blanket and uncovered her leg trying to keep much of her body hidden. He started up high on her leg and started to work down as he had done with the arm. When he got to the bruised area she tightened up and with a chilling moan she passed out. Mike finished what he was doing and managed to wrap the bruised area before she came to.

"Are you all done?" she asked. "Did you feel anything unusual?"

"No. You have very beautiful legs. There was nothing I could feel that was out of place."

"You are enjoying this aren't you?" she said with a forced smile. "Well great," he answered. "You have your sense of humor back.

You are going to be fine. Let's get some sleep. It's been a long day. " "I am very tired and feel very weak."

"I'm not surprised," said Mike. "With what you have gone through, I don't know how you can even stay awake." Mike got his blanket and positioned it next to Sarah. He stretched out beside her and covered himself with the blanket. He tucked her blanket closely under her chin.

Soon, they were both asleep. The next morning, when Mike woke up, he found that Sarah was already awake.

"How are you this morning?" he asked

"I'm alive and feeling a little better. I don't feel very strong." "I suppose now you are getting hungry."

"Now that you mention it, I am kind of hungry. What do you have?" "I only asked if you were hungry. I didn't say I had something to eat."

"Whose sense of humor were you talking about last night—yours of mine? I think you are enjoying my predicament too much."

"I'm sorry, Sarah," said Mike. "It isn't what you think. I thought that I had lost you. You can't imagine the thrill I feel knowing that you are alive and going to get well. You may not understand this, but I have very strong feelings for you."

"I love you too, now go get us something to eat. It's past eight, I'm guessing"

"You'll be all right if I leave you by yourself?"

"Did you see any people in town? Who is going to disturb me?" Mike smiled at her. He bent over and kissed her on the forehead.

"Don't go anywhere," he said.

"I never thought of you as a comedian," she countered.

Mike left before she could say more. He checked the radiation level as soon as he got upstairs. It was about half way to the danger point. It had gone down considerably. He went outside and spotted what looked like a grocery store. The store had severe damage, but some soup and vegetable cans were still intact. The meat in the display case was covered with glass. It didn't look too good anyway. In the rear of the store, he found a freezer compartment. He opened it and it was still very cold inside. It had frozen meat and shelves of products that had to be kept cold. Mike grabbed a quart of milk and closed the freezer quickly. On the shelf across from the freezer, he found some cereal. Next, he went into a store that carried household items like dishes and utensils. He picked up two bowls and silverware and returned to the drug store basement.

"I will have to lift you to a sitting position," said Mike. "You can't eat while lying down."

"No way," she said. "I can't hold the blanket with my left hand and eat, and I can't lift my right arm."

"I can hold the blanket while you eat, or you hold the blanket with your left hand and I will feed you," suggested Mike.

"All right let's try," she said.

Mike started to lift her to a sitting position. The blanket slipped several times, and Sarah quickly pulled it back up. He finally got her sitting up, but she couldn't stay up on her own. Mike put his arms around her waist and pulled her up against the wall. Sarah tried to use her right hand to help hold up the blanket. It was too awkward for her.

"This isn't going to work," she complained.

"I have only one suggestion," offered Mike. "We can try to get some clothes on you. If you can handle the embarrassment one last time, I can help you get dressed."

"I suppose that is the only answer."

"Well, tell me what you want me to do," said Mike.

"Look in my backpack. I have my other set of clothes there." Mike did what she asked. He gingerly helped her get dressed.

"Now please feed me. I'm getting tired and would like to lie down and rest." Mike had many questions, so while she was eating he decided to get some answers.

"Tell me, Sarah," he started. "What happened? How did they catch you out there? I know that you are a very careful person, so how did it all happen?"

"When I was on my way back, a very dark thick cloud covered the moon. It was absolutely black out. I couldn't see my hand before my face."

"Yes," said Mike. "I remember that. I was worried that I wouldn't be able to see you."

"It was so dark I couldn't find the airfield. I stumbled around until my feet told me I was on plowed ground. I managed to get across the field until I felt grass under my feet. Then, as if someone turned on a light, the moon came out. I found that I was next to a tent. The guard was right there, and he grabbed me. Then another one must have come up behind me because everything went black. The next thing I remember, I was in the back of the Jeep and thinking, due to the pain, that I was just about to die. Now you answer my question. How did you get me away from them, and how did I end up in a Jeep?"

"Apparently, the men were from the Jeep that we lost track of on the road," answered Mike. "They must have pulled up there after we lost them. You came out about three hundred feet from where I was waiting." Mike then related all that went on from the time he heard the noise to the time she awoke in the Jeep.

After he had finished feeding her, she stretched out on her blanket and went to sleep. Mike left to go outside to see what he could find that would be useful. He found a hardware store and found a plastic hose and a gas can. He siphoned gas from abandoned cars and filled the jeep. He also found a portable propane gas grill. It came in handy to cook some of the meat that was available in the grocery store freezer. There was plenty of good food for them to eat.

As the days turned to weeks, Sarah got stronger and stronger. After about two weeks, Sarah was able to get up and eat at a table that Mike had set up. She still held tightly to her blanket. Soon, the time had come for them to consider moving on.

CHAPTER FIVE

Into the Shadow of Death

IT WAS EARLY ONE MORNING after they had finished breakfast that Mike brought up the subject of their moving on.

"Sarah," he said. "I think that we should talk about getting back on the road. That is, if you feel up to it."

"I feel much better, but I won't really know until we remove the bandages from my ribs, my arm and my leg. I've been afraid to remove them. If you were right and there were no serious breaks, then we should try to remove them. First, remove the bandage from my arm."

"Do you want me to do it now?" asked Mike.

"Now is as good a time as ever," she said. Mike turned her around so that her bad arm faced him. He slowly unwrapped the gauze from her arm.

"The swelling is gone, but I still see a little black and blue areas," said Mike.

"That is to be expected," she said, moving her arm up and down. "It is a little weak. I will need a little therapy. I think I can remove the rest if you just start the rib gauze." Mike did as she asked. "Now if you will take all my clothes out of my backpack and leave so I can get dressed."

"Will you need any help?"

"Just don't go too far. I'll call you if I need you." Mike went out to the Jeep. He checked the oil and the coolant. Everything was in order. They were ready to travel whenever Sarah was ready. He went into the drug store and sat on the stool that he had previously found there. It was almost a half hour later when he heard Sarah calling him.

"Mike, you can come down now. I need your help."

Mike ran down the steps and found her sitting on the chair fully dressed. She had on a pair of jeans and a light blouse.

"What is the problem?" he asked. "What do you need?"

"I need you to put on my shoes. I can't bend over to put them on." "How did you put on your panty hose and your jeans?

"I didn't put on any panty hose; I had some socks. I put on my jeans with great difficulty."

Mike put on her shoes. She then attempted to stand. "I'm going to need your help to walk," she said. "My leg is very weak." Mike put her good arm over his neck and helped her up the stairs.

"It's so good to get out of the stuffy basement," she said when she had reached the upper level. With Mike's help she walked to the stool that Mike had been sitting on.

"Let me rest a minute." She rubbed her bad leg. "What do you want to do now?" asked Mike.

"Let me rest for a few minutes. Then I would like to walk to a clothing store. Before we can travel, I'll need a change of clothes."

"I don't think we can do that today," said Mike. "You can't even walk. How are you going to try on clothes?"

"With your help I hope. Look, I want to get out of here and get to a motel and take a shower or bath. I feel like I've been swimming in oil."

"How do you think I feel? I've been without washing even my face as long as you."

"I know you want to get out of here as much as I do, but you are a man. You can get along without washing longer that a woman can."

"Perhaps that's true with an old-time farmer, but I'm not a farmer." "So help me. We will travel south to an area that has not been devastated by the enemy. We can then get cleaned up."

"Remember my theory?" said Mike. "I believe that there are four armies. Two armies attack from the East and two armies attack from the West. The armies from the east, divide the country, one attacks the northern states and the other the southern states. The two armies from the West will divide the states the same way."

"That's just your theory," said Sarah. "I'm praying that you are wrong."

"I hope so too. It doesn't matter. We can't go north after what we did. We don't know how much damage was done. They may be looking for us as we speak."

"Help me walk," said Sarah as she got up and tried to put weight on her bad leg. She had a bad limp, but she was moving forward. "Okay, I can walk. With your help, I would like to walk down the street."

"If you insist, but I think you should wait until tomorrow." "At least let's see how far I can go."

Mike took her outside, and they walked down the street. They got as far as the clothing store when she stopped.

"What's the problem?" asked Mike.

"I think you were right," she said leaning heavily on his shoulder. "I'm getting pretty tired."

"You did better than I expected," commented Mike. "Your muscles are weak. We will go back and after you have rested, we can do some leg exercises."

"Right now, I'm getting pretty hungry," said Sarah sounding out of breath.

"Next stop, the classy café at the drug store," said Mike. "But it is only eleven. Isn't it a little early for lunch?"

"I can't help it, I'm hungry now. Can we also move out of the basement?" requested Sarah. "There is a lot of room on the side where the tables are. Why are the tables there anyway?"

"Yes, I can move some of the tables and sweep the floor," he said. "There is some broken glass on the floor. The tables are there because the store has a soda fountain. I don't think they served food."

"Let me sit at one of the tables. I don't want to lie down. I felt very dizzy when I first got up. I have to get used to sitting up."

"Your wish is my command," said Mike with a smile. It made Sarah smile also. Mike warmed up the portable grill he had found in one of the stores that he had searched through. He also found an extra, full propane tank. He decided to save it for when they would travel. The tank that he found with the grill had enough gas for the next couple of meals.

After they had eaten, Mike made Sarah exercise her legs by lifting them against his pressure holding them down. It was light at first but as they repeated it Mike made it tougher. Later that day she went for a short walk. It wasn't until the next afternoon that she was able to walk to the store and try on some clothes. She insisted that Mike wait outside.

"What's your problem?" kidded Mike. "I've seen everything you have and you don't have anything I haven't seen before."

"I like to ration what I have carefully and only on very special occasions," she responded knowing that he was kidding her.

"So that is the way it is," said Mike

"Yes, so skidoo."

Mike went outside and leaned against the wall. His thought drifted to the fact that they should leave. They were comfortable here, but they were running out of food, and the radiation was still a little high. Sarah was walking with only a slight limp. He decided that it was time to go. He also had to do something to find his son, but he didn't know what that was. He was moving farther away from where he thought his son would be. He had to depend on God leading him.

It was nearly an hour later when Sarah came out with a package of clothes.

"I thought you had moved in there. I was about to come in and find out what happened to you."

"I had a difficult time getting in and out of the clothes," she answered. "But now I have everything I need except a bath."

"While I was waiting for you, I was thinking that it was time for us to move on. That is, if you feel you are ready to travel."

"I think I'm ready. You are right. We should be moving south and away from the radiation."

"Let's see how you feel tomorrow morning. I'll get everything in the Jeep that we are going to take with us like the grill and medical supplies."

"Sounds like a good plan. I will be ready to travel. I was thinking the same thing this morning."

After he sat Sarah at a table she liked and got her a cup of coffee, Mike put everything in the jeep that he could except the grill and their backpacks. He also went to the clothing store and obtained a set of clothes for himself. He needed a set of lighter clothes for the warmer weather they would be driving into.

The next morning, Mike got up at the first sign of light. It was about six. He made some breakfast and, after it cooled a little, he packed the grill in the Jeep. Next he put his backpack in the Jeep, and when he returned, he found that Sarah had gotten up and was setting the table with the breakfast that Mike had made.

After they ate, Sarah packed some sandwiches, fruit, and vegetables for lunch while Mike finished packing their belongings in the Jeep. They didn't know where they would be at noon that day.

By seven-thirty they were back on the road. Mike remembered that the sign just north of the town they were in had an arrow that pointed east to Route 59. He headed north out of the town until he got to the country road. There he saw the sign to Route 59. He turned right and followed the sign. He was soon traveling south on Route 59. Mike followed 59 into Missouri until 59 turned east at Route 4. Mike turned west on 4 for about ten miles into Kansas. There he found Route 73 and 159, which went south. He headed south following Route 159. At about noon they arrived at Reserve, a small town off the highway. They stopped there for lunch.

"Have you been aware that things have not changed?" said Sarah sadly.

"Are you pointing to the fact that we have not been able to travel much over twenty miles an hour because of the damaged cars and bad roads, or are you referring to the cities and towns that are in ruins every were we go?"

"I am wondering where all the people are," said Sarah, ignoring Mike's sarcasm. "Do you realize that we haven't seen another man or beast for the last four hours?"

"I know," he answered. "Have you noticed that everything is still smoking? It seems like the attack has only been a few hours ago."

"Could that be true?" asked Sarah thoughtfully. "If that is true, where are the bodies? In the other places up north, there were many dead people."

"There are two things that come to my mind," said Mike. "First, it seems that this army has traveled much slower than the northern one. I believe this because we can still see the smoke from the ruins. Secondly, being slower, it would allow people to get warnings from others that were hit first. I think that the people who live here have run for their lives."

"That makes a lot of sense," she said. "However, I think some must have found places to hide."

They ate the lunches that Sarah had prepared and were soon back on the road. Mike followed Route 159 until about two miles past Effingham. There, they picked up Route 59 again.

It was about four-thirty when they got to the city of Lawrence. Driving down the main street, they found some activity. A few men and women were trying to put out fires and others were trying to salvage their belongings. They stopped to talk to one of the men coming out of a clothing store with a box of things he was salvaging.

"Sir," said Mike. "Can you help us?" "What can I do for you?" he asked "First, how long ago did the attack on your community take place?"

"They came by here early this morning. We were advised by people east of us that were running to get ahead of the attackers. Most of our people ran southwest to get away from them, but many of us hid and weren't discovered. We had too much to lose if we left. We understand that aircrafts attacked all of the cars on the road. We have no idea how many of our people actually escaped. It was better to stay put and take a chance by hiding. Where did you guys come from, and how did you evade the aircraft?"

"We come from northeast," said Mike. "The aircrafts attacked west of us. We were lucky. Can you tell us if there is a motel or hotel where we can get a room?"

"Yes, there is a classy motel just on the other side of town," he answered.

"Thank you," said Mike and drove off.

It was just a few miles down the road when they saw the motel right where the man had said it was.

Once they had cleaned up, they were eager to go to sleep. These were the most comfortable beds they had slept in for weeks. They were soon fast asleep.

The next morning Mike woke up first. It was eight. It was so comfortable that he just lay there until he heard Sarah stirring.

"Sarah, are you awake?"

I've been awake for a little while," she answered. "I just can't get up. This is so nice. Don't you find it delightful?"

"It's great," said Mike. "The only thing I liked better was being under a rock or in a dark basement with a beautiful girl in my arms."

"You're so funny," she answered.

"It's nice but we have to leave," he said being serious. "I think God has more work for us."

Shortly, they were going south on Route 59. It was after noon before they stopped for lunch. They pulled off the road at Route 54 just before the town of Moran and ate the great lunch that Marie, owner of the motel they slept in last night, had packed for them. It was in an insulated canvas bag. The food was still warm.

"What wonderful people there are in this world," said Sarah.

"I know," agreed Mike. "I only wonder where God is taking us. Do we just keep going south?"

They had been in kind of a daze all morning.

"Let me check the map," said Sarah. "Maybe something will come to mind."

"What concerns me is that I think my son is north and we are traveling south." Sarah took out the map they kept in their backpack and planned their route.

"If we continue going south on 59 and change to Route 2, in Oklahoma, we can get to the Welch by this evening. There, we can figure out our next move. Route 2 will take us to Route 69, and that will take us pretty far south. I think we have to continue going south."

As Sarah had predicted, they got to Welch that evening. After eating what was left of the food Marie had packed for them, they sat in the Jeep to discuss their future plans.

"Why do you think we have to continue going south?" asked Mike. "Haven't you noticed that everywhere we go we still see heavy destruction?"

"That's what I've been telling you all along," said Mike. "There is another army taking care of the southern part of our country. What does that have to do with our going south?"

"Don't you see?" asked Sarah, deep in thought. "That's where I think God wants us to go. Let's see where the center of this army is." "Dear Lord," said Mike, "you're not thinking of going in and doing the same thing with this army as we did up north?" "Why not, if it's possible?" asked Sarah.

"We don't know if this army acts like the northern army. They may not congregate. They are led by different leaders."

"We won't know until we get there," said Sarah. "What have we to lose? Maybe we can only get a part of the army, but that is better than none. Anyway Mike, you don't have to go with me. You can continue going south, or you can go back up north and see if you can find your son."

"Why do you even consider that?" asked Mike. "You know that I will never desert you. You know that I'm just as crazy as you are. You're stuck with me."

"I'm willing to discuss this," said Sarah. "What do you think we should do?"

"I know you are right," he answered. "I don't have to like it. Let's continue going south for now and see what develops."

Welch was in as bad a condition as all of the other towns they had been through. They found an empty building and spent the night. The next morning they followed the route Sarah had planned and, as she had said, Route 2 led them to Route 69. They continued to Wagner and found a grocery store that was still in pretty good condition. They had some lunch, and at around one, they continued going south on Route 69. It was about three-thirty. Mike was getting bored with the scenery. The destruction along the way was not even slightly diminished or relieved. Mike had just headed under an underpass for Route 40 when Sarah shouted out.

"Michael!" she yelled out. She had never called him Michael before. "Stop!"

Alarmed by her sudden outburst, Mike slammed on the brakes. "What is wrong," responded Mike.

"Didn't you see that?" she answered. "See what?"

"Just back up to the entrance ramp for Route 40," she answered. "You'll see it then."

Mike backed the car up to the entrance ramp. It was difficult because of all the wrecked cars on the road.

"Do you see now?" asked Sarah. "What am I looking for?"

"Don't you see that Route 40 has been cleared of the damaged cars? They have all been plowed off the road."

"By George, you are right," he answered, his face showing his sudden realization. "It has to be the supply line route."

"We have no choice but get on Route 40 and follow the road west," said Sarah.

"Are you sure you want to do this?" asked Mike. "We got away with damaging the northern army. We don't know if this army was trained the same way."

"We will soon find out."

"All right," said Mike as he headed the Jeep onto the ramp to Route 40. There were many more damaged cars on Route 40. They were all, however, pushed to the side of the road.

"It looks like the cars were shot up from the air," said Mike. "See how a lot of the cars have bullet holes in their roofs. The airfield should be close." Mike pulled over to the edge of the road. "I think you should drive. I need to get my powerful binoculars and keep a close eye on the road ahead of us."

"Good idea," said Sarah. "We don't want the aircrafts coming home to catch us on the road." Sarah drove slowly and as close to the edge of the road as the damaged cars would let her.

"Stop," said Mike after they had driven about two hours. "I see the jeep up ahead. It looks like they have stopped for the night. It's now about a quarter to six. There is a turnaround up ahead. I saw an exit about a mile back. We have about six hours before we can do anything. Let's get off the road and see if we can get something to eat."

"It's a good idea," agreed Sarah. "We can hide for a while and maybe get a couple of hours sleep. It may be a long night."

"You're at the wheel," said Mike.

Sarah pulled to the turnaround and headed west. Just as Mike had said, she came to an off-ramp. She took it and they drove down a small country road for about ten miles. They came to a small crossroad community. There were only about eight buildings including a gas station.

"I don't think we should go any farther away," said Mike. "Pull in beside that gas station. There are several cars around it. I may be able to get some gas. We may need a full tank for our escape."

"And look across the street," added Sarah. "That looks like a delicatessen. You get gas while I go and see if I can dig up some food."

Mike went into the station. Everything inside was badly damaged. However, he was able to find a five-gallon container. With the cars around the station and those in the street, Mike was able to fill the gas tank of their Jeep. Then he went into the deli. Sarah had found a small table and was in the process of setting up two places for dinner.

"Hi," she said. "You are just in time. I found a lot of lunch meat and a few slightly stale buns. There is a lot of corned beef and enough rye bread for two large sandwiches. This must have been a kosher deli."

"I thought most of them were," said Mike. "Whatever, I do like corned beef sandwiches." They ate as much as they could get down.

After setting up their blankets on the floor, they went to sleep.

Sarah woke up first. She checked the time. It was about eleven. She woke Mike.

"I think we had better get moving," she said

"Why did you have to wake me now?" he complained. "I was just about to undress her."

"Very funny," she said. "Aren't you glad I kept you from sinning?"
"It was only a dream. I can't control my dreams," he said jokingly.
"Well it is almost eleven. It's dark out, so I think the aircrafts are
already on the ground and the pilots are asleep."

They got back on Route 40 and were soon near the spot where they had turned around.

"Better go slow here," instructed Mike as he tried to see ahead in the dark. "Better turn the headlights off. We don't want to announce our arrival."

"Speaking of arrival," said Sarah. "I wonder where the rear guards are?"

"I hope they are parked around the air strip somewhere," said Mike. "We better keep our eyes open for them."

Sarah crept slowly down Route 40, watching what she could see in the moonlight. Mike also looked down the road. It was Mike who saw it first.

"Stop, Sarah," he said. "It looks like the road ends up ahead. I think they plowed dirt over the road for the airfield. Pull over to the left. I think I see what looks like a flag that way."

"Yes, I think I see it too," she said as she looked for a spot between damaged cars that had been plowed to the side of the road. She went almost up to the end of the airfield before she was able to pull onto the side of the road. The field was pretty flat, so she pulled In far off the road so they could not be seen from the road in case the read guard jeep would go by.

"We should be reasonably safe here. If the rear guard is behind us, they will have trouble seeing our Jeep."

"Even if they see it, would they know that it's an enemy?" asked Mike. "It is, after all, one of their Jeeps."

"You never know what will go through their crippled minds," responded Sarah.

They walked south along the air strip until they felt they were opposite what they thought was the flag of the main tent. That would put them closest to the commanding officers position. Mike found a large shrub by a tree.

"I think I will lie here between this tree and shrub. I can see clearly from here, and I am also hidden pretty well."

"You understand that if I'm not back within about an hour, you are to get into the Jeep and get as far away as you can," instructed Sarah. "You won't know if I was caught before or after I set the bomb."

"Never mind all this *what if*," said Mike. "Just get back here as soon as you can."

"I see a tent to our left," she said, ignoring Mike's comment. She realized that he was intelligent enough to know what to do. "I'll sneak up to it. If there is a guard, I'll take care of him. Can you see the tent clearly?"

"Yes, I can. I'll keep you covered." He positioned himself in a prone position with the rife aimed directly at the tent. "I can also get anyone that comes out of the tent."

Sarah left sliding on her belly toward the tent. Mike was amazed at how quickly she moved flat against the ground. The thin clouds had moved away, and the moonlight gave them a good view of the area. Mike kept his eye on Sarah. Suddenly, he saw her raise her arm. Mike assumed that she had the pistol in it. She unexpectedly got on her feet and entered the tent. A few minutes later, she came out and raised her hand with her thumb up. She then disappeared into the open airfield.

Sarah ran across most of the field, but as she got close to the other side she got down on her belly. The moon had come out very bright as the clouds cleared from the sky, and she was afraid that there would be a guard at the other side of the runway. She was right. As she got to the other side, she crawled on her belly behind a small shrub.

There was one guard, who was apparently very confident because he wasn't paying any attention to the surrounding area. It was very easy for her to put him to sleep. She then entered the nearest tent and found that one bed was empty. She quickly shot all the others with her stun gun and after dragging the outside guard into his bed, she proceeded from tent to tent until she got to the main tent.

The main tent was going to be a problem because there was a large distance between the tent that she was hiding behind and the guard. She had no choice. She waited until the guard had turned around and started in the other direction before she quickly ran up behind him and shot him in the neck. He started to yell out but couldn't get much more out than a loud burp.

Sarah waited, hiding against the tent away from the entrance. After a few minutes, she accepted the fact that no one had heard the noise. She entered the tent and quickly shot the five men with her stun gun. She searched under the main bed and found two backpacks. They were what she was looking for. She set the timers to two hours and checked her watch. It was one fifteen. She was about fifteen minutes behind schedule. She left the tent cautiously. She now had to find the tent the guard came from.

She entered the tent closest to her. There were four beds, and they were all occupied. She put them to a permanent sleep with her gun anyway. She moved on to the next tent. She injected them as she had done to the first tent. She entered four tents before she found one with an empty bed. She put the guard in the bed and started to make her way back to the runway.

She was three quarters of the way across the runway when the clouds cleared away from the moon again. Something told her to get back on her belly. She didn't understand why she had gotten the feeling; she was almost home. She and Mike had only to drive over fifty miles away from there, and they would be safe. Listening to her instinct, she crawled on her belly until she got near the edge of the runway. There, she heard voices.

She slowly approached the sounds. She waited until the thin clouds reduced the moon's light. She then moved back to the area where she had left Mike. His rifle was still there between the tree and the large shrub, but Mike was not there. She saw that there were three men who had captured Mike. One was a distance from the others watching to make sure that Mike was alone. The other two had Mike on the ground and were hitting him with the butt-end of their rifle.

The smaller one was hitting Mike on his upper torso, and the other was trying to get his blows in by hitting him around the legs.

Terror filled Sarah's heart. What would she do without Mike? She took a deep breath. She found it hard to breathe. She almost yelled out. It took her a few seconds to gain control and start to think about how to save Mike. The other man was too far from the others for her to shoot them all without being noticed. Sarah started to pray for God's assistance. She waited about two minutes, but time was running out. The men were still hitting Mike. Mike was a big man, and he could take a good beating, but soon the beating would kill him. She had to do something now. She considered running out to the man watching and hope that she could get back to get the others in time to put them to sleep. She was about to run out when the third man turned around and started back toward the other two. This was her chance. As the man reached the other two, she ran out and shot all three before they could react. She had an advantage that Mike didn't have when he rescued her; her pistol had multiple shots.

She ran up to Mike. He was unresponsive. She checked his pulse. He was still alive. Hope filled her heart. It was clear that his arm was broken between the shoulder and the elbow; below the elbow it was swollen and getting black and blue. She couldn't tell if anything else was broken. She quickly untied his hands. Using the same rope, she bound his arm so that the broken area was unmovable. She was concerned that there were breaks in his legs also so, using the belts of the three men, she secured his lower arm and his legs together. She grabbed him under the shoulders and dragged him to the rear guard's Jeep that was closer than their jeep. She knew that she could not get him to their Jeep.

Sarah dragged the three men into their tent and left them on the floor of the tent. She checked the men for the keys to the Jeep and found the keys on the tallest man. She placed the backpacks and the rifle in the Jeep and drove them to their Jeep since it had a full tank of gas. She dragged Mike into their Jeep with all the other equipment and was soon going east on Route 40.

See looked at her watch. It was two-twenty. She had less than an hour to get over fifty miles away from the explosion, but it was going to be difficult to average more than fifty miles an hour. She drove as fast as she could. She decided to get off of Route 40 back on to Route 69. She was hoping that she could find a place to hide from the effects of the blast in one of the towns along the way. She didn't think Route 40, being a divided highway, had anything that would work toward their safety.

It was ten after three when she came to a small town. She had no choice but to stop there. She had failed to check the mileage on the Jeep. She had no idea how far they had traveled, but she was sure that it wasn't far enough. She looked for a place between two buildings. There wasn't any.

She spotted a sign that read "Crowder Butcher Shop". She pulled over the curb and stopped to the right of the front door. She grabbed both flashlights and set them on the counter of the store. She noticed, as she had hoped, that there was a walk-in freezer in the rear of the store. She opened the door. It was still cool inside. The area was quite small. There was one post in the center and a butcher block near the front door. There was also a water cooler just outside the door. Knowing they would need water, she moved the water cooler inside. She then went out and dragged Mike into the freezer. Next, she brought in the backpacks and everything she thought they would need. Her hope was that the insulation of the freezer would protect them from the effects of the blast.

She looked at her watch. She had a few minutes left. She needed medical supplies for Mike. Putting one of the flashlights in the freezer, she took the other and started to run across the street to what looked like a drug store. However, as she got to the other side of the road, she saw a sign next to the drug store that read "Doctor Wilson." She decided that he would be more likely to have the kind of medical material that she needed. Inside, she found that he had a lab. Inside the lab, she found everything she had hoped for. Most important, she found four-inch pre-impregnated gauze bandages. She grabbed a bowl and all the materials she needed and raced back to the freezer.

She just closed the freezer door when she was knocked over by the earthquake-type shaking of the whole building. The shaking threw her across the room. She could hear the rushing of air like that of a full hurricane. All the flashlights were also thrown around, but they remained on. Next, an almost unbearable heat engulfed the room. A few minutes later, everything except for the heat became calm as if it had never happened. Sarah picked up the larger flashlight and surveyed the room. All seemed to be as before. She checked Mike. He was still unconscious.

She had to help him. She checked the Geiger counter. The radiation was near the dangerous level, but for the moment they were safe. Sarah moved Mike so he was between the post and the leg of the butcher block. She stripped Mike down to his shorts. She placed one of the belts across his chest and under his arms, tying him tightly to the pole so that his left shoulder was up against it. She then took the rope and tied it tightly around his wrist. She pulled the rope around the leg of the butcher's block and pulled hard. She felt Mike's arm snap back into place. She checked Mike's arm with her fingers as she was taught in medical school. She could feel the break, but everything seemed in place. She took the prepared gauze and soaked it in the water she had placed in the bowl. She then wrapped it around Mike's arm from his shoulder to his elbow. Using the same technique she had used to examine his upper arm, she checked the area below his elbow. She could feel a rupture, but the bone was not separated. She wrapped it as she had done to the upper arm. She checked his legs and found the same problem that she had found in his arm. After pulling his legs back in place, she tied them to the other leg of the butcher's block and wrapped them as she did the arm. She put Band-Aids on his head and side wounds. Now there was only the waiting until the Gauze hardened into the hard cast.

She drank some water and sat in the dark having turned off the flashlights to preserve the batteries. Every half hour or so she would check the hardness of the leg cast since it was the last one done. It was several hours later when she concluded that the casts had hardened sufficiently to remove the rope and pull Mike down to a comfortable position.

She folded his trousers and placed them under his head as a pillow. She then undressed to her underwear and took a last drink of water. She placed herself next to Mike's good side. She pulled his left arm around her and snuggled next to him, her nearly bare body touching him with her arm across his chest. She loved the feel of his body against hers.

"Mike," she said out loud, "I love you and need you. Please come back to me. Don't leave me." With that, she nestled her face into his neck and holding him tight she fell asleep.

CHAPTER SIX

Revelations

SARAH WOKE UP AFTER WHAT seemed to her to be a short time. She reached for the flashlight that she had put near her head and turned it on. To her amazement, it was three in the afternoon. She checked Mike's pulse. It was still beating faster than it should. She called out to him, but there was no answer. She was concerned about the blow to his head. She knew that a blow could cause the brain to swell, causing death hours after the blow. She didn't bother to dress. She liked the feeling of being free of clothes. It was too hot anyway. She got up and checked the radiation. It had come down about a third from where it was. That was good news for Sarah. She took the Geiger counter to the freezer door and opened the door slightly. The meter read in the danger area. Sarah closed the door immediately. They had to get out of there. With the radiation that high, it could take months to drop to livable levels.

She was getting hungry but only saw uncooked beef and chicken in the freezer. Taking the larger flashlight, she explored every corner of the freezer. In a corner under the area that the chicken was stored she found a round piece of meat that looked like some kind of lunchmeat. She took the knife from the butcher block and cut off a slice. It looked like corned beef. It tasted like corned beef, but they had no bread, and she couldn't go out for bread. There probably wasn't any that was edible because of the heat. She ate a couple of slices and decided that it would have to do for the present.

"Please wake up, Michael," she said to him. "I need you to tell me what to do."

She spent the afternoon just hanging around in the dark. She had shut off the flashlights to preserve the batteries. She felt her way to the butcher block and sat on it for a while with her back against the freezer wall. She got bored and finally, in the late afternoon, she cuddled up to Mike's body as she had done overnight and took an afternoon nap.

When she awoke, she turned on a flashlight and checked Mike. There was little change. She checked the time. It was ten after eight. She was still concerned about Mike, but she had calmed down sufficiently to start thinking logically. What was she going to do next? She realized that they had to get out of there. There were two choices. One, she could drag Mike to the Jeep and drive south to a safer area. Or, two, she could wait until Mike awoke and then leave the area. She decided she would wait awhile. She decided that they should go south to the Mexican border, try to head west from there, and then head north toward the mountains where she'd felt the secret base was located. She had made a habit of calling the base from her cell phone every day at least once. It would always ring, but no one would answer. She tried from the freezer, but she couldn't get a signal. She would have to wait until they left the area. At about ten, she nestled against Mike's body and planned on going to sleep, but she couldn't sleep since she had taken a long nap in the afternoon. She enjoyed the feel of Mike's warm body. She rubbed his chest with her hand. She hugged him tightly and eventually went to sleep dreaming of the future with Mike.

The next day was a complete repetition of the day before. She had to sneak out a few times to the bathroom, which was next to the freezer. She couldn't worry about the radiation. The third day started out the same except that Sarah had decided to follow her first plan of dragging Mike to the Jeep and leaving the area. She checked Mike's pulse. To her delight, it was back to normal—72 beats per minute. It was a change in the right direction. She tried to wake him to no avail. She decided to check the outside radiation level. It was just under the danger level. That was also good news.

She got dressed and went out to the main area of the store. It looked like it had been on fire. She went out to the Jeep. It looked like it had gone through a fire too. The paint on the outside was all peeling.

Would it start? She asked herself.

She put the key in the ignition. After a few minutes, it kicked over, but it seemed to be running on half of the cylinders. At least it would get them out of there. She went back to get the backpacks and other items. As she started to gather them, she heard a moaning coming from Mike. She dropped everything and rushed to his side.

"Mike, honey, are you awake?" she asked. Mike opened his eyes, moaned, and closed his eyes again. "Mike, how do you feel?"

"Where am I?" he asked

"You're here with me in a little town. How do you feel?"

"Head hurts very bad," he answered in a very low and slow whisper. Then he opened his eyes and continued. "Sarah, is that you?"

"I'm right here," she answered. "Can I do anything for you?" "Thirsty," he said. Sarah quickly got him some water from the water

cooler and, raising his head, she fed him the water. Mike closed his eyes and went back to sleep. Sarah checked his pulse again. It was normal.

Sarah felt better than she had felt in days. She had high hopes now that Mike would survive. She now had a lot to do. She found that the radiation had dissipated faster then she had anticipated. She ran out to the grocery store down the street. She found cans of soup that were still intact, not compromised by the heat or radiation. That is probably all that Mike could tolerate anyway after not eating for three days. She also found some bread, vegetables, and fruit that were back behind others and the fruit at the bottom of the barrels were still good having been sheltered by the fruit around it. The temperature outside was almost back to normal. The heat wave must have come as a wave and dispersed as quickly as it came .

She stopped at the drug store and grabbed all the flashlight batteries they had. She was not going to spend another moment in the dark.

As she was leaving she saw a clothing store. Quickly she entered the store to see what was available. The only things she found were two pillows. Then she returned to the freezer. Mike was still asleep. Sarah set everything she'd grabbed on the butcher block and turned on both flashlights. After setting a pillow under Mike's head, she had a sandwich and fruit for lunch. She set everything up to feed Mike some soup as soon as he woke up. It was past six when Mike woke up.

"Could I have some water?" he asked.

"Don't you want something to eat? You haven't had anything to eat for almost four days. You need some nourishment."

"I'm not hungry," he replied.

"Well, you are going eat some soup whether you are hungry or not," said Sarah, trying to be tough. Mike didn't respond. He was too tired to answer. Sarah grabbed him by the armpits and pulled him up so that he was leaning on the pole. Mike tried to help pushing with his good leg.

"What is wrong with my arm?" he asked. "I can't move it. My leg is heavy and it hurts. What has happened to me?"

"That is what I was going to ask you," she said. "Don't you remember what happened at the airfield?"

"The last thing I remember is that I was lying between the tree and a shrub looking out for you and the next thing I remember is waking up here. What happened out there?"

"Somehow we missed the rear guard. They must have seen our

Jeep. I think they snuck up on you and hit you over the head." "Where are we? What is this area we are in?" he asked.

"We are in the freezer of a butcher shop. We are lucky to be alive. I couldn't get us far enough from the site of the explosion. The insulation of this freezer has saved us, but as soon as you can walk we have to leave this area. The radiation outside is a little higher than I like."

Mike tried to get up but almost slipped off the post he was leaning on.

"I can't get up," he complained.

"Don't try yet," she advised. "You are not strong enough. That's why you need to eat something. Here drink some of this soup. It will give you some strength."

Mike didn't resist. Sarah fed him a full bowl of soup, and he accepted it without trouble. After he had eaten, she slid him back down and covered him with the blanket. Within seconds, he was fast asleep.

Sarah was feeling hungry herself. She had some soup, but it wasn't enough for her. She decided to check the freezer area again and found some chicken that was still a little cool. Setting up a grill outside the store, she lit it and left it to warm up. She cut up the chicken and, after the grill had gotten hot, she placed the chicken legs and wings on it and cooked them to her satisfaction. Minutes later, she finished eating. Being nice and full, she laid down next to Mike for an afternoon nap.

She woke up at about seven. She cooked the rest of the chicken and ate some fruit.

It was about ten-thirty that evening, when she undressed and snuggled up to Mike, as she had done the previous nights, and fell asleep. The next morning, Sarah woke up first. It was a very hot morning. She dressed and went to the grocery store. In the backroom she found some cereal. She also found a milk bottle that had not been distorted. The milk had been heated.

So what? she thought. *That could make it better.*

She returned to the freezer, and woke Mike.

"Mike, I have some cereal for your breakfast. You need some substance. This will be your first semi-solid food."

"I am a little hungry," he responded. "What time is it?" "It's a quarter past ten," she said looking at her watch.

She raised Mike to a sitting position and started to feed him. He stopped her with his good hand.

"Wait awhile," he said. "I'm feeling a little dizzy. Put the bowl on my lap. I'll feed myself when I feel better."

"You are getting better," she said with a smile.

Little by little he fed himself. After he had finished eating, Sarah asked him, "Do you want me to help you lie down again?"

"No, let me get used to being up. Besides, I'm tired of sleeping." "Good," said Sarah. "We have to get out of here as soon as you can walk."

"I'm getting tired of this place myself," said Mike. "I would like to see some sunshine."

Sarah got up early the next morning. She couldn't sleep. She was eager to get away from that area. She said her morning prayers, got fully dressed, and started to put everything she could in the Jeep. She made breakfast with the remainder of the cereal and made sandwiches from what was left of the meat. She didn't know if they would have an occasion to stop for lunch somewhere. She then woke up Mike.

"I'm sorry to wake you so early, but we have to get on the road." "What time is it?" he asked.

"It's seven thirty. I have breakfast for you. I've packed everything but your clothes so we are almost ready to go."

"Wow," said Mike. "You are really eager to leave this place. Why?" "I'm eager because the radiation is very high. It has hardly come

down since we got here. Since it is accumulative, we have to get away from here. If you ever want to have more children, we have to get away as soon as possible."

After they had eaten, she helped Mike get dressed. Mike stood up with Sarah's help. With his left arm around Sarah's neck, he hopped on his good leg until he was comfortably seated in the Jeep.

"The Jeep looks like it has been on fire," said Mike. "Will it run?" "We will see in a minute," answered Sarah. "I'm going back inside to make sure we've got everything we need." Getting back she got in the Jeep and started the engine. "It looks like we have everything."

She backed the jeep and got on the road. The Jeep was shaking from the poorly running engine and felt like it was going to fall apart.

"What's the problem with the engine?" asked Mike, becoming concerned about their safety. "It sounds like it's running on half of its cylinders."

"This is a four cylinder engine. It has to run on at least three cylinders. You're a man, you tell me what is happening."

"Since you asked me, I'll tell you what I think," said Mike, hesitating to think about it. As an engineer, he should have a logical answer.

"I think that all the cylinders are working. They are not all working at the same time."

"This is all we have and as long as it's moving, we don't have any choice," said Sarah.

"I think what happened is that the heat has melted all the plastic on the ignition wires. With the shaking of the engine, they short out occasionally. As time goes by, it will only get worse."

Sarah turned the Jeep down Route 69. The best speed the Jeep could average, with the bad engine and the bad road conditions, was approximately twenty miles an hour. About an hour and a half later, they got to the outskirts of McAlister. It was about ten. They had reached a point where the road was completely blocked. Even the Jeep couldn't get through. Sarah had placed the Geiger counter between the front seats where she could keep a running value of the reading. It had come down considerably, but not enough to satisfy Sarah. She backed up and took a narrow country road still going south. The Jeep was going slower and slower. The engine sounded like it would soon stop.

"I don't know how far we can get down this country road, but I would like to get to the point where the radiation is down to zero. On the other hand, we have to find a place to stay until we can take your cast off."

"And how long could that be? asked Mike.

"It will take a total of about six weeks," she answered. "We have barely a week toward this healing time."

They drove as fast as the Jeep would go, but they were barely averaging ten miles an hour. They had made it to a place where the radiation dropped to zero, but they were in the middle of nowhere.

"The meter reads zero," advised Mike.

"We have to continue down this road. I'm hoping that we can get to a small village." However, it sounded like the Jeep wasn't going to cooperate. The engine was now stopping and restarting from its forward motion.

"I don't think it's going to go much farther," said Mike.

"It has to," said Sarah in a state of panic. "I can't drag you to the next town."

She started to pray out loud. Soon, the Jeep could hardly move. Sarah was about to give up when Mike spoke.

"Look, Sarah," he said with a happy voice. "There is a farmhouse just ahead. Try to get up its driveway."

"I don't know if we can get that far."

"There is a little slope in the road up to the drive way. See if we have enough speed so you can coast there."

The Jeep, with its last sign of life, went about twenty feet up the driveway and died.

"It's about a hundred feet to the porch of the farm house," said Sarah. "Do you think you can make it?"

"Do we have any other choice? With your help, we will be able to make it." Sarah went around the passenger side of the Jeep and helped Mike get out. Mike almost fell, but Sarah grabbed him and held him up.

"I don't know if I can make it up to the house," said Mike

"We can go a little at a time," answered Sarah. "It's barely twelve. We have all afternoon to get there. And think of how nice it's going to be to sit on the front porch." Mike tried to walk, but he couldn't put weight on his bad left leg.

"I can't do it," he responded.

"We have done this before. Remember, I got you outside yesterday."

"Yes, but that was about ten feet. This is about a hundred feet."

"Put your bad arm around my neck as far as you can. I'll try to carry you under your shoulder. Now let me be your left leg." They started up the drive. They went one step at a time. As Sarah moved forward, Mike would hop on his right leg. They were about halfway up the driveway when they heard a sound like a truck coming their way.

"What is that?" asked Mike. "I hope it isn't a tank coming this way." "Could it be an aircraft?" asked Sarah. "It would be terrible if we came all this way and get killed by an aircraft."

"It doesn't sound like an aircraft," said Mike. "This sounds like an ordinary truck."

Just as he said that, a truck came over the hill, across the road, toward the south side of the farmhouse.

"It's a weapons carrier," remarked Mike having recognized the vehicle. "Look, it's carrying a bunch of soldiers in the back. They are all Arabs. We are like sitting ducks here in the open."

"I'm not worried about them," said Sarah. "They are going to the other side of the house. They are not paying attention to us. What I am worried about is the noise I hear straight across from us. It sounds like a lot of people yelling."

Just then, a group of soldiers on foot came out over a little hill on the other side of the road heading straight for them.

"They are also Arab soldiers," said Mike with panic in his voice. "Oh no," said Sarah. "We have to get out of here."

Mike tried to walk fast but tripped on his own feet and fell. As he fell, he turned so he ended up in a sitting position. His weight pulled Sarah down with him.

"I can't make it!" he yelled to Sarah. "Go and save yourself." "No, I won't leave you."

"Don't be silly. Save yourself. Go hide in the basement or somewhere by the barn."

"I won't leave you," she insisted. "Let me help you up." She got up and tried to lift him. She ended up falling back beside him.

"Sarah, please go. I love you. You can't help me."

"It's too late," said Sarah wondering why she really didn't go. "I love you too. We will go together."

"I can't believe that God is finished with us," said Mike. "There is so much work to be done. We are not only needed to help in defeating the enemy, but we will be needed to help in all the reconstruction that has to be done."

Sarah was not thinking of work. Though she had told Mike she loved him, her thoughts were of Tom. Tom was the only one she had really loved with all of her heart. He was the only one that had given her butterflies in her stomach and a lump in her throat. She wondered if he was still alive. If not, would she meet him in heaven?

"There are about a half dozen coming our way," she said, coming out of her thoughts. "We only have a few minutes left. I'm sorry I brought you out here. We should have stayed in the freezer."

"How could you have known?" asked Mike. "Don't think about that. The soldiers have just reached the road. Let's pray." Mike said a quick prayer, since he didn't have much time. Sarah prayed with him.

I don't want to die, decided Sarah as the realization of what was about to happen began to sink in. The soldiers had reached the Jeep and were coming very fast. The fear and the horror of the possible pain of dying overwhelmed her. She closed her eyes. She didn't want to see it coming. She started to tremble. Her imagination went wild. She began to think of the pain of the bullets entering her flesh.

Her heart began to beat furiously. The stress overcame her, and she slumped into Mike's arms unconscious.

"Thank God," said Mike out loud. "You won't feel any pain now, sweetheart." He hugged her tightly. She felt so perfect in his arms. His thoughts however, were on Tara. She was his true love. Had she died in Chicago? Would he see her now in heaven? The soldiers were now just feet away. He was going to die without seeing his son again.

As they got closer, he became angry. He remembered that the Bible said to love your enemies. He wasn't going to close his eyes; he was going to stare right into their eyes.

"Oh, help me, dear Lord," he said out loud. "It's too hard not to hate them. Come on, you wicked animals. Pave your road into hell." As they come up to him, he looked into their faces. He saw something that he had not expected. He had seen it before, but he couldn't remember what it was. The first man that came upon him and Sarah side stepped him and ran past.

"Leaving us to your companion are you?" Mike yelled at him. The last two came right at him. One side stepped them and the other jumped over them. Mike turned his head and saw them run past the house and down toward the cornfield. Mike was amazed. The soldiers had completely ignored them.

How was that possible? he asked himself. *What is going on?*

He then remembered the look on their faces. He remembered what it was. He had seen it on the face of some of the soldiers earlier.

It was fear.

The soldiers were scared to death. He looked down the area from where they had come to see if anything was chasing them. He visualized an American army chasing them, but he saw nothing.

"Sarah, wake up," he said as he patted her on her cheek. It took a few minutes before she came to.

"Are we dead?" she asked, still in a daze.

"No," said Mike happily. "We can't be dead because my leg still hurts."

"What happened?" she asked. "Why aren't we dead?"

"I shook my fist at them and scared them away," joked Mike.

"Come on Mike," she said getting upset with him. "What happened?"

"I don't really know," he answered truthfully. "We will have to sit down and think about this."

"Well, tell me what you do know. Did God make us invisible?"

"No, I know they saw us because they jumped over us when they got here. The only thing I do know is that they looked scared to death. It was like the devil was chasing them. I thought maybe our army had come to the rescue, but I looked back and didn't see anyone chasing them."

"I can't believe we are still alive," said Sarah in a state of confusion.

"Shall we try to get to the farm house?" asked Mike, almost fully recovered from the incident.

"I'm still feeling drained. My heart is still beating out of control. Let me rest here with you for a while. It is only a little past noon. We have all afternoon to get there. I've got to get over the fact that we are not dead."

She nestled into Mike's arms. She felt comfortable there. She fit perfectly. As she lay there she remembered her thoughts on Tom.

Well, she thought. *Mike is a very close second choice.*

Mike liked the situation also. He wrapped his good arm around her and enjoyed being alive. Ten minutes later, they both fell asleep. It was about three when they both woke up. They looked around. They were alone. The air was deadly silent.

"Let see if we can get to the porch," suggested Mike.

"I don't know how to do that," said Sarah. "I tried to lift you before, and I couldn't."

"Well we have to think of something," said Mike. "We can't spend the next five weeks here on the front lawn."

"Very funny," said Sarah with a slight smile on her face. "Why don't you roll over and try to get up on your knees. If you can't get up from that position, you can sleep on your stomach."

"Now who is the joker?" asked Mike. He rolled over on his stomach and drew up his legs. Sarah grabbed him under the armpits and pulled him to an upright position.

One step at a time, they slowly make it to the porch steps.

It was easy for Mike to sit on the step. Sarah went behind him and grabbed him under the armpits. One step at a time, they started up the steps.

Resting a few minutes between steps, they soon had Mike sitting on the front porch swing. Sarah sat beside him.

"I have to rest a while," she said as she relaxed, exhausted. "Go ahead," said Mike. "What else do you have to do?" Sarah didn't answer him. She was deep in thought.

"The thing that puzzles me," she said, "is why didn't they shoot us? They just ran past us. It wouldn't have taken two seconds to get rid of us."

"They were no longer worried about us," suggested Mike. "They were running for their lives. What I can't figure out is why."

"Or, for that matter," continued Sarah, "why didn't they shoot us when they had us at the airfields, once when they had me and once when they had you? Was it that they enjoyed beating us to death?"

"I think that was part of it. They surely looked like they enjoyed beating us, but I think there was more to it. Just think about it, what would have happened if they had shot us? They were in the vicinity of around five hundred thousand soldiers sleeping across the field. What would have happened at the sound of shooting?"

"I see what you mean," said Sarah. "They probably would have shot them for getting them all excited."

"I can just imagine the anger that the big brass would experience," said Mike. Sarah didn't answer. She was too tired. After sitting there for about a half hour, Sarah said, "I'm too restless sitting here. I'm going to look around. Will you be all right here for a while?"

"Sure. Go ahead, I'll be all right," agreed Mike.

"I'll be back soon," she added and left through the open front door. About fifteen minutes later, she came back outside where Mike was sitting.

"What's it like?" asked Mike. "Is anyone here? Any bodies lying around that we have to clean up?"

"No, there are no bodies," said Sarah "It's not too bad. There are two bedrooms, a living area, a nice kitchen, a breakfast nook, and a nice screened in porch in the back just outside of the kitchen. I can take you there if you wish. That would get you out of the sun."

"No, I'm comfortable here. The sun is partially blocked by the two trees in front."

"As you wish," said Sarah. "I'm going to get our stuff out of the Jeep. It looks like we are going to stick around for a little while."

At that, she went down to the Jeep and carried all of their belongings into the house. She made two trips, lastly bringing in the grill. She was sure that if they could find food, they would need the grill. Besides, why leave anything in the Jeep? It wasn't any good anyway.

"I'm going to look around the place," said Sarah after she had brought everything inside.

"Go ahead," said Mike. "Keep an eye out for something for dinner." "Take a nap. I won't be long," assured Sarah. She went back inside.

It was about seven before Sarah came back to the front porch. "Where have you been?" asked Mike. "I was getting worried about you. You have been gone for nearly four hours."

"You said that you wanted me to look for food," said Sarah with a happy face, something that Mike had not seen for a long time. "So I found some."

"Tell me about it," said Mike.

"First, what would you like to eat? It's after seven, and I don't know about you, but after all the hard work I've been through, I'm very hungry."

"Well what have you got?" asked Mike.

"How would you like a rib steak and some potatoes and some spinach? I also have some fruit for dessert."

"That is very cruel, and it's not funny," said Mike getting angry. "Why are you doing this? When will we ever see a dinner like that?"

"You don't believe me?" said Sarah with wonderment. "Have I ever lied to you? Have I ever been cruel to you?"

"I don't understand," said Mike puzzled

"Come on with me, and I'll explain on the way in the house." She grabbed Mike under his left armpit, and with his help, she brought him into the house and into the kitchen. When Mike entered the kitchen, he hesitated and almost fell. If not for Sarah's strength, he would have fallen on his face.

"Wow!" he exclaimed. "You weren't lying. What? How? Where?" is all that he could say.

"Just sit here and I'll explain."

Mike sat still dazzled by what he saw.

"I guessed that you like your steak medium rare," she said. "Anyway that is how I cooked it."

"Yes," responded Mike. Sarah put a potato in his dish and a fork full of spinach.

"Now, if you will say grace, we can eat before it gets cold."

Mike said a grace that was almost incoherent. However, the basic theme was giving thanks to God for Sarah and the food. Mike ate as he had never eaten before. As he was eating, he slowly came to his senses.

"I'm sorry I didn't believe you," he said. "Sometimes I can be such a jerk."

"Not at all," said Sarah. "I wanted to surprise you, but I probably should have handled it better."

"Now that I'm full and can't move, please tell me the whole story." "Well, when I went back in I explored a little more closely," began Sarah. "I found that there was a pantry next to the kitchen. I also found a laundry room across the hall from the kitchen. Just as you enter the laundry room, there is a little wall protruding from the left wall. In the area behind it is a freezer chest. I checked inside, and I found it to be full of food. When I touched it, I found that it was still pretty frozen. I wondered why. I know that the enemy army had gone through before we set the last explosion. How could the food still be frozen?"

"Maybe the electricity wasn't cut somehow until after the army went through," said Mike interrupting her.

"That doesn't sound logical," responded Sarah. "Let me tell you the rest of what I found. I checked the kitchen refrigerator. The food was still cool. That's when I went outside. Behind the house on the left is a shed. The shed was divided in two sections. On the right section, the door faced the house. I went in there first. Inside, I found a small six-cylinder engine attached to a generator. The engine was off. I checked the wire from the generator and I found that it had been cut outside of the shed. It was probably done by the invading army. Well, I didn't know how to repair a cut wire."

"So what did you do?" asked Mike.

"I ignored it for the time being, and I checked the other side of the shed. The door to that section faced the barn, and I could see why. It had a tractor inside. It was also the tool shed. I never saw so many tools. I found a box that had, 'Three wire no 14' stamped on it. I opened it, and inside, I found wire that looked like the one that was cut."

"Don't tell me that you rewired the house," said Mike with admiration written all over his face.

"I could disconnect the old wire. All I needed was a screwdriver. I had dozens of screwdrivers to choose from, so I disconnected the old wire. I was about to connect the new wire when I realized that I couldn't climb up the side of the house to thread the wire through the eyelets near the roof. So I connected one end of the wire in the box to the other end of the old wire. I then went to the other end of the wire and guess what I found?"

"Are you purposely keeping me in suspense?" asked Mike. Sarah ignored him.

"I found a trap door that went down to a small basement. Down there, I found a small rack of twelve-volt batteries. Ten were connected in series and in parallel with two other, similar racks."

"You know about series and parallel connections?" asked Mike with astonishment. "You never cease to amaze me."

"I knew that if you connect ten twelve volt batteries in series, you get one hundred twenty volts, and tying three banks in parallel will get you even more current. The wire was connected to the batteries through a wire terminal. I disconnected the wire and pulled it until the new wire showed up at the terminal. You understand that pulling the wire wasn't an easy job; it took me a lot of effort pushing and pulling. It took me about a half hour or more. However, I connected the wire and checked on ways to start the engine."

"So what you're telling me is that the batteries kept the freezer and refrigerator powered even though the engine was off," said Mike. "That is ingenious."

"The batteries are connected only to the freezer and refrigerator. The lights in the house are on only during the hours that the engine is running. What is ingenious is that the engine is automatically started at dusk and turned off around midnight."

"Do you know how that was done?" asked Mike.

"I think so," said Sarah. "I found an electric eye on the other side of the shed. I covered it with black tape and the engine started. I don't know what will make it stop."

"I think I can help you there," said Mike. "Being an electrical engineer has its advantages. Tell me, you said that the cable had three wires in it. Is that correct?"

"Well it really had four wires," said Sarah. "That is, if you count the bare copper wire."

"Was there one black wire, one white wire, one green wire, and the bare wire?"

"Yes that is correct," said Sarah. "What does that mean?"

"It means that I can tell you how the engine gets turned off," he answered with a smile. "I think that they are using the green wire to tell the engine when the batteries are fully charged. The engine may go on and off during the night if the battery voltage drops below a predetermined level."

"That sounds like a good explanation," said Sarah. "Do you know what else I found? I went into the barn and found two horses. The poor things were almost dead. I feed them. They may come in handy since we don't have a vehicle."

"Right now, I want to call the secret base. I have tried to call every day, but I always get the same results. It rings, but no one answers. By the way, there is a live receptacle in the kitchen that is connected to the batteries. That way we can have coffee in the morning without all of the electricity on. Anyway, I'm going to use it to hook my cell phone charger to it." After she tried to call, she plugged in the phone and helped Mike out to the back porch.

"Would you like me to look for something for you to read?"

She was about to go inside when she was shocked by the sound of the phone ringing. She picked it up and answered.

"Hello," Sarah said. "Yes, this is Doctor Anders." Mike could hear her from the porch.

"Doctor Anders?" he said out loud. He didn't know she was a doctor. He should have known after she had fixed his broken body. He leaned over. He wanted to hear everything that went on.

"Is that right?" she said. "That's amazing. I had no idea. Yes, Mike and I set off their own nuclear weapons, both in the northern and the southern army. We had no idea of the damage we did. Who's Mike? Mike is a fellow that I met on the way to the Chicago meeting. His full name is Michael Mills. I don't really know. Just a minute, and I'll ask him. Michael!" she yelled out to Mike. "Are you Colonel Michael Mills, the colonel that set the trap in Afghanistan that destroyed the back of the insurgents? The one that's called the Desert Fox?"

"Oh no, not that name," said Mike. "I was Colonel Mills, but I'm retired. It was no big deal."

"Yes that was him," continued Sarah on the phone. "Really, I'll let you talk to him after you tell me what is going on. I have been trying to call you ever since I found out about the destruction of Chicago. What is going on?" Sarah listened intensely for about fifteen minutes, not speaking except every so often she would say, "Yes" or "I understand."

Mike could no longer get any information from the conversation. Finally, she spoke again. "Do you want me to leave Mike and come to meet you?" She listened for a while, and then she explained the problems they had and how badly Mike had been hurt. "As you wish." She finally ended her conversation and walked out to the porch and handed Mike the phone. "Here, this is General William McGard. He is in charge of the secret base. He wants to talk with you."

"Hello," said Mike. "How are you, sir?"

"I'm fine, Colonel. Doctor Anders told me of your injuries. I told her to stick with you until you can travel. We urgently need you here. Doctor Anders will fill you in on all that has happened. I will only take the time to tell you what we need you for. Our base has several fighters and bombers. We couldn't get help to the eastern states and could only hit most of the enemy ships on the western US coast before they could land. We used nuclear bombs to destroy their ships at sea. However, a group of ships made it through and unloaded about two hundred thousand soldiers at the southern end of California. The Texas and Arizona State troopers that were on leave or training have been assembled and are heroically slowing them down.

"Sarah will give you the details, but every army, navy and air force base has been destroyed except ours. The army base in Seattle was nuked, but a company of about one hundred thousand soldiers was out of the base on a training mission. They are presently located just south of Spokane. The high-ranking officers went home for the weekend and left the troops in the hands of lieutenants. You see why we need you.

"News of the invasion got out to the Midwest, and the people have all run to the borders. Now, we have announced over TV, radio, and whatever else we could use to tell people that the eastern army has been defeated and that we need every available young man to come to Spokane. We also told the other people to go back home. The enemy has also heard this message. They are now headed north to attack us in Spokane. Our air force and the Texas and Arizona armies are also headed north and are slowing down the enemy advance. There is something else that you have to do before you come here. Doctor Anders will fill you in; I have to leave on a mission. By the way, you are in the reserves are you not?"

"Yes, sir."

"Well, as of now you are on active duty, Colonel. Talk to you later." The General then hung up.

"Well, I guess I'm in the army again," said Mike. "The general says that I am, as of now, reactivated."

"Tell me what else he told you," urged Sarah.

"You first," said Mike. "You were on the phone with him forever. You have a lot more information then I have."

"All right," agreed Sarah. "First, he told me that we destroyed the complete northern and southern invading armies. He said that we eliminated somewhere between one and one and a half million enemy solders. There were only about a hundred left on the fringes of the camps. He said that the ones that were left were running to get back to their ships to get home."

"The solders that ran past us on the front lawn must have been some of those that survived. I thought I saw fear in their faces," said Mike.

"Not only that," continued Sarah, "but the general said that many of them were exposed to so much radiation that they may not make it to the east coast."

"What did he tell you about the cities that were nuked?"

"It wasn't just the ten cities that we thought were nuked," said Sarah. "It was in the hundreds. Every large city was hit. All of the coastal cities were bombed."

"What did he say about what he needed you for, and where he wants you to go?"

"First," answered Sarah, "he wants us to go south and get all the people who are trying to get into Mexico to go back to their homes. We're supposed to get all eligible young men to come to Spokane to help win back our country. Then, I am needed to help with the nuclear devices that only I know how to operate."

"Where was he all the times that you tried to call him?"

"He was on several missions," explained Sarah. "He had to fly an aircraft to stop the west coast invasion. Now he is going on another mission that he couldn't tell me about. Oh, there is more news that he told me. He said the Arabs got their time difference messed up by an hour. Our troops and air bases in the Middle East heard about the nuking of our cities, so they sent men fifty miles outside of our bases. They shot anyone approaching with any kind of a backpack. I'm sure they killed a lot of innocent people, but they did get four nuclear backpacks. Israel also obtained three nuclear backpacks. They are already on their way to retaliate. Now it's your turn. What did General McGard tell you, and what does he want you to do?"

Mike related to her every detail of the conversation he had with the general.

"That's why I have to get well as soon as I can," finished Mike. "First of all we have to find some kind of transportation."

"I have another question for you," said Sarah. "What is this 'Desert Fox' thing about?"

"Some stupid reporter started it," said Mike. "In this dumb story, he compared what I did to the action of the German General Rommel in the African desert during World War 2. He inflicted heavy loses to the superior US and British forces by hitting and running with his small army. He was called the Desert Fox. Please don't repeat that to anyone. It embarrasses me because I don't feel worthy."

"Well, let's forget that for now," said Sarah. "Tell me, have you ever gone horseback riding?"

"Of course, I've gone many times as a young man."

"Good, because we have two horses in the barn. We can use them to get to a town where we can obtain a vehicle."

"Now then, all that is left is for me to get well."

"Only until you can ride a horse," said Sarah in humor.

"Very funny," said Mike. "That could be tomorrow, unless the horse doesn't like the casts beating him in his sides."

"Seriously," said Sarah. "It is almost nine, and I have to unpack, make the beds, and get everything ready for tomorrow."

"Why? What's happening tomorrow?" asked Mike.

"I have to get up early to take care of the farm animals and see if I can rustle up some breakfast for my man. Do you want to come inside while I do some work?"

"No I'll stay on the back porch. This swing is very comfortable. She left him there and went inside. Mike felt very comfortable and was content to sit and enjoy the serenity of the open farmland. He listened to the chirping of the birds and squirrels. It was after eleven when Sarah came back out and sat with Mike for a while.

"I'm tired," she said. "I would like to sit here with you and dream that someday this may be the type of life that will return to America."

"I'm confident that it will," said Mike with assurance in his tone. "It will just take hard work. Americans are born survivors."

"I know," said Sarah. "We come from a strong blood line, from brave parents that had the courage to leave their homes in Europe and start a new life in a wilderness."

"Before I forget," said Mike changing the subject. "Why didn't you tell me you were a doctor? I thought you were a nuclear scientist."

"After I completed my undergraduate, I went to medical school for a year where I was intrigued with the nuclear devices used in the medical labs. I then changed my major to study towards a PhD in physics. My intentions were to stay in the medical field, but God had other ideas. You should talk. You didn't tell me you were a war hero." "That's because I'm not. I just followed the example in the Bible of the plan that Joshua used against the city of Ai. Like Joshua, I set a trap in the mountains and then sent in a small force to attack the enemy. After a short battle, my men retreated, and the enemy followed, thinking that they had defeated me, and walked right into my trap."

"I don't care where you got the idea," said Sarah. "I just think it was ingenious."

They sat there is silence, enjoying the cool night air for about a half-hour. Then Sarah got up and faced Mike.

"Come on, Mike. Let me take you to your bed. It is getting pretty late."

"My bed?" asked Mike. "Isn't my bed your bed also?"

"I made up a bed for you in the front bedroom," said Sarah. "I'm going to sleep in the back bedroom."

"Why?" asked Mike partly in jest. "You slept practically naked, huddled up to me in the freezer, and now you are getting a purity syndrome."

"What are you talking about?" asked Sarah, surprised at his statement. "When did I do that?"

"It was the night that we blew up the southern enemy army."

"Are you talking about the first night we spent in the freezer?" she asked. "You were out cold that night and the next two days."

"I know," answered Mike. "I did wake up once that night in severe pain, but it was very comforting to feel your warm body hugging me so tight. It gave me a feeling of safety, of being cared for. That's why I fell asleep for so long. Thank you, by the way."

"You actually woke up once that night?" asked Sarah in a state of shock and embarrassment. "Did you really?"

"So why don't we cuddle up together in the same bed?" said Mike, knowing that it would not happen."

"That will never happen again," said Sarah turning red. "That was a special occasion. I thought you were going to die. Never mind the small talk," she continued. "Let me take you to bed now, or I will leave you out here all night."

"Here, I'm being very romantic and you are acting so cold." Sarah grabbed him by the shoulder and helped him get up.

"We have too much to do to get romantic. Besides, we are just friends."

"Just friends?" said Mike. "Just a few days ago you declared that you loved me."

"That was when I thought that we were going to die," she answered.

"I see," said Mike. "You only love me when we are going to die. The rest of the time, we are just friends. Well I love you all the time. Didn't you really mean it?"

"Will you stop it already? I do love you. I love you as my best friend."

"No," he answered, "I will not stop. I am hurting all over my body and now you want to hurt me in my heart. I just need a little affection."

"Are you serious?" she questioned.

"The only other time I was this serious is when I said, 'I do.'"

"I'll compromise," said Sarah, softening to his advances. "You sleep in the back bedroom, and I'll give you a hug and kiss good night."

"I guess I don't have any choice," he answered. "If that is the best I'm going to get."

"We can't let ourselves get too involved. We can't take our mind off the difficult task we have ahead of us." She helped Mike get into bed, and after she helped him undress to his shorts, she covered him and gave him a big hug and a kiss on the cheek. Mike was not satisfied with the kiss on the cheek. With his good arm he held her from getting up. They looked each other in the eyes. Their faces were only an inch apart. Neither could resist the temptation. Their lips touched. Passion rose in their hearts. The kiss lasted for minutes. Sarah pulled about an inch away. She looked lovingly into his eyes.

"To answer the question you asked earlier, yes, I meant it."

Mike understood what she meant. Sarah then got up and headed to her room. "Good night," she said as she left the room.

CHAPTER SEVEN

On the Road Again

IT WAS SEVERAL DAYS LATER that Mike found he could walk on the leg using a cane that Sarah had made. In the evenings, they would sit on the back porch. Mike would put his good arm around her and pull her close to him. Sarah would smile. She liked to place her head on his shoulder. She felt so safe in his embrace.

Mike, however, knew when to stop. Mike had promised her that he would never dishonor her, and he meant to keep his promise. Sarah was in touch with the general every day that he was at the base and not on a mission, which was about every second or third day. On the last day, he told her that they were running out of ammunitions and bombs. He said that the enemy army had stayed hidden and stayed back for some unknown reason. One reason may have been due to their aircraft attacks. However, now that our aircraft have decreased hits on them, they are starting to slowly move north. Several men had united with the enemy army, increasing their ranks. He felt that these were the infiltrators that set the bombs in the large cities and were now rejoining their own people. He emphasized that they needed her right away. He said the Texas and Arizona soldiers were on the way north to join the soldiers in Spokane.

"We have to leave very soon," said Sarah one evening. "We can't delay much longer."

"I wish we could stay here a little longer," voiced Mike affectionately.

"I would love that too," said Sarah. "I could live here the rest of my life with you. I would like to just be domestic."

"Like a mother and wife?" asked Mike.

"Yes, like a mother and wife, but it will never happen I'm afraid," she said sadly. "I am too educated. They would never let me. I wouldn't be able to resist the demand for my type of training. My training would be in too great in demand."

"There is no reason that you couldn't do both," said Mike. "I know the days of the stay-at-home wife is not as common as it used to be, but it is done every day. I am, therefore, planning on helping my partner do some of the domestic part of living together. By the way, did you say that you would like to spend the rest of your life here with me? Do you love me that much?"

"You know that I do," she said with a shy look about her, "but I wouldn't want to deceive you. I love you very much. You are a great guy. You are very intelligent and romantic and very handsome."

"I heard a *but* in there somewhere," said Mike.

"I just want you to know that I will always love Tom. We had some kind of magic between us that I have never felt before."

"That hurt," said Mike sadly.

"Don't worry, I'll get over it, but tell me that you don't still have feelings for Tara. You once told me that you had a special love for her, that she gave you butterflies in your stomach. You don't have to answer me. Just think about it. I think you love me as much as I love you. Tom is gone, and so is Tara if she lived in Chicago. I'm just moving on."

Mike didn't answer her, but he knew she was right. However, his thoughts were more about Annie. He missed and thought of her every night. His thoughts of Tara were diminishing every day.

The next day was a day of preparation. They planned on taking everything they could on the horses' saddlebags.

Sarah cooked the best breakfast, lunch and dinner she knew how. They didn't know where their next meal would come from. Mike said grace at every meal thanking God for the farm that he provided and the food that he made available to them. Lastly, he prayed that God would guide them on the path that would fulfill the purpose he had for keeping them alive. That evening, Sarah removed the cast from Mike's leg.

"This is the final test," said Sarah. "It will tell us if we can leave tomorrow."

"How do you know I won't fail on purpose?" said Mike, kidding her. "Because I know that you are a good Christian and you wouldn't fake a problem," she said. "Now cut the bull and let's see you walk out to the back porch where we will spend our last night together on the swing."

"Boy, you know how to use all the tricks, don't you," he said affectionately.

"I know what you like," she said with a smile. Mike got up and started to walk around. He was still limping a little, but he got around without trouble though rather slowly.

"I guess I'm all right," he said after taking a few steps around the kitchen.

"Do you have any pain?" asked Sarah.

"No," he answered. "It's just that the legs don't have much strength."

"Do you think you can ride the horse?"

"I don't think that will be a problem," he said, "but what about the arm, can you remove that cast?"

"I think we should leave that on for a while longer. The arm was hurt more seriously. I'll bring the required tools with me, and we will take that cast off later."

"Then there is nothing left to do but sit on the porch and rest," said Mike.

"I don't think that rest is the right word," said Sarah. "However, I'm going to see that we go to bed early. We have to get up early tomorrow."

Mike didn't say a word. He was through speaking. If Sarah was going to see that he got to bed early he didn't want to waste anymore time talking. They sat on the rear porch swing in one another's arms, and their lips didn't have any trouble finding each other. They wondered when they would have the opportunity to be safely embraced romantically like this again. The next morning Sarah got up first.

They put on their empty backpacks, and they mounted and started south down the road heading for Route 59. They walked their horses when the soft shoulder wasn't flat. They didn't want to run the horses on the pavement. They exchanged small talk about feeling strange traveling on horseback. About two miles down the road, they came to the town of Saris. It was in ruins and also deserted. They didn't find a vehicle that was drivable. From Saris, the road turned southwest. At about ten o'clock they came to the town of Adel. It was pretty much like Saris; there was no one around. There were also no bodies around.

"Do you think they all got away from the enemy army?" asked Sarah.

"I wondered about that too. I suspect that they all got away, or they cleaned up before they left," answered Mike. "I don't think there is a crew that goes around cleaning up. What bothers me is that there are no drivable cars around. In fact, since there aren't too many cars around, seems to indicate that a lot of people drove away. Whether or not they got away alive is another question."

"Do you think that they could have been bombed by the aircraft?" asked Sarah.

"We won't know that until we get to the main highway."

It was almost five when they reached the freeway Route 69 at the town of Stringtown. They got on the freeway, and since the soft shoulder was hard, they were able to make better time.

"Look," said Sarah. "There are two cars going the other way on the freeway."

"I noticed that as we approached it before. At least I saw one car go by. That is very strange."

At about six, they reached the town of Atoka.

"I see that this town is not in bad shape," said Mike. "We have been traveling southwest. I think we have gotten far enough west to get to the towns that the invaders had not gotten to yet. The little damage that we see is probably from the bomb blast."

"I think you are right, but why aren't there more people around here?"

"They probably went south to escape the invading army," said Mike. "They had no idea that the army would be stopped before it got to them."

"There seems to be some cars parked along the road that look perfectly good," said Sarah. "I wonder if we can obtain one."

"Not if the owners are inside that building," said Mike. "It looks like a restaurant. The sign says 'Sweet Pea.' What I would like to get is a small truck like that one parked on the other side of the street."

They had dismounted and were walking toward the restaurant. "What I want to know is, what should we do with the horses?" asked Sarah.

"First we have to find water and food for them," said Mike.

"I'm not worried about that," said Sarah. "I'm wondering where to settle them for the night, or, for that matter, where do we tie them while we go in to dine."

Just as they had said that, a man in his mid to late thirties came around the corner and saw them with the horses.

" Hi," he said. "Are you guys traveling by house back?"

"Only until we can find another methods of transportation," said Sarah.

"May I ask you a question?" "How can I help you?" he asked.

"If you are from this area and are familiar with the people would you know who owns that truck across the street?"

"First of all I'm not from this area," he said. "In any case, it doesn't matter because the truck is mine. Why do you ask?"

"Would you like to sell it?" asked Mike.

The man laughed. "You want to trade it for the horses?" he asked, still laughing loudly. "No way, I need the truck for my farm."

"Tell me," said Mike, "what has made you decide to go home at this time? What told you that the problem is over?"

"I heard it on the radio," he answered. "I understand that it even got announced on TV."

"What did you hear?" asked Mike, very puzzled, not only that the radios and TV stations were already back in service, but that the news had gotten out already.

"The radio news commentator said that the invading army had been pushed back into the Atlantic Ocean. Why do you ask?"

"We were given the job of informing the people who have run to the Mexican border to escape the invaders that the threat is over and they could go home," said Mike. "We need a car to get down there. Would you happen to know where we could purchase a car?"

"There is a gas station just around the corner," he said. "He may be able to help you. Come to think of it, Durant, the town I just came through, had a used car lot just off the highway. I'm sure you could buy a car there."

"Sure but how can we get there?" asked Mike.

"Buy me dinner, and I'll take you there. It's only about 25 miles. It should only take about twenty minutes."

"That's a deal," said Mike. "My name is Mike. Do you want to eat first?"

"My name is Sam." He looked at his watch. "It's almost six. I think we should go there first. I don't know how late he will be open, or if in fact he is open. There isn't that much traffic, as you can imagine."

Mike turned to Sarah. "Sarah, honey, do you want to come?"

"Why don't you go, honey?" said Sarah, kidding Mike about his honey thing. She knew that Mike was telling Sam to forget it. He could see how Sam was looking at Sarah. "I'll see if I can find some food and water for the horses."

"Are you sure?" asked Mike.

"Yes, I'm sure, go, and I'll meet you inside. I'll take care of the horses while you are gone."

Mike and Sam walked across the street and got into the truck. Soon, they were on their way to Durant.

"How did you get trapped into the job of going along the border informing people?" asked Sam. "That's a big job."

"I know it is, but we are really needed up north to help defeat the western invading army," said Mike. "This is only a job on the way."

"How are you two going to help fight the army?"

"Sarah is a weapons expert, and I have been drafted to join the US Army."

"Wait," said Sam getting excited. "You aren't Colonel Mills, the Desert Fox, are you? Is Sarah, Doctor Sarah Anders or something like that?"

"You have heard of us?" asked Mike caught completely by surprise.

"Yes, the radio said that a Colonel Mills, the Desert Fox, and a Doctor Sarah Anders were coming to help fight the western army. They said that you were going to command the US Army, and that the doctor was a nuclear expert. It asked that we help you in any way we can."

"I can't believe that information got out," said Mike. "If you heard it, so has the invading army. What else have you heard over the radio?" "Well, they said that an army made up of Texas and Arizona State troopers, were to hold them back until the enemy disengaged and slowly headed north." Sam hesitated, thinking if there was anything else he had left out. "Oh yes, there was one more thing. They asked all able men to go to Spokane and join the US Army that is preparing to engage the enemy."

"We will have to be on our toes from here on in," said Mike almost to himself.

"Why are you worried?" asked Sam not understanding Mike's concerns.

"Well if the enemy knows about us, then they are going to try to stop us."

"The radio also asked that we all were to help you get to your destination," added Sam.

They were soon on the outskirts of the city. Sam got off the highway and turned down a small street to a used car lot. The sign read "Quality Auto." Mike got out and started to look over the autos on display. He spotted a cream colored car that had just been washed.

"We just got it in," said a voice behind Mike. "We will make you a very good deal on this car. It is only six years old and has a little over thirty thousand miles on it.

"How much?" asked Mike.

"Twelve thousand," said the salesman. "I'll give you eight thousand," he said.

"You drive a hard bargain. Let's split the difference. Give me ten thousand and you have a deal." asked Walter.

"You have a deal," said Mike as he wrote out a check. "Can you get me a license?"

"By the way, my name is Walter. Wait here a minute. I'll get a form for a license application. You fill it out and sign it. I'll go to a tag agency, tomorrow and get a plate." When he got the form, Mike filled it out and gave it to Walter, with cash for the plates.

"I'll see you in the morning," said Mike. Getting in the car, Mike followed Sam back to Atoka.

Sarah was waiting in front of the restaurant. She had both backpacks by her feet.

"Sarah, what is going on?" asked Mike after he and Sam found parking spots and walked to where Sarah was standing. "What have you been up to all this time and where are the horses?"

"One question at a time please," she said with a smile. "I fed the horses from a field not too far from here. Then, I took them to the gas station just around the corner and got water for them. The nice fellow at the station offered to keep them in the station overnight. I gathered all of our belongings and packed our backpacks, so if you would just put them in the trunk of the car, we can go inside and have dinner."

"Why do I even bother to ask?" asked Mike. "I should know by now that you will take care of all that has to be done. Let's go eat. Come along Sam. We will buy you that dinner we promised."

"Right behind you," said Sam.

Inside they were quickly seated and the waiter gave them a menu. "My name is Fred, and I'll be your waiter this evening. I'm sorry, however, that we only have the chicken dinners and Atlantic salmon dishes available. The chicken dinners available are these two up here," he said pointing to the top of the menu.

"I'll have the Chicken Milanese dinner," said Sarah. "They are always good. I'll also have Italian on my salad and coffee."

"That sounds good," said Mike. "I'll have the same, except decaf coffee."

"I'll have the salmon with ranch dressing on my salad and regular coffee," said Sam.

While they were eating their meal, Mike and Sam brought Sarah up to date on all that Sam had heard on the radio and what he had heard about what people had told him they saw on TV about Mike and Sarah and about the fact that the war was over in the East. Then they sat and discussed the ramifications of that information being out where the invaders could have it available to them.

"I don't understand how the information got out," said Sarah. "I'm sure that General McGard would never let that information out. I'll have to call him and see if he has any ideas on where and how that leak got out. I tried to call him earlier, but no one answered. I'll call him later.

"Well, it is important that we find that out of course," said Mike. "But more important is that we have to be very careful from here on out, because I'm sure that the enemy will want to stop us. I think they know what Sam has told us because, as Sam said, they have disengaged with the Texas and Arizona troops and are moving north. That means also that we have to hurry, or we will be late for the battle."

"What are your plans, Sam?" asked Sarah.

"First, I'm going home to make sure my parents are all right. I was on a trip to El Paso Texas, when I heard of the invasion of the eastern US. A friend called me and told me what was happening. I called my parents and told them to hide in the bomb shelter that my great-grandfather built around the World War 2 era. It is hidden behind the shed. You have to know where it is to find it. I'm only worried that they didn't listen to me. Anyway, after I see that they are okay, and that they can take care of themselves, I'm going to Spokane and join the army there."

"It's getting late," said Mike. "We have to find a place to stay tonight and get up early tomorrow."

"There is a very nice motel just down 4th street just past the gas station," said Sam. "That's where I'm going to stay tonight."

"Sounds great," said Mike. "We will follow you there."

"Thanks for the dinner," said Sam. "It was very nice to have your company too."

"You have got to be kidding," said Mike. "I feel like I still owe you. It was so nice of you to drive me to get a car."

"No problem," said Sam. "Glad I could help." Having said that, Sam left.

At the motel, Sam found a parking place in front and went in first. Mike was surprised at the number of cars in the parking lot. He wondered if some of those cars were abandoned. Apparently, he found out once inside, they belonged to people staying in the motel. It wasn't very big to start with.

"There must be a lot of people that heard the radio news and are heading home," said Sarah. Inside, Sam had already registered and had gone to his room.

"We would like two rooms with showers," said Mike.

"All our rooms have showers," said the clerk showing his irritation at the request. "I only have one room left, and it's on the upper floor." "You only have one room?" said Mike thinking that he must have misunderstood him.

"Yes," said the clerk. "It does have twin beds if that helps."

"We will take it," said Sarah saving Mike the effort of asking her. They paid in advance and went to their room. They were fast asleep as soon as they hit the beds. It had been a long day.

The next morning, Mike woke to the sound of the shower. He took what he needed from his backpack and waited for Sarah to finish. After Mike had showered, he started to dress when Sarah stopped him. He was still in his underwear

"I think that it's time to remove the cast from your arm," she said. "I think it has healed enough by now."

She took the tools out of her backpack and started to remove the cast.

"Do you always carry tools to remove casts?" he said in jest.

"You'd be surprised as to how many tasks these tools will do. This saw blade could come in handy some day."

Mike tried to flex his arm now that the cast was removed.

"My arm seems to have grown stiff. I find it hard to move," he complained to Sarah.

"Don't worry, it will be as good as new in a few hours."

After Mike finished dressing they packed their backpacks and went to the restaurant for breakfast. Sam had apparently already eaten and left for his home.

After breakfast they placed their backpacks in the car and left for Durant. They arrived in Durant at about nine thirty. Walter was waiting for them.

"This is Sarah," said Mike introducing his companion. "Do you have my plates ready?"

"Yes I do," responded Walter. "I'll put them on in just a minute. I also checked your bank. They are three hours ahead of us, you know, and were open when I called this morning. They verified that your check is good."

Walter took off his dealer plates and put on Mike's. They shook hands and left.

They followed Route 75 into Texas and continued for about twenty miles to the city of Denison, then they stopped at a gas station to get directions. They were told that the only way south was by taking Route 69. They said that all the roads into Dallas end at the big hole that used to be Dallas.

They followed 69 for the next two hours. All the towns were partially deserted. Only a few stores and gas stations were opened.

They were soon headed south on Route 69. It was twelve thirty.

"I think I'd better look at the map," suggested Sarah. "I don't think we want to end up in a big hole that used to be a large city."

"That's a good idea," said Mike. "Do you want me to pull over?"

"No, I can check it while we are moving. I don't want to waste any time. We have to get to Spokane as soon as we alert the folks at the border. I've tried to call the general several times, but no one answered. I guess he is on a mission. With the invaders moving north,

I wonder if he still wants us to go to the border. Not only that, but I want to know how the news of our situation got out."

"I know. That has been on my mind also. I am starting to formulate a plan, and I need to talk to him," said Mike

"We are almost to the town of Jacksonville," said Sarah. "We have to take Route 79 from there on. It looks like it misses most of the large cities in Texas."

"I'm glad you told me," said Mike. "The sign we just passed says that Jacksonville is just ahead. We can just take the exit to 79 south. Good work."

They followed 79 past all the large cities. At Rockdale, they switched to route 77. They noticed that there weren't many cars on the road. The few they saw were all going north. No one was going south. Also, they noticed that after entering Texas, they didn't see many damaged cars on the road, and the amount of city property damage declined the farther they got south.

They arrived at Robstown around six thirty. Robstown was just about ten miles from Corpus Christi.

They didn't feel like tackling a large town. They were both tired of driving and very hungry. They had to try several restaurants before they could find one that was serving anyone. After a satisfying dinner, they searched around for a motel that was open for business. All they could find was an old hotel that had rooms available.

"We could drive a little way out of town to see if we could find a nice motel," said Mike.

"I'm too tired," said Sarah "I'm too tired to go any further. Let's stay here. We have had worse accommodations and probably will have worse yet."

"Whatever you say," responded Mike. "I'm pretty tired too."

"I bet you are," said Sarah. "You have done all the driving." They got rooms and immediately went to sleep.

It was 9:00 a.m. when they left Robstown the next morning. Traffic heading north became heavier as they traveled south, but traffic going south was still very scarce. The towns they traveled through were still mostly deserted until they got to Raymondville.

From there south to Brownsville the roads and cities were very congested. They found a place to eat lunch in Brownsville and then started west along Highway 83 which ran along the border. It was about three 3 in the afternoon when they got to within five miles of McAllen.

The road from Brownsville was very close to the border; they began seeing cars parked along the road and tents on both sides of the road. There were many trucks and vans trying to sell anything from food to tents; they congested the highway so that it was difficult to travel. Mike and Sarah made several stops along the road to inform people that the eastern invaders had been driven back to the Atlantic. As they stopped on the side of the road, Sarah would contact the people on the north side of the road, and Mike would inform the people on the south side of the road. The people, upon hearing the news, started to pack to go home.

It worked pretty well until they got to the point where the highway turned north toward McAllen. The road went north about five miles and away from the border. Because of the stops and the traffic, it took them three hours to get to McAllen. They decided to find a place to stop for the night and continue traveling the next day. They were both very tired. They found a fast food diner and a motel about five miles west of McAllen. It was full, so they had to rent a storage area where the owner had put in two roller beds for them. They finally turned in for the night.

The next morning, they left early and started west on 83. It wasn't as easy as the day before. The highway varied from two to five miles from the border.

"This is not acceptable," said Mike. "At this rate, we will never get to Spokane."

"What are you suggesting?" asked Sarah.

"I don't have an answer yet," he responded. "I just know that we can't get to all the people when we have to walk two or more miles to contact many of them."

Not having any alternatives, they continued until they got to Laredo. They did the best they could. It took over eight hours to go about one hundred and fifty miles to Laredo. It was after six when they got there.

"Now we have to get an alternative," said Sarah looking at the map.

"What's the problem now?" asked Mike.

"Well the problem is that route 83 heads north, and there isn't a road that goes along the border. The highway gets about thirty to fifty miles from the border. I suspect that there are farms in between. We could be shot trespassing on a farmer's land."

"You are right," said Mike. "I'm too tired to worry about it now though. Let's find a place to eat and spend the night."

They found a motel and then walked down the street to a small restaurant. It was while they were walking to the restaurant for breakfast the next morning that Mike got an idea of what to do. It came to him when he saw an off-road vehicle across the street from the restaurant.

"That's what we need," he said. "With a machine like that, we could go anywhere." Mike walked across the street to get a closer look at it. It was a two-seater with a removal top. As he was looking at it, a young man walked up to him.

"Do you like my four wheel dirt bike?" he asked.

"Yes, I do," answered Mike. "Would you like to sell it?"

"Not on your life," he answered. "This is my right arm. It has seen more beaches than a lifeguard. Why would you want one anyway? You don't look like a beach type."

"I have to go along the border and tell the people that ran there to escape the invaders, that the war is over and the enemy has been pushed back into the Atlantic."

"Wait a minute," said the young man. "You aren't Colonel Mills, are you?" He looked across the street and saw Sarah. "I know you. You were on TV yesterday. That's why I am going home. I'm making sure my parents get home safely, and then I'm going to Spokane and join the army there. My name is Jimmy Holten."

"Well, Jimmy, you can help right here if you really want to help your country," said Mike.

"What can I do to help?" he asked.

"Would you consider following the border up to California and informing people that the war is over, that the enemy has been defeated? Ask them all to go home and start reconstruction, then come back and take your parents home."

"My parents have their own car, I just want to follow them home and make sure everything is all right. Besides, that is a long way, and I don't have any money for gas. I could sleep in my car, but it needs fuel."

"What do you think you will need?" asked Mike. "Perhaps I could help."

"First, let's figure how far I really have to go," said Jimmy. "I come from a trip to El Paso. Most of the people for about a hundred miles on this side of El Paso come from the California-Arizona area. Some of them headed back when they heard that the invading army had pulled back to California and was headed north toward Spokane. I suppose they heard the news also."

"That's why we have to get this job done and head north," said Mike.

Jimmy started to calculate what it would take to cover the area Mike had described. He figured that the complete trip would be about six hundred miles and that it would take about ten days. At fifty dollars per day that it would cost Mike five hundred dollars.

"How far is it from here to your home?" asked Mike.

"I live just south of Savanna, Georgia," said Jimmy. "It's over a thousand miles from here, but my parents will feed me if they are willing to wait for me. Let me call them, and then we will talk."

He walked away from Mike and rang a number on his cell phone. A few minutes later he returned to Mike who had been joined by Sarah.

"My parents said that they will wait for me," said Jimmy. "So, I'm ready to do my part. How can you help me economically?"

"Well," said Mike, "you said it would take you about ten days to do what I asked and about two days to get home. At fifty dollars a day, you'd get five hundred for the job. How does six hundred sound to you? That way, it will help you get home."

"That's more than fair," said Jimmy. "You have a deal."

Mike headed west on Route 83. They were surprised to see a few cars and tents that were parked along both sides of the road all the way to Eagle Pass.

At Carrizo Springs, they changed to Route 277 that led them to Eagle Pass. They arrived at Eagle Pass at a little past noon. They ate lunch and headed up 277 to Route 90 at Del Rio. The highway came pretty close to the border for about sixty miles. They didn't see Jimmy at all during the leg of the trip that took them close to the border. They took 90 to Route 10 and into El Paso. It took a day and a half to get there. They arrived about noon. Jimmy was right about the people from about one hundred miles east of Laredo coming from the West and not from the East. El Paso was the worst they had seen on the complete trip up to now. It was so crowded from people that came from the West that you couldn't get into any restaurant.

"I've never seen it this bad," said Sarah. "Even Brownsville wasn't this bad."

"I don't think we have time to wait to get fed here. Let's head north and see if we can stop along the way. I don't think it will be this crowded much farther north."

"I sure hope not," responded Sarah. "I'm not really that hungry anyway. I agree, let's move on."

It took a little while to get out of the city. Soon, they were traveling at highway speeds up Route 85 into New Mexico to Las Cruces. They stopped at a fast food restaurant, had a short lunch, and were soon back on the road. It was duck soup from here, they thought. There was no traffic and the towns they passed were partly deserted. Either they were working their land, or they were south running from the invaders.

The roads were clear. In two days they would be in Spokane. Little did they know what was ahead for them.

CHAPTER EIGHT

Road of Terror

MIKE AND SARAH FOLLOWED ROUTE 85 to about fifty miles south of Albuquerque where they were stopped by a roadblock and a sign that said that the road was closed. An arrow pointed to the exit from Route 85 to Route 60. The sign indicated that the exit led to 60 east.

"I guess that Albuquerque no longer exists," commented Sarah.

"I think you are right. I think they targeted all of the large cities," said Mike. "What I hope now is that 60 will take us back north at some point.

"It almost has to," said Sarah. "This looks like a country road. That means it will be slow going. Perhaps I should try to contact the general again," said Sarah. "I've been trying to call every chance I could get, but there is never anyone to answer."

"I think it is a good idea," said Mike. "I think I'll pull over and rest anyway. We've been driving for over four hours." Mike pulled to the side of the road, and they got out to stretch their feet. Sarah dialed the general.

"Hello, General," said Sarah surprised that anyone answered. "I've been trying to contact you for several days. I know…you have missions to go on. Here, please talk to Colonel Mills. He needs to talk with you."

Sarah handed the phone to Mike. "Good day, General, how are you?"

"I'm, fine," answered the general. "Where are you guys? We need you up here yesterday."

"We are presently traveling north. Barring any problems, we should be there in about two or three days. General, are you aware that the news has been announcing our existence and plans not only on the radio, but they have our pictures on TV? I thought that our phones were encrypted."

"Yes, I'm very much aware of the situation," said the general. "We have investigated the source of the leak. Our phones are safe; the problem is that our army phones are not. It was an oversight on my part. I've communicated with First Lieutenant Furgason. I told him of your coming and that he was to report to you. I told him that you would be accompanied by Doctor Anders. He informed his second lieutenants of your coming. One of the second lieutenants is from Texas, and he made contact with one of his friends in Major Brandon Rangers. The information got picked up by an alert newsman and was reported. Apparently, the newsman did his homework to know so much of your and Doctor Anders's histories. Sorry about that. You will have to keep your eyes open at all times. I'm sure the enemy has picked up the phone call as well and probably the news casts."

"General, does First Lieutenant Furgason have a safe phone?" "Yes, he does, and I have sent a safe phone to Major Brandon by

air drop. He should have it by now. I'm going to give you the phone number of each. I'm sure you will want to contact them. I suspect you have a plan already worked out in your mind."

"Yes, I do, sir. I need to get them in line with my plan." Mike pulled out a small pad he had and wrote down the numbers he was given by the general. "I'll call them right away."

"Good," said the general. "I'll let you go, then. Good Luck." Mike hung up and turned to Sarah.

"What should we do next?" he asked. "It is getting late, it's after five. I would like to call the two armies."

"I think that you should," said Sarah. "I think that is much more important than where we eat or sleep at this time."

"Glad to hear you say that," responded Mike as he started to dial the number the general had given him for the Spokane divisions.

"Lieutenant Selontti here, what can I do for you?"

"I'd like to talk to Lieutenant Furgason," said Mike. "Lieutenant Furgason is in a meeting," he responded. "Well, get him out!" yelled Mike. "This is Colonel Mills." "Yes, sir. Right away, sir."

A few minutes later, Lieutenant Furgason answered the phone.

"Yes sir, this is Lieutenant Furgason," he responded. "How are you sir?"

"I'm fine," said Mike. "Lieutenant, I have a plan to trap the invading army and I need you to prepare for it."

"Yes sir," said the lieutenant. "I will do whatever you need." "Here is what I need you to do—got a pencil and pad?" "Yes sir, I'm ready."

"First, I want you to look at the map of California and find a place where there is a valley with two rather steep mountains on both sides. I want you to divide your people in four groups. I want the northern group to be divided into a heavy, fixed group to protect the northern part of the valley. Then, I want a fast moving, hard hitting group that can hit and run to draw the enemy into the valley. I then want two groups of about a thousand men each to be planted on top of each mountain. I would like them to be able to fire down at the enemy in the valley with mortars and light missiles. I want them to be able to move very quickly when ordered. I would also like you to see what you can find that can drill holes in the side of the mountain. Whatever you find, make sure that you find people to man them. Do you get the picture?"

"Yes sir," he answered. "I get the picture perfectly clear."

Mike then explained in detail what he needed the drilling equipment for and how it was to be used. He also described the complete plan and other preparations that he wanted him to do. He also explained that he was going to contact the Texas Rangers and set them up to protect the southern end of the valley once it is selected.

"Oh, before I forget," added Mike. "I want each of the teams to have regular cell phones that I can give instructions through for the enemy to pick up. I will code the instructions over those phones so that you will do other than what the instruction asks. Do you understand what I want?"

"Yes, sir. I understand perfectly. I will start on it immediately."

"We can go over it when I get there," said Mike. "I should be there in a few days. Colonel Mills out."

They hung up, and Mike immediately called Major Brandon.

"Major Brandon here," said the voice over the phone. "How can I help you?"

"This is colonel Mills," said Mike. "What is your position, and what are your current plans?"

"We are about even with the north moving enemy and are endeavoring to meet with the forces at Spokane."

"Negative, Major. I want you to reverse your direction and head south so that at a point I want you to move west and come up behind the enemy." Mike then explained his plan and how they were to help. "I also would like you to divide your forces into two groups like the northern army is doing. I want the stronger, slower moving force to stay well behind the enemy. I would like a fast moving group to hit the enemy from behind and run only enough to slow them down but not enough to entice them to chase you. I don't want you to fight them by yourself."

He explained the cell phone plan and emphasized that they should not discuss any of their plans on standard cell phones. "We will contact each other by the safe phone. Is the plan clear to you? Do you have any questions?"

"No sir, I know exactly what I have to do. It's a great plan. I'm glad that I will play a part in it. I will keep you up to date. Major Brandon out."

"Well Sarah, the plan is in action," said Mike. "They seem like pretty intelligent men. I think we are in good shape. Now all that is left is for us is to get there."

"Right now, I would like to get to the next town and find something to eat and a place to sleep," said Sarah.

They got back on the road and arrived at the junction of Route 60 and Route 285 at Encino at a little after six. They left Encino at seven-thirty the next morning anxious to get to Spokane. They followed Route 285 into Colorado where they switched to Route

160. They headed west on 160 that took them to Durango, where they stopped to find food.

Mike had not let the warning that the general had given him sink into his heart. If he had, he would have noticed the little black foreign car that had been following them since they turned onto Route 160. Mike spotted a grocery store and turned into the parking lot across the street from the store and parked the car.

"Take your backpack and let's go shopping," said Mike. "The backpack is too important to leave behind."

Mike put his backpack on, but Sarah decided to carry hers in her hand. She didn't feel at home with a backpack on as Mike did. The side road was much wider than the Ohio roads they were used to. As they walked across the street, Sarah's backpack strap hung down and dragged across the ground. On the other side of the road was a sewer at the street curb that made the curb higher than normal. As Sarah was about to step up on the curb she accidently stepped on the backpack strap causing her to stumble and trip on the curb. She fell flat on her face. Mike, already at the store doorway, rushed to help her. Just as he had gotten to her, the store blew up. Mike fell on top of Sarah trying to protect her. Good thing Mike had his backpack on. It protected him from flying glass and other debris. As Mike looked up, he saw a man with a rocket launcher, probably a bazooka, on the opposite side of the street. He had apparently launched a rocket into the store trying to assassinate Mike and Sarah. Mike quickly grabbed Sarah and, forcing her in front of him, threw her behind the brick wall that had held the store window.

Bullets were whistling past them as they ran for cover. When they fell to the ground, Sarah noticed that Mike's arm was bleeding.

"Mike, you have been shot," she said painfully.

"Don't worry," he said. "It's only a flesh wound. Keep your head down. We have to worry if that fellow launches another rocket at us. Too bad we left the rifle in the car. Do you still have the zoo stun gun?"

"Yes," she said as she searched through her backpack. "Quickly, let me have it."

She handed him the pistol.

"Dear Lord," he said out loud, "please let my aim be precise."

He lifted up his head only to duck it down quickly. Bullets rang out from all around him. He had looked long enough to see that there were three men. The one with the bazooka was slowly approaching them, one was behind a car in the parking lot, and the third man was on the side of a little building past the parking lot. Mike chanced another look and a storm of bullets rang past him. One bullet just missed his ear. He had seen what he had hoped he wouldn't see: he saw the man with the bazooka place another rocket into the launcher.

"It's now or never," he said as he moved from the position he had to the end of the wall next to the door. He aimed the pistol and shot twice to make sure that one hit the man with the rocket. His aim was good. The man stopped and slowly fell on his face. All was quiet for what seemed hours. Then the man behind the car stepped out cautiously.

"He didn't hear a gunshot so he apparently thinks we don't have a weapon," whispered Mike to Sarah. "Keep your head down and keep as still as you can."

The man walked slowly toward his friend. His rifle was up and ready to fire at a blink of an eye. When he got to his friend, he lowered his rifle and turned his friend over to see if he was hit. Seeing no bullet holes, he raised his head in wonderment. That was his mistake. Mike was quick and accurate. He never knew what hit him.

The third man suddenly lowered his rifle, jumped in his car, and was soon out of sight. Mike wondered if it was because of fear, or because he heard the siren of a police car. Mike ran out onto the street and retrieved both the rocket launcher and the only rocket the man had. He searched the men and found some cash.

"We can use this," he said almost to himself. Before he could put the rocket and the launcher into their car, the police car came to a screeching stop.

An officer jumped out and yelled, "Put your hands on you heads, and don't make a move." Mike and Sarah complied. As the officer approached them he recognized Sarah. "Are you Doctor Anders?"

"Yes I am," said Sarah. "How do you know me?"

"Your picture and Colonel Mills's picture are plastered all over the TV," said the officer as he put his gun away. "What is happening here?"

"These men tried to ambush us," said Mike. "I believe they are part of the terrorist group that nuked our big cities and our military bases. There were three of them. One got away in a small, foreign, black car."

"I suppose they are after you after hearing about you on the TV. That makes sense. One of the benefits of the free press," said the officer. "I'm Sergeant Posts. How can I help you?"

"First of all, you can take these men into custody. We only shot them with a stun gun. They will be awake in about two hours. We were able to shot them because they were sure we had no weapons. Speaking of weapons, I would like to keep what we find on them. I don't think our problems are over. There must be hundreds of them." The officer walked up to the men who were lying on their backs in the street. He suddenly pulled out his gun and shot them both in the heart.

"Oh, they were trying to escape," said the officer.

"I can't believe you did that," said Sarah in amazement. "Why did you do that?"

"I don't trust our liberal judges. A good lawyer will have them free as prisoners of war. They apparently killed thousands of Americans. They are not American citizens and do not deserve protection under our constitution. They have been executed as spies."

"Is it all right for me to take the weapons?" asked Mike.

"Sure, take them," said the officer. "They won't need them anymore."

"Before you do anything, I have to take care of your wound," said Sarah. "Sit here on the curb."

She took out her medical kit from her backpack and unbuttoned Mike's shirt. She pulled the shirt from his left arm.

"It's not too bad," she said looking the wound over. "It's a clean cut all the way across the arm." She applied a disinfecting ointment and soon had it dressed. Then she slipped the shirt back over his arm. "You are going to need to wash this shirt at our next stop," she said.

Mike picked up the rocket and launcher and threw them and his backpack in the back seat. Sarah put away her medical kit, grabbed the rifles, and put them in the car's trunk, out of sight. She then put her backpack in the back seat.

"Listen," said the officer. "I'll follow you down the road a ways just to make sure no one is following you. I can't go too far. I have to get back before my shift is over, or the lieutenant will have my head."

"That would be great," said Mike. "It would be greatly appreciated. Thank you very much."

"I will turn on my flashers and pull over to the side of the road when I am about to turn around. That will be my good-bye signal. Good luck to you both."

Mike and Sarah got into the car and proceeded north on Route 550. Sarah had determined from the map they had that Route 550 would lead them to Route 50. Route 50 would eventually lead them to Route 91 north. Mike kept his eyes on his rear view mirror to make sure that the officer was still bringing up the rear. The road was winding and traveling was very slow.

It was about an hour later that Mike noticed the police car pull over to the side of the road and turn on its flashers. Mike also noticed a sign ahead that read, "Leaving Ouray County." Just below that was a sign that pointed the way to Route 50. Mike turned his turn signal from left to right, signaling good-bye. Mike watched the police car turn around and it soon disappeared from view.

"I hear a helicopter," he said to Sarah about ten minutes later. "Do you think the general has sent a copter to meet us?" She never got a chance to answer. Mike, upon hearing the familiar sound of a machine gun, swerved to the side of the road. He slammed on the brakes and opened his door as the helicopter flew over them.

"Grab your backpack and head for the field on your side," Mike said.

Sarah complied and was soon deep into the high growth in the field. Mike got out of the car and, taking good aim from a kneeling position, fired a shot from the pistol that he had obtained from the terrorist in Durango. He hit the windshield, which made the pilot take evasive action. This gave Mike a chance to grab the rocket launcher with the only rocket available and joined Sarah in the field. When he was well into the field, he turned to see where the helicopter had gone. He saw that the helicopter had landed across the street, and two men with rifles had gotten out and were running toward them. The helicopter took off and acted like a look out for the men on the ground. Mike knew that they didn't have a chance with the helicopter as a look out. He was sure the pilot was in constant communication with the men on the ground.

Mike sat down on the ground with the rocket launcher on his shoulder ready to fire as soon as the helicopter came into view. This was his last chance. If he missed, it was all over. The other problem he worried about was would the men get to him before the helicopter came into view. Suddenly, he saw the helicopter come low over the street toward his location. Apparently, the pilot had seen Sarah but had missed Mike who was hidden by high grass. Mike took carful aim. He fired just as the pilot turned his craft back toward the street. He had seen Mike with the launcher and was trying to escape. He was too late. The rocket hit him midship. The helicopter blew up, and part of the tail fell on Mike's side of the road. The main part fell on the other side of the road. The two men chasing them were surprised by the explosion of their craft. One ran across the street to check on his companion. This gave Mike the chance to catch up to Sarah.

"Head for the house," he ordered her. "When you get to the other side, continue running through the field. I think it is a cornfield. Whatever it is, make a lot of action so they think that we are continuing running to the other side. Stop when you hear my pistol go off and quickly come back to me."

"Got you," she said as she sped up to get well ahead of him.

Mike then hid behind the rear of the house. As soon as the first man got across from him, Mike shot him. He was dead before he hit the ground. Sarah quickly ran back to Mike keeping the house between her and the other man.

"I think he is trying to outsmart us by coming around from the front of the house," said Mike. "Well, we will fool him."

As soon as he turned to run in front of the house, Mike grabbed Sarah's hand and slowly pulled her so that the house stayed between them and the pursuer. When they were away from the house, on the way back to the street, Mike yelled to Sarah, "Run as fast as you can toward our car!" As they were running Mike handed Sarah the keys to the car. "Get into the car and start down the street."

"Where are you going?" she asked.

"I'm going to hide behind the burning tail of the copter. We want him to think that we are getting away."

Sarah did as Mike asked. As soon as she got to the street she ran to the car, got into the front seat, started the car, and sped down the street. The pursuer ran into the street watching the car start to pull away. As lifted his rifle to take aim at Sarah, Mike ran out into the street behind him.

"Are you looking for me?" asked Mike with his pistol aimed at the man's back. The man was well trained. At the first word out of Mike's mouth, he quickly spun around with his rifle up and ready to fire. Mike, although surprised by his quickness, got off his shot. The man had already pulled the trigger. The bullet tore through Mike's shirt but missed his flesh. The man fell. His body twisted a little and then was still. Sarah, having seen everything from the rear view mirror, backed up the car and met Mike who had picked up the other man's rifle and was running toward Sarah. Mike jumped in the passenger seat and closed the door.

"Do you want to drive?" asked Sarah.

"No, I think from here on out you'd better drive. I'll get my binoculars and watch the road. I don't think they are finished with us. It is imperative to them that we don't get to our destination. I think the worst is yet to come."

"Please don't say that," said Sarah softly, showing how tired she was. Mike took off his backpack and helped Sarah remove hers. He then reached into his backpack and removed the big binoculars.

"I think that from now on, I will wear this around my neck," said Mike as he put the binocular strap around his neck. "I'm going to carry the pistol in my pocket too. We should also get the rifles out of the trunk and put them in the back seat where we can reach them quickly."

"Do you really think they are going to make a last-ditch effort to kill us?" asked Sarah, hoping for a negative answer.

"I have no doubt of it," said Mike. "I surely would if I were in their place. Can't you see? Their success or failure depends on us getting to our destination. Unfortunately, thanks to our freedom of the press, they have more information on us than I would like."

"What are we going to do?" asked Sarah, now frightfully worried.

"First, we have to contact the general," said Mike. "I'm sure he knows how important it is for us to get to Spokane."

Sarah tried to reach the general as they spoke.

"There is no answer," she informed Mike. "I'll keep trying as often as I can."

"Do you think that the mountains between us and the secret base could create a problem in communication?" asked Mike.

"I don't think so," she answered. "Remember that my communication is through a satellite. A bad storm or heavy clouds could have an effect, but I don't think so."

They were about five miles from Montrose when they had been attacked by the helicopter. It was three-thirty when they started back on the road. The helicopter incident took less than a half hour, though it felt like a half day. They went through Montrose and arrived at Delta at about four.

They drove through Grand Junction, continued on, and arrived at the Utah border at about five-thirty. They decided to keep driving. It was six when they arrived at the little town of Cisco. They stopped, got something to eat, and found a place to sleep.

They left at seven-ten the next morning. They arrived at Provo at ten twenty-five. There, they picked up Route 91 only to be side tracked about two miles north of Provo. There, a detour sign led them around Salt Lake City. They took Route 189 to Route 80 and back to Route 91. They reached Ogden at 11:18. They stopped for lunch there at a fast food restaurant. They crossed the border into Idaho at about one pm. The road north from there was full of beautiful scenery. The road took them over many rivers and through many mountain passes. The area, however, was covered with forests. Sarah, for some reason, was uneasy about the forests.

"Let's get through this part of the country," she said. "I find the forest very scary."

"Why?" asked Mike, "I find it very beautiful."

"It's too dark and wild with bears and the like," answered Sarah. "I never felt safe in a wooded area. I was always scared of the woods even when we were kids and my parents took us on a picnic in the forests of Ohio. I always checked for snakes and wild animals."

"There aren't any poisonous snakes in Ohio," said Mike with a smile on his face.

"I don't care," she said with a finality that ended the discussion. "Well, you're driving," Mike said. "I'll go where ever you take me." They had to detour around Pocatello and Idaho Falls. They were soon back on Route 91. It was about four forty-five when they crossed into Montana.

"It's about one hundred miles to Butte," said Sarah. "At the rate we are going we should get there about seven-thirty. I don't want to stop anywhere before we get there. I suggest that we keep going until we get there. We pick up Route 10 there. Route 10 takes us right into Spokane. I would like to stop at Butte, have something to eat, and stay there tonight. We can get an early start in the morning and be in Spokane before noon. That is if Butte looks safe. If it doesn't look good we can continue and get to Spokane before midnight. In fact, the more I think of it, the more I like it. "

"That's fine with me," said Mike. "Like I said, you're driving. I'll just keep watch for enemy attackers. This area would be a terrible place to be caught. There isn't much around, not even traffic."

"I wish you wouldn't talk like that," said Sarah. "I don't want to be anywhere around this lonely place." As she said that, she sped up to seventy miles an hour. "Try calling the general. As close as we are now, perhaps he could escort us in or pick us up."

"There isn't much room around here for a helicopter to land except on the road," said Mike. "I'll be darned," he said out loud. "They have an answering machine. It's about time." Without any other comment, he left a message. "General McGard, this is Colonel Mills. We are on Route 91. We just crossed the border into Montana. We need your help. We have been attacked twice by terrorist groups. The first time was in Durango, Colorado. The second time was about five miles south of Montrose. We are sure they haven't given up. Colonel Mills out." Mike hung up the phone and smiled at Sarah. "They finally got an answering machine," he repeated.

"Well, I hope they get the message soon," said Sarah. "I have this very uneasy feeling."

"Come on now," said Mike. "Where is that brave woman that was willing to give up her life back awhile ago?"

"She disappears when it comes to forests," she answered. "That is my hang up."

Driving north into Montana, they realized that they were in the foothills of the Rockies. The terrain became very mountainous, and the road very hilly and winding. On both sides of the highway there was nothing but wilderness. A few open spaces with high grass were seen occasionally, but they were rare. Thick forests and mountain peaks were the more prevalent scenery.

"Wow," said Sarah. "Look at how dark it is up ahead. There is a fierce storm in the mountains. There is nothing but mountains ahead."

"I'm sure there is a pass that this road goes through," said Mike. "There is," said Sarah. "It showed it on the map. I think it is called

Pipestone pass. I would check it, but it's getting to dark. It's only six thirty."

"Yes, but look up at the mountains ahead," said Mike. "There is a lot of lightning, and it's coming our way, or we are going into it, and look at the trees. It must be getting very windy," "It's getting very windy down here too," added Sarah. "I can feel it in the steering wheel. I need to compensate for the wind pushing the car off the road."

It suddenly started to rain. Sarah turned on the windshield wipers. "It looks like the last leg of our trip is going to be miserable." Sarah had no idea of what was to come. The road started a downhill trend until they reached a bridge. They crossed the bridge, and the road started an uphill climb. The rain was coming down heavily. Lightning was flashing every few seconds. Loud thunder followed so closely that it shook the car. They were just coming over the crest of the hill when Mike, who had been looking ahead with his powerful binoculars, suddenly grabbed the wheel and pulled the car off the road. He grabbed Sarah by the arm and pulled her down in the seat just as bullets shattered the windshield barely missing Sarah's head. The car went off the road, down into a field, and landed at a forty-five degree angle. As Mike opened the door on his side, they both started to slide out of the front seat. Mike grabbed the backpacks as he fell out of the car.

"There are four cars blocking the road and coming right at us," said Mike. "Put on your backpack and run toward the woods. The backpack can protect you from a stray bullet. It will absorb some of the impact."

"What's happening?" she asked as she put on her backpack almost crawling on all fours to keep hidden in the tall grass.

"Keep low," he answered as he pushed her forward. "Run for your life."

Mike was running just behind her, pushing her to run faster. Bullets flew over their heads and around them. After a few minutes, as Sarah reached the woods, Mike stopped to look behind them to see what the attackers were doing.

"Dear Lord," he said out loud. "They have another vehicle. It is an all terrain vehicle."

"What did you say?" asked Sarah, as Mike caught up to her.

"They have an all-terrain vehicle," he repeated. "It looks like a dune buggy. It is coming after us and is trying to cut us off."

Sarah was now into the forest. The high growth was slowing her down. She got to a patch that had low limbs and some sort of brier that was grabbing and tearing at her blouse.

"Mike," she shouted. "Help me, Mike help me. Mike!" Mike was a few feet to her left. He had wandered left to see where the buggy was. In doing so, he accidentally ran across a narrow path. He ran to where Sarah was and, by stomping down on the overgrowth, made a path for her to him. He then pulled her onto the path.

"Run as fast as you can," he told Sarah. "That buggy can out run us on level ground, but here we have a chance because he has to get around the trees. Some areas of this path are too narrow for the buggy to get through."

"What are we going to do, Mike?" she asked, her voice filled with fear.

"We are going to run as fast as we can, and for the rest, we will trust God," said Mike.

"Where will this path take us?" she asked.

"I think this could be an old Indian path that is used as a game path in modern times."

Sarah was getting tired. They had been running for almost an hour. Mike could still hear the engine of the buggy following them. On top of that, the rain had begun to get heavier. It was now coming down in buckets. They were soaked to the skin. The backpacks were advertized as waterproof, but how much could they take? It became very dark. They could hardly see enough to follow the path. It also got very narrow, and the low-hanging branches were invisible until they whipped their faces. This was a constant danger. They still kept running, keeping their hands in front of their faces for protection. The ground became very soft and sticky wet from the heavy rain. Twice, Sarah tripped over a root or ground vine. She fell on her face and got mud on her hands and face. Every once in a while, the lightning would light up the area so they could see that they were running toward the mountains. The sound of the thunder was so close that it shook the ground. It seemed as if it was on top of them. The terror of it caused Sarah to panic and stop in her tracks.

Mike pushed her on. The thought of the attacker chasing them with the intention of killing them gave them strength to keep going on. Sarah was too tired to ask questions anymore. She did wonder what they would do when they got to the mountains, if they didn't get caught by the attackers or some fierce animal before they got there.

Their journey became even more difficult as they ran deep into the wilderness. The rain hammered down on them slowing them down. The forest was alive with noise from the rain and wind and the sound of a falling trees. Branches being struck by lightning and breaking or being snapped by the severity of the storm's wind added to the terror of the night. The rain was coming down so hard that it ran down their face and blurred their vision.

Mike listened for the sound of the buggy. The sound had faded. It was hard to hear with all the noise of the storm. He looked around and saw the headlights of the buggy in the distance. They were still chasing them. It was very dark among the trees and now Mike noticed that it had started to get foggy. They slowed down to rest a minute. The rain seemed to get stronger.

"Why don't the trees offer some protection from the rain? People generally duck under a tree to get out of the rain," said Sarah without thinking it out.

"First of all, these are mostly pine and fir trees. They don't have leaves to cover you, and secondly, the worst place to be in an electric storm is under a tree. If you are under a tree, the lightning always finds that human flesh is of less resistance to the ground then the wood of a tree."

"I wish you hadn't reminded me of that," said Sarah.

"Let's keep running," said Mike. "I looked back and saw the headlights of the buggy. We are gaining ground on them, but they are still following us."

Mike looked at his watch and waited for the lightning to light up the area so that he could see what time it was. It came sooner than he wanted. He was surprised that it was after ten. They had been running for almost four hours. It seemed that the land was sloping upwards. Mike wondered if it really was sloping upwards or if it was that he was so tired. They had no idea as to what direction they were going. The lightning showed them that they were going toward the mountains, deeper into the ghostly wilderness, but were they going north or west toward their attackers? They kept moving along the trail, but they soon noticed that they were running onto rocky ground. By the light of the lightning, they became aware of large rocks appearing. It also became cooler as they got closer to the mountains. Their clothes were so wet that they stuck to their bodies. It caused Sarah to start shivering.

"I'm getting very cold," she said. "When is it going to stop raining?" Mike didn't pay attention to her. He was looking around to see if he could hear the buggy or see its headlights.

"I think they have stopped chasing us," he finally said. "We can slow down. We can start looking for a place to spend the night. It's after eleven."

"Where are we going to spend the night in this God forsaken wilderness?" asked Sarah getting very discouraged.

"Trust me," said Mike. "Have I let you down yet?"

"I'm sorry," she answered. "I do trust you. Don't listen to this—" "Concerned lovely lady," said Mike, continuing her sentence. "You

just need time to adjust. Let's continue up to the foot of the mountain. We will look for a large rock with some kind of an overhang." They continued walking up the trail.

"How are we going to find a large rock in this pitch black darkness?"

"Stop being so negative," he said, finally getting tired of her complaining. "We will bump into it when we get to it." There was silence for a brief moment, and then they both started to laugh. They didn't understand how they could laugh. It was a release of tension. Mike reached over and hugged Sarah. "We will be okay. Trust me."

"I'll behave from now on," she said. "I promise!" They stood there in one another's arms when Mike heard a sound. The rain had changed to a slow drizzle. The storm had, for the time being, subsided somewhat.

"Do you hear that sound?" asked Mike. "Yes," said Sarah. "What is it?"

"It sounds like running water," he answered. "I think we are near a river."

"I take it that's good," said Sarah.

"Well a river generally takes you to a road or city," said Mike, "but for now it will take us through this mountain. Since the rain is light, I can get out my flashlight. However, before we continue, let's see if we can reach the general."

Sarah handed Mike the cell phone, and Mike placed the call. "I got the answering machine again. General McGard," he said after the tone. "This is Colonel Mills. We were attacked on Route 91. We were just north of a place called Divide. We had just driven over a bridge called the Double Bridge. We had to leave our car and escape into the forest. They were chasing us until it got dark. We got lost in the storm but will try to go north as soon as the weather clears up. Look for us. I will try to call later." After he hung up the phone, he turned to Sarah. "Let's go investigate, " he said.

He took out his flashlight. It lit without any problem. The light showed that in front of them was a very large rock. The game path led to the left of it. The river sound came from the right. They walked along the side of the rock, since there was less wild growth there, and soon Mike noticed that a larger rock was leaning forward with about three or four feet of overhang, providing a shelter beneath it. Mike checked the ground under it. It was wet but not as wet as the rest of the ground around it.

"Sarah, this a good place to spend the night. Why don't you rest here while I go look for the river?"

"Not on your life!" she exclaimed. "I'm never going to be more than five feet from you. I'm going with you."

"Okay, if you feel up to it," he said. "I just thought you were too tired to go on. You can leave you backpack here if you like. We are coming back here."

Sarah put down her backpack and followed Mike. They traveled along the rock and finally came to the edge of the river. Sarah stopped short of the river.

"Wow," she said. "What is that foul smell?"

"That is the smell of fish. Some may have been killed by the storm, though that does smell terrible." Mike kept searching the ground with the flashlight. Soon he found what it was that smelled so badly. There was a very large, dead trout that was on the shore of the river. He went toward it and bent over to view it up close.

"Mike," said Sarah. "What are you doing?" "I'm looking to see what killed it."

"What do you care what killed it?" she asked, holding her nose. "You'll see later in our journey through this period of life's experience."

"Whatever are you talking about?" asked Sarah. "Are you all right?"

"This fish died by the effect of a fish hook in its mouth. He was too big for the fishing line that the fisherman used. It broke the line and came here to die. I am removing the hook that has about twenty to thirty feet of fishing line attached to it. It may come handy later on down the river."

Mike washed the hook the best he could in the river and, after winding up the line, stored it in his backpack. "Now let's go back to the area where we left your backpack."

Sarah followed without question. She decided to keep her mouth shut from here on. When they got back to the leaning rock, Mike took off his backpack and headed out away from the area.

"Where are you going?" asked Sarah getting panicky again.

"Just lay out your blanket there, as close to the rock as you can, and we will use mine to cover us," Mike instructed her. "I'll be right back." As Mike left, Sarah placed her hand over her mouth. She promised to keep quiet and trust Mike. Mike returned about five minutes later carrying a small, but obviously heavy, log. He leaned it against the rock and left again. After bringing a third log Sarah couldn't hold her tongue.

"What are you doing Mike?" she asked. "You want to build a log cabin?"

"I am building a lean-to," he said. "I don't think the rain is over. I want to give us as much protection as I can." An hour later, he had brought eight logs. After that, he brought several branches that he had found deep in the woods that had broad leaves. He placed them on top of the logs.

"You are a genius," said Sarah. "This is really nice under here." Mike put the flashlight on the ground shining toward his backpack.

"Now let's see how good these backpacks are," he said as he took out his change of clothes. "Not too bad. They are pretty dry. I think we should get out of these wet clothes before we try to sleep. It's after midnight." Mike began changing his clothes. As he was changing, he could tell by the rustling noise of Sarah in the dark that she was doing the same thing.

"That feels a lot better," said Sarah almost to herself when she had finished. Mike placed his backpack nearest to the rock to use as a pillow. Sarah's blanket was already on the ground. Mike laid down with his head on the backpack.

"Use your backpack as a pillow," suggested Mike. "Grab the end of my blanket and pull it over you."

"Okay," she said. "I'm ready to go to sleep. I'm so tired I don't think I'll get up until noon."

Sarah laid herself down next to Mike but she didn't place her head on her backpack. She laid her head on Mike's chest. Mike didn't mind. He wrapped his arms around her, and they both went to sleep. Mike had been correct. As they fell asleep, the rain started to come down heavily. It didn't bother them at all. They were too tired, and the branches with the broad leaves kept them relatively dry.

It was sometime in the early morning that Sarah opened her eyes. She looked out from under the lean-to and saw that it was daylight, though very foggy. It was still raining cats and dogs. It was a loud clap of thunder that awoke her.

It is too stormy and rainy to get up, she thought.

She nestled snug to Mike and went back to sleep. Mike instinctively tightened his arms around her. It wasn't until late morning that Mike awoke. The rain had subsided. However, it was still very foggy.

"Sarah," he called, "we had better get up and be on our way while it isn't raining too hard."

"Do we have to?" she asked still half asleep. "I could stay this way for the rest of the day."

"If you did," said Mike, "it would probably be for the rest of your life. Aren't you even a little hungry?"

"I wasn't until you brought it up," she answered starting to get up. "I don't look forward to the rest of the day."

"Let's see if we can follow the river to a road or, if we are lucky, to a city," said Mike ignoring her comment. "We first have to get over this mountain range."

Mike and Sarah folded up their blankets, and, after brushing themselves off, put on their backpacks and retraced their steps to the river. When they got there, they were disappointed. The river went through the mountain, but on both sides of the river were high cliffs. There was no way that they could follow the river that way.

"We can't go that way," said Sarah. "I guess we have to find another way through these mountains."

"We just have to go back and follow the game trail," said Mike as he walked up to the river and used the water to wash his hands and face.

"That's a good idea," said Sarah washing herself. "Wow, that water is very cold." Mike smiled, wondering why Sarah was making such a fuss. He suspected that she needed to say them to keep her sanity.

He realized that this was a very difficult time for her. He knew she wasn't a coward, she just hated the wilderness.

Come to think of it, he thought. *I don't like it much myself.*

He turned around and headed back to the trail, past the lean-to. The fog was so thick they could hardly see the path. The trail was, evidently, leading them up the side of the mountain. They walked up and along the trail with a deep cliff on their left and jagged rocks on their right. It was a couple of hours later that the sky before them got very dark.

"I think our luck is running out," said Mike. "It looks like a storm is moving in."

Sarah didn't say a word. A few minutes later, the lightning and thunder ahead on the mountains became fearsome. As they walked along the edge of the narrow path, it became harder to see the path in front of them due to the heavy fog.

"Sarah," said Mike, "please be very careful here where it is very narrow. I kicked a rock over the edge, and it took minutes for it to hit the bottom. We have to be extra careful until the path gets wider. Keep your right arm against the side of the mountain so in the fog you don't wander too far to your left."

"Will do," answered Sarah. They followed the narrow ledge for a few minutes; then the trail came to a dead end. Sarah stopped at a rock formation that blocked the path.

"Why are you stopping?" asked Mike, not being able to see beyond Sarah's back.

"The trail ends here," she answered. "There is nothing but a blank wall in front of me."

"I guess the heavy rain has caused some erosion," said Mike. "We have to try to climb over it."

Sarah placed her foot up on the small edge on the rock. She needed a small lift from Mike to go up onto the next level.

"Why is it so foggy?" asked Sarah. "It would be nice to be able to see where we are going."

"I think that it's a low-hanging cloud caused by the storm. I'm sure that after we start going downhill, the fog will be behind us. We just have to be careful."

Sarah reached what looked like the top. She turned and faced Mike as she started down the other side. She felt around with her foot for a footing to hold her. Mike came closer to her to help in case she started to slide. Sarah had just turned to look down for the path, when the edge she had put her weight on gave way. She gave out a yell. Mike grabbed the strap of her backpack and kept her from falling down the deep canyon.

"I've got you," he said. "Try to find better footing while I hold you." Mike soon felt the release of her weight as she stepped down to the path.

"I think I'm on solid ground," she said. "You can let go now."

"Just stay where you're at," instructed Mike. "Wait for me to join you." Slowly, Mike came down to where Sarah was hugging the side of the mountain. "Continue around carefully," Mike continued.

Slowly, they continued along the edge. Mike noticed that the path was getting wider, but the storm was getting closer. It was getting very close to five, and they were far from getting over the mountain. It would be impossible to sleep on the edge of the mountain especially during a storm.

Suddenly, it started to rain very hard. For the first time, Mike began to worry about ever getting out of the wilderness alive. He started to pray. As if God was answering his prayer, he heard Sarah call out to him.

"Mike!" she yelled. "Come here, quick, look at what I found!" Mike hurried to where Sarah was. She was pointing to her right. "Look, I think it is an Indian cave. It has paintings on the walls."

"How do you know that there are paintings on the walls?" asked Mike.

"I was in there," answered Sarah. "I came out to call for you." They quickly entered the cave out of the heavy rain.

"This is an act of God," said Mike. "God has provided a place for us to spend the night and get out of the storm. It's kind of early to stop, but we would be foolish to keep going down the side of the mountain in this terrible storm."

Sarah checked the clothes that she had wrung out at the lean-to. They were still a little damp but better than the water soaked ones she had on. She took off the clothes she had on down to her underwear, and, after wringing them out, she laid them on a flat spot back in the cave. Mike did the same thing.

"Mike, are you hungry?" asked Sarah.

"Are you kidding?" he answered. "We haven't had anything to eat in two days."

"Well, it hasn't been exactly two days, but, whatever, I'm willing to share anything I have with you."

"Have you been holding out on me?" asked Mike with a smile. "When, during the last two days, have we had time to sit down and have a bite?"

"You have a valid point," said Mike. "Now what do you have?"

"I'm sorry if I misled you into thinking that I had a lot," said Sarah. "I don't have much, but I'll share it with you. I have several cookies and a candy bar."

She dug deep into her backpack and pulled out six large cookies and a large almond chocolate bar. She handed Mike three of the cookies. She then broke the bar in half and handed one piece to Mike. Mike sat down on the blanket that Sarah had set down in a cozy part of the cave away from the entrance and gave thanks to God for the food and asked him to bless it.

"This is a lot of rich food," said Mike. "We will get a lot of energy from this."

"And probably a stomach ache too," added Sarah.

They ate slowly so as not to overwhelm their stomachs with too much at one time.

"Well, I think this will give me a good night's sleep."

"It's too early to sleep," said Mike. "If we go to sleep now, we will wake up in the middle of the night."

"Not me," said Sarah. "I could sleep all day tomorrow."

"If we were on vacation, I might let you do just that; however, we have an enemy to stop. The longer we delay, the harder it's going to be."

"What do you think the general will do when he gets your message?" asked Sarah.

"I think he will send a search aircraft to try and locate us. He would also try to locate the assailants and take them out at the same time to give us protection from additional attacks."

"How soon do you think that will be?" asked Sarah. "I mean, how long does the type of missions he goes on last? That should determine how soon he gets the message and starts his search."

"I don't think a flight would last more than a day," said Mike. "He probably has already heard my message. The bad news is that until the storm clears up, he can't do much searching."

"Tell me, Mike, what do you think of this cave?" asked Sarah changing the subject. "Do you think that some wild animals could live in here? Are we safe?" Mike took out his powerful flashlight and started to search the inside of the cave.

"The cave does seem to have several tunnels. It goes in pretty far. Even with this powerful light, I can't see the end. This one across from us curves in so I can't see too far into it. Do you want me to search each one?"

"Do you think it is a good idea?" asked Sarah, putting the load on him.

"No, if there are animals in here, we don't want to disturb them. They have not been bothering us up until now. Let us not press our luck. What would we do anyway, go out into the storm?"

"I guess you're right," she answered, "but we had better be prepared in case one shows up."

"Now you are thinking like the Sarah I know and love. We should get our pistols out and make sure they are not too wet and are still working."

Sarah pulled out the stun gun and checked it carefully. Then she set it next to her backpack where it would be handy if she needed it. Mike took out the pistol that he had obtained from the attackers at Durango. It was pretty dry. However, when Mike checked the chamber, he found that it only had one bullet left. He set it next to his backpack. He decided not to tell Sarah. He just had to be careful to use accurately and only when absolutely necessary. The storm had gotten worse as night permeated the area. Lightning and thunder filled the air like cannon fire in a war zone.

"Mike, what are your thoughts on why God has done this to America? I know that it has turned its back to God, but have you any other thoughts?" asked Sarah. "I mean why hasn't he initiated the rapture?"

"Well, to answer your first question," said Mike, "look at what God did to Israel. He almost destroyed them three times. God was always giving them a chance to repent. Perhaps he is doing the same thing to America. Actually, if what I suspect is be true, He will test the whole world."

"What makes you say that?" asked Sarah.

"Well, do you think that the people being attacked, especially the US, would just sit if any of them survive and recover?" suggested Mike. "We are not going to give them another chance. I think this is the atomic World War 3 that everyone has been afraid of since the atomic age started. There was never a question in my mind that if the Arab terrorists obtained the atomic bomb, they would use it. Why do you think you are so valuable to the general? Do you think he is thinking of anything else? I think retaliation is his number one priority after defending his country."

"I guess you are right," said Sarah. "I was hoping that the rapture would be the next event."

"God has his own plan for what and when things will happen," said Mike. "We are just not privy to it."

"If what you are saying is true, then God has plans for us to be a part of the retaliation," said Sarah feeling better.

"Let that give you encouragement," said Mike.

"Then why is he making it so hard on us?" asked Sarah. She was speaking of the storm that was raging outside of the cave.

"I know," said Mike. "That is a terrible storm. However, it may be over in the morning. Besides, God did give us this cave. Could you imagine what it would have been like if we were still outside on the side of the mountain?"

"I don't even want to think about it," she said. "I remember some very severe storms we had back in Ohio. I was caught out in one once. I've been afraid of storms every since."

After some small talk they decided to try to sleep. Mike lay on Sarah's blanket with his head on his backpack and pulled his blanket over himself. Sarah put her head on Mike's shoulder and pressed her body tight to his. Mike wasn't sure he could go to sleep with this arrangement. Somehow, after a few minutes, he did fall asleep to the beating of Sarah's heart and the constant sound of thunder.

"Yes, like a mother and wife, but it will never happen I'm afraid," she said sadly. "I am too educated. They would never let me. I wouldn't be able to resist the demand for my type of training. My training would be in too great in demand."

"There is no reason that you couldn't do both," said Mike. "I know the days of the stay-at-home wife is not as common as it used to be, but it is done every day. I am, therefore, planning on helping my partner do some of the domestic part of living together. By the way, did you say that you would like to spend the rest of your life here with me? Do you love me that much?"

"You know that I do," she said with a shy look about her, "but I wouldn't want to deceive you. I love you very much. You are a great guy. You are very intelligent and romantic and very handsome."

"I heard a *but* in there somewhere," said Mike.

"I just want you to know that I will always love Tom. We had some kind of magic between us that I have never felt before."

"That hurt," said Mike sadly.

"Don't worry, I'll get over it, but tell me that you don't still have feelings for Tara. You once told me that you had a special love for her, that she gave you butterflies in your stomach. You don't have to answer me. Just think about it. I think you love me as much as I love you. Tom is gone, and so is Tara if she lived in Chicago. I'm just moving on."

Mike didn't answer her, but he knew she was right. However, his thoughts were more about Annie. He missed and thought of her every night. His thoughts of Tara were diminishing every day.

The next day was a day of preparation. They planned on taking everything they could on the horses' saddlebags.

Sarah cooked the best breakfast, lunch and dinner she knew how. They didn't know where their next meal would come from. Mike said grace at every meal thanking God for the farm that he provided and the food that he made available to them. Lastly, he prayed that God would guide them on the path that would fulfill the purpose he had for keeping them alive. That evening, Sarah removed the cast from Mike's leg.

"This is the final test," said Sarah. "It will tell us if we can leave tomorrow."

"How do you know I won't fail on purpose?" said Mike, kidding her. "Because I know that you are a good Christian and you wouldn't fake a problem," she said. "Now cut the bull and let's see you walk out to the back porch where we will spend our last night together on the swing."

"Boy, you know how to use all the tricks, don't you," he said affectionately.

"I know what you like," she said with a smile. Mike got up and started to walk around. He was still limping a little, but he got around without trouble though rather slowly.

"I guess I'm all right," he said after taking a few steps around the kitchen.

"Do you have any pain?" asked Sarah.

"No," he answered. "It's just that the legs don't have much strength."

"Do you think you can ride the horse?"

"I don't think that will be a problem," he said, "but what about the arm, can you remove that cast?"

"I think we should leave that on for a while longer. The arm was hurt more seriously. I'll bring the required tools with me, and we will take that cast off later."

"Then there is nothing left to do but sit on the porch and rest," said Mike.

"I don't think that rest is the right word," said Sarah. "However, I'm going to see that we go to bed early. We have to get up early tomorrow."

Mike didn't say a word. He was through speaking. If Sarah was going to see that he got to bed early he didn't want to waste anymore time talking. They sat on the rear porch swing in one another's arms, and their lips didn't have any trouble finding each other. They wondered when they would have the opportunity to be safely embraced romantically like this again. The next morning Sarah got up first.

They put on their empty backpacks, and they mounted and started south down the road heading for Route 59. They walked their horses when the soft shoulder wasn't flat. They didn't want to run the horses on the pavement. They exchanged small talk about feeling strange traveling on horseback. About two miles down the road, they came to the town of Saris. It was in ruins and also deserted. They didn't find a vehicle that was drivable. From Saris, the road turned southwest. At about ten o'clock they came to the town of Adel. It was pretty much like Saris; there was no one around. There were also no bodies around.

"Do you think they all got away from the enemy army?" asked Sarah.

"I wondered about that too. I suspect that they all got away, or they cleaned up before they left," answered Mike. "I don't think there is a crew that goes around cleaning up. What bothers me is that there are no drivable cars around. In fact, since there aren't too many cars around, seems to indicate that a lot of people drove away. Whether or not they got away alive is another question."

"Do you think that they could have been bombed by the aircraft?" asked Sarah.

"We won't know that until we get to the main highway."

It was almost five when they reached the freeway Route 69 at the town of Stringtown. They got on the freeway, and since the soft shoulder was hard, they were able to make better time.

"Look," said Sarah. "There are two cars going the other way on the freeway."

"I noticed that as we approached it before. At least I saw one car go by. That is very strange."

At about six, they reached the town of Atoka.

"I see that this town is not in bad shape," said Mike. "We have been traveling southwest. I think we have gotten far enough west to get to the towns that the invaders had not gotten to yet. The little damage that we see is probably from the bomb blast."

"I think you are right, but why aren't there more people around here?"

"They probably went south to escape the invading army," said Mike. "They had no idea that the army would be stopped before it got to them."

"There seems to be some cars parked along the road that look perfectly good," said Sarah. "I wonder if we can obtain one."

"Not if the owners are inside that building," said Mike. "It looks like a restaurant. The sign says 'Sweet Pea.' What I would like to get is a small truck like that one parked on the other side of the street."

They had dismounted and were walking toward the restaurant. "What I want to know is, what should we do with the horses?" asked Sarah.

"First we have to find water and food for them," said Mike.

"I'm not worried about that," said Sarah. "I'm wondering where to settle them for the night, or, for that matter, where do we tie them while we go in to dine."

Just as they had said that, a man in his mid to late thirties came around the corner and saw them with the horses.

" Hi," he said. "Are you guys traveling by house back?"

"Only until we can find another methods of transportation," said Sarah.

"May I ask you a question?" "How can I help you?" he asked.

"If you are from this area and are familiar with the people would you know who owns that truck across the street?"

"First of all I'm not from this area," he said. "In any case, it doesn't matter because the truck is mine. Why do you ask?"

"Would you like to sell it?" asked Mike.

The man laughed. "You want to trade it for the horses?" he asked, still laughing loudly. "No way, I need the truck for my farm."

"Tell me," said Mike, "what has made you decide to go home at this time? What told you that the problem is over?"

"I heard it on the radio," he answered. "I understand that it even got announced on TV."

"What did you hear?" asked Mike, very puzzled, not only that the radios and TV stations were already back in service, but that the news had gotten out already.

"The radio news commentator said that the invading army had been pushed back into the Atlantic Ocean. Why do you ask?"

"We were given the job of informing the people who have run to the Mexican border to escape the invaders that the threat is over and they could go home," said Mike. "We need a car to get down there. Would you happen to know where we could purchase a car?"

"There is a gas station just around the corner," he said. "He may be able to help you. Come to think of it, Durant, the town I just came through, had a used car lot just off the highway. I'm sure you could buy a car there."

"Sure but how can we get there?" asked Mike.

"Buy me dinner, and I'll take you there. It's only about 25 miles. It should only take about twenty minutes."

"That's a deal," said Mike. "My name is Mike. Do you want to eat first?"

"My name is Sam." He looked at his watch. "It's almost six. I think we should go there first. I don't know how late he will be open, or if in fact he is open. There isn't that much traffic, as you can imagine."

Mike turned to Sarah. "Sarah, honey, do you want to come?"

"Why don't you go, honey?" said Sarah, kidding Mike about his honey thing. She knew that Mike was telling Sam to forget it. He could see how Sam was looking at Sarah. "I'll see if I can find some food and water for the horses."

"Are you sure?" asked Mike.

"Yes, I'm sure, go, and I'll meet you inside. I'll take care of the horses while you are gone."

Mike and Sam walked across the street and got into the truck. Soon, they were on their way to Durant.

"How did you get trapped into the job of going along the border informing people?" asked Sam. "That's a big job."

"I know it is, but we are really needed up north to help defeat the western invading army," said Mike. "This is only a job on the way."

"How are you two going to help fight the army?"

"Sarah is a weapons expert, and I have been drafted to join the US Army."

"Wait," said Sam getting excited. "You aren't Colonel Mills, the Desert Fox, are you? Is Sarah, Doctor Sarah Anders or something like that?"

"You have heard of us?" asked Mike caught completely by surprise.

"Yes, the radio said that a Colonel Mills, the Desert Fox, and a Doctor Sarah Anders were coming to help fight the western army. They said that you were going to command the US Army, and that the doctor was a nuclear expert. It asked that we help you in any way we can."

"I can't believe that information got out," said Mike. "If you heard it, so has the invading army. What else have you heard over the radio?"

"Well, they said that an army made up of Texas and Arizona State troopers, were to hold them back until the enemy disengaged and slowly headed north." Sam hesitated, thinking if there was anything else he had left out. "Oh yes, there was one more thing. They asked all able men to go to Spokane and join the US Army that is preparing to engage the enemy."

"We will have to be on our toes from here on in," said Mike almost to himself.

"Why are you worried?" asked Sam not understanding Mike's concerns.

"Well if the enemy knows about us, then they are going to try to stop us."

"The radio also asked that we all were to help you get to your destination," added Sam.

They were soon on the outskirts of the city. Sam got off the highway and turned down a small street to a used car lot. The sign read "Quality Auto." Mike got out and started to look over the autos on display. He spotted a cream colored car that had just been washed.

"We just got it in," said a voice behind Mike. "We will make you a very good deal on this car. It is only six years old and has a little over thirty thousand miles on it.

"How much?" asked Mike.

"Twelve thousand," said the salesman. "I'll give you eight thousand," he said.

"You drive a hard bargain. Let's split the difference. Give me ten thousand and you have a deal." asked Walter.

"You have a deal," said Mike as he wrote out a check. "Can you get me a license?"

"By the way, my name is Walter. Wait here a minute. I'll get a form for a license application. You fill it out and sign it. I'll go to a tag agency, tomorrow and get a plate." When he got the form, Mike filled it out and gave it to Walter, with cash for the plates.

"I'll see you in the morning," said Mike. Getting in the car, Mike followed Sam back to Atoka.

Sarah was waiting in front of the restaurant. She had both backpacks by her feet.

"Sarah, what is going on?" asked Mike after he and Sam found parking spots and walked to where Sarah was standing. "What have you been up to all this time and where are the horses?"

"One question at a time please," she said with a smile. "I fed the horses from a field not too far from here. Then, I took them to the gas station just around the corner and got water for them. The nice fellow at the station offered to keep them in the station overnight. I gathered all of our belongings and packed our backpacks, so if you would just put them in the trunk of the car, we can go inside and have dinner."

"Why do I even bother to ask?" asked Mike. "I should know by now that you will take care of all that has to be done. Let's go eat. Come along Sam. We will buy you that dinner we promised."

"Right behind you," said Sam.

Inside they were quickly seated and the waiter gave them a menu. "My name is Fred, and I'll be your waiter this evening. I'm sorry,

however, that we only have the chicken dinners and Atlantic salmon dishes available. The chicken dinners available are these two up here," he said pointing to the top of the menu.

"I'll have the Chicken Milanese dinner," said Sarah. "They are always good. I'll also have Italian on my salad and coffee."

"That sounds good," said Mike. "I'll have the same, except decaf coffee."

"I'll have the salmon with ranch dressing on my salad and regular coffee," said Sam.

While they were eating their meal, Mike and Sam brought Sarah up to date on all that Sam had heard on the radio and what he had heard about what people had told him they saw on TV about Mike and Sarah and about the fact that the war was over in the East. Then they sat and discussed the ramifications of that information being out where the invaders could have it available to them.

"I don't understand how the information got out," said Sarah. "I'm sure that General McGard would never let that information out. I'll have to call him and see if he has any ideas on where and how that leak got out. I tried to call him earlier, but no one answered. I'll call him later.

"Well, it is important that we find that out of course," said Mike. "But more important is that we have to be very careful from here on out, because I'm sure that the enemy will want to stop us. I think they know what Sam has told us because, as Sam said, they have disengaged with the Texas and Arizona troops and are moving north. That means also that we have to hurry, or we will be late for the battle."

"What are your plans, Sam?" asked Sarah.

"First, I'm going home to make sure my parents are all right. I was on a trip to El Paso Texas, when I heard of the invasion of the eastern US. A friend called me and told me what was happening. I called my parents and told them to hide in the bomb shelter that my great-grandfather built around the World War 2 era. It is hidden behind the shed. You have to know where it is to find it. I'm only worried that they didn't listen to me. Anyway, after I see that they are okay, and that they can take care of themselves, I'm going to Spokane and join the army there."

"It's getting late," said Mike. "We have to find a place to stay tonight and get up early tomorrow."

"There is a very nice motel just down 4th street just past the gas station," said Sam. "That's where I'm going to stay tonight."

"Sounds great," said Mike. "We will follow you there."

"Thanks for the dinner," said Sam. "It was very nice to have your company too."

"You have got to be kidding," said Mike. "I feel like I still owe you. It was so nice of you to drive me to get a car."

"No problem," said Sam. "Glad I could help." Having said that, Sam left.

At the motel, Sam found a parking place in front and went in first. Mike was surprised at the number of cars in the parking lot. He wondered if some of those cars were abandoned. Apparently, he found out once inside, they belonged to people staying in the motel. It wasn't very big to start with.

"There must be a lot of people that heard the radio news and are heading home," said Sarah. Inside, Sam had already registered and had gone to his room.

"We would like two rooms with showers," said Mike.

"All our rooms have showers," said the clerk showing his irritation at the request. "I only have one room left, and it's on the upper floor." "You only have one room?" said Mike thinking that he must have misunderstood him.

"Yes," said the clerk. "It does have twin beds if that helps."

"We will take it," said Sarah saving Mike the effort of asking her. They paid in advance and went to their room. They were fast asleep as soon as they hit the beds. It had been a long day.

The next morning, Mike woke to the sound of the shower. He took what he needed from his backpack and waited for Sarah to finish. After Mike had showered, he started to dress when Sarah stopped him. He was still in his underwear

"I think that it's time to remove the cast from your arm," she said. "I think it has healed enough by now."

She took the tools out of her backpack and started to remove the cast.

"Do you always carry tools to remove casts?" he said in jest.

"You'd be surprised as to how many tasks these tools will do. This saw blade could come in handy some day."

Mike tried to flex his arm now that the cast was removed.

"My arm seems to have grown stiff. I find it hard to move," he complained to Sarah.

"Don't worry, it will be as good as new in a few hours."

After Mike finished dressing they packed their backpacks and went to the restaurant for breakfast. Sam had apparently already eaten and left for his home.

After breakfast they placed their backpacks in the car and left for Durant. They arrived in Durant at about nine thirty. Walter was waiting for them.

"This is Sarah," said Mike introducing his companion. "Do you have my plates ready?"

"Yes I do," responded Walter. "I'll put them on in just a minute. I also checked your bank. They are three hours ahead of us, you know, and were open when I called this morning. They verified that your check is good."

Walter took off his dealer plates and put on Mike's. They shook hands and left.

They followed Route 75 into Texas and continued for about twenty miles to the city of Denison, then they stopped at a gas station to get directions. They were told that the only way south was by taking Route 69. They said that all the roads into Dallas end at the big hole that used to be Dallas.

They followed 69 for the next two hours. All the towns were partially deserted. Only a few stores and gas stations were opened.

They were soon headed south on Route 69. It was twelve thirty.

"I think I'd better look at the map," suggested Sarah. "I don't think we want to end up in a big hole that used to be a large city."

"That's a good idea," said Mike. "Do you want me to pull over?"

"No, I can check it while we are moving. I don't want to waste any time. We have to get to Spokane as soon as we alert the folks at the border. I've tried to call the general several times, but no one answered. I guess he is on a mission. With the invaders moving north, I wonder if he still wants us to go to the border. Not only that, but I want to know how the news of our situation got out."

"I know. That has been on my mind also. I am starting to formulate a plan, and I need to talk to him," said Mike

"We are almost to the town of Jacksonville," said Sarah. "We have to take Route 79 from there on. It looks like it misses most of the large cities in Texas."

"I'm glad you told me," said Mike. "The sign we just passed says that Jacksonville is just ahead. We can just take the exit to 79 south. Good work."

They followed 79 past all the large cities. At Rockdale, they switched to route 77. They noticed that there weren't many cars on the road. The few they saw were all going north. No one was going south. Also, they noticed that after entering Texas, they didn't see many damaged cars on the road, and the amount of city property damage declined the farther they got south.

They arrived at Robstown around six thirty. Robstown was just about ten miles from Corpus Christi.

They didn't feel like tackling a large town. They were both tired of driving and very hungry. They had to try several restaurants before they could find one that was serving anyone. After a satisfying dinner, they searched around for a motel that was open for business. All they could find was an old hotel that had rooms available.

"We could drive a little way out of town to see if we could find a nice motel," said Mike.

"I'm too tired," said Sarah "I'm too tired to go any further. Let's stay here. We have had worse accommodations and probably will have worse yet."

"Whatever you say," responded Mike. "I'm pretty tired too."

"I bet you are," said Sarah. "You have done all the driving." They got rooms and immediately went to sleep.

It was 9:00 a.m. when they left Robstown the next morning. Traffic heading north became heavier as they traveled south, but traffic going south was still very scarce. The towns they traveled through were still mostly deserted until they got to Raymondville. From there south to Brownsville the roads and cities were very congested. They found a place to eat lunch in Brownsville and then started west along Highway 83 which ran along the border. It was about three 3 in the afternoon when they got to within five miles of McAllen.

The road from Brownsville was very close to the border; they began seeing cars parked along the road and tents on both sides of the road. There were many trucks and vans trying to sell anything from food to tents; they congested the highway so that it was difficult to travel. Mike and Sarah made several stops along the road to inform people that the eastern invaders had been driven back to the Atlantic. As they stopped on the side of the road, Sarah would contact the people on the north side of the road, and Mike would inform the people on the south side of the road. The people, upon hearing the news, started to pack to go home.

It worked pretty well until they got to the point where the highway turned north toward McAllen. The road went north about five miles and away from the border. Because of the stops and the traffic, it took them three hours to get to McAllen. They decided to find a place to stop for the night and continue traveling the next day. They were both very tired. They found a fast food diner and a motel about five miles west of McAllen. It was full, so they had to rent a storage area where the owner had put in two roller beds for them. They finally turned in for the night.

The next morning, they left early and started west on 83. It wasn't as easy as the day before. The highway varied from two to five miles from the border.

"This is not acceptable," said Mike. "At this rate, we will never get to Spokane."

"What are you suggesting?" asked Sarah.

"I don't have an answer yet," he responded. "I just know that we can't get to all the people when we have to walk two or more miles to contact many of them."

Not having any alternatives, they continued until they got to Laredo. They did the best they could. It took over eight hours to go about one hundred and fifty miles to Laredo. It was after six when they got there.

"Now we have to get an alternative," said Sarah looking at the map.

"What's the problem now?" asked Mike.

"Well the problem is that route 83 heads north, and there isn't a road that goes along the border. The highway gets about thirty to fifty miles from the border. I suspect that there are farms in between. We could be shot trespassing on a farmer's land."

"You are right," said Mike. "I'm too tired to worry about it now though. Let's find a place to eat and spend the night."

They found a motel and then walked down the street to a small restaurant. It was while they were walking to the restaurant for breakfast the next morning that Mike got an idea of what to do. It came to him when he saw an off-road vehicle across the street from the restaurant.

"That's what we need," he said. "With a machine like that, we could go anywhere." Mike walked across the street to get a closer look at it. It was a two-seater with a removal top. As he was looking at it, a young man walked up to him.

"Do you like my four wheel dirt bike?" he asked.

"Yes, I do," answered Mike. "Would you like to sell it?"

"Not on your life," he answered. "This is my right arm. It has seen more beaches than a lifeguard. Why would you want one anyway? You don't look like a beach type."

"I have to go along the border and tell the people that ran there to escape the invaders, that the war is over and the enemy has been pushed back into the Atlantic."

"Wait a minute," said the young man. "You aren't Colonel Mills, are you?" He looked across the street and saw Sarah. "I know you. You were on TV yesterday. That's why I am going home. I'm making sure my parents get home safely, and then I'm going to Spokane and join the army there. My name is Jimmy Holten."

"Well, Jimmy, you can help right here if you really want to help your country," said Mike.

"What can I do to help?" he asked.

"Would you consider following the border up to California and informing people that the war is over, that the enemy has been defeated? Ask them all to go home and start reconstruction, then come back and take your parents home."

"My parents have their own car, I just want to follow them home and make sure everything is all right. Besides, that is a long way, and I don't have any money for gas. I could sleep in my car, but it needs fuel."

"What do you think you will need?" asked Mike. "Perhaps I could help."

"First, let's figure how far I really have to go," said Jimmy. "I come from a trip to El Paso. Most of the people for about a hundred miles on this side of El Paso come from the California-Arizona area. Some of them headed back when they heard that the invading army had pulled back to California and was headed north toward Spokane. I suppose they heard the news also."

"That's why we have to get this job done and head north," said Mike.

Jimmy started to calculate what it would take to cover the area Mike had described. He figured that the complete trip would be about six hundred miles and that it would take about ten days. At fifty dollars per day that it would cost Mike five hundred dollars.

"How far is it from here to your home?" asked Mike.

"I live just south of Savanna, Georgia," said Jimmy. "It's over a thousand miles from here, but my parents will feed me if they are willing to wait for me. Let me call them, and then we will talk."

He walked away from Mike and rang a number on his cell phone. A few minutes later he returned to Mike who had been joined by Sarah.

"My parents said that they will wait for me," said Jimmy. "So, I'm ready to do my part. How can you help me economically?"

"Well," said Mike, "you said it would take you about ten days to do what I asked and about two days to get home. At fifty dollars a day, you'd get five hundred for the job. How does six hundred sound to you? That way, it will help you get home."

"That's more than fair," said Jimmy. "You have a deal."

Mike headed west on Route 83. They were surprised to see a few cars and tents that were parked along both sides of the road all the way to Eagle Pass.

At Carrizo Springs, they changed to Route 277 that led them to Eagle Pass. They arrived at Eagle Pass at a little past noon. They ate lunch and headed up 277 to Route 90 at Del Rio. The highway came pretty close to the border for about sixty miles. They didn't see Jimmy at all during the leg of the trip that took them close to the border. They took 90 to Route 10 and into El Paso. It took a day and a half to get there. They arrived about noon. Jimmy was right about the people from about one hundred miles east of Laredo coming from the West and not from the East. El Paso was the worst they had seen on the complete trip up to now. It was so crowded from people that came from the West that you couldn't get into any restaurant.

"I've never seen it this bad," said Sarah. "Even Brownsville wasn't this bad."

"I don't think we have time to wait to get fed here. Let's head north and see if we can stop along the way. I don't think it will be this crowded much farther north."

"I sure hope not," responded Sarah. "I'm not really that hungry anyway. I agree, let's move on."

It took a little while to get out of the city. Soon, they were traveling at highway speeds up Route 85 into New Mexico to Las Cruces. They stopped at a fast food restaurant, had a short lunch, and were soon back on the road. It was duck soup from here, they thought. There was no traffic and the towns they passed were partly deserted. Either they were working their land, or they were south running from the invaders.

The roads were clear. In two days they would be in Spokane. Little did they know what was ahead for them.

CHAPTER NINE

Lost in the Forest

SOME TIME LATER, SARAH OPENED her eyes and saw bright sunlight entering the opening of the cave. Sarah reached for Mike, but, to her surprise, he wasn't there beside her.

"Mike!" she yelled out. There was no response. "Mike!" she called out again. She sat up on her blanket. "Mike, where are you?" she said with a voice in panic. "Mike, you wouldn't leave without me," she said almost to herself. She got up and went to where her clothes were drying. Panic hit her harder than before when she noticed that all of Mike's clothes were gone. "Mike!" she yelled out loud. "Mike," she repeated as she started to cry. She quickly walked out of the entrance to the cave. The sun was bright and high in the sky. She could see the mountains and the valley below with a great gorge between her and the mountain on other side. On the other side, she also noticed that there was a large flat area with a helicopter sitting on it. She took out her binoculars and noticed that a single person was in the helicopter. It was the pilot waving for her to come to him. She could hear him yelling.

"Hurry, come, we have to go now!" His voice came to her as if he were in a long tin tube.

"How am I going to get there?" she yelled out as loud as she could. All he did was continue waving for her to come to him. The sun was high in the sky. She was able to see clearly. She looked at the side of the mountain the helicopter was on. She noticed a narrow path going down to the valley floor. She carefully walked to the edge of the cliff she was on. Sure enough, she saw a similar path going down from her position.

That's where Mike must have started down, she thought. Why he would leave her by herself was still the question on her mind. *Perhaps he wanted me to depend on myself if something happened to him*, she decided, thinking almost out loud. She then realized what she had to do. She had to pack her backpack and follow Mike down the side of the mountain she was on and climb up the other side where the helicopter was waiting for them.

She ran into the cave. She dressed and started to fold her blanket when she heard a loud explosion. It was followed by a series of explosions. She looked out and the helicopter was not there. Pieces of it were lying all over the mountain. It sounded like a barrage of rocket fire. Had they found them? The next thing she heard and felt was the largest explosion yet. It seemed as if it was right on top of her.

She fell onto her blanket on her side. She stayed as still as she could, waiting for the next barrage. Then suddenly, her heart stopped as she became alarmed at what she felt on her face. Something under her cheek was warm. She slowly raised her hand to feel above her face and felt something hairy. She became panicky. Had some furry animal come into the cave and fallen asleep on her blanket? She slowly lowered her hand and, lifting up her head, she opened her eyes. She was startled at what she saw at the cave entrance. The wind was blowing, and there was a violent downpour of rain. She could hear the rain beating down on the edge of the path just outside of the cave. It was pitch dark outside except for the occasional lightning that lit up the area. It was one of these lightning events that caused her to break out with laughter. During the short instant that the lightning lit up the area, she recognized the animal that was sleeping on her blanket. It was Mike. She felt his face. It was his beard she felt. He hadn't shaved in a couple of days. She started to laugh out loud again. She felt so foolish. It had all been a bad dream. She wondered if she would ever tell Mike about it.

She closed her eyes, and relaxed, although she was afraid to sleep for fear of dreaming again. She did snooze a little, and when she opened her eyes it was brighter outside, but the rain was still pouring down in buckets.

Why should we get up? she asked herself. *We won't be going out in this rain and fog. It would be suicide.* With this, she went back to sleep. She woke again when Mike stirred and called her name.

"Sarah, are you awake?" he asked.

"Yes," she answered. "I've been awake on and off all morning. It's been raining so hard I thought it would be silly to try to go out into it. Besides, the fog was and is still very thick."

"It's after-ten thirty," he said, his voice indicating surprise. "We have to get going no matter what the weather is like."

"I know," said Sarah, getting up. She was about to get dressed when they heard a loud howling noise.

"Stay absolutely still, Sarah," he instructed. "Don't move a muscle. I think it is a bear. If we stay absolutely still, he will realize that we mean him no harm. Where is your zoo gun?"

"My gun is over there, under my backpack," said Sarah as calmly as she could, but her heart was traumatized.

Was it all going to end here?

Mike slowly and carefully reached under Sarah's backpack and retrieved her pistol. The bear came out of his tunnel and slowly approached Mike growling continually. They had invaded its home. When he got to within fifteen feet of Mike, he arose on his hind legs and growled as loudly as he could. He looked like he was about to attack so Mike had no other choice. He aimed the pistol at the bear's open mouth. He fired once and, seeing that it didn't have any effect, he fired twice more. He then reached for his pistol. He had wanted to keep that one bullet for as long as he could, but could there be a greater emergency? He was about to fire when the bear came down onto all four feet and slowly backed up until he got to the entrance to his tunnel. Then, he turned around and slowly disappeared into the dark tunnel.

"What happened?" asked Sarah, surprised that they were spared the wrath of the bear.

"I guess the drug began working, and the bear smartly decided he would be safer in his tunnel," said Mike. "For whatever reason it did what it did, we have to get out of here as fast as we can. He may change his mind. We have no idea how long the drug will last."

They got dressed, packed the rest of their clothes and left the cave. The fog was still very thick. They walked slowly along the narrow path, though the path seemed to disappear every so often.

"Mike," said Sarah. "How strong are your feelings for me?" "What makes you ask such a question?" asked Mike. "Because I want to know," she said. "Now tell me the truth."

"I like you very much," said Mike. "To me, you are the most beautiful woman I know.."

"You really won't answer me, will you?" "I thought I just did," said Mike.

"You should have been a politician, do you know that?" said Sarah

"Now why would you say that?" he asked.

"Because you speak a lot of words but tell me nothing," she answered. "By the way, I love you too."

"Well let's concentrate on the path," said Mike. "It is getting hard to find in this fog."

After about a half hour, the path was completely gone. They had to climb down the side of the mountain as the rocks permitted. However, they liked the fact that they were going down. That reduced the fear of dropping down the gorge. As they climbed along the side of the mountain, the going became very slow. They had to find their footing every step of the way. They were at a point where they had started dropping below the clouds. They now could see their feet. Sarah stepped on a rock that protruded out from the side of the mountain. As she put weight on it, it gave way. She started to slide down the hill. She was able to yell out as she began to slide.

"Mike!" she yelled in panic. Mike grabbed at her and caught the strap of her backpack. He stopped her slide.

"Got you," he said. "Now try to get a footing on the rock next to you." She moved her feet in a searching pattern and found a footing. She put her weight on it and it held. Slowly, she recovered her balance and proceeded to the next position. Mike followed her, never letting go of her backpack strap.

As they worked their way along the rim of the mountain, two things began to become apparent. First, they were going downhill because they soon were below the clouds that hovered over the mountain. Secondly, a trail was beginning to emerge as they got closer to the lower level of the mountain. They were still pretty high. They could look down on the valley below and see the forest that they will have to travel through to get to the other mountain.

"I don't know about you, Mike, but I'm pretty hungry," Sarah said.

"I know, so am I," said Mike. "I'm keeping my eyes open for any vegetation that we can eat to keep us going. I think we will have to wait until we get down to the forest. Maybe we can shoot a rabbit down there." As they walked down the trail, suddenly, Mike took off to the right down the opposite way from where the trail led.

"Mike!" yelled Sarah. "Where are you going?"

"I'm going to get you something to eat," he replied.

"Not without me," she said as she followed him. She stepped down a few rocks and caught up to Mike at the bottom of a small cliff. There, in the shadow of the cliff, was what looked like a large brier plant. It was a mulberry bush. Mike was picking mulberries and putting them in the cup that held their canteen.

"You want food?" asked Mike. "Start picking and storing some for later in case we do not find anything for dinner." Sarah did not have to be told twice. She got her cup and would eat one and store one.

"Don't overeat," warned Mike. "We won't want a stomach ache this evening."

"How in the world did you find these berries? The bush was not in view from where we were."

"You have to have eagle eyes," said Mike teasing her.

"Aren't you the smart one," she answered. "Don't you ever give a straight answer to a question?"

"Sorry," said Mike. "Sometimes I can't help myself. I saw a flock of birds feeding on something, so I figured if whatever they were eating was good for them, it may be good for us."

"Please remind me never to question you again," said Sarah feeling dumb.

"Don't be silly," said Mike. "I was just fooling around with you. I do that when I find something that makes me happy. I was happy because I knew you were very hungry. The bad news is that the satisfaction from fruit or vegetation doesn't last very long. You will soon be very hungry again."

"That's why you want us to store some for later," said Sarah.

"That's right," he answered. "Now let's get moving. It is already past four."

"What do we do with this cup full of berries?" asked Sarah. "We can put the cup in the side pocket of our backpack, but will our canteen fit in the place for it without the cup it normally sits in?"

"It will sit in there kind of loose, but we can button the flap over it and it should stay okay."

They tried it, and it worked satisfactorily. They then went back to the trail and headed down to the forest below. They were about level with the treetops when Sarah noticed something in the open field near the other end of the valley.

"Look at that large field," said Sarah. "And look, what is that dust being raised at the left side of the field?"

Mike took out his binoculars and focused on the dusty area.

"It's a bunch of wild horses running east to what I believe is water," said Mike. "I also see a herd of deer going in the same direction." "Now you are making me hungry," said Sarah. "How I would like a venison steak."

"I could shoot one, but then wouldn't that be a waste of food," said Mike. "We couldn't eat a whole deer."

"Speak for yourself," said Sarah. "I would love to try, but I guess you are right," she said admitting that she was kidding. They continued walking down when Sarah suddenly stopped.

"What's up?" asked Mike wondering why she had stopped.

"A thought just came to me," she said. "You said that the animals were heading east. How did you know that they were heading east? We have been going around the mountain in circles as we come down. I have no idea in what direction we are headed."

"We are presently headed east also, as we climb down the mountain. When we cross the valley we will be going north. When we head up the mountain on the other side, we will again be heading east and turning north as we round over that steep gorge on the right side of the mountain."

"Is this one of those questions that you really will not answer?" asked Sarah.

"Not at all," said Mike. "See the bright spot in the sky? That's the sun. You can't really see it through the haze, but you can see where it is. I have been watching it travel as we come down the mountain. It is coming from the east and traveling to the west. As I watched it, I could see that it was a little south, which is where it travels during the later part of the year. That tells me where south is. From the trajectory of the sun, I can see that the mountains' range is east and west with a slight tilt to the north. Therefore, the left side is northwest and the right side is southeast. I would guess that the tilt is about thirty degrees."

"What surprises me is that I followed all that," said Sarah. However, her countenance was not able to hide the admiration she had for Mike.

They got to the bottom and started to cross the valley. The forest here was not as thick as the forest on the other side of the mountain. There were a lot of open areas as they crossed over to the other side. As they neared the foothills on the other side of the valley, Mike stopped.

"Sarah," he said, "give me the zoo gun."

She handed it to him without question. She had learned finally to trust that he had a good reason for everything he did. She only had to wait, and she would find out what it was.

Mike stooped down walking back toward the trees they had just left. He slowly fell down on his stomach. Sarah stooped down behind the high grass. She couldn't hear the zoo gun go off, but she knew it had because Mike suddenly got up and ran to the nearest tree. He stooped down on the ground. Sarah couldn't see what he was doing too well because of the high grass. She saw him however, with the saw on his Swiss knife cutting high branches off the nearest tree.

When he started walking toward her, she noticed that in his right hand he was carrying two branches that were cut like two wyes and one very straight branch. In his other hand, he was carrying a rabbit. He had cut off its head, gutted, and skinned it.

"I thought you were going to bring me a deer," said Sarah in jest. "Is that going to be enough for both of us?"

"I'll let you eat whatever you can, and I'll eat the left over if there is any," he said playing along.

"I'll tell you what," said Sarah. "If you will cook it, I'll share it with you." Then, getting serious she added, "I haven't the slightest idea of how to cook it out here."

"If you want to help," he said, "look around on the ground and gather all the dry branches you can find. The ones I cut are still very green and moist. They will not burn as fast as the dry ones."

He found a large rock and pounded the wye branches into the ground about two feet apart. He then skewed the straight branch through the length of the rabbit. Soon, there was a hot fire burning under the rabbit. Every so often, Mike turned the branch that the rabbit was on so that it would cook evenly on all sides.

They didn't say a word while they ate the rabbit. They finished by licking the bones.

"Where did you get the matches?" asked Sarah. "I was surprised to see you with matches. Didn't they get wet with all the rain we were in?"

"I had them in a little tin can," said Mike. "They stayed pretty dry." "You looked like you knew what you were doing," said Sarah in admiration. "Have you done this many times before?"

"As a matter of fact, I've never done it before," confessed Mike. "I did read up on it for one of my books. It worked great in my book." They both laughed. It was easy to laugh with their belly full. "By the way, do you want desert?"

"That's right," said Sarah. "We have the berries still in our canteen cup. Should we eat them or save them till later?"

"I don't know how good they will be later."

"I think we should save them. We don't need them now," said Sarah giving her opinion. "Whatever they are like later, they may be better than nothing."

"All right," said Mike "let's get moving. We don't want to be caught on this side of the mountain when it gets completely dark. I would like us to get to the other side before dark."

They started to walk up the side of the mountain. The path was pretty clear at the beginning, but as they moved farther up, it became harder to find.

About a half hour later, they found themselves at the base of the valley between the two peaks they were trying to cross. The trail seemed to go around to the west and then to the east up above the high cliffs that Mike and Sarah were facing.

"Can we stay down below the cliffs and cross there between the peaks?" asked Sarah.

"I don't know," said Mike. "The trail doesn't go that way. There must be a reason. Look at how the sides of each peak slope down toward each other. I suspect that there is a steep drop off, probably toward a river. I vote that we follow the trail."

"Whatever you say," agreed Sarah. "I've been lost since last week."

"That is a slight exaggeration," said Mike, "but I get what you mean." They back-tracked to where the trail led up the side of the mountain. As they climbed up, the trail became more difficult. It was soon obvious that the heavy rain had taken a toll on the trail. Every so often, they would run into a part of the trail that was washed away. There, they would have to cling to the rocks on the side of the mountain and search with their feet for a rock to step on to jump to a place on the trail that was good. This slowed them down considerably. Mike was concerned that what he had been afraid of was going to happen. He felt they were going to be stuck on the steep side of the mountain over night.

As they progressed, not only was time going by too fast, but the cloud was coming down to mar their vision too. They soon could hardly see their feet. They were running out of time. They came to a place where Sarah couldn't find a way to the step across a wash out.

"Mike, hold on to me," she said. "I can't find a footing."

Mike moved up close to her. He grabbed her backpack. As he moved toward her he stepped on a large rock that came loose and fell. They heard the rock roll down the side of the cliff, and then it became silent.

"Mike, did you hear the rock hit bottom?" she asked.

"No, I didn't," he answered. "I can't believe that it is that deep." "Why didn't we hear it hit the bottom?" asked Sarah in panic.

"I don't know," he said. "Let's move on. I want to get out of here. I'm sure that when we get away from this side, we will get back to the trail."

Mike held on to Sarah as she reached for footing. Finally, she was able to move to a wider section, and they began to move faster. It wasn't going to be that easy though. After a few minutes, they came to another part of the trail that had been washed out.

"Mike, hold me," she said as the rock she had put her weight on gave way and she started to slide down the cliff. Mike grabbed her hand as she slid.

"Give me your other hand," he requested. She reached out with her other hand, and Mike pulled her up to his level. She let go of one hand and slipped again, but was held up by Mike's hand. "Give me your other hand again," he asked. As Mike tried to grab her other hand, the rock he was standing on gave way. They both started to slide down. Sometime during their slide Sarah lost grip of Mike's hand. She was now in free fall.

"Mike!" she yelled out, but there was no response from Mike. As she was falling, she noticed a rock sticking out below her; but she was falling too hard to dodge it, and she hit the rock with her shoulder. She not only received a severe pain, but by hitting the rock, she was bounced away from the side of the mountain and was in free fall away from anything she could grab.

She yelled out the name of Jesus. She started to imagine the pain she would receive when she hits the ground.

Is it all going to end this way? she asked herself as she hurdled down to certain death. She started to think of how she had failed to help her country. Then suddenly, she found herself screaming. She was now waiting for the pain that was certain to come. It seemed like she was taking forever to hit the bottom. She decided that hitting headfirst would give her less pain. She remembered one very early morning when she got up to get ready for a trip. It was still dark out. She was taking off her pajama top when she tripped over her suitcase she had left on the floor. She tried to shield her fall with her hands but they were restricted by the half removed pajama top. She fell right on her face. The only thing she remembers is that she saw a light flash like the flash of a camera. There was no pain until she came to. Only this time she wasn't going to come to again.

She was falling feet first. She tried to turn around so that she would hit headfirst, but she was unable to turn. She had nothing to grab. She started pray, then she felt her feet hit something hard. The pain traveled up her whole body as she went deeper into whatever she had hit. It took a while for her to come to enough to realize that she had fallen into a river. She was underwater and couldn't breathe. She had taken in a mouth full of water. She struggled, trying to get to the surface. She was almost completely out of breath when she bobbed out of the water. The waterproof backpack helped her to the surface, but the river current was moving swiftly down through rapids and jagged rocks. She could hardly keep her head above water. If it wasn't for the buoyancy of the backpack, she would have drowned immediately. The backpack also provided a lifting force when she was on her back, but, due to the rapids, she had little control of her position. However, she managed to position herself in the center of the river so that when the river went through a narrow passage between two protruding rock formations, she passed through the rapids without being slammed against one of the rocks.

It seemed like hours that she struggled to stay alive. Several times she went through a rapid, was plunged deep into the river, and managed to come up for a breath of air. Her arms and legs were getting tired though; she couldn't keep this up to much longer. She was being tossed about like an apple.

She had other dangerous elements in the river that threatened her life. There were tree branches and limbs that were being washed down the river with her. Ahead of her, she saw that the river was turning to the right, and she was heading head first into a rock wall. With all of the strength she had left, she managed to turn around just in time to push herself off with her feet.

The impact was like jumping off of an eight-foot wall. The pain almost caused her to pass out. She floated for a few minutes with her head under water and lost all awareness of where she was. Fortunately, the river flowed down a small rapid, which turned her on her back so that her lungs automatically took a deep breath. She felt dizzy. She was on the verge of passing out. She didn't know what position she was in. Everything started to spin around. Her head went under water. The water in her face brought her around again.

Full of pain, Sarah realized that she was out of strength. She couldn't move her hands or feet. She had been in the water for several hours now. She accepted the fact she was going to die. She almost wished it; she couldn't take any more. The flow of the river slowed down. Sarah just floated on her back. She was alive only because the river flow and her backpack kept her head above water.

She became aware that she was on the other side of the mountain. She saw trees on both sides of her. She saw the branch of a tree sticking out into the water. She attempted to grab it, but she couldn't get her hand out. She had floated for about a half hour more when the river took a sharp turn to the right. Sarah was swept onto the shore with several branches. The rest had given her enough strength that she was able to manage to crawl up the bank onto an open spot away from the water. The sand felt so warm against her soaking wet body. She placed her cheeks on the warm earth and passed out.

It was several hours later that Sarah became conscious. She looked around at the forest in front of her. The sky was bright and the sun was high in the sky. She just lay there for a while. She didn't have enough energy to think. She was surprised when she noticed that her clothes were almost dry. She looked at her watch. It was still working. It was almost eight.

"Dear Lord," she said out loud. "It was about six or seven when I fell in the river yesterday. I've been in the river all night."

She sat up and realized that she had to start thinking for herself. She had depended on Mike so much.

"Mike where are you?"

She fought thinking of all the possibilities, but couldn't help it. She started to consider all the possibilities. He could still be up in the mountain trying to come down, or he could have fallen into the water as she did and, being a stronger male, swam ashore closer to the mountain and could now be on his way to her. It's not very likely that he stayed up on the mountain. She remembered that he slid down with her. If he had made his way to the shore, he would have caught up to her by now. The most likely possibility was that Mike was dead. It was a miracle that she was alive. Could Mike have been as fortunate?

We are all in God's hands, she told herself.

She began visualizing Mike's body washing up on a shore someplace. She could possibly find his body down river somewhere. She started to think about what she had to do when tears started to run down her face. She had to stop thinking of Mike. She will pray that he is all right, but for now, she had to think about what she should do.

She started to walk away from the mountains. She never wanted to go back there. As she walked she found that her mind went back to Mike. Tears started to run down her cheeks. She wished she had the cell phone. She remembered that Mike had it last. No matter, if she had it with her, it would have probably been destroyed by the hours in the water.

The trees in this area were not as thick as the forest on the other side of the mountains, but the wild growth was just as severe. She struggled to get through the growth until she found a trail. It was also full of wild growth, but not as thick. The bad thing was that it led away from the river. She followed it, keeping an eye on the river that seemed to move farther from her with every step.

A couple of hours later, she reached a point where large rock formations started to appear. She found that climbing the rocks was better than fighting the brush. It also brought her back toward the river. She climbed up the higher rocks so she could look farther down the river, but the growth and trees were too high. As she proceeded, she found that the land sloped gently downhill. The trees became less dense as she progressed down the river. The rock formations were found less often, but when she did come across one, it was much larger.

Later that morning, Sarah started to get hungry. She had only eaten berries since noon the day before. She was also getting very tired. The pain all over her body, especially the pain in her knees, wasn't helping very much. She took out her pistol with the intent of perhaps shooting a rabbit. She hadn't seen anything but birds, but a large bird would do in a pinch. She slowly, and as quietly as she could, bent down low. She searched the ground around the trees for rabbit tracks. She had seen what Mike had done earlier, and she was sure she could repeat the task. As she walked, she came to a large rock that extended over the river.

I can see a ways down the river from there, she thought as she climbed up to the top.

She also decided to rest up there since she didn't think she had the energy to climb both up and down the rock. When she got to the top, she wandered to the very edge by the river. As she looked down the river, her heart stopped.

Down the river, about a mile or so, she saw smoke rising from the side of the river. The river had taken a sharp turn and left a wash on the left like the one that had landed her on shore. The muscles of her stomach tightened up. A wave of great joy filled her soul.

Was there someone out there? she asked herself. *Am I saved? Maybe he can help me find Mike.*

She began hoping that things were finally going her way. Her body was revived with new strength. She almost slid down the rock and started running through the thicket unconcerned if the branches and over growth hit her in the face or tore at her clothes, but she began to worry that whoever started the fire was long gone. Then she remembered that a good hunter would never leave a fire unattended.

As she got closer, she noticed that there was a person next to the fire. He or she was holding something over the fire. She wondered whether it was an Indian or not when she noticed that he didn't have much clothes on.

Soon, she was at the edge of the forest. The tall grass was much easier to run in. Sarah wondered where she had gotten the energy to continue running. As she got closer to the fire, she noticed it was a man who, upon hearing the rustle of the grass, turned, took out his pistol, and pointed it at Sarah. Sarah's heart almost jumped out of her body. The joy she felt now, she had never felt before in her life. It was Mike.

"Mike!" she yelled out. "Oh, Mike," she repeated and fell on top of him. They both fell over onto the sand. She started to kiss him all over his face, first his eyes, then his cheeks, then his nose, and finally his lips. Mike was the first one to speak when her lips moved from his lips.

"I thought I had lost you," he said with large tears in his eyes. "I thought I had lost you." She didn't bother to answer him; she just kept on kissing him, now on his neck and then on his chest. After she was completely exhausted, Mike was able to turn her around so that he was on top.

"How did you get here?" she asked.

"Where did you come from?" he asked feeling foolish asking it. "I have been waiting for you. See I have lunch ready for you." "Where did you get lunch from?" she asked.

"From the river," said Mike. "Let's eat and then we can talk."

"Who wants to eat or talk?" she asked as she kissed him again this time hard on his lips. He returned the passion, but soon broke it off. Getting up, he turned to the fire.

"We'd better eat first. We don't want our lunch to burn."

The lunch was on a thin, flat slab of rock that looked like a large piece of slate. On each side of the fire were two large rocks about a foot high. The flat rock was resting on these rocks which set it about a foot above the fire. Mike had a roaring fire under it. It looked very hot. On top of the flat rock were two halves of a large fish. He moved half of the fish off the rock using a long branch in which he had whittled away the bark onto a smaller flat rock. He handed this to Sarah and slid the other half onto another small flat rock for himself.

"Were did you get the fish?" asked Sarah. "This wasn't another dead fish you found by the side of the river is it?"

"No of course not," answered Mike starting to laugh at the idea. "Remember when I took the hook from the fish on the other side of the mountain? Well its string, on a thin branch, makes a great fishing pole. Look out there," he said pointing to the edge of the river where a branch was sticking out of the ground. Suddenly, the stick started shaking furiously. "Look, I think we have another one. We are going to have a full lunch after all." He got up and pulled in another fish. He quickly took out his knife and soon had two other halves on the make shift grill.

"You had better eat the fish on your plate before it gets cold," said Sarah as she started to eat her fish using a knife and fork.

"Where did you get a fork and knife?" asked Mike amazed at what he saw.

"Haven't you looked behind your canteen holder? There are three little pockets that hold a knife, a spoon, and a fork. Just flip up the flap that covers them."

"I didn't know we had them there," he said finding them in his backpack. "Why didn't you tell me when we were eating the rabbit? Come to think of it, why didn't you use them then?"

"We didn't need them then," she answered. "We ate the rabbits like they were chicken legs remember?"

"It doesn't matter," he concluded. "Now tell me, what happened to you after you fell off the mountain?"

"I fell into the river," she said. "I'm surprised that I'm still alive. I struggled against the rapids all night. I was washed up on a small inlet where the river turned sharply to the right, just like you have here. This inlet is different because it was caused by the river being diverted by that big rock sticking out into the river. The results, however, are the same. I crawled on land and passed out. I woke up about eight this morning. I remembered someone once said, 'If you are lost in the forest, find a river and follow it.' I followed it until these rock formations started to show up. I climbed up one and saw the smoke from your fire. You know the rest. How about you? How did you get here?"

"When I was trying to bring you up and keep you from falling, I stepped on a rock to get a solid footing. It gave way, and I came falling after you. While falling, I saw the rock that you hit. I turned around and pushed myself away from the rock with my feet. That took me way out into the middle of the river. That's probably why I was carried farther down the river then you were."

"Why did you want to push yourself away from the wall?" Sarah asked. "I would think that you would want to stay close for the possible chance of grabbing on to something."

"I knew the river was down there," he said. "I wanted to get as far out as I could. I was worried that if I didn't go far enough, I could fall on the edge of the river that could have been too shallow or even dry. That's what I was afraid had happened to you. I was worried that your body would soon wash up here. Apparently, hitting the rock shoved you far enough away from the edge for you to survive."

"Well let's eat the fish," said Sarah changing the subject. "I think it is done."

They ate the fish and rested on the sand a while. Sarah noticed that the rock that was diverting the river was very large and very flat on top. She looked down at her clothes, and they were very dirty and still very moist. She got up and checked her backpack. It was so muddy you couldn't tell what color it was. She empted it of everything and carried her spare clothes, her blanket, and the backpack to the edge of the water. She grabbed the soap she had in her backpack and started to wash the bag inside and out. She also washed her blanket. After rinsing them, she carried them to the top of the big rock where the sun was beating down on it. It was very warm, especially on top the rock. After setting the backpack as far up the rock nearest to the edge by the river as she could, she laid the blanket at the other end of the rock away from the river. She then returned to the edge of the river.

"What are you doing?" asked Mike, watching her as he sat near the fire. "I thought you wanted to rest a while."

"I will," she answered, "after I clean up a few things. Listen Mike, I am very exhausted, and every muscle in my body aches. Let's stay here tonight. I need a good night's rest and a chance for my body to heal, or do you think the terrorists are still after us?

"Okay," he said. "I guess one day may not matter. As for the terrorists, they won't matter either. I forgot to tell you. I did contact the general. He got our message and sent a couple of jets out on Highway 91. He saw the four cars but didn't know it was the terrorists until they started to shoot rockets at him. The jets shot back and destroyed all four cars and their occupants. The second jet saw the off road buggy returning to the highway, and destroyed it also. So, none of those fellows will be chasing anybody."

"That's great," said Sarah as she walked to the water's edge carrying her alternate set of clothes. She washed them and set them out on the rock to dry. When they had dried, she changed clothes behind a rock and washed the rest of her clothes. She then returned to the top of the rock and set them down in the sun. She also laid herself down in the sun. Mike decided that it was a smart thing to do, so he washed all his clothes the same way.

"Do you expect to spend the night up here?" asked Mike. "I don't think it is safe out in the open like this."

"Can you build a lean-to like you did before?" she asked.

"Understand that I too had to swim all night and am just as pooped as you are. Besides, it will be harder to find the logs here, even if I could drag them to the side of this rock."

"I'm sorry," said Sarah. "That was so thoughtless of me. Of course, you must be as sore as I am. What do you recommend?"

"There is a slight stone overhang near the water. I think we can lay our blankets there and be safe at least on the one side. I can build a fire for protection from the front. Keep your gun near you while I look around to see what I can find.

Mike left and wandered into the woods. Sarah fell asleep. When she awoke she climbed down to where Mike was working.

"What are you doing?" she asked. "Where did you get those leafy branches?" She noticed that Mike had built a lean-to with small branches.

"They're not as good as the logs," Mike answered, "but I don't think it will rain overnight. They will hide us from predators."

"What predators?" asked Sarah quickly, with alarm in her voice. "There are mountain lions in this part of the country," said Mike.

"We didn't see any up in the mountains," said Sarah. "Shouldn't we have seen them up there?"

"There is little food up in the mountains. They may live up there. I don't know very much about mountain lions, but I think they would come down to the forest to catch their food."

"What would they eat down here?" she asked.

"Well, I would guess that deer would be their preferred food," said Mike. "That is just a guess. As I said, I don't know much about this kind of thing. I would also guess that rabbits, squirrels, and that sort would be fair hunting for them."

"It's about six, and I'm getting hungry," said Sarah. She didn't want to hear any more about forest animals.

"I've got the fishing line in the water," said Mike. "I've not had time to hunt rabbit."

"That's okay," said Sarah facetiously. "I love fish"

"I'm sure you do," said Mike with an understanding smile. As he was pulling in the fish, Sarah started to think of where they were going from there.

"Did the general say anything about trying to find us?" she asked. "I'm sorry," said Mike. "In the joy of finding you alive and all that has happened I forgot to tell you. The general knows about where we are. He suggested that we follow the river north. It will lead us to Route 10. He will have someone there to meet us."

"You'll never guess how much better that makes me feel," said Sarah. "I had almost given up hope of ever being rescued."

Mike cleaned the fish and soon had a roaring fire burning under the flat rock. After they ate, they sat on the high point of the rock and watched the sun go down, though, couldn't see much of the sunset because of the trees west of their position. Mike put his arm around Sarah and squeezed her tight.

"Never thought that I would be able to put my arms around you," said Mike getting romantic. "I missed you so much. I miss the times we had at the farmhouse."

"I know," said Sarah. "That was a very good time."

"Can't we pretend that we are sitting on the back porch of the farm house?" he asked. Sarah looked at him.

"Are you getting romantic on me?" she asked.

"Is there anything wrong with that?" asked Mike. "Are you no longer able to feel romantic?"

"As a matter of fact, that is the problem," said Sarah. "I am feeling too romantic. I don't want us to get into trouble out here where we need God more than ever."

"Don't you trust me?" asked Mike. "I promised you back at the farmhouse, and I will again now: I promise that I will never do anything to dishonor you."

"You don't understand," she said. "It's not you that I don't trust. It's me that I don't trust."

"Well, let yourself go because I am much stronger than you. I have a very strong will. I will never let you dishonor yourself. I love you and God too much." Sarah tilted her head toward Mike so that their lips were about a half-inch apart.

"Oh Mike," she whispered. "My heart is still hurting from the thought that I had lost you."

Mike didn't let her finish whatever thought she had. Her lips were too close. Their lips touched. Mike wrapped his arms around her. back. She felt so good in his arms. He felt his will weakening.

He wanted her so badly, especially when she opened her mouth and played with his tongue. His hands touched her bra. It would have been so easy to unhook it. Then he remembered his promise. Her kisses made it even harder. She had completely accepted his promise and let herself go. She rubbed her body against his, back and forth until her excitement began to show in her kisses. Mike felt his excitement beginning to get out of control. He knew they had to stop. He pulled away from her lips and kissed her on the cheek and then on the neck. He pulled her head tight against his chest.

"Sarah, I love you so much," he said, feeling that it would let her know why he stopped kissing her.

"Did I get too passionate?" she asked.

"You can never get too passionate," said Mike. "You're lucky that I made that promise to you."

"You're a man of your word," she said. "You were right. I never would have been able to stop. Let's just sit here in each other's arms. It's starting to get chilly. Your arms and body will keep me warm."

They sat there on the end of the rock in one another's arms, feeling warmth in their hearts. Every once in a while, Mike would rub his hands up and down her back. She would occasionally do the same to Mike. They marveled at the comfort it gave them. When it became almost completely dark, they grabbed Sarah's blanket and went down to the lean-to. Mike had already spread his blanket on the ground next to the rock. Sarah made herself comfortable on Mike's blanket. Mike started a fire on the west side of the lean-to and then joined Sarah who covered them both with her blanket. They fell asleep in one another's arms.

The early morning light shining on Sarah's face caused her to wake. She noticed that Mike was not beside her, but she could see through the branches that someone was moving around outside. The embers, just west of the lean-to, were still smoldering from the night's fire. Sarah got up and started to walk to the river to wash her hands and face. As she walked by Mike, she stopped and smiled at him.

"Good morning Mike," she said as she continued down to the river. "What are you up to this early in the morning?"

"I want to get an early start," he said. "I have started a fire in our homemade grill and am fishing for a fish for breakfast."

After eating, they got dressed and packed their backpacks.

"This has been like a vacation from misery," said Sarah. "I wonder if it's going to get better or worse."

"How do you feel?" asked Mike, worried of her physical condition. "I'm a little stiff but the pain is much less."

"I'm all right," said Sarah. "How far would you guess it is from here to Route 10?"

"I told the general that we were just over the mountain," explained Mike. "He said that we were between ten to twenty miles from the highway. Let's take the average, say fifteen miles. If we make about two miles an hour, it will take approximately seven hours. It is now eight, so we should be over halfway by noon. Let's give ourselves a couple of hours to rest and eat. We should resume our travel by two. If my calculations are correct, we should get there three hours later, say about five o'clock."

"That sounds so good," said Sarah. "Let's get going."

"That is good news, and, at least to me, it is also bad news," said Mike sadly.

"Why is that?" asked Sarah. "Are you worried about the task before you?"

"No, not that at all," said Mike. "Don't you realize that we will be parted for what could be a long time?"

"Gosh, I hadn't thought of that," said Sarah. "I'm beginning to miss you already. I'll never forget you. Do you think that after a while you will forget me?"

"I will never forget you or stop loving you, even if you found your first love, Tom, and married him. I'd still love you like my baby sister." "That doesn't seem likely," said Sarah sadly. "Tom probably doesn't even remember me. How about you and Tara, what would happen if you came across her?"

"Tara was an engineer for her father in the center of Chicago. There is zero chance that she is still alive, but your point is well taken. Also, as much as I love you, I could never forget Annie."

They walked around the rock they had spent the evening on and continued north along the river. The land around the river was clear of a lot of growth and trees. To the west was a plain of high grass that varied from about two feet to as much as four feet high. Beyond the grass, about 100 feet, was a forest. It was as overgrown as the forest they first ran into by Route 91.

"Isn't this unusual," said Sarah after they had traveled a couple of hours. "Why is the land around the river clear? Shouldn't there be more trees and brush near the water?"

"Normally that is true," said Mike. "I don't know the answer. My guess would be that when it rains hard up in the mountains, the river overflows and covers the land around the sides of the river. The grass and other plants need air to survive. Notice that there are some trees that are at the edge of the river in some places. That is probably where the river doesn't swamp the land as bad."

They did, eventually, come to higher ground where the trees and shrubs made it tough for them to walk next to the river. They had to walk through the woods, keeping an eye on the river. It would have been so easy to get turned around in the forest.

It was around noon when they came to a fairly flat, dry area next to the river. It had short grass that covered the area about twenty feet from the river. West of them was about fifty feet of very tall grass. Beyond the grass was the usual forest full of trees and shrubs.

"I'm going to find you something different to eat," said Mike. He disappeared into the woods.

When Sarah saw him he was carrying two wye sticks, a long straight stick, and the dressed rabbit.

Mike placed the rabbit on the stick and started to gather dry leaves and short, small branches for the fire. He was starting to light the leaves when Sarah tapped him on the shoulder.

"What?" asked Mike.

"Look at the tall grass between us and the woods," she said being as still and quiet as she could. "I see something moving in the grass. Right across from us."

"Look closely," said Sarah. "Notice how once in a while the valley or hole in the grass is moving toward us?"

They sat there waiting for the event, whatever it was, to happen. They watched the hole in the grass slowly move toward them. Sarah stiffened in expectation of certain terror. She clenched her teeth. They both slowly lifted up their gun when the hole came close to the edge of the grass. It seemed like they were frozen there forever holding their breath. A chill ran down Sarah's back as if she knew the attack was to occur at that moment. Mike, who was calmer and had more faith in their ability to survive an attack, was completely taken by surprise by the speed at which the attack occurred.

It was a mountain lion. Sarah got out several shots, but due to the speed of the attack, they had no effect. The animal was in the air above Mike before he could aim and fire. The bullet entered the lion's mouth and settled in its brain. Mike rolled over onto his side, just missing the falling lion. It fell next to Mike, kicked a few seconds, and then went still. Sarah jumped into Mike's arms, crying from the release of tension.

"Let's quickly pack and get out of here," said Mike.

They waited for about an hour, and then, deciding that there was no mate, they packed up and started walking north following the river. Both kept looking back, behind them to make sure they were not being followed. Whenever they reached slightly higher ground, Mike would check the area ahead of them using his binoculars.

"Did you see anything?" Sarah would always ask.

It was on one of these occasions that Mike saw what looked like a bridge over the river.

"Before you ask me," said Mike, "let me tell you what I think I see. It is still pretty far away, but I think I see a bridge up ahead. I think it could only be the bridge on Route 10."

"Could it really be?" asked Sarah. "Could this terror-driven experience be over?"

"Let's move west," said Mike. "From here, the bridge looks pretty high. Notice that the land west of us is slightly sloping uphill? We have to be west of the bridge and on higher ground to get on it."

They started moving faster than they had been. They suddenly obtained energy they didn't know they had. They both wanted this nightmare to be over.

CHAPTER TEN

Back in Action

IT WAS AROUND FOUR WHEN they started climbing uphill with the bridge and several army trucks within their sight. A few minutes later, they were greeted by the soldiers on the bridge. As they stepped onto the pavement, a sergeant stepped up to Mike and saluted him.

"Sergeant Maxwell, sir," he said.

"At ease soldier," responded Mike. "Are you to escort us to Spokane?"

"No sir," said the sergeant. "The General has requested that we protect your position here and said that he will send a helicopter to pick you up. We have already notified him of your arrival, and a copter is on its way."

"Thank you, Sergeant," said Mike.

"Also, Colonel Mills, Spokane no longer exists," continued the sergeant. "We moved just in time. The General felt that, since radio and television gave away our position, the terrorists with backpack devices might come looking for us."

"That was pretty smart," said Mike. "The general is one in a million."

"Yes he is, sir," said the sergeant. The sergeant then turned to Sarah. "How are you, Doctor Anders? I hope you are well."

"Thank you, Sergeant. I'm as well as can be under the circumstances." As they talked, Mike could hear the sound of the helicopter above them. It landed on the highway and the sergeant led them to it.

"We will see you at the base, Sergeant Maxwell," said Mike. "Thank you."

"Your welcome, sir," said the sergeant. "Have a safe flight." The helicopter took off and was in the air flying west in seconds.

"I'm Captain Comins, sir," said the pilot. "Sorry to rush off without ceremony, but the general said that a small well armed force was moving north looking for you two. He said that I should get you to the base as soon as possible."

"Ceremony," said Mike. "I don't need any ceremony. I do need to get to the base as soon as possible, and Doctor Anders needs to get to the secret base as soon as possible. Ceremony is the last thing we need."

"By the way, sir," added the pilot. "The duffel bag just behind you has your fatigues and dress uniform in it. You may want to change as soon as we get to the base."

"Thank you, Captain," said Mike. "How long will it take to get us to the base?"

"I'm not sure, sir," said the pilot, "I would guess it will take about four to five hours depending on the prevailing wind. I don't know because I have never made the trip before. I come from the secret base."

"How far are we going?" asked Mike. "Can you tell us where we are going?"

"Yes sir," said the pilot. "We are going to northern California. That's where Lieutenant Furgason will be waiting for you." Sarah noticed that the pilot was constantly on the radio speaking with someone.

"Who is he in contact with constantly?" she asked Mike. "It can't be the Spokane tower."

"I have no idea," said Mike. "Perhaps he's in constant contact with the secret base." The helicopter varied dramatically every once in awhile from a straight path. It caused either Mike or Sarah to be suddenly thrown around against the side of the aircraft or one another.

"I'm sorry about that," is all the pilot would say. After a few sharp turns Mike became impatient.

"What is going on?" he asked the pilot. "Why are you performing these severe maneuvers?"

"Sorry about that, sir," he said. "I am aware that you and the doctor are the most wanted people in the country. You two are considered most valuable to us, and as the general made clear, probably the only chance we have of wining this war. The enemy also knows this, and would do anything to stop you. Therefore, I have to take every evasive action that I need to take. I love my country. I appreciate what you can do for it."

"I don't understand," said Mike. "We haven't been under attack have we?"

"No sir," he said, "but whenever I see a puff of smoke or anything on the ground that's suspicious, I take evasive action. I can't wait until a missile is in the air."

"Carry on," said Mike.

It was about an hour later when the pilot took a very sharp maneuver to the left. It caused Sarah to be thrown on Mike's lap. The helicopter then took a sharp dive toward the ground. At the last minute, it leveled off as Mike noticed some kind of missile whiz past them. The pilot was yelling on the phone, asking for help and giving his position. The pilot made a few more severe maneuvers and, again, just escaped being hit with a missile. Next, he took a sharp turn to the left trying to get out of sight of the vehicle that was shooting missiles at them. He was flying low and zigzagging to give the shooter an unsteady target. Suddenly, the helicopter turned on its side and dropped like a sack of potatoes. Sarah screamed and grabbed Mike.

"Have we been hit?" she asked.

"Not yet," said Mike, trying to hide the fear that he also felt. The helicopter straightened up just in time to miss the treetops.

"Everyone okay?" asked the pilot. He maneuvered the helicopter back into the air where it seemed to continue on to its destination.

"Thank God," said the pilot. "The fighters are here."

Mike and Sarah looked back. They were still close enough to the ground to see two fighters blast the ground vehicles out of existence.

"Thanks, fellows," Mike heard the pilot say over his radio.

"How in the world did they get here so fast?" Mike asked the pilot. "They have been around us since we took off," said the pilot. "I've been talking to them. I knew they were close. The general wasn't going to take any chances. They will fly a few minutes behind us until we get to the base."

"How will they be able to fly this slowly?" asked Sarah

"They will be flying in circles back out of sight. Their goal is twofold. First, it is their job to protect us. Secondly, by staying out of sight behind us, they let the enemy feel free to attack so that our fighters can eliminate them at the same time. The general believes that these are the terrorists that carried the backpack devices that destroyed our cities and military bases, and that they are now heading to join the main body of the attackers."

"How can they keep flying that long?" asked Mike.

"Oh, they don't fly behind us on the complete trip," said the pilot. "They are replaced when they get low on fuel. They go back to refuel and another two take their place. They will do that until we get to our destination."

"I see that they trust you to protect us until they can catch up," said Mike, impressed with their plan.

"I've been flying helicopters since I was sixteen. My father ran a small airport in Virginia."

"Are there many terrorists that are headed to join the main invading army?" asked Sarah.

"The general says that, watching via satellite, they see hundreds of them join every day."

"Good," said Mike. "We can get rid of them all at once." "I like the way you think, Colonel," said the pilot.

No one spoke for the next couple of hours, nor did they encounter any other problems along the way. Finally, they came within sight of the camp.

"We are almost there," said the pilot.

"Yes," said Mike, "I can see the camp site. They look like they are ready to travel."

"You'll know what is going on as soon as you see the commanding officer," said the pilot. "I'm not sure who is in charge at present." A few minutes later, they landed near what looked like the command center. They were met by a lieutenant when Mike and Sarah stepped onto the ground.

"I'm First Lieutenant Jeffery Furgason," he said. "I'm so glad to see you Colonel Mills. If you will follow me, I will take you to your quarters where you can change. I presume that you are also very hungry. Afterwards, I'll take you to the command center and bring you up to date."

"Just give me a few minutes to say good-bye to Doctor Anders," requested Mike.

"Of course, sir," said the lieutenant. He then walked a few paces away to give him privacy. Mike turned to Sarah.

"I miss you already," he said as he embraced her. "Take care of yourself."

"I'll miss you terribly," she answered. "I don't know what I will do without you. I've depended on you so much."

"You are a very strong, intelligent woman who can be very gentle and sweet when you want to be." He said, pulling back to look into her eyes. "On top of that, you are very beautiful. You will do fine." Their lips met and turned into a very passionate farewell kiss. When their lips parted, Sarah looked like she was going to say good-bye. "Don't say good-bye, ever," Mike added and kissed her one last time. "Here, better take your cell phone. I'll not need it here."

She took the phone, turned, and started up to the helicopter. When she got there she turned back and yelled back.

"You take care of yourself," she said over the noise of the helicopter engine. "Be safe and come back to me."

Mike waved as she fastened her seat belt and as the craft started to lift into the air.

"Call me when you get to the secret base!" he yelled back. He wasn't sure she heard him. He watched as the helicopter flew out of sight. He felt like his heart went with her. He turned to the lieutenant.

"Do you want to freshen up first?" asked the lieutenant.

"No, I'm too concerned about what is going on and where the enemy is at present. Let's go to the command center."

"As you wish, sir," responded the lieutenant.

When they got to the command center, Lieutenant Furgason unfolded a large map of the area.

"We are right here," he said pointing to a spot on the map. "Sir, I didn't know when you were going to get here, or if you would even make it before it was too late. Since you had explained your plan in great detail, and I understood what you wanted, I was sure that I could get things going until you arrived. I hope I haven't stepped out of bounds."

"Let me know what you have done so far," said Mike, not wanting to commit himself to an answer until he knew what the lieutenant had accomplished.

"First, I assembled all of my officers, and we went through the map trying to find a good place for the trap. We all agreed that this area here was the best place." He pointed to the area in the Trinity Mountains he was describing. "The valley here is very narrow, and the two mountains on each side are very steep and pretty clear of shrubs and trees. It is at the very northern end of the Sacramento River valley. That's the area the invading army is coming up. Route 5 goes through the valley just east of the one I'm recommending and is a better pass through the mountains. So, I had General McGard nuke a big hole in the pass and bomb the area so the mountain has blocked the pass. So even if they can climb in and out of that big hole, they would have to climb over the rocks blocking the pass too.

"Seems like you have everything under control," said Mike, astonished at the job that the lieutenant had done so far. "What have you done about the equipment that I asked you to find, and what I wanted you to do with it?"

"I found twenty-five mining machines, but I could only find twenty men that knew how to run them. So I sent ten to the west side of the mountain and ten to the east side of the mountain and instructed them on what you wanted. They are almost finished as we speak. I have also sent eight hundred men to the west mountaintop and eight hundred men to the eastern slope and have ordered them to dig in so they are not visible. They have hidden mortar and missile power to rain down on any one in the valley below."

"You have done a fantastic job," said Mike. "I commend you on your efforts. Now, what I need is a secure cell phone."

"I have one the general sent for you," said the lieutenant. "It has every officer individually set in and a conference button that will address us all at once."

"Can you get me a commercial one just like this?" asked Mike. "I want one that the invaders can surely read so we can lie to them about our action."

"Great idea," said Lieutenant Furgason. "I'll have one made up for you."

"Now, tell me about your officers," said Mike. "Where are they?" "Right, sir," he answered. "I have divided the men into four groups.

I am in command of the group here, at the north end of the valley. I have sent a mobile hit-and-run group that is located at the south end of the valley. That group is commanded by Second Lieutenant Richard Selontti. The eight hundred men on the western mountain are commanded by Second Lieutenant Brandon Brice. The eight hundred men on the eastern mountain are led by Second Lieutenant Sam Sorenson."

"Looks like you have everything in place," said Mike. "You don't really need me."

"Thank you, sir," said the lieutenant. "I'm very glad you are here."

"If you will show me my quarters, I'll change and be ready to travel in a few minutes. I want to be on the top of the east mountain at the southern end so that, with my powerful binoculars, I can see and direct the action."

"You're not going to stay here, sir?" the Lieutenant said, surprised at the colonel's request.

"No, you can handle everything here. I need to be where I can see the battle take place."

"We will make arrangements for you to travel."

"When can you take me up on the mountain where I need to go?"

asked Mike.

"You will have to climb up the northern end of the mountain. The eastern end is too steep," he answered. "It will be too dark to go tonight. You will never be able to climb the mountainside in the dark. It is too steep even on the northern side. I'll see that you get there at first light in the morning."

Mike ate and went to bed. The canvas bunk was like a feather bed in comparison with where he had been sleeping.

"Good morning, Colonel," said the lieutenant the next morning. "Are you ready to travel?"

"Good morning," said Mike. "I just have to get my backpack." When Mike returned, the lieutenant introduced him to his companion. "Colonel Mills," he said. "This is Sergeant Bruce Bane. He will take you up the mountain to Lieutenant Sam Sorensen. It is a rugged climb so be prepared."

"I just came from climbing over a set of mountains," said Mike with a smile. "I'm prepared."

"Sergeant Bane and his squad are our supply line," continued Lieutenant Furgason. "They make the trip nearly every day. They are pretty well supplied up there now except for today's lunch and dinner.

"Thank you, Lieutenant," said Mike.

"Sir, here are the phones you requested. They are all programmed as I informed you last night. I made sure all the leaders have one of each phone."

"Very good," said Mike.

"I think we'd better be on our way," said the sergeant. "We will go by Jeep until we get to the place we found that is easiest to climb."

"Lead on," said Mike as he got into the Jeep.

They drove for about twenty minutes down the center of the valley between the two mountains. There were three Jeeps in the group required to carry the supplies to the troops. Mike was impressed at the choice Lieutenant Furgason had made for the trap. The mountains were very steep and very close together. That would require an advancing army to travel in a long narrow column. That also made fighting more difficult. When they got to the point about one-third down the valley, they stopped and unpacked. Sergeant Bane led the way with Mike following. The others, hauling the supplies in backpacks, followed behind. It was a rough climb that reminded Mike of the climb he and Sarah had to do the last few days.

It took about fifteen minutes to get to the top. At the top, he was met by Lieutenant Sorensen.

"Glad to have you here, sir," he said. "We all feel a lot better with you here. The men have been asking me about you."

"Nice to meet you, Lieutenant," said Mike. "I hope that I can live up to your expectations."

"I understand that you wish to set up at the south end of the mountain top."

"That's right," said Mike. "I want to be able to have the trailing units in my sight. It is always the commanding officer's position. I want to be able to observe their every move."

"If you will follow me, I will take you to that area. I see that you have a very powerful pair of binoculars around your neck. I'm sure with those you can keep good track of them." "I sure hope so," said Mike.

When they got to the other end, the mountain started to slope down rapidly. Mike stopped by a large rock that blocked their way.

"I think that here, north of this rock, will be a good place for me to set up. I can see the bottom clearly, and I will be hidden from anyone approaching from the south. Yes, this is the place. Can you get one of your men to dig down a little so I can lay prone here, observing everything that goes on below?"

"Yes sir," said the lieutenant. He quickly got one of his men to dig down by the rock so Mike could settle there for the duration of the mission.

A few minutes later, Mike was sitting in his trench, happy with his position. He pulled out his secure phone and hit the button that called all the troop leaders. He introduced himself and explained his plan. He explained the reason for the commercial phone. He outlined the plan to use the commercial phone to provide false information to the enemy. He informed them that he would direct them individually on the secure phone in to what to say as occasions arose. Then he discussed a few code words that he would use on the commercial phone to mislead the enemy, commands that he will give that require the troop leaders to do the exact opposite. He would explain every command on the secure phone before speaking on the commercial phone whenever there is time. Two commands, however, would have no warnings. They must do the opposite if given these commands on the commercial phone. Mike then relaxed into his observation position and waited for the enemy to walk into his trap.

Sarah had arrived at the secret base the day before and was met by a soldier who introduced himself as Sergeant McLeary. He showed her to her quarters and explained that the general was busy and would see her in the morning. In the morning, after dressing, she started to leave her quarters to find the cafeteria when she saw Sergeant McLeary waiting for her.

"Have you been waiting here very long?" asked Sarah, surprised to see him.

"No, Doctor Anders," he said. "The general sent me to get you, and I was ready to knock when I heard activity inside your quarters. I thought I would wait until you came out so as not to rush you."

"Thank you, Sergeant," said Sarah. "I'm not in the military, so you can call me Sarah."

"I'm not sure that the general would like that," said the sergeant. "Then just call me Doctor when he is around," she answered. "Do you wish to have breakfast first?" he asked.

"Should we make the general wait?" she asked.

"The general said that I should ask you if you wanted breakfast first and take you to the cafeteria if you did."

"Then let's go get something to eat. I didn't have supper last night," said Sarah, suddenly feeling hunger pangs.

The sergeant took her to the cafeteria. "Will you join me?" she asked.

"I've eaten already," said the sergeant. "I'll come back for you in a half hour." After saying that, the sergeant left. After breakfast the sergeant took Sarah to the general's office.

"Welcome, Doctor Anders," said the general as he got up from his desk and put out his hand. "It's so nice to finally meet you. I've been looking forward to this for months." Sarah accepted his hand.

"It's nice to meet you too, General McGard. I thought we would never get here."

"Yes, you two had quite an exciting trip," said the general. "When we have a little time, I would like to hear all about it. However, right now we have a very urgent mission." He then turned to Sergeant McLeary. "Sergeant," he instructed, "I would like you to monitor the army position using the satellite observation camera station. Go to the station, and I'll be there after I get Doctor Anders started with her training class."

"General," said Sarah. "The training will be different for the bombardiers and the weapons crew than it will be for the pilots. The pilots don't need the technical information the weapons people do. The pilots need to know how high they'll need to be and how to fly out of the area of danger they created."

"That's perfect," said the general, "because some of the pilots aren't here yet. I'll assemble the others after I take you to the class room."

"General, I would like to inform Colonel Mills that I arrived here safely. I promised to inform him."

"I need to talk with him too," said the general. "After I get you started, I'll tell him of my plans.

"Are your plans a secret?" asked Sarah, wanting to know what was in store for them.

"Nothing here will be held from you, Doctor. After you train the men, we are going on a very dangerous retaliatory mission. Not retaliatory in the sense of getting even but in the sense of preventing them to build weapons to use against us in our weakened condition." "What is happening in the Middle East?" asked Sarah, taking advantage of the general's informative mood.

"The army there is doing the same thing that we are. They are using the captured nuclear backpacks to destroy the Middle East's ability to fight back. They have an escaped citizen of Russia who knows where all the nuclear weapons have been stored underground. He is taking a backpack to eliminate their nuclear capability. They found another that knows where the nuclear backpacks are being built. He is going to give them a taste of their own medicine."

They arrived at the classroom, and Sarah wanted to get in one more question in before the general left.

"How about me and Colonel Mills? What have you got planned for us?"

"If I survive this last mission, I am going to start a temporary government. I need the colonel to help me form the state and federal organizations. As for you, after you finish with us, I'm sending you on a very safe mission. It seems that we found a small enemy force that has kidnapped a few young Americans as their slaves to set up a large farm to provide food for their troops. You will have to organize a group to continue the farming activities using volunteer farmers while trying to find the relatives of the enslaved group. After that, I want you to be in charge of providing power using your new nuclear technology as well as any other method you can come up with."

"Sounds interesting but a little out of my line," said Sarah. "I don't know anything about farming.

"You don't have to know anything about farming," said the general. "You are going to be the organizer. I will replace you as soon as I can find someone to take your place. Getting power across the country is just as important."

The general left and soon soldiers started to pour into the room. When it looked like everyone was there, Sarah introduced herself and started to teach them the technology of the new device.

The general went into the satellite station and asked the sergeant what was going on.

"The enemy army seems to be stalled about two-thirds up the river valley," said the sergeant. "Using the telescopic capability, I can observe them for about ten to fifteen minutes every ninety minutes."

"That's great," said the general. "Have you been in touch with Colonel Mills?"

"No, not yet," said the sergeant. "I didn't have anything to report." "Let me call him, and I'll tell him about your task here so he can

call you if necessary." The general picked up the secure phone and dialed Mike's number.

"Colonel Mills speaking," said Mike.

"Colonel," said the general, "this is General McGard. How is the situation out there?"

"Apparently, from the information we have been able to gather from Lieutenant Selontti, the enemy is stalled while probably waiting to pick up all the backpack bombers that are still at large. I think that is good. This way, we can destroy them all at once."

"That's the thinking I like to hear," said the general. "The reason I called is to inform you that Doctor Anders is here safely and is currently bringing my non-pilot staff up to date on the new equipment. Tomorrow, she will train the pilots. After that, I will be leading my air force on a very dangerous mission. I have left instructions that if I don't come back, they are to pick you up, and you are to take over the secret base. I will leave complete instructions on what you are to do. Now, before you object, I must tell you that we don't have any other choice. Lieutenant Furgason and Doctor Anders will be a great help to you in you doing what has to be done."

"I'd rather believe that you would be back to take control yourself," said Mike.

"You can be sure that I wish the same thing, however, just in case the worst happens, you are next in the control seat."

"You can be sure I don't want it," said Mike. "I just want to look for my son and go home."

"We all have great and wonderful dreams," said the general. "I also wanted to inform you that your contact with this base will be through Sergeant McLeary now. He will constantly monitor the battle through the satellite. If you need anything, please contact him. Do you have any questions?"

"No," said Mike. "You have made yourself perfectly clear. God willing, I'll see you in a week."

The general then hung up and proceed to his office. At about six thirty, Sarah knocked on his door.

"Come in," said the general. Sarah walked in and greeted him.

"I'm all finished with instructing your people in the use and handling of the nuclear weapon," said Sarah. "I am heading to the cafeteria for some dinner. And thank you, by the way, for the lunch you sent to us in the training room."

"Wait," said the general. "I'll go with you. I want to hear the details of what you've accomplished."

"Of course, sir," said Sarah, feeling a little intimidated by being accompanied by a general. The general noticed her nervousness.

"Please relax, Doctor," said the general. "You're not in the military, so you don't have to be formal with me."

It didn't help Sarah. She was still overwhelmed with that much authority around her. In the cafeteria, they sat at the general's table and ordered their food.

"Now tell me," started the general, "what are your thoughts on today's progress?"

"I was very surprised and very pleased to find that all the men were extremely intelligent and very well informed," said Sarah. "They all seemed to follow me without any problems."

"I'm very happy to hear that," said the general. "Tomorrow, I will assemble all the pilots that will be going with me on the next mission. I'm aware that you know your way around here by now, but before you go to the training room, I would like you to come to my office. Let's say around eight. That should give you enough time to get up and have breakfast."

"I'll be there," said Sarah.

"Now tell me about the problems you ran into getting here," requested the general. Sarah related in detail their adventure from the time they met on the way to Chicago to the time they met the soldiers on Route 10.

Sarah returned to her quarters around eight and spent the next couple of hours planning for the next day's class. She set her alarm clock for six and went to sleep. The next morning, Sarah got up, showered, went to the cafeteria, ate breakfast, and presented herself at the general's office at precisely eight a.m.

"You are punctual, aren't you," said the general. "I like that. Now if you will follow me, I would like you to meet one of the pilots. I want you to talk to him before you go down to the training room. I'll have the rest of the pilots there at nine."

"Who is it that you want me to talk to before the training session?" asked Sarah.

"I'll meet you at nine in the training room, and I'll introduce you to all the pilots. After the training, I will have the helicopter take you to your next assignment, if that is acceptable with you."

"Yes, of course," said Sarah.

Before she could say anything else, the general pointed to the door at the end of the hall.

"Just go in the room at the end of the hall," instructed the general. "The pilot is there waiting for you. I'll meet you in the training room at nine."

With that, the general turned and left her wondering what was going on. She walked to the end of the hall and opened the door. As she entered the room, she recognized the pilot and turned to leave. He quickly put his hand on the door preventing her from leaving.

"Please," he said, "we have to talk."

"There is nothing to talk about," responded Sarah.

"Please," he repeated, "the Sarah I knew was gentle, kind, and would listen to a person's explanation."

"What explanation?" asked Sarah angrily. "What happened, were you dumped by your new girlfriend?"

"There was never anyone but you," he said.

"Boy, you have a real way of showing it," she answered. "Why should I believe anything you say?"

"Give me a chance to give you my explanation," he said. "Please, let me explain."

"Explain what?" asked Sarah. "You want to explain how you suddenly decided that you wanted me back or why you don't want the other girl anymore?"

"The last time you saw me, it was Saturday and remember, I left early because I told you I had something important to do." Sarah didn't say a word. "What it was that I had to do is pick up the one and a half-carat engagement ring I had ordered for you."

"That sounds like a lot of bull droppings," said Sarah, interrupting him.

"I was going to ask you to marry me," he continued, ignoring her comment.

"What happened? Did you get cold feet?" asked Sarah, still distraught.

"When I got back to my quarters, I was met by two soldiers who said that I had been called to the general's office. The general told me that I was being reassigned to a secret base. I told him that I had to inform my girlfriend that I was being reassigned, but he said that the base was a secret and that he couldn't let me do that. They confiscated my cell phone. He said that not only was no one to know where the base was, but no one was to know that the base even existed. They shoved me into a helicopter, blindfolded me, and brought me here. I have never had the chance to contact you."

"I want to believe you," said Sarah.

"You can verify everything by asking the general," he said. "Besides, look at me. Have you ever seen a man more in love than I am? Sarah, you are my whole life. The battle that we are going on, I'm fighting for you first and my country next. I have butterflies in my stomach and a lump in my throat, and I can hardly keep from throwing my arms around you. Don't you have butterflies in your stomach too?"

"No," said Sarah. Oh, Tom, I never stopped loving you." Sarah slid down the wall, sat with her knees up to her chest, and started to cry.

"Sarah, what's the matter?" Tom asked.

"I can't do this," is all she could say. "Can't do what?" asked Tom.

"I can't handle this," she said.

"Dear Lord," said Tom. "There is someone else?" "Yes," she said starting to cry even harder.

"Are you married?" asked Tom also getting tears in his eyes.

"No," she said, "nothing like that. It's just that we have been through so much together, and he loves me very much. I love him too. I can't handle this. I'm very confused. I need some time to think about this. I love both of you."

"Have you two made love?" asked Tom in deep pain himself.

"How can you ask that?" asked Sarah. "Don't you know me at all? I'm a Christian. I would never do that outside of marriage."

"I'm sorry," said Tom. "I'm in such a state right now that I don't know anything."

"Oh, Tom," said Sarah, realizing the pain he must be feeling. "I'm sorry. I should have thought of you. It's just that I don't know how to tell him. I do love him, and I don't want to hurt either of you."

"Do you love him more than you ever loved me?" asked Tom, the hurt showing in his face.

"I'm not sure," she answered. "I will never love anyone as much as I loved you. I had built my whole future on you and our love. Don't get me wrong. I love Mike very much. I will never forget him.

"Have you ever told him about me?"

"Yes," she answered. "That's a very good point. I never lied to him. I told him that you were the only one that gave me goose pimples and butterflies. I never had that with him. However, he was the next best. I was willing to spend the rest of my life with him. I know that I would have been happy with him. He is so gentle, yet very strong. He is lovable, caring, considerate, and affectionate. I know that he would have done everything he could to make me happy. I love him too with all of my heart."

"Who is the guy?" he asked. "Do I know him?"

"I'm sure you have heard of him," said Sarah. "He is Colonel Michael Mills."

"Oh my," said Tom in desperation. "You mean the Desert Fox? How could I ever compete with him?"

"This is not a competition," said Sarah. "Can't I love more than one person? Now that I think of it," she said, stopping to quietly assess the situation "I've been so traumatized by seeing you that I have been very confused and not thinking straight. However, now

I'm thinking seriously. I think that you and I have to spend more time together. We have to find out if what we had is still there. Are we both living in the past? I do love both of you very much. We had passionate kissing sessions, and I thought he was the only one. I need more time, do you understand?

"No, not really," said Tom. "What does all this mean?"

"Let me explain it this way," she said, "There is no doubt in my mind that you are the one I wanted and have always wanted. I wanted to spend the rest of my life with you. Yet, I love Mike and will always want him around. Mike is like family. I'll always love him because I admire him and look up to him. He is someone very special. You are a very special fellow too, and I admire you also, but I would still love both of you even if you were a nobody. Do you get the picture?"

"I think so," said Tom. "What matters is that you are telling me that I still have a chance with you."

"Good," said Sarah. "I'm sure you will love Mike also through admiration of him. Now, enough said, we are wasting time. We will soon be expected in the training room."

She threw her arms around him and planted a sweet kiss on his lips. He responded lovingly.

Nine came around too soon. They had almost forgotten their duty to their country.

"I've been dreaming of this moment every night for almost four years," said Tom. "I'm glad we had this time together. I urged the general to give us this time seeing that we are going on a very dangerous mission."

"Now that I've found you, please take care of yourself.

"Before we go to the training room," said Tom, taking out the engagement ring, "it is over ten years old but as good as new. When you make up your mind, it is ready to be put on your finger.

"Thank you for understanding. I need to see Mike before I make a decision. I'm leaning toward you if that will help you. We had better go, or we will forget where to go."

They arrived at the training room a little after nine. Tom joined the other pilots, and the general introduced them and left.

That evening, after the training was complete, Sarah, Tom, and the general had dinner together. Sarah informed the general that the pilots had all been briefed, and she was very pleased with their intelligence. The general warned Tom that they were going to leave very early the next morning and asked him not stay too long with Sarah.

"Tom, I need you very well rested. I need you to lead the fighters in eliminating the missile sites and to protect the bombers from the enemy fighters. I need you wide awake."

"Don't worry, General," said Sarah. "I want him to come back to me. I will not keep him out long."

She kept her word and sent him to bed early. The next morning when she arose she found the sergeant waiting for her.

"Good morning, Sergeant," said Sarah. "Is the general still around?"

"No, Doctor Anders," he said. "They left early this morning. The base is very empty."

He took her to breakfast. After breakfast he took her to the landing platform. There, she met Captain Cumins.

"Good morning, Captain Cumins," said Sarah.

"Good morning, Doctor Anders," said the captain. "I'm flattered that you remember me."

"How could I forget the man who rescued me from the wild forest?" asked Sarah. "Where are we bound for this morning?" "To a new adventure," said the captain.

Sarah, after getting into the helicopter, turned to the sergeant and waved good-bye as the copter lifted from the platform and headed for her new adventure.

Mike was getting very anxious. It had been two days since he had heard anything from the secret base. Even with his very powerful binoculars, he could not see any activity in the direction the invading forces were coming from. Everything was ready. He had achieved very close connections with his officers. They had all their signals down pat. They each knew what to do under all possible situations. They practiced every possible variation in the invading forces' actions.

They were more than ready. He was about to call the base when his phone rang.

"Colonel Mills here," he answered.

"Colonel, this is Sergeant McLeary. I'm sorry that I have not called you sooner, but there has been no activity from the enemy. They have been absolutely fixed in their position until now. They are moving, but not toward you. They are heading east across Route 5. They are going around the mountain range you are in."

"Thank you, Sergeant," said Mike. "We know what to do. Keep me informed of their movements." Mike hung up and immediately contacted all his officers on the secure phone.

"Colonel Mills here," he said. "This is it, fellows. The enemy is moving across Route 5. We have to stop them. We practiced this, but I will keep repeating the required action. Lieutenant Selontti, you are to hit them from the west and run when they start pursuing you, but don't run too fast. You have to make them think that they will overrun you without trouble. This is as we practiced. You know what to do to entice them to follow you. Lieutenant Furgason, you know what to do. I will direct you when the time is right. The rest of you: be informed and stay ready."

It only took Lieutenant Selontti fifteen minutes to get his fast-moving troops west of the enemy forces and start attacking them with heavy artillery. The enemy retaliated. Slowly, Selontti's forces started to retreat west. The enemy didn't seem to want to follow. Mike contacted Selontti on the secure phone.

"Lieutenant," he said, "now is the time you ask for help on the commercial phone."

"Right away, sir," he said and hung up. Selontti called Mike on his commercial phone.

"Colonel Mills," said Selontti, "we are in trouble. We are running out of ammunition, and we have encountered heavy losses. We need help in both manpower and supplies. We are being backed up to the sea."

"Lieutenant," said Mike, "try to hold on. I'll see if I can get some help for you." Mike then called Lieutenant Furgason on the commercial phone.

"Lieutenant Furgason," said Mike, "Lieutenant Selontti in the Sacramento river valley, is in trouble. Can you help him?"

"Sir," responded Furgason, "we had heavy losses in the Spokane bombing, but will try to help the best we can. We are at the north side of the Trinity Mountain area. I am at the north end of the valley next to the Route 5 valley. Tell Lieutenant Selontti to find the southern end of the valley and come north. I will bring my forces south, and we will meet in the middle and combine our forces. Colonel, can we have air support?"

"Thank you," said Mike, "unfortunately the air force is unavailable at this time. As soon as it returns, I will send it your way. I will try to get you whatever help and supplies I can muster."

Mike hung up and called Selontti on the commercial phone. He related the conversation he had with Furgason. Selontti had already heard it and knew what to do. Mike then called Major Brandon on the commercial phone.

"Major Brandon," said Mike. Our troops in the Trinity Mountains are in trouble. I was wondering if you could provide them with some help."

"I'm sorry, sir," said Brandon. "Most of my men have gone back to Texas. Our main objective is to protect Texas, and even if I wanted to help, I don't have the manpower or the supplies. We are currently on our way back to Texas. Sorry sir."

"Thanks anyway," said Mike and hung up. He knew that, in reality, Major Brandon and his men were right behind the enemy with the directions to prevent a retreat of the enemy and, when given the orders from Mike, to blow the charges they had planted on the south end of the valley and block any possible retreat. Immediately after he hung up, Sergeant McLeary called on the secure phone.

"Sir," he said, "I am almost out of range, but I can see the enemy forces moving fast toward the west."

"How long before you will have us in view again?" asked Mike

"It takes the satellite ninety minutes to make one revolution around the earth. Thanks to the telescopic capability, I can view you for about twenty minutes. Therefore, I will be in range again in about an hour and ten minutes."

"Thank you," said Mike. "Keep watch as best as you can. You have been of great service already."

Selontti was able to run ahead of the enemy and turned into the valley about fifteen minutes later. That did make it a little safer for them since the enemy could not have a wide array against them. Their front line had to be restricted to the width of the valley floor.

Fergason's forces did not go south into the valley, they went farther north, as Mike had directed him. Selontti's forces retreated as fast as they could. To their surprise, the enemy forces moved faster than Mike thought the enemy force could with the heavy equipment they carried. Selontti had no problem, however, pulling away from them. Mike watched them chase Selontti up the valley. The enemy had a greater force than he had realized. He waited until the trailing edge of the force was clear of the southern end of the valley, and the main force was about in the center of the valley before he gave orders to Brandon to blow the southern entrance.

The explosion rocked even Mike and his mountain personnel. The enemy was surprised by the explosion but soon realized that they had walked into a trap. All hell broke loose. They moved rapidly to the north to exit the trap. As soon as Selontti cleared the northern end of the valley, Furgason blew the northern entrance. The enemy was trapped in the valley. Mike gave the command to fire all that they could. It was obvious that the enemy was being decimated. Mike kept close watch of the enemy's commander's vehicle. His attention never left the commander. What the commander did was the only thing that concerned Mike.

The battle was almost over. It had been over an hour since he last heard from Sergeant McLeary. Mike wondered if he was watching the battle.

CHAPTER ELEVEN

Road to Recovery

IT WAS TWO DAYS LATER that General McGard returned from his dangerous mission. He was worn out and tired. Though the mission was a greater success than he had expected, he was depressed because of the losses they had experienced to achieve their victory.

During the flight there and back, he had plenty of time to think of his next move. He had decided that the army had to take over the country. There was no one else that could be trusted. The Pentagon was destroyed as was all of Washington DC including the White House. Of all the personnel at the secret base and the few state officials he had contacted, all requested that the general take over as a temporary president. He didn't really want the job. All he dreamed of was to retire and spent the rest of his life on his farm with his wife. However, He decided that he had no alternative but to accept the responsibility at least until election could be arranged. He also stated that he wanted Colonel Mills as his temporary vice president. He needed Colonel Mills to manage and organize the state governments. He trusted Mike and felt that his high moral standard was a necessary requirement. He also respected Mike for his gentle and persuasive personality. He knew that Mike was not a politician but a diplomat. His men loved and respected him. He was a caring man. The general felt he also needed him to review the constitution, not to rewrite it, but to expand and clarify every amendment and article of freedom it guarantees, especially the freedom of religion. Although he was completely exhausted, he couldn't rest without knowing what had transpired in the battle conducted by Colonel Mills. Upon landing, he went directly to the satellite monitoring area.

"Hello, Sergeant," said the general. "Are you holding down the fort?"

"Doing my best sir," he replied. "How was the mission to China? Did you bring them down to their knees?"

"We were successful in our mission, but we had high losses," said the general. "We lost seven aircraft and too many good men. One of the aircrafts we lost was a bomber. At least two fighter pilots are trying to get home on foot. I have sent a rescue team out to try and find them. Fortunately, we destroyed their air power."

"I'm sorry, sir," said the sergeant. "Unfortunately, I can say the same thing. The army's losses here were too many."

"Tell me what has happened since I was gone?"

"I have it all on DVD so you can see everything I observed," said the sergeant.

"I'll review them later when I can study them. I'm too exhausted now anyway. I'm going to bed as soon as I leave here. Just give me a general account of what has transpired."

"First of all, the enemy started to cross Route 5 away from the trap. Colonel had anticipated that and had a small force, led by Lieutenant Selontti, at the southern end of the valley. This force, with false information on the commercial phone, which the colonel anticipated that they were listening to, enticed them to try to overrun the small force. By running from them at just the right speed, they led them into the valley. Once they were inside, Major Brandon ignited a set of charges that they had set on the southern end of the two mountains. This caused an avalanche of rocks and dirt that sealed off the southern end of the valley. The enemy, realizing what was going on, ran for the northern end of the valley. As soon as Lieutenant Selontti cleared the north end, Lieutenant Furgason set off a charge there that sealed off the north exit. Then, Colonel Mills ordered the men on the mountain to rain down on the enemy with everything they had."

"Sounds like a perfectly intelligent plan, executed with precision," said the general, feeling extreme excitement. "Did they wipe them out?"

"The satellite was just overhead, which made my view fantastic. I could look right down on the action. Our men had almost wiped out the enemy when Colonel Mills yelled, 'Charge.' At that moment, the troops on top of each mountain started running down the hill to finish wiping them out. I couldn't actually see the men, but they raised a lot of dust and dirt as they ran down the hill at a fantastic speed. It was almost like they were rolling down or sliding down on their butts. Just as they were about to reach the bottom, my view was obscured by a large billow of black smoke. Though I couldn't see through the smoke, I could see that at least a large part of the tops of the mountains had disappeared. The nuclear explosion took place near the center of the valley. The seals at each end of the valley had disappeared." The general, who had been sitting at the edge of the chair, suddenly fell back. With a trembling voice, he asked, "Have you heard from Colonel Mills?"

"I tried to call him, but there was no answer," said the sergeant. "I called Lieutenant Furgason. He said that he and his men are still running north away from the blast. The seals at the ends of the valley took up a lot of their energy. They are just at a point of high but acceptable radiation. I asked about Colonel Mills. He said he didn't know, and he couldn't investigate for at least two weeks or until the radiation was lower. I got the same response from Major Brandon."

The general was speechless. He just sat there and looked blank. Sergeant McLeary thought he saw tears in the general's eyes. "Are you all right, sir?" he asked.

"Yes, I'm all right," he said finally. "It's just that I am very disappointed in the results. I'm not disappointed in our wining the battle, of course, but in the probable loss of the colonel. Is there any way that he could have survived?"

"I don't see how sir," answered the sergeant. "I've looked at the site every ninety minutes. Several feet have been blown off the top of the mountains. The dirt and rocks from the top are scattered down the sides, so there are no trees or brush visible anywhere on either side of the valley. Nothing could have survived the force of the bomb."

"That blows my plan to pieces," said the general. "I was very concerned that I wouldn't return from the last mission, so I left detailed instructions for Colonel Mills to take over in case I didn't return. God has strange ways of doing things. It looks like everything happened in reverse. I thought I would die. Instead it was the Colonel. I don't know what I'm going to do without him. He was the main part of my plan. I'm going to bed. I don't think I could eat anything, the way I feel."

"I'll see you in the morning," said the sergeant. "Have a good evening, sir."

The general didn't respond. He just dragged himself to bed. He was sure that he couldn't sleep a wink. However, as his head hit the pillow, he was fast asleep.

The next morning, before breakfast, he went to the satellite monitoring room. The sergeant wasn't there yet. He searched the room and found the DVDs on a shelf. They were well labeled. He found the ones of the Trinity Mountain battle and studied them. It was just as the sergeant had described. He couldn't see any possible way that the Colonel could have survived. He called First Lieutenant Furgason.

Lieutenant Furgason answered the phone.

"This is General McGard. I would like to talk to Major Furgason," he said, announcing Jeffery Furgason's promotion in his strange way.

"This is Lieutenant Furgason sir," he said, puzzled by the general's statement.

"Not anymore," said the general with a giggle in his voice. "You are now a major in the US Army. I suspect it will be your rank for a short time, but forget that for now. I want to know how you and your men are, and whether you are ready to come to the secret base. I also want to know what has happened to Colonel Mills."

"Well sir, to start with, my men and I are all fine. Major Brandon assures me that he and his men are also fine. We discussed his next move. He tells me that he has been informed that the Mexicans have assembled somewhere around a hundred thousand soldiers on the border. His informants tell him that they feel the Mexicans are considering attacking us in our weakened state. He decided to go back to protect the border. He says that he has many men with construction experience, so he is going to build a wall across the complete southern border to free his soldiers from protecting the border. He only lacks finances. I agreed with him since I didn't know if you were going to come back."

"You did the right thing," said the general. "I will take care of the Mexicans. I'll tell their president to get in touch with the Chinese. I'll tell him about our air force and the number of atomic weapons we have left. That will make him withdraw his army with its tail between its legs. Now tell me about Colonel Mills. Is there any chance of his survival?"

"Colonel had anticipated every action that the enemy could take. I know that he was aware of the enemy having atomic weapons. He had a contingency plan. I don't know if it worked or not. I cannot investigate for about two weeks or until my men tell me that the area is safe. I have men about twenty miles around the valley. I would like to stay here and complete the investigation, and after that, I would like to reorganize the army. I have new men coming into my camp every day wanting to join my group. I plan on setting up a training program for all new men."

"That will be fine," said the general. "Before I hang up, do you have any questions?"

"Yes sir, I have a couple of questions," he answered. "First, intending no disrespect to you, without Colonel Mills, who is my commanding officer? You are a general in the air force. Is that correct?"

"As of this morning, that was correct," said the general. "However, when you were promoted to Major I was promoted to Commander of the Armed Forces. Soon, I expect to be Commander in Chief and you will be Commander of the Armed Forces."

"That is my next question," said Furgason. "What has happened to our navy?"

"The only navy we've been able to communicate with is in the Middle East. All the other ships, I believe, have been destroyed. That is what is holding up the reorganization of the armed forces. Admiral Kane, however, has voiced his desire to stay as an admiral in the navy. As soon as the task in the Middle East is complete, we will sit down and reorganize. The goal is to appoint an acting temporary president to reorganize the state and federal systems. In the mean time, you can reorganize the present troops you have under your command. I would like you to reorganize your men into four groups if possible. I would like men who come from the four parts of the US to be teamed together. I will need to eventually come up with a small force to police each part of the country. The division I would like is a group from the Atlantic states; a group from the eastern mid-states like Ohio, Illinois, Indiana; a group from the western mid-states; and a group from the Pacific states."

"I will do my best, sir. Good luck on your new job," said Furgason, then he hung up.

The next two weeks were very busy for the general. He got more accomplished then he had hoped. He met with all the officers he could find that were Colonel or higher rank. Basically, it included the Admiral and six of the ship commanders under his command. These represented the navy. It also included three army officers who returned from the Middle East. The general represented the army.

He had promoted Captain Tom Corrie to Lieutenant Colonel and put him in charge of the air force.

The meeting went well. It only lasted two days. Admiral Kane was happy in the position he had and so were his officers. He said he wanted to go to Hawaii and investigate the reason the ships weren't responding to his calls. He suspected that the officers were in Honolulu, which was nuked, and the sailors aboard the ships don't know what to do.

At the meeting, they all voted for General McGard to be acting temporary president of the USA and commander in chief. The general accepted. The only question that the admiral had was where the financing of the services was coming from. The general explained that he had a financial member of his team that was reviewing the records that were collected by one of his agents before the terrible bombing of the country's military bases and large cities. He said that the investigation was taking place in two areas. The first was to take over Fort Knox and come out with silver and gold certificates.

The second effort was to calculate the amount of money that was destroyed in the banks of the nuked cities. This money would be distributed to any surviving members of the depositor, and the remainder would be used to rebuild the nation and to pay for the maintenance of the military.

The meeting closed with the members happy with the general's answers. The general then started to set up his cabinet. He found a very intelligent and competent electronic engineer who had much experience with television and radio transmitters. He put her in charge of getting all the communication of the country working again, especially in the east since the rest of the country was in fair shape. She assembled a team and started to rebuild communications in the most important areas first. Tom was also made a cabinet member and was put in charge of all transportation. Tom was already rebuilding the more important airfields. He also found a plant in California that had been used at one time to build DC9 aircrafts. Tom found enough men with experience to start building a few commercial passenger aircrafts. The problem was that the general really needed Mike for the reorganization of the state and federal governments. He could not find anyone he thought was sufficiently competent. He did find four congressmen who had been out of Washington and in a safe area, but he didn't want a politician in that position. He wanted a military man because military training made men think more logically. He planned on making Furgason the head of the army when he had finished the investigation and reorganization of his men. What he needed now was someone to take charge of rebuilding and providing the country's energy. And he knew exactly the person for that job. He also needed to find an area to rebuild Washington DC. The area where it had been was too disseminated to rebuild anything there anytime soon. He didn't like that area anyway.

The next morning, he got Captain Comins to take him to the farm in Iowa where he had sent Sarah. They got there about four thirty that afternoon. Sarah was there to greet him. To Sarah's surprise, he hugged her.

"How are you, Doctor?" he asked, releasing her. "I'm so glad to see you."

"I'm glad to see you too, General," said Sarah. "What brings you here on this cold afternoon?"

"I have a serious request to ask of you as well as to inform you of all the developments that have occurred since you left the secret base. First of all, we brought China to its knees. It will not disturb anyone soon. Unfortunately, the cost was too high. We lost too many planes and men."

"Is Captain Corrie all right?" asked Sarah with a worrying frown. "Yes, he's fine except it isn't Captain Corrie, it's Lieutenant Colonel Thomas Corrie now. He is on a mission to rebuild our country's transportation system. His real title is Secretary of Transportation."

The general explained about the meeting he had and that they had nominated him as temporary acting president. He explained that he was in the process of forming a new government."

"Then do I call you Mr. President or General?" asked Sarah. "Why don't you just call me Bill?"

"Only if you call me Sarah."

"Agreed," said President McGard. They had just entered the cafeteria and were standing by a table, when Sarah asked the question she had wanted to ask from the beginning.

"What has happened in the battle of the enemy in California?" asked Sarah, really wanting to know about Mike but ashamed to ask since the general knew about her relationship with Tom.

"There is no enemy left in California or anywhere in the US. They were completely destroyed. Unfortunately, the cost was very high. We lost about two thousand men, and the most important loss was the loss of Colonel Mills."

It was fortunate that the general was right behind her so he could catch her as she started to fall. She had almost passed out. He sat her on a chair and noticed that she was crying.

"Oh, Mike," she said repeatedly. "You promised to come back."

After about fifteen minutes, she had recovered enough to ask what had happened. President McGard told her everything he knew.

"Isn't there any chance he survived?" she asked finally. "I don't see how," he said.

"But he knew that they would be carrying a nuclear backpacks," said Sarah, still showing much pain. "He knew that."

"Please, don't think I'm being insensitive, but aren't you and Colonel Corrie engaged?"

Sarah gave a sad and forced smile. I haven't accepted yet," she said. "I love Mike with all of my heart. I will never forget him. We went through so much together. We saved each other's life several times at the risk of our own."

"I understand completely. I had tears in my eyes when I heard of it."

"You know what?" said Sarah, brightening up somewhat. "I don't believe it. Mike is too smart to be caught in that kind of a situation. He is too brilliant. I just don't believe it. It is too simple. I'm sure that he is trapped someplace safe waiting until the radiation has dissipated sufficiently for him to come out. I just won't accept that he didn't prepare for the possibility. He would never put that many men in danger."

"I hope you are right," said President McGard, refusing to discuss it any longer. "Listen, in the meantime I have to organize a new government. I need a secretary of energy. That is, you if you will accept."

"What would my duties be?"

"We will give you a team with knowledge of the different types of electric plants. You will personally handle getting energy to the people. You will start with the standard and, nuclear plants and maybe, using the new technology, create a better, more efficient, and less dangerous power system."

"When would I have to start?"

"Why? Do you have something else you want to do, or do you just want to think about it?"

"No, I accept the position without question. Let me tell you why I asked. I've already met your young financial officer. I had Captain Comins take me back to the secret base. I saw the DVDs that you made before the disaster. Rose made me a copy of the disks that showed the tax files of all the people. You see, the slaves the Chinese kidnapped and brought here are all children from nine to sixteen years of age. There are about two hundred of them. We have found families or relatives for twenty-nine of them. In the mean time, we have recruited about twenty farmers to take their place. We are also setting up schools for the kids we still have not found homes for. I would like to complete this task."

"I agree," said President McGard. "It is a very important job, and it should be completed. I will agree under one condition: I will give you a month to continue the job here and train someone to replace your job here. Do you agree?"

"That sounds reasonable," said Sarah. "I'm sure I can find someone to do this. I am looking for teachers anyway, and I have some pretty competent helpers now that I can train.

"Sounds great," said President McGard. "Now let's get something to eat."

They had dinner, and afterwards they sat with a cup of coffee and enjoyed some small talk.

"Is there anything I can help you with?" asked Sarah, after the president was settled with his briefcase in the corner of the cafeteria. "Now that you brought it up, maybe you can help," said President McGard.

"I'll be glad to help in any way I can," said Sarah.

"The place I really wish you could help is to find a replacement for Mike. I needed him as my vice president and temporary secretary of state. I need someone to supervise the reorganization of the federal government and all the state governments."

"Bill," said Sarah, "will you do me a favor? Hold off on filling those positions until the investigation of the battle area is complete. I spent a year with Mike. I know him better than anyone."

"You got it," said President McGard. "Now, in my spare time, when I can find some, and when I'm in a situation where I can't do anything else, I will review the Constitution. I don't want to change it; I just want to clarify it. I could use your input on some of the changes I want to make. I feel that the freedom of speech and religion has been chipped away with loop holes that they have created. I am trying to assemble all of my cabinet members, all the governors, and all the congress men, we could find and discuss all possible clarification that need to be done."

Sarah and the president discussed all the freedoms guaranteed by the Constitution. They were both equally conservative and agreed on most points. The president was very pleased with the discussion they had and with Sarah's contributions.

It was nearly twelve when they quit and turned in for the night. The next morning, President McGard got up early and, after thanking Sarah, said good-bye and left to go back to the secret base. He got there about five in the evening. He was very weary from the trip and the thought of the work ahead of him. He was met by Sergeant McLeary.

"Welcome home, sir," he said, not knowing how to address him. "Captain Cumins," he added turning to the pilot, "there was a call for you. It was from Lieutenant, or is it Colonel, Furgason. He says he needs your services right away."

"Go ahead and call him back," said President McGard. "Go and help him in any way you can. I won't need you for awhile."

President McGard then went into the cafeteria and had a quick dinner, and afterward, he went to his office to check on his messages. He reviewed the notes he had made during the discussion with Sarah and went to bed early. He went to sleep thinking of who he was going to put in place he had reserved for Colonel Mike Mills. In the morning, he was on the way to breakfast when he was called by Sergeant McLeary.

"Sir," he said, "Captain Comins called and said that, because of a very important guest he is carrying, you will be required to meet the helicopter that will land in about fifteen minutes."

President McGard went directly to the landing pad, wondering who the important guest could be. A few minutes later, he heard and saw the helicopter come into view.

After the helicopter landed, the door opened and a soldier in dress uniform descended from the airship. When president McGard recognized who it was, his skin got goose pimples, he felt a knot in his stomach, and a lump in his throat. He couldn't speak. As he walked toward him, the chill down his spine made him stop and look. Then, without warning, he grabbed him and hugged him with all of his might as if he would disappear if he let him go.

"I missed you too General or, should I say, Mister President."

"Just call me Bill," said President McGard. "I'm so glad to see you. You can't imagine how good it is to see you. I thought you were dead."

"As Mark Twain said, 'My death was greatly exaggerated.'"

"I've missed you so much," repeated President McGard. "I need you so badly. I couldn't find anyone to replace you."

"Replace me for what?"

"Never mind that for now," said President McGard. "We have so much to talk about."

"Now Mike, tell me how it is that you are still alive after being through hell. How did you manage not to be burned to death by the radiation if not by the explosion itself?"

"You can give all the credit to Lieutenant Furgason," said Mike. "He is a fantastic soldier. I just had to tell him the basic plan, and he worked out the details to perfection."

"Based on your last recommendation he is now a colonel," said President McGard. "I just haven't told him yet."

"When I was in the forest, I contacted him and asked him to find a valley to set the trap. I also asked him to find some mining equipment to dig tunnels on the outside of each mountain. He not only got a perfect spot, but he got twenty cave diggers, ten on each side. He did that but, also realizing what I had in mind he got twenty, four-inch flexible plastic hoses, and placed them in each tunnel with about a hundred feet sticking out of the tunnels. That way, the eight hundred men on top of each mountain had a place to hide and the hoses would provide oxygen if needed. We did need it, as it turned out."

"But we heard you yell 'Charge' and saw the dust as your men ran down the mountain to the bottom of the valley," said president McGard, puzzled by the information.

"All of that was for the benefit of the enemy. You didn't notice that the orders were given through the commercial phone. We used the commercial phones to mislead the enemy. My commands were all in code. When I yelled, 'Charge,' it meant retreat to the tunnels for the men on top of the mountain. It also meant that Fugason should flee as fast as he could north, and that Brandon should flee as fast as he could to the south. I was watching the enemy's commander throughout the battle. I knew that when he saw that the battle was lost, he might take drastic action. We had decimated his forces. We shot everything we had down on them. We had killed at least seventy percent of his men. The men that had come to the east side of the valley to take shelter were decimated by the men on top of the west mountain, and when they tried to take shelter on the west side, they were a perfect target for the men on the east mountain. I guess the enemy's commander figured it was all over and decided to take us with him. I saw him take out the backpack and knew what it was he had in mind. That's when I gave the command to retreat."

"But we saw the dust on both sides of the valley," said President McGard, still confused.

"When I first got to the top of the mountain, I ordered the men to bring up large rocks that we could roll down the mountain to look like our men were attacking on my command. I needed this so the enemy commander would not change his mind by thinking that his demise was eminent. I didn't want him to change his mind when we were all in the tunnels or far away. He would have escaped my trap." "That is the most fantastic story I've ever heard," said McGard.

"Sarah was right. You are a genius." "When did you talk to Sarah?"

"I just saw her yesterday at the place she is stationed." said President McGard. "She almost passed out when I told her that you hadn't made it out of the battle. I kept her from falling. Then she sank to her knees and cried like a baby, but you know, when she recovered from the initial shock, she brightened up and said that she didn't believe it. She said that you, of all people, knew that they carried nuclear backpack bombs. She said that you were too smart to be caught like that. She also said that you would never put that many men in danger. She said that you were probably laid out somewhere waiting for the radiation to subside. She asked me not to find a replacement for you until the investigation was complete. I did what she asked, but I didn't really believe her."

"Does she know that I'm okay?" asked Mike.

"No, I didn't know myself until I saw you get off the helicopter. I was really surprised to see you."

"Well don't tell her. I'd like to go and see her," said Mike.

"First, what happened when you went into the tunnels?" asked the president.

"We had to stay in the tunnel until the radiation cleared. The explosion had covered all of the tunnel entrances. We couldn't get out. Furgason had instructed the tunnel diggers to pull to about twenty miles away from the mountain until they heard from him. Yesterday, Furgason came and had the diggers dig us out. Thanks to the forethought of Furgason, the four inch pipe gave us enough oxygen to survive."

"Did all the men survive?" asked President McGard.

"No, two of the tunnels that were in line with the nuclear blast collapsed, and no one in those two survived."

"How many men altogether did we lose?"

"We lost about two hundred altogether. We lost a hundred and sixty in the tunnels and forty in the battle. Now, what is this about replacing me?"

"I have been planning for the reorganization of the new federal government. I want you to be my Vice President, and I want you to temporarily assume the duties of the Secretary of State."

"Why me?" asked Mike. "I have no experience in that area."

"I need a man of integrity," said the president. "Our task will not only be to set up a federal government, but to assist the states to get set up. Like I told Sarah, I need a diplomat not a politician."

President McGard then explained all that he had done thus far. He told him of all the secretary positions he had filled. He explained that Sarah had accepted the position of Secretary of Energy with the request to finish the job she was presently involved in. He showed him the notes he had taken from his discussion with Sarah. Feeling that he had given Mike enough to think about, he asked what he thought.

"I think you have everything going in the right direction," said Mike. "I see a lot of work ahead for you."

"Not me alone," said the president. "I need all of you. My plan is to get everyone together on the first of next month and we all contribute to clarification of the Constitution; then, a working plan to form the federal government and how to help the states form their governments in the case that they don't have one anymore. That is, for those states whose capitals were destroyed. The others, we will review to make sure they follow the clairified Constitution. I think that after we have all agreed, we will get together and visit one state at a time doing what is necessary to bring that area back to acceptable operation."

"Is there a reason for waiting until the first of next month?" asked Mike.

"It isn't that things are at a standstill," said the president. "I have most of the cabinet working. I also have all the military leaders rebuilding their divisions. I have many other people working on different aspects of reforming the government. I have a military squad checking briefly the conditions of each state's needs for food, medicine, and governmental functions. However, I think you, Sarah, and some of the others who have been working very hard need a vacation. I, for example, need to spend time with my family. I haven't seen my wife in almost a year. She doesn't even know that she is the First Lady. I am going to take two weeks off. At this point, however, I would like to know if you have accepted the position I am offering you."

"Yes, of course I accept," said Mike. "I'll do whatever you want me to do."

"I want you to study the constitution, review the notes I gave you, and get together with Rose the secretary of finance," said the President. "See you in two weeks."

"Yes sir," said Mike, starting to look forward to seeing Sarah again.

Tom's work took him to an airport near the Idaho camp where Sarah was stationed. He took two weeks and decided to spend them with Sarah. Sarah was happy to see him but his being there reminded her of Mike. She started to cry.

"Is that the affect I have on you," said Tom. "When you see me you start to cry. Am I that bad to be around?" Sarah managed a smile.

"It's just that seeing you, reminds me of Mike." She then told him of Mike's death.

"Oh, Sarah, I'm so sorry" said Tom "I can feel your pain."

"Thanks," said Sarah. "What are you doing here anyway? I thought that you were busy rebuilding airports and aircrafts."

"I am but we are working on an airport near here, besides I have a team of great men working for me. Besides, it gave me the change of being with you. You said that you wanted some time to think it over and that we had to spend some time together. Well, now I'm taking two weeks."

"I'm so glad you're here," said Sarah. "I've been so depressed since Mike died. I really need some company." Tom and Sarah spent the two week together. There was some romantic time and some just getting reacquainted time. Their romantic time got pretty passionate at times. They spent the two week always being together. It was the last day before Tom had to leave that Sarah asked Tom to go for a walk with her.

"Tom," she said, "we have to talk."

"Sure, Sarah," he responded, wondering if she was going to ask for the ring.

"Tom," she repeated, "when we first fell in love, I was very young, and I was infatuated with you. I thought the whole world of you. You were also very young. Tom, we are not the same people that we were then. That was over ten years ago. You are not the same and I am not the same. I don't want to hurt you but I don't feel the same now as I did then."

"Oh, Sarah," said Tom, looking relieved. "I'm so glad you said that. I didn't know how to tell you. I feel the same way, especially as I see how much you love Mike."

"You know, Tom, Mike once told me that he didn't know how much he loved his wife Annie, until he lost her. I didn't know how much I loved Mike until I lost him."

"I feel so much better," said Tom. "We can still be friends" "Of course," she answered. "I will always feel love for you"

Mike did as the president asked. He didn't hear from the president again for two weeks. He met with Rose, the secretary of finance. They spent the best part of the week together. She supplied Mike with a description of the financial condition of the country and each state. Near the end of the second week, he studied the notes he was given. He was impressed by the knowledge and understanding that Sarah showed in the notes. The next day he received a call from the president.

"I want you to rest the remainder of the day and be ready to travel tomorrow morning," said the president. "I will take you to where Sarah is working."

The next morning, he got up early, had breakfast, and proceeded to the helicopter pad. The president was nowhere around.

"Is the president coming with us?" Mike asked Captain Comins, the pilot of the helicopter.

"No," answered the pilot. "We have been able to obtain a second helicopter, and the President is off to check out a possible area for the new capital. I was told to take you to the Idaho Camp as soon as you were ready. He said that you should be sure to take enough clothes in case you have to stay a few days."

"Everything I own is here in this small suitcase," said Mike. "I'm ready now."

They left at about eight and stopped in a small town that Tom had set up for refueling. There, they had a quick lunch. They arrived at the campsite early that afternoon. Sarah was told to meet the helicopter but was not notified as to who would be on it. When she saw Mike step out of the helicopter, her heart skipped a beat. She ran as fast as she could and threw herself in his arms.

"Michael!" she yelled with tears in her eyes. "I knew you would be okay."

"I missed you too," said Mike. "I heard from McGard that you didn't believe him, so why are you making such a fuss?"

"I was afraid I was wrong," said Sarah as they walked away from the helicopter. "It was really more of a wish than a prediction. I'm so happy to see you. I love you with all of my heart, but there is something I have to tell you."

"I think I heard a *but* in there."

"Did McGard tell you anything about my time here?" said Sarah, wondering if he already knew about Tom.

"He only told me to come here," said Mike. "He was off on a special mission. I think it had something to do with the location of the new capital. He did tell me that he wanted me to be his vice president with the added task of secretary of state until he could find a suitable replacement. Why, what is going on?"

"Let me explain."

"*Explain*, that's another word that starts me worrying," said Mike.

"You said that you loved me with all your heart," said Mike. "Therefore, can I assume that it has nothing to do with our relationship?"

"Mike," answered Sarah, "I do love you very much. You have taken care of me for the last year. You've saved my life and cared for me. I don't want that relationship to ever end."

"What I don't understand," said Mike, "Is why you are being so evasive. Why are you beating around the bush?"

"There is something I have to tell you."

"Uh oh," said Mike. "Do I hear another *but*? Have you found someone new that you love more than me?"

"No," said Sarah, "not someone new, someone old."

"Someone old," said Mike thinking hard. Sarah could tell by the sudden shocked look in his face that he had realized what she was telling him. "What I don't understand is why you told me that you loved me with all of your heart."

"Because I do," said Sarah. "I love you both with all of my heart. "I never lied to you. I always told you that we were second choices. I have suffered for over a month thinking of how I was going to tell one of you without hurting you. Then I hear that you had died. I was very lost. I was even ready to tell Tom to forget it, that I couldn't hurt you. He talked me out of it. He said that I should talk to you.

"Oh sure, live with the thought of my wife unhappy because she married the wrong man."

"Mike," said Sarah. "You are such a wonderful person. You are gentle, loving, romantic, caring and extremely intelligent. I would never be unhappy with you. I know that you would do everything you could to make me happy."

"Does Tom still give you butterflies in your stomach?" Sarah didn't answer. She was fishing to see how much Mike loved her. She wanted to know how he felt.

"Did you know that Tom proposed to me?

"What did you say?" asked Mike, showing the hurt in his face.

"I haven't answered him yet. I wanted to know what you think about it"

"How can I answer that, Sarah? I can't see in your heart." "What are your feelings about me and Tom?"

"My heart is broken but in a good way. You see, a half of my heart is hurting, but the other half is joyful. I'm like a woman who has sorrow in labor, but, at the same time, great joy in the delivery of her child. Sarah, the thing I want most in this world at this moment is your happiness.

Then, as if a light came on in her mind, she exclaimed, "Dear Lord! With all of this on in my mind and being so happy to see you, I forgot the most important thing I have to do. Come with me," she said, grabbing his hand and pulling him outside. "There is someone special I want you to meet. You know that the Chinese took slaves to do the farming to supply food for their armies"

"I heard very little," said Mike. "I don't have any details."

"Just come with me, and you will learn all the details of this situation."

She walked Mike down past several small buildings and stopped in front of one. She checked it out very carefully to make sure she had the right one. They all looked so much alike. They did have a number on each building, but it was in Chinese.

"What are we doing here?" asked Mike, seeing Sarah hesitate in front of the building.

"It's kind of a welcome home prize. Just wait out here. I'll just be a minute," said Sarah.

She entered the building and closed the door behind her. Mike was puzzled. Why was he standing out on the dirt road? He turned and looked behind him to look at the miles of what he thought were wheat or corn fields. Every plant was growing neatly in a straight row. The soft, gentle breeze caressed the rows of plants so that they swayed in unison. It gave Mike a feeling of belonging; that God was at work here. He felt a sudden peace.

He was so engrossed with the peacefulness of the moment that he barely heard the door open behind him. He slowly turned around to see someone run out of the building at full speed.

"Daddy," said the voice of a young boy as he jumped into his arms. "Benny," said Mike, tears flowing like a river. "How are you, sweetheart? I thought I would never see you again."

"Daddy, the bad men shot Mama," said Benny. "She tried to save me, but the bad man shot her once in the neck, and then, when she was on the ground, he shot her in the chest."

"I know, honey," said Mike. "I came home right after it happened. I saw Mom. I buried her in the cemetery near our house. We will go see her when we get home."

"Daddy," said Benny, "I want to go home. When can we go home?" "Soon," said Mike. "I'm in the army now, and I have to get permission from the president to leave. I promise you, we will go home soon."

Sarah walked up to them slowly and quietly so as not to disturb their reunion. Benny saw her and pointed to her.

"Daddy, do you know Aunt Sarah?" he asked. "She has been taking care of me. She promised to get you here. Thanks, Aunt Sarah. You kept you word."

"She is quite a woman isn't she?" said Mike. "She is something else. Do you know that she and I will be working together?"

"I'm glad, Daddy," said Benny. "I like her a lot."

"Me too," added Mike. "So, Sarah, how can I ever thank you?" "Thank God," she said, "He brought me here. I had no idea that your son was here. Though, when I found out that the slaves were children, I was hoping, from the story you told me, that Ben would be here. So, I started asking for the names of the children, and when I heard the name Ben Mills I started to cry. I knew how much he meant to you."

"Come here," said Mike to Sarah. With Ben still in his arms, he hugged Sarah with great affection. Ben also put his arm around her.

"I only wish I could get my hands on the man that shot my Annie when she was on the ground fighting for her life," said Mike with anger in his voice.

"You don't have to, Daddy," said Ben. "Why do you say that, Benny?" said Mike.

"Because, Daddy, before Aunt Sarah got here, a bunch of soldiers came and there was a big fight. I watched the man who killed Mama every day. I was hoping that I would get a chance to get a gun and shoot him myself. I was hiding behind the woodpile over by the cafeteria. The soldiers shot him and he fell. I ran up to him when the others ran away, and the soldiers followed them. When I got to him, he was dying. He asked me to help him, that he was badly hurt. I asked him if he helped my mom when she was shot. I told him that I saw how he helped her by shooting her. He tried to say he was sorry. I took his gun, and was going to shot him when I noticed that he had already died. I felt bad because I wanted to shoot him."

"God wouldn't let you do it," said Mike. "Don't you understand? Murder is wrong, no matter how you do it except in self defense. I'm glad you didn't do it. Thank God that he kept you from doing it."

"I'm glad he is dead," said Ben.

"Well, Sarah," asked Mike. "Since you are in control here, what happens next?"

"I don't know that I'm in control, but for now, I advise you to get settled in your bungalow. After you get Benny settled in, and if you are still awake, come to the cafeteria for a cup of coffee. We can talk about the future. Tomorrow, you and your son can get reacquainted, and if you want me to join you, you have but to ask."

"We want you to join us," said Ben. And then, turning to his father he asked, "Don't we Dad?"

"Of course we do," said Mike. "We may not see much of you soon, and we want to get as much time with you as we can."

"Well then, I'll see you guys for breakfast if you get up early enough. I have breakfast at around eight. Tomorrow, about dinnertime, we will have company. The president and his Secretary of Transportation will arrive about then."

"I'll get to meet the legendary Colonel Tom Corrie," said Mike.

"You certainly will," said Sarah. Ben did not understand the significance of the statement.

Sarah showed them their quarters for the night, and, after Ben fell asleep, Mike joined Sarah, and they talked until about eleven. Sarah managed to stay away from the questions about Tom and her. The next morning, Mike and Ben met Sarah at the cafeteria for breakfast. After breakfast, since the topics they could discuss with Ben were limited, Sarah decided to show them around.

"You know that the Chinese kidnapped young children to farm the land they had chosen to grow food for their troops. What you don't know is that they also brought Christian nuns from China to take care of the children. They brought the nuns not only to take care of the children, but, at the same time, to get rid of the Christian element they hated. These nuns were educated, and most importantly, they were taught English. I am using them as teachers for the children. That's where Ben was when I got him for you. The children work in the mornings and early afternoon, and then they go to school. I am assembling farmers who are willing to help to replace the children so they can spend more time in school. I am also trying, with the help of volunteer women, to find the children's relatives. We have found homes for quite a few already. We have a long way to go yet."

They spent most of the morning just getting to know each other better. After lunch, Sarah took them out to the fields to show them the wonderful job the children had done.

"I was trying to figure out what type of plants these were," said Mike. "They are beautiful. What are they?"

"Well the biggest crop is potatoes. There is a smaller area with wheat, and another small area with corn."

The afternoon slipped by faster than they wanted it to. At six, Sarah got a phone call that told her that the helicopter was scheduled to arrive about six-thirty. Sarah and Mike dropped Ben off at his classroom and waited at the helicopter pad. The helicopter arrived a little past six-thirty. Tom was the first to jump down to the ground. Sarah ran up to him and hugged him.

After a few minutes, Sarah led Tom to Mike. Before she could introduce them, Tom blurted out, "Colonel Mills, I've been looking forward to this meeting with great anticipation." He then stuck his hand out to Mike. Mike grabbed it only to pull Tom up to him so he could hug him.

"My name is Mike. You are a friend. Friends should not be formal." "Please call me Tom. However, I feel a little humbled and inferior in your presence. I've heard so much about you in the Middle East and now in California. President McGard didn't stop talking about you throughout our trip.

"He likes to exaggerate," said Mike. "Did he tell you that Furgason did most of the implementation? Don't worry, you'll get over that inferior feeling once you get to know me and find that I am just an average guy."

"I doubt that, besides there is a certain amount of pride in being here with you. I can tell my children when they read about you in their history books."

Mike turned to Sarah. "I like this guy.

"I do too," said Sarah. "Where is the president?"

"He is in the helicopter giving instructions to the pilot," said Tom. "Do you have any idea what he has planned for us?" asked Mike. "No idea at all," said Tom. Just then, the president stepped down from the helicopter.

"Hello, Mike, Sarah," he said. "How are you guys?"

Sarah went up to him and hugged him. "We are fine. We are waiting for your instructions."

"How are you, Mike?" he asked, knowing of the situation between Sarah and Mike.

"I am delirious," said Mike. "Did you know that Sarah found my son? I have been looking for him for a year."

"That is wonderful," said the president. Then, turning back to Sarah he asked, "Is there a place we can meet to discuss the job in front of us?"

"We can get together in the cafeteria," said Sarah. "The children and the staff eat around five. I think it is empty. If there are any stragglers, I can get rid of them. Besides, don't you think we should all get something to eat first?"

"I guess that would be the smart thing to do," he said. Sarah led them to the cafeteria and asked the help to serve them.

"Will Ben get anything to eat?" Mike asked Sarah.

"Yes, I told the teacher to see that he is fed," responded Sarah. After they had dinner, the president got right to the point.

"Just to bring you up to date," he said. "I want to tell you that we need to decide on a location for the District of Columbia, for the new Washington. I thought we should move it to a place I found that

I liked. It was at the far western end of Virginia. It's a narrow piece of land at the border of Ohio, Kentucky, and Virginia. However, the other cabinet members objected. They think it should stay where it is. I wanted to change it for two reasons. First, in effect, we are rebuilding our nation, and most importantly the cost to rebuild where it is now would cost ten times more. A new location will be much cheaper. What do you fellows think?"

"What about the people in the new location? Do they like the idea of being taken over?" asked Tom.

"How much more do you think it will cost and why?" asked Mike. "Was everything in Washington DC destroyed? I'm thinking of all the monuments. They will be hard to replace. We should be able to save some unless they are all completely destroyed, and I can't believe that they were."

"There were about three or four nuclear devices set off in the area," said the president. "It is devastated. However, I didn't look close enough to see all the monuments. The cost will be very high because, where the White House, the Capital buildings, and the Pentagon used to be are now large holes. We would have to fill these holes so they will be solid enough to build on. What do you think, Sarah? We haven't heard from you yet."

"My first thoughts are to forget the costs," she said. "It's like changing our flag. If we are creating a new country then why not change the flag? We wouldn't change the flag because it is the symbol of our freedom. Where Washington is located is a symbol of this country. I know that all the other countries at this time are not looking at us. They all have their own problems. But how long will that last? I guess what I'm saying is do we want the other countries of the world to know how badly we were damaged? Do we want to show that we lost our whole government?"

"You all make good points," said the president. "Does anyone have any more questions?"

"Why are we moving so fast on this? Shouldn't we take more time to think about it?" said Tom.

"No, I think we need a central government before we can do anything else. We need the states to feel that there is a central government, and that we are in charge. Don't misunderstand. I believe in a central government that is small when it comes to power and the states getting back the constitution guaranteed them. We need a capital. As Sarah says, we need a symbol. Let's vote on it. All in favor of rebuilding the capital where it was before, please raise your hand."

Everyone raised their hands.

"Then we will build where it is now. I was hoping to get someplace for us to meet and receive guests soon. I'll put people on it right away. There is only one other thing I have to cover. I need the cabinet, and all the other I will invite, to meet somewhere to finalize our plans. We need information on the needs of each state. I have people going through each state to determine their needs. That will take about a month. When I get this information, I will contact you, and we will all meet. By then, I will have found a central location where we can meet. After we examine the information, we will go to each state, and each of us will do what we were trained to do in accordance with to your position in the cabinet. The eastern states will be the biggest job; the other states didn't get overrun by the invading army. So, here is what I want each of you to do. Sarah, I have sent for Carol Wenton. She is very competent. I want you and Tom to train her to do the job here so she can relieve you by the first of next month. Mike, I am sending you by helicopter to Bloomington, Illinois. There, we have arranged for you to get an automobile. Drive home and find a place to keep your son while you are away. While there, would you find a good place for us to meet at the end of the month? Ohio is pretty centrally located to the worst damaged areas. Do you both know what you are supposed to do?"

They said, "Yes."

They all went to bed wondering what the future would bring. Two helicopters arrived that night. The next morning, when Mike got up, the president was already gone in one of the helicopters. Sarah showed up at the helicopter pad with Carol. The pilot was ready to take Mike and Ben to get the car. Sarah introduced Carol to Mike. Mike and Sarah hugged for a long time. Nether wanted to let go. They both had tears in their eyes. They said good-bye. Mike watched her from the copter window as long as he could. He was missing her already.

CHAPTER TWELVE

A New Beginning

WHEN MIKE DROVE INTO HIS driveway it was dark. His watch read nine fifty-seven. Ben was fast asleep in the front seat. Mike wondered if the extra key was still under the porch rug. He didn't find out because Sally noticed the car pull into the drive. She didn't know the car, but as Mike got out, the auto lights were enough for Sally to recognize Mike. Before Mike could open the porch door, she ran out and threw herself into his arms.

"Mike," she said. "I would never have believed that I would see you again. That was such a big risk, setting out to find your son. What a wonderful surprise. How are you?"

"I'm fine, but please, look in the front seat and tell me that it was a foolish effort." Sally looked in the front seat, but she couldn't see anything in the dark.

"What do you have in there?" she asked.

"Do you have my keys?" asked Mike with a joyful smile on his face. "When we get inside, I will show you what I got for my efforts."

Sally ran home and was back in a few seconds. Mike opened the door and reached for the light switch. The lights came on. He noted that the electricity was on, so he turned on the outside garage lights and opened the garage door.

"Sally will you bring in what I have in the front seat, please?" asked Mike.

"Of course," said Sally, having no idea what was in the front seat. The outside light made it very clear what was in the front seat.

When Sally opened the door, her jaw dropped. She hesitated for a minute to digest what she saw. Then, with tears swelling in her eyes, she grabbed Ben and hugged him "Benny," she yelled. "Is it really you?"

Poor Ben, who had been asleep, wondered what had grabbed him. At first, he struggled, but then he recognized Aunt Sally.

"Aunt Sally," he said with joy. "I know now that I am home."

"It's a miracle," said Sally. "I never believed that your father would find you in all the mess that has happened in this country. It's so good to see you. Wait until I see your father. He almost gave me a heart attack."

They went inside and found Mike laughing. "Well, do you think my search was in vain?'

"You almost gave me a heart attack," said Sally. "I'll never forgive you." That said, she walked up to him and gave him another affectionate hug. "You're so sneaky."

"How have you been?" asked Mike. "Have you heard anything about Bill?"

"I wish I could be sneaky like you, but I don't know how. Yes, I heard from Bill. He was seriously shot. The people who found him, nursed him back to health. He was delirious for a couple of weeks, they told me. They thought that he wouldn't recover, but thank God he did."

"I was wondering, since I thought that he would be here with you," said Mike. "Where is he?"

"He has been working late, working for the same company. They are trying to rebuild the buildings and offices, and of course the business."

"They are very lucky to have him," said Mike. "I'm so looking forward to seeing him."

"He will be surprised and happy to see you too."

"What have you been doing?" asked Mike. "I see my electricity and gas are on, and that the place is spotless. I was afraid that the pipes would have burst during the cold weather."

"Dearest, Mike," said Sally. "I've been cleaning your house and paying your bills for over a year. I wouldn't let your pipes freeze."

"I don't know how to thank you," said Mike. "You didn't have to do this. I feel bad that you've had to take care of two houses. I am very grateful."

"While you were basking in the sun in California, we were freezing up here. If it wasn't for your gas-powered electric generator, I don't know what we would have done. We lived in your house until the electricity was restored."

"Didn't you have gas so that you could keep warm during the cold months?"

"Yes," said Sally, "however, our furnace needs electricity to operate. We had to blow all our pipes free of water in order to keep them from freezing. By the way, we not only lived in your house, but we also ate all the food you had in the freezer and refrigerator."

"That's good," said Mike. "I'm glad it didn't go to waste. How is the food supply around here?"

"It was pretty bad for a while," said Sally. "It is getting better now. The grocery stores have been rebuilt, and they have established suppliers from the western farmers and cattlemen. We can't get everything we could before, but we have enough to survive."

"We will talk more in the morning," said Mike. "I have something to ask of you. First, I must go out and get some food and take Ben to school if there is one."

"Yes, I think there is. I've seen children going down the street in the morning. I assume that they are going to school. Well, I'll let you get some sleep. I'm sure you are dead tired from driving. I'll see you in the morning. Welcome home."

She was barely out the door when Mike and Ben were fast asleep.

The next morning, after making breakfast for Ben and himself, Mike decided to check out the town and get some food.

"Benny," he said, "I know that you are a big boy now, so, it won't be a problem leaving you alone for a while, will it?"

"No, Dad," said Ben. "I can take care of myself. Where are you going?"

"I need to see about your school and get some groceries for us," said Mike. "We were lucky that Aunt Sally brought us some milk and eggs this morning."

"Okay, Dad," said Ben. "I'll be okay. I'll watch a little TV while you are gone."

Mike was about to leave when the phone rang.

"Mike," said the voice at the other end, "this is Sarah. I see that you got home safely."

"Yes, we had a good trip. We got home about ten last night. How are you guys doing?"

"Tom and I have trained Carol as well as we could. She is a fantastic person. She has picked it up so fast that she is doing a better job than I did. That's why I'm calling. Mike, I need a favor from you."

"I'll be glad to do anything I can to help," promised Mike.

"Since we are finished here, and since we'll have a lot of work ahead of us, and since Cleveland doesn't exist, we wondered if you could make arrangements for us. We will need a place to stay, and a church whose pastor is a born again Christian.."

"I'm sure that you will be happy with my pastor," assured Mike. "I'm looking into a local hotel for a possible meeting room for our cabinet meeting with the president. I'll see what they have available for other members of the cabinet. As for you and Tom, I have a five-bedroom house. You can stay with me for the few days you will be here."

"I don't think it would be proper for us to stay at your house," said Sarah.

"Well, at least till you find a place you can stay here. How soon can you get here?"

"We were thinking that we would leave as soon as the helicopter can get here. Hopefully, we can leave tomorrow morning. We will pick up a car where you did. Therefore, we should get there tomorrow night."

"I'm looking forward to seeing you. Have a safe trip. Good-bye." Mike hung up and looked at his son.

"We are going to have company tomorrow night. I have a lot of work to do today. I'll probably be gone until noon. I'll bring lunch for us then. Will you be all right?"

"I'll be okay," said Ben as he turned on the TV. Mike went into the garage and opened the garage door. He had to do it manually. The automatic garage openers were built into his car and Annie's car, but both of those cars were gone. The hand held control was somewhere in the house. They had never used it, so he wasn't sure where it was. He didn't have the time to look for it now. He pulled the car out of the garage, and got out to close the garage door when he heard his name.

"Hey, Mike, you old son-of-a-gun, how are you?" asked Bill. He ran up to Mike and gave him a big hug. "I never expected to see you again. Sally told me that you came home last night. You could have knocked me over with a feather."

"You're the one that is here by a miracle, Sally told me of your traumatic experience."

"Yes it was nip-and-tuck for awhile," said Bill, "but God didn't think it was my time."

"You will have to tell me all about it some time," said Mike in a hurry.

"There is not much to tell," said Bill. "Henry, my boss, and Betty the accountant ran into the boiler room in the basement. I was right behind them, but didn't make it. I was shot in the back. They apparently took care of me after the invaders left. I don't remember anything until several weeks later. That's all there is to it."

"I have to go," said Mike finally. "I have guests coming tomorrow night and I have nothing in the house."

"Who do you have coming, anyone important?"

"It's a long story, and I will fill you in later. I'm a cabinet member of the new president's cabinet. I have two of the other members coming tomorrow. I'll introduce you to all of the members when they get here."

"Go do your thing," said Bill. "It's just that I've missed you so much. Is there anything I can do to help?"

"God knows that I've missed you and Sally. We had such good times together, and you can help. Do you know if any of the hotels in the area are open for business, and what is the story on the area schools?"

"I know that the Hilton is still operating. It always has a few cars in the parking lot. I'm sure it is hurting like all the other business though. As for the school, I know that children are going to school, but that is all I can tell you. I think a Martha something is running the school."

As Bill started to walk away, Mike yelled to him.

"Bill, how secure is your job with your old company? Sally tells me that you have been working till late at night."

"That is about to end. They only have one factory that is workable. That is the one I've been helping to set up. The company is hurting very badly. Henry, the owner has not only lost buildings, but very knowledgeable people. Also, he has no customers, except the few from the one we are repairing now. It is a tool company. Henry thinks that he will probably end up running it by himself. The only business he can get is for building tools and maybe industrial tools. He said that after this is complete, he has nothing for me, but if I'm really in need, he is willing to give me a day a week. He says that he will be starting from scratch. He's not sure he can support himself."

"That's all right," said Mike. "You have a job with me. I need a staff to help me with my job. I'll fill you in later if you accept."

"Are you kidding? Of course I accept. When do I start?"

"You start right now. However, I don't know what the salary will be yet. I don't even know what mine is going to be."

Mike drove off happier that he had been a few minutes ago. He admired Bill for his salesmanship, his down to earth common sense, and his honesty. He would be a great secretary of state. Mike, first, went to the hotel. He was told that if the majority of the people that attend the meeting stayed there, they would provide a conference room free of cost.

"Will there be any one that is well known in the meeting?" asked the Manager.

"I don't know how well known everyone is, but the one that will head the meeting is the acting president," said Mike, not expecting the clerk to know him. He was wrong.

"President McGard is coming here?" said the manager, getting all excited. "When will he be here? Who is coming with him? We have to prepare for him."

"It will be about the end of the month, probably after the Fourth of July," said Mike. "He is going to meet with all of his cabinet members and a few other officials he has found. I'm surprised that you have heard of him."

"Are you kidding?" asked the manager. "There has been nothing else on the radio and the television. We have been following the defeat of the enemy in the Midwest and in California, by the famous Colonel Mills, now vice president. We only saw them in uniform, but you look a little like him." Then, with a shocked look on her face, she got all giddy and added, "You're not Vice President Mills are you?"

"Guilty," said Mike as he turned to leave.

"We will have everything ready," she said. "Just call us."

Next, Mike went to the church, and as luck had it, the minister was there.

"Good morning, Pastor Anthony," said Mike upon entering his office. "How are things this morning?"

"Well good morning," said the pastor. "To what do I owe the honor of your visit this morning?"

"Okay, you can stop it now," said Mike with a smile. "So you've heard of my experiences."

"Every day on every radio and television station," said the pastor, kidding Mike.

"All kidding aside," said Mike. "I need a favor."

"All kidding aside," said the pastor. "We are very proud of you. I know that you will do the right thing for this country. So what can I do for you?"

"Tomorrow night, two very good friends of mine, both members of the president's cabinet, I believe will want to get married before they have to start the tough job ahead for them. How soon can you marry them?"

"Tomorrow is Thursday," said the pastor thinking out loud. "If they can get a marriage license sometime next week, I can marry them the following Saturday."

"If they wanted to get married sooner, could you marry them during the week?"

"I'd rather not," said the pastor. "First, try to sell them on the following Saturday."

Next, Mike went to the school. On the way, he phoned McGard and notified him that the meeting place had been confirmed. Mike also told him about Bill Walters, his neighbor. He told McGard that Bill was a great salesman and corporate manager who, Mike thought, due to his diplomatic personality and experience would make a great Secretary of State. McGard said that Mike should hire him, bring him to the meeting, and that they would talk about it then. McGard also added that any one named Bill had to be a good man. When he got to the school, he went into the principal's office. In the office, he found Martha standing by the door ready to leave.

"Hello Mike," she said and gave him a warm hug. "How are you? Have you found any track of your son, Ben?"

"I not only found tracks I also found him," said Mike. "That is why I'm here. I would like to register him for school. Are you the new principal?"

"I'm the new principal and the only math teacher," she said. "I have both jobs, and it is getting to be too much. Send Ben here tomorrow. I'll see that he gets back where he left off. Has he had any education while he has been gone?"

"He had some where he was held, but I don't know how much," said Mike. "Do you have a lot of students?"

"We have about a third of what we had. However, I heard from a Doctor Anders that she is sending home another fourteen children. I am trying to find their parents or relatives for them."

"I see that you are going to a class, so I'll let you go. I'll send or bring Ben tomorrow morning at eight."

"That will be fine," said Martha. "Good to see you again."

Mike then went to the grocery store and bought enough food for four for a week. When he got home, Ben was watching a cartoon on television. After lunch, Mike went to the city hall. He found that Robert Barton was moved up to mayor and that Steven Briggs was Council Chairman. Unfortunately, they only had two other council members. They were in the process of redistricting by population and setting up a procedure for elections. It was very difficult because the population was changing daily. It seemed that some of the people that had run ahead or gone south of the invading army where now coming back. It made the count of residents very difficult.

Mike learned what he came for. He was told that the Akron Courthouse was open, and that if he wanted a marriage license, he would have to go there. When Mike got home, he noticed that Bill was working in his back yard.

"Bill, what are you up to?" he asked. "Are you all finished with rebuilding the old factory plant?"

"Hi, Mike," Bill answered. "I hope you weren't pulling my leg about working for you, because I quit my job. I told him I got a full time job. I was worried when I came home, and you weren't here. Sally has faith in you, so on her word, I quit my job."

"That's okay. I talked to the president about you. He said that I should hire you, and that you can aid me as my assistant in my duties as Secretary of State. Come over and I'll explain everything I know about what we are expected to do."

Mike made some coffee, and they settled down in Mike's office. "Tomorrow night, the secretary of energy and the secretary of transportation will be here. There are two or three more that I have not met yet. I'll meet them at the end of the month. The two that are coming tomorrow are originally from Cleveland. They asked me to make arrangements for them here."

They spent the rest of the afternoon talking about what was going on. Mike explained everything he knew about the plans that the president had. They got so into talking the problems that needed to be solved that they didn't realize what time it was. Sally brought dinner to them at about seven in the evening.

"Don't you guys want anything to eat?" she asked. "At least think of poor Benny. He has been patiently waiting on you two. I'll go up and set the table. I made some meatloaf. I'll call you when everything is ready."

Mike and Bill moved to the family room.

"Remember the last time we sat here talking?" asked Mike.

"Don't remind me," said Bill. "I thought your idea was ridiculous. My non-belief almost cost me my life. I'll never doubt you again."

"I won't say I told you so, because I don't know if I believed it myself. If I had, Annie would still be alive.

"It is wonderful sitting here like this again after a year. I never even dreamed it would happen," said Bill. "It is wonderful, but it's not the same without Annie."

They all ate dinner, and after dinner, Bill and Sally decided to go home early. Bill hadn't been home before bedtime in over a month. They needed some time alone together.

"Listen," said Mike as they were leaving, "my guests are arriving late tomorrow night. If you don't mind eating late, we would like you to have dinner with us."

"I'm sorry, we can't tomorrow night," said Sally. "We have made arrangements to go to dinner with my aunt. She is so alone since my uncle was killed by those monsters that tried to wipe us out. I promised that we would spend the day with her."

The next morning, Mike met Bill. They spoke for a while about the tasks ahead of them. Bill and Sally then left for the little town of Findlay to be with their aunt. It was one of the few towns that were still prospering. Its main product was cement vaults and coffins.

Mike dropped Ben off at school and returned home to look over the notes McGard left him. It was a long and lonely day. The anticipation of seeing Sarah again that evening made the day even longer. He ate lunch at noon and went to pick up Ben at three-thirty. He tried to study the notes, hoping to come up with thought of his own, but it was to no avail. He was too nervous, waiting on the arrival of his guests. It was a little after seven when Mike heard a car in his driveway. He rushed outside to see who it was.

"Sarah," he said as he grabbed her in a tender hug. "It's so good to see you." He then turned to Tom who was just coming around the car. "Tom, it's so good to see both of you." Mike then gave Tom a friendly hug.

"It's good to see you too," said Tom. "It's good to meet friends that are in civilians clothes."

"Yes, I know what you mean," said Mike. "Come on inside. It's still a little chilly out here." Tom opened the trunk, and Mike helped him bring in their suitcases. "I guess you two are pretty hungry."

"I'm almost too tired to be hungry," said Sarah. "What do you have planned?"

"We're even picky now, are we?" asked Mike in jest. "If you must know, I have my indoor grill heated up and have four juicy rib steaks ready to grill. However, if you are too tired..."

"I think we just got real hungry," said Tom interrupting him. "We really didn't have much of a lunch at the car pickup city. I don't even remember its name, we are so very hungry."

"I know what you both mean," said Mike. "I made that trip myself not too long ago. Besides, Sarah and I have a lot of good eating to catch up on."

"You can say that again," said Sarah. When Mike opened his mouth to say it again, she added, "But, I wish you wouldn't." They all laughed and settled down in the family room.

When dinner was ready, Mike called Ben to eat. Ben wasn't aware that Tom and Sarah were there. When he came down he instantly recognized them.

"Hi, Aunt Sarah," he said. "It's so good to see you."

"It's good to see you too. How does it feel to be home?" "It's good, but I miss my mom."

"Let's eat," said Mike. "You know that Uncle Tom and Aunt Sarah have just come from the same place we came from after we got our car. Remember how tired we were?"

Hi, Uncle Tom," said Ben and gave Tom a hug also. Mike served them soup and salad and, after that, served each a rib steak.

They talked a little after dinner was over, but it was obvious that Tom and Sarah were very tired.

"I put you two in rooms at the end of the hall so that you will not be disturbed until you get up late tomorrow," said Mike.

"Tom," said Mike. Did you have a brother or sister?" "No," said Tom. "I was an only child."

"I had a sister. She lived in Cleveland. Her house was in an area that is now a big hole. I loved her very much.

"I miss her very much. Anyway I think you should go to bed. I know how tired you must be."

They went up stairs, both feeling very tired. Mike stayed downstairs until he no longer heard any activity up stairs. Ben had gone to bed earlier and had closed his door.

The next morning, Mike made breakfast for Ben then drove Ben to school, and when he got back, Tom and Sarah were just getting up. He made them coffee and some home fries. Sarah came down first.

"Good morning," said Mike, to which she replied the same. "I was sure that Tom would come down first."

"I had the bathroom tied up, so he had to wait," said Sarah. "What's for breakfast?"

"I have coffee, and I'll make some eggs if you like," said Mike.

"I'd love two eggs, sunny side up," said Sarah. "Tom likes them the same way."

Tom was down soon and they ate breakfast together.

"I have two very intelligent and competent neighbors I want you to meet. I want to recommend them for positions on the cabinet. I would like your opinions on them."

"We would be glad to, but we want to go to the hotel and get acquainted with the area."

"Of course," said Mike. "We still have about three weeks before the president gets here. We have plenty of time. After they ate and freshened up, Mike gave them directions to the hotel they would be meeting.

"Don't wait up for us for lunch," said Sarah. "It is now past ten. We are going to have lunch in Akron and look around for the city, besides Tom and I have some talking to do."

"Have a nice day," said Mike as they left.

The hours slipped by slowly. Mike ate lunch and sat in his office contemplating the future. It was about two-thirty when he heard someone knocking loudly on the rear door. Mike ran to find out what all the raucous was about. It was Sally.

"What's the matter?" asked Mike opening the door.

"Mike," she said out of breath, "do you remember that while you were on your honeymoon, a woman with a cane came asking for you? When I told her you were on your honeymoon, she started to cry and left. Well, if you want to see who it was, she is just leaving your front yard."

Mike quickly ran to the front door and out. The woman had just gotten into her car and was about to drive out of the turnaround in front of Mike's house. He ran after the car and caught up to it as it reached the main road. He knocked on the window. The woman stopped her car and turned to see who was knocking on her window. When Mike saw the woman's face, his head started to spin. He stepped backwards and, tripping over his own feet, he fell to the ground. The woman, worried that he had hurt himself, rushed out of her car and was at his side. Sally was just coming around the corner of the house and saw what had happened.

"Call his wife!" yelled the woman as Sally ran up to them. "Call his wife," said the woman again.

"What happened?" asked Sally, grabbing Mike's left arm. The woman was holding his right arm. This prevented Mike from helping himself to get up.

"Isn't his wife at home?" asked the woman.

"He doesn't have a wife," said Sally finally. "She was killed by the invaders a year ago."

"Oh Lord," said the woman. "I'm so sorry. Let's get him inside." Mike, still dazed, let them lead him through the front door which he had left open. They didn't let go until he was sitting comfortably in his family room.

"What are you doing here?" asked Mike of the woman.

"I just wanted to see that you were all right," said the woman. "With all the frightful killings and bombings that have occurred in the last year, I was worried about you and your family. I was in the area and decided to see if you were all right. I'm so sorry about your wife."

"What happened? Was your husband killed by the invaders?" asked Mike with anger starting to build up in his voice. "No," said the woman with tears showing in her eyes.

"So, he dumped you as you dumped me," said Mike, his voice showing his disdain for the woman.

"There never was anyone else," said the woman, her voice quivering, showing her uneasiness with the questions.

"Why are you lying to me?" asked Mike. "I talked to your friend Laura. She told me that you had gotten back together with an old high school sweetheart and were going to get married that June."

"She lied to you," said the woman.

"Why would she lie to me?" asked Mike "I don't understand."

"I told her to lie to you," said the woman. "I know that you were hurt very badly and may never forgive me, but I did what I thought was best for us both. I know that you will never agree with me, but at the time, it seemed like the right thing to do. I know now that I made the biggest mistake of my life. Please, let me explain."

"Explain what?" said Mike, still showing anger. "Explain why you dumped me without an explanation, without a good-bye. You could have at least written a Dear John letter. You disappeared out of the world and left me heartbroken and feeling lost."

"Dear God," said Sally, showing great surprise. "You can't be Tara. We thought you were dead. You are the love of his life, the one that forgot him and dumped him overnight."

"Speaking of forgetting," said Tara, "you were pretty fast in getting married to someone else."

"I'm going to leave you lovers to work this out for yourselves," said Sally, "but before I leave, I have to say this in his defense: Tara, ask yourself how I knew who you were. He has never stopped talking about you. I have talked to Annie, his wife. She knew all about you. She knew that Mike's heart belonged to you. She told me that she loved Mike so much that she was willing to live with that. By the way, Mike. I am going to cook dinner, and, seeing that it's time to pick up Ben, I'll do it for you." After saying that, Sally left.

"Why did you marry someone so soon?" said Tara.

"So now it's my fault," said Mike in disgust. "I didn't dump you."

"I could explain that if you would keep your mouth shut and let me explain," said Tara.

"Now you tell me to shut up."

"Yes, until I've explained," said Tara. "Then, I want to know if you had a girlfriend on the side."

"All right, explain," said Mike. "I can't see how anything that you say could possibly make a difference, but I'll keep quiet."

"You may never forgive me, but I want you to know why I did what I did."

"Go ahead," said Mike. "I'm listening."

"Remember when we were together the last time that I left early because I had a bad headache?"

"Yes," said Mike. "You had headaches all the time."

"Well, when I got home they got more severe. It got so bad that I found I was losing my balance. Remember, I also had that problem. You used to kid me about being clumsy. Anyway, it got so bad that I finally went to the doctor." Tara lowered her head. She was going to tell her story without looking at Mike. "The doctor ran several tests on me," she continued. "He sent me to a specialist who took X-rays, ultrasounds, CAT scans, and MRIs. He said that I had a tumor in the center of my brain, between the two lobes. He said that he thought it might be malignant because it had grown so fast. He sent me to California to a special brain surgeon, Doctor Dane. He reviewed the test results and ran several tests himself. The results, he said, were that no one would attempt the surgery. It was too risky. He said that the chance of a successful surgery was only about fifty percent. Even if it was successful, there was a fifty percent chance of my losing some motor control, like speech or the ability to walk. I asked him what would be the results of doing nothing. He said, 'There isn't anything that we can do. At best you have two to three months of life. For the last month or so, you will lose all memory, motor controls, and the ability to eat.' Mike, I couldn't put you through seeing me degenerate before your very eyes. I couldn't take knowing that you were there suffering with me. I was in agony not only that I was going to die, but that I would never see you again. Mike, I just couldn't let you see me like that." She looked up at Mike. She saw tears streaming down his cheeks and into the corner of his mouth. As soon as she looked up, Mike grabbed her and hugged her.

"I'm so sorry for your pain," he said finally. "I would have died right with you. Are you all right?"

"If you let me, I'll tell you the rest of the story," said Tara. "Go ahead," said Mike with tears still in his eyes.

"I went home, ready to die," continued Tara. "My father didn't know what to do. We had both given up. Thank God, however, Doctor Dane didn't give up on me. Several days later, he called and told us that he had searched the Internet and every other place he could. He said he found a surgeon in Sweden who had done several similar surgeries and had a high percentage of success. He said he was willing to operate after seeing the test results the doctor sent him. My father took me there as fast as he could. After examining all the test results, Doctor Pulsen explained that it was a serious problem. He told us that it was a colloid cyst. He said that it wasn't malignant. He informed us that the recovery could take six months to a year. Loss of memory was common, and he said that I could lose motor control. "Doctor Pulsen operated on me. It was over a month before I was conscious and able to understand what was going on. He said it was probably there from birth. He said that it came out easily, not having a tight hold of any part of my brain. He said that he got it all, and, barring any complications, that I would make a complete recovery. However, he said that it would take a lot of time. It had damaged the motor nerves, and they need time to heal.

"When I became completely conscious, I found that I couldn't talk or move my arms or feet. It took three more weeks before I could eat. The first time they tried to feed me soup, I threw it up. After several months, I was able to walk with the help of a cane, and I came looking for you. I almost died on the spot when I learned that you were on your honeymoon. Realizing that I had made the biggest mistake of my life, I kicked myself. I thought then that I would never marry. My career was going to be my life. Now it's your turn." Why did you marry so soon after our break up?"

"I was like you," started Mike. "You left me hurting very badly. One day, I could see my whole life ahead of me, and the next I couldn't see to the next minute. I thought then, like you that I could never love anyone like I loved you. I had a hole in my heart that as big as the Grand Canyon. I began to doubt myself. I believed that I was unlovable. I needed something to fill that hole. You had your career. I didn't like my career that much. It couldn't fill the void I had in my life. For several weeks, I would cry myself to sleep. I would dream that I found you, and that you rejected me. You would tell me that you didn't love me anymore. I had that dream so often that I believed that it really happened. When my parents decided to visit my Aunt Millie, I decided to go with them just to get away for a while. You remember my Aunt Millie and Uncle Alfred don't you?"

"Yes, they lived in Pennsylvania, in the city of Jennet I believe." "That's correct. Aunt Millie, if you remember was married to an Italian."

"Yes, a Sicilian if I remember correctly," said Tara.

"Well, your memory wasn't affected," said Mike. "What you didn't know was that Uncle Alfred had a brother that lived in the same city. My Uncle decided to have a family cookout for us, and he invited his brother and his family. They had a daughter that was single and a couple of years younger than I. I noticed that she was very pretty, but I wasn't interested. My parents, however, were formulating plans of their own. They knew if they suggested anything between us, I would run for cover. I didn't want a family fixed marriage. I don't know if my parents and her parents talked when we weren't around, but they decided to let the two children Anna and her brother Sam come to Cleveland and spend a couple of weeks with us. I could tell that Annie liked me, because whenever I looked at her she would look down. I didn't care. My ego needed that. In those two weeks, Annie made it pretty clear that she loved me. She showered me with more love than I ever expected. I needed that so badly that I told my mother that I liked her. I never asked Annie to marry me. Our parents planned the whole wedding. I went along. I felt that, though I didn't love her, I couldn't do any better. The first night we were together after the wedding, I closed my eyes and pretended it was you I was making love to. But Tara, I won't lie to you. After seeing how much love she had for me and how sweet and lovable she was to me, I started having feelings for her. She was a terrific wife. I realized that I loved her with all my heart after our son, Ben was born."

"You have a son?" asked Tara.

"Yes, that's who Sally volunteered to pick up," said Mike. "That is my son, Ben. As soon as she picks him up, I'll introduce him to you. He is ten years old."

"Now I have another question for you," said Mike. "I thought for sure you were dead. How did you escape the Chicago disaster?"

"I poured myself into the job. I became an authority on TV transmitters. I had been on a job in Rochester, New York, and my plane had taken off to fly home when the aircraft lost contact with Cleveland. The pilot informed us of the problem. He said not to worry because he could fly by the seat of his pants. However, about five minutes later, a couple of fighters started to shoot at us. Our pilot was an old fighter pilot. He flew the plane down toward the ground with the plan of landing somewhere if the plane was disabled. Well, the engines were shot up, and he glided the plane to a small clearing. He slid the plane on the ground, but the clearing was too small so it slid through a wooded area and into an open field beyond the woods. The plane was demolished. The wings were torn off and the fuselage was opened wide. Most of the people survived the crash. However, most didn't survive the fighters that had started to strafe the ground with machine gun fire. They killed many of the people who had tried to run back to the woods. I ran in the opposite direction. I hid under one of the wing parts that had been dragged along with the aircraft. I spent two weeks trying to find my way back to civilization."

"My dear Tara," said Mike with tears starting to show again. "You have had more than your share of problems."

"So have you, and some of it from me," said Tara.

"I'm afraid we have a problem," said Mike. "I'm working with the president. I will have to leave town pretty soon."

"That reminds me," said Tara. "I know that the name Mills is a very common name, but do you have any relatives that have been working with the president when he was still a general?"

"Why do you ask?" said Mike.

"Well I've heard so much about a Colonel Mills," said Tara. "I just wondered if he was a relative." Mike started to laugh.

"Don't you watch television?" asked Mike. "His picture has been plastered all over the tube. Haven't you seen his face?"

"I've seen his picture from afar but not his face," said Tara. "Why, is he a relative?"

"He is the closest relative I will ever have," said Mike, starting to laugh out loud. Tara was no dummy. She suddenly realized why Mike was laughing.

"Oh my," she said with a shocked look on her face. "Was that you —I mean is that you? Are you the Desert Fox?"

"I hate that name, but yes, I'm guilty," he said still laughing.

"My hero," said Tara, "I should have known, but the information that I got last was that the Colonel was killed in a nuclear blast in California."

"The reports of my death, as Mark Twain said, were greatly exaggerated."

"Now what are you doing for the president?" she asked.

"I'm his vice president and temporary secretary of state. We are going to meet on July fifth to formulate our strategy. All of the president's cabinet members will be there. We are then going from state to state to help with the reconstruction of each state and eventually our country."

Now it was Tara's turn to laugh. It startled him. "Honey," she said, "we are going to be together forever. No one is going to separate us for long."

"How can you say that?" asked Mike. "Don't you understand what I just said?"

"Do you know where I'm staying tonight?" He shook his head indicating, no. "I'm staying at the Hilton, and I have a very important meeting to go to on July fifth." Since Mike just sat there in a state of shock, she continued. "We will always be together, because I'm the secretary of communication. I've been putting stations back on the air for a month now. I'm going to go with you everywhere."

"That's fantastic," said Mike. "But I have a problem with that. You see, I'm in love with someone else. I don't have the same feeling for you as I had back then. We were only kids."

"Oh, Mike, I'm sorry I didn't come here to win you back. I'm sorry if I misled you. I was just so happy to see you and that you were alive Do you see why I came by to see if you were okay? I thought you were married, but since I was in the neighborhood I couldn't resist checking up on you. I had no idea that you were widowed. I also had no idea that you were the nation's hero."

"You know what?" asked Mike. "I think we are talking too much." He grabbed her and hugged her. We will always be friends.

"There is another thing I should tell you," said Tara. "About two years later after I got over finding out that you were married, I met Ralph. We dated for about six months and were married. I have two children. Thanks to God they survived the attack. We now live in a little town about 70 miles northwest of Chicago. Just then Sally came back with Ben."

"Am I interrupting anything?" asked Sally.

"Yes, but you're forgiven," said Mike. Then, turning to Ben, he said, "Benny, I want you to meet a girl I was engaged to before I met your mother. Her name is Miss Garfinger. Tara, this is my son Ben."

"How do you do?" asked Ben, "I'm so glad to meet you. Are you going to be my new mother?"

"Benny," said Sally. "That's not a proper question."

"Your father proposed to me over ten years ago," said Tara. "I don't think it is still good."

"It doesn't matter now. We have both moved on," said Tara.

"I take it that you two have made up?" asked Sally. "You were fighting when I left. You were arguing about being dumped."

"It turns out that she didn't really dump me," explained Mike. "She became very ill. The doctors gave her two to three months to live. She didn't want me to see her in the state she would be in. She made the decision to keep me from knowing her dilemma. A Swedish doctor healed her, but by the time she was able to travel, I was on my honeymoon with Annie. That's why you saw her with a cane."

"Sounds intriguing," said Sally. "I would like to hear more, but I have to go cook dinner for all of you. I take it that there will be one more."

"Definitely," said Mike. "There will be six of us if Bill makes it home, plus something for Ben. "

"I'm right on it," said Sally as she left.

Mike started to reminisce with Tara when they heard a car pull into the back yard.

"Don't say anything," said Mike to Tara. "I want you to hear something that should be interesting to you about my sincerity.

"I believe everything you have told me," said Tara.

"Ben, why don't you go upstairs and do your homework?" suggested Mike.

"Do I have too?" said Ben, showing disappointment. "Ben," said Mike. That's all he had to say.

"Oh, all right," said Ben as he left the room.

Tom and Sarah walked into the family room. Mike and Tara stood up to meet them.

"Tom, Sarah, I want you to meet Miss Garfinger. She is the secretary of communications. Tom is the secretary of transportation and Sarah is the secretary of energy." They each shook hands. "Sarah, I want you to tell Miss Garfinger, what my last thoughts where when we were hanging together, thinking that we were going to die."

"I don't understand what you are asking," said Sarah.

"Did I have any romantic thoughts, like you had for Tom?"

"You mean that your last thoughts were of your old girlfriend, Tara I believe was her name. You wondered if you would see Tara in heaven, since she was killed in Chicago a year ago. You always thought of her whether we were in danger or not. Why, did Miss Garfinger know her?"

"You guessed part of the answer," said Mike. "Let me answer your question this way. Miss Garfinger's complete name is Tara Garfinger. "No," said Sarah, tears now running down her cheek. "Are you the Tara that he has been pining for all his life?" She never let Tara answer. Sarah grabbed Tara in an affectionate hug. Tara was taken by surprise. For a few seconds, her hands just hung out from her sides. "You don't know how glad I am to see you. But how can it be? We thought you were killed in Chicago. You also married someone else."

"I'm glad to see you too," said Tara. "I was out of town when Chicago was bombed." She gave Sarah a short explanation of her breaking up with Mike because of her illness. "I'm at a loss, however, to see why it means so much to you."

"I know," said Sarah. "Sometime Mike will explain it all to you." "Enough of that," said Mike, not wanting the discussion to proceed
    any further. He wanted to see what Sarah would do and say. "Let's have a drink on our friendships," said Tom.

"Let's all have one after dinner," said Sally just entering the house. "I have dinner ready. I think, if you fellows don't mind, we could eat at my house and save me the problem of bringing everything here. Bill just got home, so we are ready to eat."

"How can we resist that?" said Mike.

He got Ben, and they all went next door and had what they claimed was a fantastic dinner. It turned out to be a five-course dinner. That evening, when they got back to Mike's house, Mike found a message from the president. The president asked Mike to meet with Carol Brigs, the secretary of the treasury, who he said was handling all of the finances. He said that she would be at the Hilton in Fairlawn.

"Girls," he said after listening to the phone message. "I have to get together with the Secretary of the Treasury first thing tomorrow morning. Can you girls take care of providing breakfast and perhaps lunch while I'm gone? I have filled the refrigerator and the freezer downstairs with lots of food."

"Don't worry," said Sarah. "I'm a pretty good cook, as you know. I will take care of the men. How about you Tara?" she asked, turning to Tara, "Do you want to help or do any of the cooking?"

"I've learned to fend for myself for the last few years. Between the two of us, we will take care of everything."

"Let's all go to bed and get a good night's rest. We have a long day tomorrow." suggested Mike.

"Tara and I have decided to go to the hotel for tonight" said Tom. "Why?" asked Mike, surprised at Tom's words. "We have five bedrooms. There is plenty of room"

"You and Sarah have to talk. We have discussed this with Sarah and she needs to talk with you."

"That is no longer necessary, since Tara has come into the picture." said Sarah.

"No, I think you to need to talk" said Tara.

"What is going on?" asked Mike, being completely confused.

"Sarah and you need to talk," repeated Tara. Tom and Tara then left. Sally and Bill took the hint and also left Mike and Sarah alone.

"What is this all about?" asked Mike.

"It was something that we considered, but since Tara has come back into your life it isn't important anymore," explained Sarah showing tears in her eyes.

"I don't understand, but if Tara has changed anything then I suppose I should tell you the truth. I didn't say anything since you and Tom are so involved."

"Now, you are the one that is not making sense," said Sarah. "What are you talking about?"

"Tara and I had a long talk," said Mike. "We found that we didn't have the feelings for each other that we had as kids. We are both different people. The magic is no longer there. I don't pine for Tara anymore. That feeling is a nice memory of the past. Besides she is married with two kids."

"Oh, Mike," said Sarah. "How do you feel about that?" "Relieved," he said. "So now what is this all about?"

"Tom and I spent two wonderful weeks together in Iowa when I was teaching there," started Sarah. "We soon found out that we also were living in the past. The young woman and the young officer no longer existed. We no longer had romantic feeling for each other. It had been just childish crushes. We decided to just be good friends."

"This all happened before you found out that I was still alive?"

"Yes, that's another reason that I was so happy to see you"

"Why then didn't you tell me when I came to Iowa? Why did you lead me on thinking that you and Tom were an item? Do you know that I even arranged for your wedding?"

"I was hoping that you loved me enough that you would fight for me. That you would ask me to reconsider after all we were through together. It wasn't successful was it? "

"Even though my heart was breaking, I have always wanted your happiness before mine. I was happy that at least your dream came true."

"My dream has not come true yet," said Sarah. "Tell me something. You said that Tara brought butterflies in your stomach. Did you ever have butterflies for me?"

"I don't remember a time that I didn't have butterflies when I was with you. I didn't tell you because you were always talking about Tom. Did you ever have butterflies in your stomach for me?"

"I didn't know how much I loved you until I thought you had died. I then realized that the memory and feelings for you were much greater than they ever were for Tom. As for the butterflies in my stomach, no I don't feel them. They are more like eagles flapping their wings. By the way, those arrangements for a wedding do not have to be wasted." Mike could not hold himself back. He grabbed her and pulled her to him. Their lips met. There tongues found each other as if it had been destiny. Mike felt like he was floating above the floor. A chill ran down Sarah's spine. Her knees became wobbly. All that kept her from falling was Mike's arms around her. They forgot the time and the work they had to do the next day. They thought that they would not be able to sleep. Their dreams are being fulfilled. After they came up for air, they walked to the back porch of Mike's house and sat on the wicker couch. They continued their affectionate enjoyment. Sometime in the middle of the night they sat there with Sarah's head on Mikes shoulder as she had done on the back porch at the farm house during Mike's recovery. Sarah felt save and happier then she had ever been.

The next morning, Mike took Ben to school. Sarah went with him. She didn't want to be away from him more then necessary. At school, he walked in to the principal's office. Martha was talking to one of the students.

"Do you understand?" she was asking the student. "Yes, Miss Seaton," he said as he left.

"Mike," said Martha. "How are you? Is there something I can help you with?"

"Yes," said Mike. "I have a problem."

He then explained his job as Vice President and the traveling he would have to do. He also introduced Sarah and informed her that they were going to get married and will be on a honey moon for a couple of weeks.

"Congratulation," said Martha, "that is wonderful. I am so happy for you."

"I need someplace for Ben to stay while I finish the job we have to do to bring this country back on its feet. I was thinking of a boarding school or an academy or even a governess."

"Nonsense," said Martha. "Annie was my best friend. John and I would love to take care of Ben. He is like a son. When not in class, he used to call me Aunt Martha. We had an agreement. In class he called me Mrs. Seaton, and whenever they were at my house, he would call me Aunt Martha."

"Are you sure?" asked Mike. "Why don't you ask John first and talk it over with him?"

"That's not necessary," she said. "John and I have already discussed the possibility. We can't have children of our own, so we have even thought of adopting one of the orphaned children."

"If you are sure, I'd love that," said Mike.

"Go do your thing," she said. "Just let me know when you are leaving town, and we will do the rest. Another thing, don't offend us by offering us money."

"I wouldn't think of offending you money." From there Mike and Sarah went to the court house and got a marriage license. Next they went to the jewelry store where they bought all the rings they would need. At the store Mike offered Sarah the engagement ring.

"I can't accept that," she said with a smile. "What's the problem," he asked.

You haven't proposed to me and I haven't accepted. I need that so that I could tell my children and grandchildren.

"Sarah, darling," he said. "I love you more than I thought was possible. Will you marry me?"

"Yes, with all my heart," she said as they kissed. Mike then put the ring on her finger.

Mike dropped Sarah at his house so that she could show everyone the ring and tell them everything that had happened the night before. Mike drove directly to the Hilton. There, he met Carol who was in the lobby. She recognized Mike.

"Vice President Mills," she said as she approached him. "I'm Carol Brigs. It's so nice to meet you."

"Nice to meet you too, Carol," he said. Mike explained why he was so late. "Please call me Mike. We are going to work together for too long a time to be so formal."

"Of course," she replied. "Please follow me to my room. I have everything set up there for our meeting. President McGard wants us to communicate with him by phone."

As soon as they settled in, she contacted the president. The three of them conferred together till late afternoon. When the president was satisfied, he gave a closing statement.

"I think that the three of us have solved a lot of the problems I was worried about. You two are amazing. I'm so lucky to have you two on my side. All we really have left to do is confer the others. I am looking forward to seeing you all on July fifth. We can set up our travel plans and start our rebuilding task from there." Then, the president left a message that Mike was to pass on to the others. He then said good-bye.

Mike got back to his house around six-thirty that afternoon. Tara, Sarah, and Tom were sitting in the family room discussing the task before them.

"Hi, everyone," he said as he walked in.

"Hi, what's going on?" asked Sarah. We have been worried about you."

"Where are Bill and Sally?" asked Mike. "Let's get them, and then I can tell you all at the same time."

"They went in to call some friends about taking care of their house in case they have to leave," said Tara. "I'll go and round them up."

It was only five minutes later when Tara came back with Bill and Sally.

"First," started Mike, "let me tell you that Carol and I were on the phone with the president the entire time that I was gone. We handled a lot of things that were bothering him. He is in Washington trying to rebuild the US capital. He said that he was hauling a million tons of dirt to fill the holes that the bombs left. He is working to build the Capitol building first. He wants a place for congress to meet. Secondarily is the White House. He is also is trying to reconstruct what is left of the monuments. He feels that he will have everything in construction by the fifth of July so that he can meet everyone at the Hilton on that date."

"Why weren't we all invited in that meeting today?" asked Tom. "If we are all a part of his cabinet, why weren't we invited?"

"I guess because the main subject of the meeting was financial," said Mike. "You all would have just sat there bored to death. Besides, one of the main subjects was how we were going to pay for everything and what your salaries would be. He didn't want you in on that discussion. Does that answer your question? As I tell you the conclusions of the meeting, you will see that your presence was not necessary."

"I guess we will have to be satisfied," said Tom.

"Now, let me go on with the meat of the meeting," continued Mike. "Let me tell you that the president has appointed Bill as the secretary of the state. His area of responsibility will include the tasks done before by the secretaries of commerce and labor. Also, Sally has been appointed secretary of education. Her responsibilities will include the tasks done before by the secretary of health and human services, the secretary of education, and by welfare. He wants you two, Bill and Sally, to be working on your plans for the July fifth meeting. Don't worry I have a package that will help you. The rest of you know what your areas are."

Mike then opened the briefcase he had with him and brought out several packets. "These are your employment contracts," he said as he passed them out according to the name on the surface of the document. "It will give you, in general terms, you job description. It will also list your salary. He also wants you to know that Carol Brigs has been appointed secretary of the treasury. She will be the financial director. He has appointed General Fendon as chief of staff of the new Pentagon when it is built. His duties will include the tasks that before were done by the Secretary of War, the Secretary of Defense, and the Director of Home Land Security. He will not be at the meeting. He is currently at the United States-Mexico border. Admiral Kane will assume the position of Secretary of the Navy. He also will not be at the meeting. The president has not yet chosen the Secretaries of Agriculture or Housing and Urban Development. He will think about them later. Several months ago, the President set up a team of men and women for each state. They had no power to do anything. They were there only there to study and analyze any problems the state had due to the nuclear devastation and the invasion of foreign troops. The teams were divided into seven groups. Each was to report on its findings in the area of their expertise. Group number one was to investigate governmental, commerce, and labor problems. It also had the responsibility of organizing and executing a state census. This was necessary to determine the size of the state's wards and districts to determine the number of representatives for each state and, as a result, the size of the House of Representatives. Group two was to investigate communications. Group three was to investigate energy requirements. Group four was to investigate traveling requirements.

Group five was to investigate educational requirements. And group six was to investigate financial difficulties of the state. Each of these groups has sent in a report of their findings. Group seven was to investigate what is probably the most important to the president and that is to investigate how to set up for elections. The president wants to retire to his farm and spend time with his wife."

Mike then bent over and retrieved five folders from his brief case. "Carol already has her folder." Mike then handed each the folder with their name on it. "There are fifty reports in each of the folders. They are the findings and recommendations of the group in your field of responsibility. Now, this is the plan. You are to study these reports and be ready by July fifth to ask any questions you may come up with. The president expects it to take no more than two days. Therefore, get all your local affairs settled and be ready to travel to Maine on the morning of July seventh. We will travel from state to state, helping them with their reconstruction. In each state, we will meet the team in that state. The group in your area of responsibility will be your assistants for the time we spend in that state. The eastern states are going to be the toughest states due to the fact that they were invaded by the enemy troops. There was a lot more devastation from that area up to the middle of the country where the invading armies were finally stopped. The western states are in relatively good condition except the area around the big cities that were destroyed by nuclear bombs. From there to the Pacific should be much easier. The president and I will be working on the federal and state constitutions and setting up the election system for the states and the federal government. I now have a personal message from the president. I will quote him from my notes.

"Fellow Americans, I ask that you be ready to give your best, by studying the information you have and dedicate yourselves to the job we are destined to do. We have a monumental task ahead of us. As for you, Mike and Sarah, I ask that you get your marriage and honeymoon behind you and be ready to go to work. To all of you, we have the difficult job of rebuilding our country. We have to bring it up to the standards that our forefathers set for the country of the free, but most of all, we must reclaim this nation for God, our loving heavenly Father."

The End